THE LOEB CLASSICAL LIBRARY

FOUNDED BY JAMES LOEB 1911

EDITED BY

JEFFREY HENDERSON

EDITOR EMERITUS

G. P. GOOLD

ARISTOPHANES

IV

LCL 180

ARISTOPHANES

FROGS
ASSEMBLYWOMEN
WEALTH

EDITED AND TRANSLATED BY

JEFFREY HENDERSON

HARVARD UNIVERSITY PRESS
CAMBRIDGE, MASSACHUSETTS
LONDON, ENGLAND
2002

21.50

Library of Congress Catalog Card Number 97-24063
CIP data available from the Library of Congress

ISBN 0-674-99596-1

CONTENTS

FROGS

INTRODUCTORY NOTE

Frogs was produced by Philonides[1] at the Lenaea of 405 and won the first prize; Phrynichus was second with *Muses* (whose title suggests an artistic, and perhaps literary, theme) and Plato third with *Cleophon* (a leading politician of the time attacked also in *Frogs*). According to the Hypothesis, citing Aristotle's pupil Dicaearchus, *Frogs* was (uniquely) restaged "because of its parabasis," and the ancient *Life* (T 1.35–39), probably also deriving from Dicaearchus, informs us that Aristophanes was "officially commended and crowned with a wreath of sacred olive, considered equal in honor to a gold crown, for the lines he had spoken in *Frogs* about the disenfranchised [686 ff.]." The decree that awarded the commendation and restaging must have been passed after the autumn of 405, when by the decree of Patrocleides the Athenians enacted the measure for which Aristophanes had appealed (Andocides 1.73–79), but before the overthrow of the democracy in the spring of 404, when an appeal for equal civic rights would have been ill received, so that the play will have

---

[1] He had produced Lenaean plays for Aristophanes in 422 (either *Wasps* or *The Preview*) and 414 (*Amphiaraus*); presumably the provision of a second producer, which was in effect at the City Dionysia two months later (405 n.), did not (or not yet) apply to the Lenaea.

been restaged at the Lenaea of 404. For the restaging Aristophanes probably made only a few minor changes: lines 1251–60, 1431a-b, and 1437–53 seem to contain alternative versions of the text, but passages that would have been inappropriate at the time of the restaging remain, and there are no references to the events of early 404.

In *Frogs* Dionysus, disguised as Heracles, travels to the underworld with his cheeky slave, Xanthias, in order to retrieve his favorite tragic poet, the recently deceased Euripides. The first part of the play (1–673) chronicles their *katabasis* (descent to the underworld): a meeting with the real Heracles to obtain directions; Dionysus' voyage across the lake that leads to the underworld, ineptly rowing Charon's skiff and engaging in song with a chorus of frogs; comic terrors illustrating Dionysus' cowardice; the entry of the main chorus of Eleusinian Initiates, who live near the palace of Pluto, god of the underworld; several scenes of the sort that typically occur in the second part of a comedy, after the parabasis, in which Dionysus attempts to avoid the predicaments that await him upon arrival by exchanging his disguise with Xanthias; and finally Dionysus' admission into Pluto's palace.[2]

After the parabasis (674–737), there is a conversation between Xanthias and a slave of Pluto's that amounts to a second prologue introducing a new situation: Dionysus has been recruited by Pluto to judge a contest for the underworld Chair of Tragedy between Aeschylus, its longtime incumbent, and Euripides, who upon arrival has laid claim to preeminence in the art. Much of the ensuing con-

[2] The anti-heroic and burlesque portrayal of Dionysus in the first part of the play was long familiar in comedy and satyr drama.

test focuses on the rivals' poetic techniques, with detailed critiques of actual passages from their plays and parody of their characteristic styles. But Aeschylus and Euripides also emerge as representatives of the character, both poetic and civic, of their respective eras, and the decisive test turns on which poet is more able to effect "the salvation of Athens and the continuation of her choral festivals" (1418–19). On this criterion Dionysus chooses Aeschylus, and Pluto tells him that he may take Aeschylus with him back to Athens; Sophocles, also recently deceased, will hold the Chair of Tragedy in his absence. The Chorus of Eleusinian Initiates lead Dionysus and Aeschylus off in a torchlight procession recalling the inspirational finale of Aeschylus' *Oresteia*.

Beyond being a landmark in the history of literary criticism, *Frogs* embraces two transcendent issues, the decline of Athens as a great power and the decline of tragedy as a great form of art, and connects them by portraying tragic poets as both exemplifying and shaping the moral and civic character of their times. His solution to both issues, the resurrection of Aeschylus from the dead, is both pessimistic and optimistic: if there were no longer any living poets who could inspire the Athenians to greatness, at least the works of Aeschylus lived on, and might inspire the Athenians to recapture the virtues that had made their city preeminent in his day.

The decline of Athens and its musical culture were hardly new themes in the comedies of Aristophanes and his contemporaries, and the remedy of resurrecting great men of the past had recently figured in at least two of them: in Eupolis' *Demes* (412) the hero Pyronides brings back four great leaders (Solon, Miltiades, Aristeides, and

5

Pericles), and in Aristophanes' *Gerytades* (*c.* 408) the poets of Athens send an embassy to the underworld, presumably to resurrect the goddess Poetry (cf. fr. 591.85–86); Pherecrates' *Crapataloi* (date unknown but probably before *Frogs*) may have been similar, since Aeschylus' ghost is a character, and someone is told what to expect in the underworld (frs. 86, 100). But these themes had taken on a special urgency at the time of *Frogs*, for a shortage both of reliable manpower and trustworthy leadership threatened Athenian prospects for surviving the war, and both Euripides and Sophocles had recently died.

The Athenians' military and political situation had not improved since the Sicilian disaster of 413 and now threatened to deteriorate. The naval victory at Arginusae the previous summer had given Athens control of the Aegean but came at a crippling cost: after all available manpower had been mobilized, including slaves enlisted as rowers on the promise of freedom and even citizenship,[3] twenty-five ships and some five thousand men were lost, and in the subsequent recriminations all eight commanders were rashly condemned to death by the Assembly; in their ensuing remorse the Athenians compounded this mistake by denying commands to those they held responsible for the condemnations, including two exceptionally qualified captains, Theramenes and Thrasybulus. Alcibiades, who had capably led the Athenian naval effort since 411, had gone into voluntary exile in 407, and the question of his recall figures prominently in the decision between Aeschylus

[3] This extraordinary action was no doubt a factor in the unusually prominent and complex characterization of Xanthias (cf. esp. 33, 693–99).

and Euripides (1422–32); and the men who had been dis-
enfranchised for their association with the oligarchy of
411, and on whose behalf Aristophanes appeals in the
parabasis, were still debarred from civic life. Meanwhile,
the Peloponnesians had finally begun to receive significant
financial support from Persia, while the Athenians' finan-
cial situation steadily worsened: they were unable to re-
store their fleet to its pre-Arginusae strength, and their tra-
ditional silver coinage, augmented by an emergency issue
of gold coins made by melting down the plating on the Vic-
tory statues in the Parthenon, had to be spent abroad to
pay military expenses, and to be replaced at home by an is-
sue of silver-plated bronze coins.

But even in this perilous situation, the popular leader
Cleophon managed to persuade the Athenians to reject
the chance of a negotiated peace offered by Sparta after
Arginusae ([Aristotle], *Constitution of Athens* 34.1). No
wonder the Athenians responded so warmly to the para-
basis of *Frogs*, where the Chorus aptly upbraids them for
choosing as leaders and fighters not the best men but the
worst, just as they have traded their gold and silver coinage
for base metal (686–705, 717–37).

The situation on the tragic stage was comparable, for
Euripides had died early in 406 in his late seventies, and
Sophocles a few months later in his early nineties. Both
were international celebrities, and had long been consid-
ered the preeminent living masters of the art, with Aeschy-
lus (who had died in the mid-450's) as the third member of
the great tragic triad. But whereas the Athenians could re-
deem their political and military situation if they turned to
the best people, who were still living among them and ea-
ger to serve (cf. 699), no such choice was available in the

case of tragic poets, for Dionysus can think of no worthy successors among those who remained (71–97), so that the redemption of tragedy could only be found beyond the grave. There seems to have been some justice in this appraisal of the prospects for tragedy, for even if the poets left in Athens were not as inferior as Dionysus claims, the fact remains that when revivals became part of the program at the City Dionysia in the early fourth century, only revivals of plays by Euripides and Sophocles are attested; Aeschylus had already (and uniquely) enjoyed this status during the fifth century.

The play assumes that Sophocles is dead, but that he is mentioned in only three detachable passages (76–82, 786–94, and 1515–19) suggests that he died too late to be incorporated more fully into the plot. Presumably the play was conceived and largely completed when he was still alive, and Aristophanes added these passages to adjust for his death. He may well have had to remove some passages as well, for the original script would somehow have acknowledged the presence of the still-productive Sophocles among living poets. But this acknowledgment need not have been very involved: in view of Sophocles' advanced age alone, Dionysus could simply have said, "there are no worthy poets left except Sophocles, and he won't be with us much longer." It is unlikely that Sophocles would have figured in the poetic contest even had he died at the same time as Euripides. In contrast to Euripides, Sophocles had never been an attractive target in comedy for either personal caricature or poetic parody, whereas the contrast between Aeschylus and Euripides personally, poetically, and as representatives of their eras ideally suited Aristophanes' purposes.

The poetic contest in *Frogs* assumes that the spectators are familiar not only with dramatic literature (as distinct from performances of drama) but also with literary criticism, and that this familiarity was relatively recently acquired: as the Chorus says, "if you're afraid of any ignorance among the spectators, that they won't appreciate your subtleties of argument, don't worry about that, because things are no longer that way: they're veterans, and each one has a book and knows the fine points" (1108–14). Critiques of poets and their poetry, including metaphorical descriptions of their qualities and techniques, had long been a feature the Greek poetic tradition, and during the latter half of the fifth century became increasingly refined, as did the study of language and its communicative powers generally: the portrayal of poets and criticism of their works, both formal and through parody, was a staple subject of comedy; the language, style, and persuasive techniques of oratory and poetry were among the principal interests of sophistic thinkers and writers; and the increasing circulation and study of books had begun to create a more sophisticated awareness of poetry as literature, and of criticism as a formal approach to it. *Frogs* both reflects this development and contributed to it.

Text

Four papyri preserve parts of 165 lines of *Frogs*, and lines 454–59 are inscribed on a Hellenistic statue base from Rhodes (cf. G. Pugliesi-Carratelli, *Dioniso* 8 [1940] 119–23). Eighty-six medieval MSS (only *Wealth* and *Clouds* are better attested) contain the whole or the greater part of the play, about half of them entirely or partly Triclinian, the rest exhibiting no consistent affiliations. Nearly all of the ancient variants not found in R or V are found in one or more of just eleven pre-Triclinian MSS (A E K M Md1 [1–959] Np1 P20[ac] U Vb3 Vs1 Θ), which in this edition (following Dover's) are represented by A and K. The Aldine *editio princeps* (1498) derived its text from the Triclinian MS L (Oxon. Bodl. Holkhamensis 88, early XIV), with additional readings from E (Estensis gr. 127 = a.U.5.10, late XIV).

Sigla

I	Rhodian inscription, lines 454–59
Π1	*POxy.* 1372 (V), lines 44–50, 85–91, 840–61, 879–902
Π2	*PBerol.* 13231 (V/VI), lines 234–63, 272–300, 404–10, 607–11
Π3	*POxy.* 4517 (IV), lines 592–605, 630–47
Π4	*POxy.* 4518 (V), lines 1244–48, 1277–81
R	Ravennas 429 (*c.* 950)
V	Venetus Marcianus 474 (XI/XII)
S	Readings found in the Suda
A	Parisinus Regius 2712 (XIII/XIV)
K	Ambrosianus C222 inf. (XIII/XIV), lines 1–1197, 1251-end
a	consensus of R V A K
t	Triclinian readings

Annotated Editions

F. H. M. Blaydes (Halle 1889).
J. van Leeuwen (Leiden 1896).
B. B. Rogers (London 1902), with English translation.

T. G. Tucker (London 1906).

L. Radermacher, rev. W. Kraus (Vienna 1954^2), commentary only.

W. B. Stanford (London 1963^2).

D. del Corno (Milan 1985), with Italian translation.

K. J. Dover (Oxford 1993).

A. H. Sommerstein (Warminster 1996), with English translation.

ΤΑ ΤΟΥ ΔΡΑΜΑΤΟΣ ΠΡΟΣΩΠΑ

ΞΑΝΘΙΑΣ, *οἰκέτης*
  Διονύσου
ΔΙΟΝΥΣΟΣ
ΗΡΑΚΛΗΣ
ΝΕΚΡΟΣ
ΧΑΡΩΝ
ΑΙΑΚΟΣ
ΘΕΡΑΠΑΙΝΑ
  Φερρεφάττης
ΠΑΝΔΟΚΕΥΤΡΙΑ
ΠΛΑΘΑΝΗ
ΟΙΚΕΤΗΣ *Πλούτωνος*
ΠΛΟΥΤΩΝ
ΕΥΡΙΠΙΔΗΣ
ΑΙΣΧΥΛΟΣ

ΧΟΡΟΣ *βατράχων*
ΧΟΡΟΣ *μυστῶν*

ΚΩΦΑ ΠΡΟΣΩΠΑ
ΟΝΟΣ *Διονύσου*
ΑΝΔΡΕΣ *τὸν νεκρὸν*
  φέροντες
ΘΕΡΑΠΑΙΝΑΙ *τῶν*
  πανδοκευτριῶν
ΟΙΚΕΤΑΙ *Πλούτωνος*
ΔΙΤΥΛΑΣ *καὶ*
  ΣΚΕΒΥΛΑΣ *καὶ*
  ΠΑΡΔΟΚΑΣ *τοξόται*
ΜΟΥΣΑ *Εὐριπίδου*

DRAMATIS PERSONAE

XANTHIAS, slave of
   Dionysus
DIONYSUS
HERACLES
CORPSE
CHARON
AEACUS
MAID of Persephone
INNKEEPER
PLATHANE
SLAVE of Pluto
EURIPIDES
AESCHYLUS

CHORUS of Frogs
CHORUS of Initiates

SILENT CHARACTERS
DONKEY of Dionysus
PALL BEARERS
MAIDS of Innkeepers
SLAVES of Pluto
DITYLAS, SCEBYLAS,
   PARDOCAS, Archers
MUSE of Euripides

ΒΑΤΡΑΧΟΙ

ΞΑΝΘΙΑΣ
εἴπω τι τῶν εἰωθότων, ὦ δέσποτα,
ἐφ᾽ οἷς ἀεὶ γελῶσιν οἱ θεώμενοι;

ΔΙΟΝΥΣΟΣ
νὴ τὸν Δί᾽ ὅ τι βούλει γε, πλὴν "πιέζομαι."
τοῦτο δὲ φύλαξαι· πάνυ γάρ ἐστ᾽ ἤδη χολή.

ΞΑΝΘΙΑΣ
μηδ᾽ ἕτερον ἀστεῖόν τι;

ΔΙΟΝΥΣΟΣ
     πλήν γ᾽ "ὡς θλίβομαι."

5

ΞΑΝΘΙΑΣ
τί δαί; τὸ πάνυ γέλοιον εἴπω;

ΔΙΟΝΥΣΟΣ
     νὴ Δία
θαρρῶν γε· μόνον ἐκεῖν᾽ ὅπως μὴ ᾽ρεῖς—

ΞΑΝΘΙΑΣ
       τὸ τί;

14

FROGS

Enter DIONYSUS *and* XANTHIAS *from the side. Dionysus, disguised as Heracles, wears a lionskin over his saffron gown and carries a club; Xanthias rides a donkey and carries baggage suspended from a pole that rests on his shoulder. They make their way toward the stage house.*

XANTHIAS
Shall I make one of the usual cracks, master, that the audience always laugh at?

DIONYSUS
Sure, any one you want, except "I'm hard pressed!" Watch out for that one; by now it's a groaner.

XANTHIAS
Then some other urbanity?

DIONYSUS
Anything but "I'm getting crushed!"

XANTHIAS
Well then, how about the really funny one?

DIONYSUS
Go right ahead, only make sure it's not the one where—

XANTHIAS
You mean—

15

ARISTOPHANES

ΔΙΟΝΥΣΟΣ

μεταβαλλόμενος τἀνάφορον ὅτι χεζητιᾷς.

ΞΑΝΘΙΑΣ

μηδ' ὅτι τοσοῦτον ἄχθος ἐπ' ἐμαυτῷ φέρων,
10   εἰ μὴ καθαιρήσει τις, ἀποπαρδήσομαι;

ΔΙΟΝΥΣΟΣ

μὴ δῆθ', ἱκετεύω, πλήν γ' ὅταν μέλλω 'ξεμεῖν.

ΞΑΝΘΙΑΣ

τί δῆτ' ἔδει με ταῦτα τὰ σκεύη φέρειν,
εἴπερ ποιήσω μηδὲν ὧνπερ Φρύνιχος
εἴωθε ποιεῖν; καὶ Λύκις κἀμειψίας
15   σκεύη φέρουσ' ἑκάστοτ' ἐν κωμῳδίᾳ;

ΔΙΟΝΥΣΟΣ

μή νυν ποιήσῃς· ὡς ἐγὼ θεώμενος,
ὅταν τι τούτων τῶν σοφισμάτων ἴδω,
πλεῖν ἢ 'νιαυτῷ πρεσβύτερος ἀπέρχομαι.

ΞΑΝΘΙΑΣ

ὦ τρισκακοδαίμων ἄρ' ὁ τράχηλος οὑτοσί,
20   ὅτι θλίβεται μέν, τὸ δὲ γέλοιον οὐκ ἐρεῖ.

ΔΙΟΝΥΣΟΣ

εἶτ' οὐχ ὕβρις ταῦτ' ἐστὶ καὶ πολλὴ τρυφή,
ὅτ' ἐγὼ μὲν ὢν Διόνυσος, υἱὸς Σταμνίου,
αὐτὸς βαδίζω καὶ πονῶ, τοῦτον δ' ὀχῶ,
ἵνα μὴ ταλαιπωροῖτο μηδ' ἄχθος φέροι;

ΞΑΝΘΙΑΣ

οὐ γὰρ φέρω 'γώ;

DIONYSUS

where you shift your baggage and say you need to shit.

XANTHIAS

Can't I even say that I've got such a load on me, if someone doesn't relieve me my rump will erupt?

DIONYSUS

Please don't! Wait till I need to puke.

XANTHIAS

Then why did I have to carry this baggage, if I'm not supposed to do any of the stuff Phrynichus always does? Lycis and Ameipsias too: people carry baggage in every one of their comedies.[1]

DIONYSUS

Just don't do it, because when I'm in the audience and see one of those clever bits, I go home a whole year older.

XANTHIAS

What a triple jinxed neck I've got then, since it's getting crushed but can't make a funny comment.

DIONYSUS

How's that for being arrogant and spoiled rotten! After I, Dionysus son of Flagon, have toiled ahead on foot and let him ride, so he wouldn't get tired or have to bear a load.

XANTHIAS

Well, aren't I bearing one?

---

[1] Three of Aristophanes' competitors; Phrynichus was competing against *Frogs* with *Muses* and would win second prize.

ΔΙΟΝΤΣΟΣ

25   πῶς φέρεις γὰρ ὅς γ' ὀχεῖ;

ΞΑΝΘΙΑΣ

φέρων γε ταυτί.

ΔΙΟΝΤΣΟΣ

τίνα τρόπον;

ΞΑΝΘΙΑΣ

βαρέως πάνυ.

ΔΙΟΝΤΣΟΣ

οὔκουν τὸ βάρος τοῦθ' ὃ σὺ φέρεις οὖνος φέρει;

ΞΑΝΘΙΑΣ

οὐ δῆθ' ὅ γ' ἔχω 'γὼ καὶ φέρω, μὰ τὸν Δί' οὔ.

ΔΙΟΝΤΣΟΣ

πῶς γὰρ φέρεις, ὅς γ' αὐτὸς ὑφ' ἑτέρου φέρει;

ΞΑΝΘΙΑΣ

30   οὐκ οἶδ'· ὁ δ' ὦμος οὑτοσὶ πιέζεται.

ΔΙΟΝΤΣΟΣ

σὺ δ' οὖν ἐπειδὴ τὸν ὄνον οὐ φῄς σ' ὠφελεῖν,
ἐν τῷ μέρει σὺ τὸν ὄνον ἀράμενος φέρε.

ΞΑΝΘΙΑΣ

οἴμοι κακοδαίμων· τί γὰρ ἐγὼ οὐκ ἐναυμάχουν;
ἦ τἄν σε κωκύειν ἂν ἐκέλευον μακρά.

DIONYSUS

How can you be bearing anything when you're riding?

XANTHIAS

Well, I'm bearing this.

DIONYSUS

How?

XANTHIAS

Quite unbearably!

DIONYSUS

But doesn't the donkey bear what you're bearing?

XANTHIAS

Not what I've got here and bear myself, it certainly doesn't.

DIONYSUS

But how can you bear anything, when something else bears you?

XANTHIAS

I don't know—but this shoulder of mine is hard pressed!

DIONYSUS

Very well, since you deny that the donkey's helping you, pick up the donkey and take your turn carrying *him*.

XANTHIAS

Blast my luck, why wasn't I in the sea battle? Then I'd be telling you to go to hell.[2]

---

[2] The Athenian fleet that was victorious at Arginusae the previous summer had been manned by a great levy that included slaves, who were then rewarded with freedom (Xenophon, *Hellenica* 1.6.24, Hellanicus *FGrH* 323a F 25).

ΔΙΟΝΤΣΟΣ

35 κατάβα, πανοῦργε. καὶ γὰρ ἐγγὺς τῆς θύρας
ἤδη βαδίζων εἰμὶ τῆσδ᾽, οἷ πρῶτά με
ἔδει τραπέσθαι. παιδίον, παῖ, ἠμί, παῖ.

ΗΡΑΚΛΗΣ

τίς τὴν θύραν ἐπάταξεν; ὡς κενταυρικῶς
ἐνήλαθ᾽ ὅστις—εἰπέ μοι, τουτὶ τί ἦν;

ΔΙΟΝΤΣΟΣ

ὁ παῖς.

ΞΑΝΘΙΑΣ

τί ἐστιν;

ΔΙΟΝΤΣΟΣ

οὐκ ἐνεθυμήθης;

ΞΑΝΘΙΑΣ

40   τὸ τί;

ΔΙΟΝΤΣΟΣ

ὡς σφόδρα μ᾽ ἔδεισε.

ΞΑΝΘΙΑΣ

νὴ Δία, μὴ μαίνοιό γε.

ΗΡΑΚΛΗΣ

οὔ τοι μὰ τὴν Δήμητρα δύναμαι μὴ γελᾶν·
καίτοι δάκνω γ᾽ ἐμαυτόν· ἀλλ᾽ ὅμως γελῶ.

ΔΙΟΝΤΣΟΣ

ὦ δαιμόνιε, πρόσελθε· δέομαι γάρ τί σου.

FROGS

DIONYSUS

Dismount, you scamp! Here I am at the door that was to be my first stop. (*knocking*) Boy! (*knocking with his club*) Boy, I say, boy!

HERACLES is heard from within, then opens the door.

HERACLES

Who banged on the door? He assaulted it like a centaur, whoever—Say now, what's this supposed to be? (*turns aside to laugh*)

DIONYSUS

Boy?

XANTHIAS

What is it?

DIONYSUS

Did you see that?

XANTHIAS

See what?

DIONYSUS

How extremely scared of me he was!

XANTHIAS

Sure, scared that you've lost your mind.

HERACLES

By Demeter, I just can't stop laughing! Even though I'm biting my lip, I can't help laughing.

DIONYSUS

(*to Heracles*) Come here, my man; I'd like a word with you.

ΗΡΑΚΛΗΣ

45 ἀλλ' οὐχ οἷός τ' εἴμ' ἀποσοβῆσαι τὸν γέλων,
ὁρῶν λεοντῆν ἐπὶ κροκωτῷ κειμένην.
τίς ὁ νοῦς; τί κόθορνος καὶ ῥόπαλον ξυνηλθέτην;
ποῖ γῆς ἀπεδήμεις;

ΔΙΟΝΤΣΟΣ
ἐπεβάτευον Κλεισθένει.

ΗΡΑΚΛΗΣ
κἀναυμάχησας;

ΔΙΟΝΤΣΟΣ
καὶ κατεδύσαμέν γε ναῦς
50 τῶν πολεμίων ἢ δώδεκ' ἢ τρεισκαίδεκα.

ΗΡΑΚΛΗΣ
σφώ;

ΔΙΟΝΤΣΟΣ
νὴ τὸν Ἀπόλλω.

ΞΑΝΘΙΑΣ
κᾆτ' ἔγωγ' ἐξηγρόμην.

ΔΙΟΝΤΣΟΣ
καὶ δῆτ' ἐπὶ τῆς νεὼς ἀναγιγνώσκοντί μοι
τὴν Ἀνδρομέδαν πρὸς ἐμαυτὸν ἐξαίφνης πόθος
τὴν καρδίαν ἐπάταξε πῶς οἴει σφόδρα.

ΗΡΑΚΛΗΣ
πόθος; πόσος τις;

---

3 Normally a woman's festive garment but regularly worn

FROGS

HERACLES

I just can't get rid of this laughter. It's the sight of that lionskin atop a yellow gown.[3] What's the idea? Why has a war club joined up with lady's boots? Where on earth have you been?

DIONYSUS

I was serving topside with Cleisthenes.[4]

HERACLES

And did you engage?

DIONYSUS

Sank some enemy ships too, twelve or thirteen of them.

HERACLES

You two?

DIONYSUS

So help me Apollo.

XANTHIAS

And then I woke up.

DIONYSUS

Anyway, as I was on deck reading *Andromeda*[5] to myself, a sudden longing struck my heart, you can't imagine how hard.

HERACLES

A longing? How big?

by Dionysus; he wore it with masculine apparel in Aeschylus' *Edonians*, parodied in *Women at the Thesmophoria* 130–45.

[4] Perennially teased for effeminacy, and a character in *Women at the Thesmophoria* (574–654).

[5] Euripides' play had been produced in 412 and parodied the following year in *Women at the Thesmophoria* (1015–1135).

ΔΙΟΝΤΣΟΣ

55   σμικρός, ἡλίκος Μόλων.

ΗΡΑΚΛΗΣ

γυναικός;

ΔΙΟΝΤΣΟΣ

οὐ δῆτ'.

ΗΡΑΚΛΗΣ

ἀλλὰ παιδός;

ΔΙΟΝΤΣΟΣ

οὐδαμῶς.

ΗΡΑΚΛΗΣ

ἀλλ' ἀνδρός;

ΔΙΟΝΤΣΟΣ

ἀπαπαῖ.

ΗΡΑΚΛΗΣ

ξυνεγένου τῷ Κλεισθένει;

ΔΙΟΝΤΣΟΣ

μὴ σκῶπτέ μ', ὠδέλφ'· οὐ γὰρ ἀλλ' ἔχω κακῶς·
τοιοῦτος ἵμερός με διαλυμαίνεται.

ΗΡΑΚΛΗΣ

ποῖός τις, ὠδελφίδιον;

ΔΙΟΝΤΣΟΣ

60   οὐκ ἔχω φράσαι.
ὅμως γε μέντοι σοι δι' αἰνιγμῶν ἐρῶ.
ἤδη ποτ' ἐπεθύμησας ἐξαίφνης ἔτνους;

24

FROGS

DIONYSUS

Small, the size of Molon.[6]

HERACLES

For a woman?

DIONYSUS

Nope.

HERACLES

Then for a boy?

DIONYSUS

Not at all.

HERACLES

For a man, then?

DIONYSUS

Ah ah!

HERACLES

Did you do it with Cleisthenes?

DIONYSUS

Don't tease me, brother; I'm truly in a bad way. That's how thoroughly this passion is messing me up.

HERACLES

What kind of passion, little brother?

DIONYSUS

I can't put it into words, but I'll try to explain it to you by analogy. Have you ever had a sudden craving for minestrone?

---

[6] A famous actor (cf. Demosthenes 19.246) and, according to the scholia, a large man.

ΗΡΑΚΛΗΣ

ἔτνους; βαβαιάξ, μυριάκις γ᾽ ἐν τῷ βίῳ.

ΔΙΟΝΥΣΟΣ

ἆρ᾽ ἐκδιδάσκω τὸ σαφές, ἢ ᾽τέρᾳ φράσω;

ΗΡΑΚΛΗΣ

65 μὴ δῆτα περὶ ἔτνους γε· πάνυ γὰρ μανθάνω.

ΔΙΟΝΥΣΟΣ

τοιουτοσὶ τοίνυν με δαρδάπτει πόθος
Εὐριπίδου.

ΗΡΑΚΛΗΣ

καὶ ταῦτα τοῦ τεθνηκότος;

ΔΙΟΝΥΣΟΣ

κοὐδείς γέ μ᾽ ἂν πείσειεν ἀνθρώπων τὸ μὴ οὐκ
ἐλθεῖν ἐπ᾽ ἐκεῖνον.

ΗΡΑΚΛΗΣ

πότερον εἰς Ἅιδου κάτω;

ΔΙΟΝΥΣΟΣ

70 καὶ νὴ Δί᾽ εἴ τί γ᾽ ἔστιν ἔτι κατωτέρω.

ΗΡΑΚΛΗΣ

τί βουλόμενος;

ΔΙΟΝΥΣΟΣ

δέομαι ποιητοῦ δεξιοῦ.
οἱ μὲν γὰρ οὐκέτ᾽ εἰσίν, οἱ δ᾽ ὄντες κακοί.

ΗΡΑΚΛΗΣ

τί δ᾽; οὐκ Ἰοφῶν ζῇ;

FROGS

HERACLES
Minestrone? Oh my, thousands of times in my life!

DIONYSUS
Am I spelling out the obvious, or should I express it another way?

HERACLES
No problem with minestrone; I get the point entirely.

DIONYSUS
Well, that's the kind of longing that's eating away at me for Euripides.

HERACLES
You mean, dead and all?

DIONYSUS
And nobody on earth can persuade me not to go after him.

HERACLES
Even below to Hades?

DIONYSUS
By heaven, even if there's somewhere below that.

HERACLES
What is it you want?

DIONYSUS
I need a talented poet, "for some are gone, and those that live are bad."[7]

HERACLES
How so? Isn't Iophon alive?[8]

---

[7] From Euripides' *Oeneus* (fr. 565).
[8] A son of Sophocles and a successful tragic poet.

ΔΙΟΝΥΣΟΣ

τοῦτο γάρ τοι καὶ μόνον

ἔτ᾽ ἐστὶ λοιπὸν ἀγαθόν, εἰ καὶ τοῦτ᾽ ἄρα·

75 οὐ γὰρ σάφ᾽ οἶδ᾽ οὐδ᾽ αὐτὸ τοῦθ᾽ ὅπως ἔχει.

ΗΡΑΚΛΗΣ

εἶτ᾽ οὐ Σοφοκλέα πρότερον ὄντ᾽ Εὐριπίδου

μέλλεις ἀναγαγεῖν, εἴπερ γ᾽ ἐκεῖθεν δεῖ σ᾽ ἄγειν;

ΔΙΟΝΥΣΟΣ

οὔ, πρίν γ᾽ ἂν Ἰοφῶντ᾽, ἀπολαβὼν αὐτὸν μόνον,

ἄνευ Σοφοκλέους ὅ τι ποιεῖ κωδωνίσω.

80 κἄλλως ὁ μέν γ᾽ Εὐριπίδης πανοῦργος ὢν

κἂν ξυναποδρᾶναι δεῦρ᾽ ἐπιχειρήσειέ μοι·

ὁ δ᾽ εὔκολος μὲν ἐνθάδ᾽, εὔκολος δ᾽ ἐκεῖ.

ΗΡΑΚΛΗΣ

Ἀγάθων δὲ ποῦ ᾽στιν;

ΔΙΟΝΥΣΟΣ

ἀπολιπών μ᾽ ἀποίχεται,

ἀγαθὸς ποιητὴς καὶ ποθεινὸς τοῖς φίλοις.

ΗΡΑΚΛΗΣ

ποῖ γῆς ὁ τλήμων;

ΔΙΟΝΥΣΟΣ

85 εἰς μακάρων εὐωχίαν.

ΗΡΑΚΛΗΣ

ὁ δὲ Ξενοκλέης;

---

[9] Agathon, victorious in his debut in 416 (commemorated in

DIONYSUS

Yes, and that's the only class act left, if it really is one; because I'm not exactly sure how that stands either.

HERACLES

If you must resurrect someone, then why not Sophocles, who's better than Euripides?

DIONYSUS

No, first I want to get Iophon alone by himself and evaluate what he produces without Sophocles. Besides, Euripides is a slippery character and would probably even help me pull off an escape, whereas Sophocles was peaceable here and will be peaceable there.

HERACLES

And where's Agathon?[9]

DIONYSUS

He's gone and left me; a fine poet and much missed by his friends.

HERACLES

Where on earth to, poor thing?

DIONYSUS

To party with the Blest.

HERACLES

What about Xenocles?[10]

Plato's *Symposium*) and famous both for his innovative style and his personal beauty, had left Athens with his lover Pausanias for the court of Archelaus of Macedon around 408; he is portrayed in *Women at the Thesmophoria*.

[10] A son of Carcinus who defeated Euripides' Trojan trilogy in 415.

ΔΙΟΝΥΣΟΣ
ἐξόλοιτο νὴ Δία.

ΗΡΑΚΛΗΣ
Πυθάγγελος δέ;

ΞΑΝΘΙΑΣ
περὶ ἐμοῦ δ᾽ οὐδεὶς λόγος
ἐπιτριβομένου τὸν ὦμον οὑτωσὶ σφόδρα.

ΗΡΑΚΛΗΣ
οὔκουν ἕτερ᾽ ἔστ᾽ ἐνταῦθα μειρακύλλια
90 τραγῳδίας ποιοῦντα πλεῖν ἢ μυρία,
Εὐριπίδου πλεῖν ἢ σταδίῳ λαλίστερα;

ΔΙΟΝΥΣΟΣ
ἐπιφυλλίδες ταῦτ᾽ ἐστὶ καὶ στωμύλματα,
χελιδόνων μουσεῖα, λωβηταὶ τέχνης,
ἃ φροῦδα θᾶττον, ἢν μόνον χορὸν λάβῃ,
95 ἅπαξ προσουρήσαντα τῇ τραγῳδίᾳ.
γόνιμον δὲ ποιητὴν ἂν οὐχ εὕροις ἔτι
ζητῶν ἄν, ὅστις ῥῆμα γενναῖον λάκοι.

ΗΡΑΚΛΗΣ
πῶς γόνιμον;

ΔΙΟΝΥΣΟΣ
ὡδὶ γόνιμον, ὅστις φθέγξεται
τοιουτονί τι παρακεκινδυνευμένον,
100 "αἰθέρα Διὸς δωμάτιον," ἢ "χρόνου πόδα,"
ἢ "φρένα μὲν οὐκ ἐθέλουσαν ὀμόσαι καθ᾽ ἱερῶν,
γλῶτταν δ᾽ ἐπιορκήσασαν ἰδίᾳ τῆς φρενός."

DIONYSUS

To hell with *him*!

HERACLES

And Pythangelus?[11]

XANTHIAS

Not a word about me, while my shoulder's getting so badly bruised?

HERACLES

Aren't there others here, lads by the thousands composing tragedies and out-blabbering Euripides by a mile?

DIONYSUS

Those are cast-offs and empty chatter, choirs of swallows, wreckers of their art, who maybe get a chorus and are soon forgotten, after their single piss against Tragedy. But if you look for a potent poet, one who could utter a lordly phrase, you won't find any left.

HERACLES

What do you mean, "potent"?

DIONYSUS

Potent, as in one who can give voice to something adventuresome, like "Aether, Bedchamber of Zeus,"[12] or "Time's Foot,"[13] or "a heart unwilling to swear upon sacrificial victims, and a tongue forsworn separately from the heart."[14]

---

[11] Otherwise unknown.

[12] Misquoting *Wise Melanippe* (fr. 487), "Aether, Zeus' abode."

[13] *Alexander* (fr. 42), *Bacchae* 889.

[14] Paraphrasing *Hippolytus* 612.

31

ARISTOPHANES

ΗΡΑΚΛΗΣ

σὲ δὲ ταῦτ' ἀρέσκει;

ΔΙΟΝΥΣΟΣ

μἀλλὰ πλεῖν ἢ μαίνομαι.

ΗΡΑΚΛΗΣ

ἦ μὴν κόβαλά γ' ἐστίν, ὡς καὶ σοὶ δοκεῖ.

ΔΙΟΝΥΣΟΣ

105 μὴ τὸν ἐμὸν οἴκει νοῦν· ἔχεις γὰρ οἰκίαν.

ΗΡΑΚΛΗΣ

καὶ μὴν ἀτεχνῶς γε παμπόνηρα φαίνεται.

ΔΙΟΝΥΣΟΣ

δειπνεῖν με δίδασκε.

ΞΑΝΘΙΑΣ

περὶ ἐμοῦ δ' οὐδεὶς λόγος.

ΔΙΟΝΥΣΟΣ

ἀλλ' ὧνπερ ἕνεκα τήνδε τὴν σκευὴν ἔχων
ἦλθον κατὰ σὴν μίμησιν, ἵνα μοι τοὺς ξένους
110 τοὺς σοὺς φράσειας, εἰ δεοίμην, οἷσι σὺ
ἐχρῶ τόθ', ἡνίκ' ἦλθες ἐπὶ τὸν Κέρβερον,
τούτους φράσον μοι, λιμένας, ἀρτοπώλια,
πορνεῖ', ἀναπαύλας, ἐκτροπάς, κρήνας, ὁδούς,
πόλεις, διαίτας, πανδοκευτρίας, ὅπου
κόρεις ὀλίγιστοι.

ΞΑΝΘΙΑΣ

115 περὶ ἐμοῦ δ' οὐδεὶς λόγος.

HERACLES

You like that stuff?

DIONYSUS

Like it? Why, I'm crazy about it!

HERACLES

It's pure blarney, and you know it as well as I do.

DIONYSUS

Don't manage my mind,[15] but mind your own business.

HERACLES

Come now, it's obviously complete rubbish.

DIONYSUS

Stick to your specialty: eating.

XANTHIAS

But not a word about me!

DIONYSUS

Well, the reason I've come wearing this outfit in imitation
of you is so you'll tell me about those friends of yours who
put you up when you went after Cerberus,[16] in case I need
them. Tell me about them, about the harbors, bakeries,
whorehouses, rest areas, directions, springs, roads, cities,
places to stay, the landladies with the fewest bedbugs.

XANTHIAS

But not a word about me!

15 *Andromeda* (fr. 144).
16 The three-headed watchdog of Hades, fetched up by
Heracles in the last of his labors.

ARISTOPHANES

ΗΡΑΚΛΗΣ

ὦ σχέτλιε, τολμήσεις γὰρ ἰέναι καὶ σύ γε;

ΔΙΟΝΥΣΟΣ

μηδὲν ἔτι πρὸς ταῦτ᾽, ἀλλὰ φράζε τῶν ὁδῶν
ὅπῃ τάχιστ᾽ ἀφίξομαι 'ς Ἅιδου κάτω·
καὶ μήτε θερμὴν μήτ᾽ ἄγαν ψυχρὰν φράσῃς.

ΗΡΑΚΛΗΣ

120 φέρε δή, τίν᾽ αὐτῶν σοι φράσω πρώτην; τίνα;
μία μὲν γὰρ ἔστιν ἀπὸ κάλω καὶ θρανίου,
κρεμάσαντι σαυτόν.

ΔΙΟΝΥΣΟΣ

π't="ε, πνιγηρὰν λέγεις.

ΗΡΑΚΛΗΣ

ἀλλ᾽ ἔστιν ἀτραπὸς ξύντομος τετριμμένη,
ἡ διὰ θυείας.

ΔΙΟΝΥΣΟΣ

ἆρα κώνειον λέγεις;

ΗΡΑΚΛΗΣ

μάλιστά γε.

ΔΙΟΝΥΣΟΣ

125 ψυχράν γε καὶ δυσχείμερον·
εὐθὺς γὰρ ἀποπήγνυσι τἀντικνήμια.

ΗΡΑΚΛΗΣ

βούλει ταχεῖαν καὶ κατάντη σοι φράσω;

HERACLES

You madcap, would you dare to go there too?[17]

DIONYSUS

Drop that subject; just give me the directions, my quickest route down to Hades, and don't give me one that's too hot or too cold.

HERACLES

Let me see, which one shall I give you first? Hmm. Well, there's one via rope and bench: you hang yourself.

DIONYSUS

Stop it, that way's too stifling.

HERACLES

Well, there's a shortcut that's well-beaten—in a mortar.

DIONYSUS

You mean hemlock?

HERACLES

Exactly.

DIONYSUS

That's a chill and wintry way! It quickly freezes your shins solid.

HERACLES

Want to hear about a quick downhill route?

17 In portraying this as Dionysus' first trip to the underworld, Aristophanes apparently ignores the myths of his rescue of Semele.

ΔΙΟΝΤΣΟΣ

νὴ τὸν Δί’, ὡς ὄντος γε μὴ βαδιστικοῦ.

ΗΡΑΚΛΗΣ

καθέρπυσόν νυν εἰς Κεραμεικόν.

ΔΙΟΝΤΣΟΣ

κᾆτα τί;

ΗΡΑΚΛΗΣ

ἀναβὰς ἐπὶ τὸν πύργον τὸν ὑψηλόν—

ΔΙΟΝΤΣΟΣ

130   τί δρῶ;

ΗΡΑΚΛΗΣ

ἀφιεμένην τὴν λαμπάδ’ ἐντεῦθεν θεῶ,
κᾄπειτ’ ἐπειδὰν φῶσιν οἱ θεώμενοι
“εἶνται,” τόθ’ εἶναι καὶ σὺ σαυτόν.

ΔΙΟΝΤΣΟΣ

ποῖ;

ΗΡΑΚΛΗΣ

κάτω.

ΔΙΟΝΤΣΟΣ

ἀλλ’ ἀπολέσαιμ’ ἂν ἐγκεφάλου θρίω δύο.
οὐκ ἂν βαδίσαιμι τὴν ὁδὸν ταύτην.

ΗΡΑΚΛΗΣ

135   τί δαί;

ΔΙΟΝΤΣΟΣ

ἥνπερ σὺ τότε κατῆλθες.

DIONYSUS

Yes indeed; I'm not much for hiking.

HERACLES

Then stroll to the Cerameicus—

DIONYSUS

Then what?

HERACLES

and climb the tower, the high one.

DIONYSUS

And do what?

HERACLES

Watch the start of the torch race, and when the spectators cry "they're off," then off you go too.

DIONYSUS

Where?

HERACLES

Down!

DIONYSUS

But I'd be wasting two brain croquettes. I'd rather not stroll that route.

HERACLES

Then how will you go?

DIONYSUS

The same way you went.

ΗΡΑΚΛΗΣ

ἀλλ' ὁ πλοῦς πολύς.
εὐθὺς γὰρ ἐπὶ λίμνην μεγάλην ἥξεις πάνυ
ἄβυσσον.

ΔΙΟΝΥΣΟΣ

εἶτα πῶς γε περαιωθήσομαι;

ΗΡΑΚΛΗΣ

ἐν πλοιαρίῳ τυννουτῳί σ' ἀνὴρ γέρων
140   ναύτης διάξει δύ' ὀβολὼ μισθὸν λαβών.

ΔΙΟΝΥΣΟΣ

φεῦ.
ὡς μέγα δύνασθον πανταχοῦ τὼ δύ' ὀβολώ.
πῶς ἠλθέτην κἀκεῖσε;

ΗΡΑΚΛΗΣ

Θησεὺς ἤγαγεν.
μετὰ ταῦτ' ὄφεις καὶ θηρί' ὄψει μυρία
δεινότατα.

ΔΙΟΝΥΣΟΣ

μή μ' ἔκπληττε μηδὲ δειμάτου·
οὐ γάρ μ' ἀποτρέψεις.

ΗΡΑΚΛΗΣ

145   εἶτα βόρβορον πολὺν
καὶ σκῶρ ἀείνων· ἐν δὲ τούτῳ κειμένους,
εἴ που ξένον τις ἠδίκησε πώποτε,
ἢ παῖδα κινῶν τἀργύριον ὑφείλετο,
ἢ μητέρ' ἠλόησεν, ἢ πατρὸς γνάθον
150   ἐπάταξεν, ἢ 'πίορκον ὅρκον ὤμοσεν,

HERACLES

That's a long voyage. First you'll come to a vast lake, quite bottomless.

DIONYSUS

Then how will I cross it?

HERACLES

An ancient mariner will ferry you across in a little boat no bigger than this, for a fare of two obols.[18]

DIONYSUS

Wow, what power those two obols have everywhere! How did they make their way down there?

HERACLES

Theseus brought them.[19] After that, you'll see an infinity of serpents and beasts most frightful.

DIONYSUS

Don't try to shock or scare me off; you'll not deter me.

HERACLES

Then you'll see lots of mud and ever-flowing shit; in it lies anyone who ever wronged a stranger, or snatched a boy's fee while screwing him, or thrashed his mother, or socked his father in the jaw, or swore a false oath, or had someone

---

[18] The traditional fare was one obol; here "two obols" probably refers to the two-obol dole introduced by Cleophon in 410 (Aristotle, *Constitution* 28.3; *IG* i³ 375–77), perhaps to the price of a theater ticket (but then "everywhere" is hard to explain).

[19] The journey of Theseus, an Athenian hero, to the underworld was well known, and was dramatized in Critias' tragedy *Perithous* (date unknown, and alternatively attributed in antiquity to Euripides).

ARISTOPHANES

ἢ Μορσίμου τις ῥῆσιν ἐξεγράψατο.

ΔΙΟΝΥΣΟΣ
νὴ τοὺς θεοὺς ἐχρῆν γε πρὸς τούτοισι κεἰ
τὴν πυρρίχην τις ἔμαθε τὴν Κινησίου.

ΗΡΑΚΛΗΣ
ἐντεῦθεν αὐλῶν τίς σε περίεισιν πνοή,
155 ὄψει τε φῶς κάλλιστον ὥσπερ ἐνθάδε,
καὶ μυρρινῶνας καὶ θιάσους εὐδαίμονας
ἀνδρῶν γυναικῶν καὶ κρότον χειρῶν πολύν.

ΔΙΟΝΥΣΟΣ
οὗτοι δὲ δὴ τίνες εἰσίν;

ΗΡΑΚΛΗΣ
οἱ μεμνημένοι—

ΞΑΝΘΙΑΣ
νὴ τὸν Δί᾽ ἐγὼ γοῦν ὄνος ἄγω μυστήρια.
160 ἀτὰρ οὐ καθέξω ταῦτα τὸν πλείω χρόνον.

ΗΡΑΚΛΗΣ
οἵ σοι φράσουσ᾽ ἁπαξάπανθ᾽ ὧν ἂν δέῃ.
οὗτοι γὰρ ἐγγύτατα παρ᾽ αὐτὴν τὴν ὁδὸν
ἐπὶ ταῖσι τοῦ Πλούτωνος οἰκοῦσιν θύραις.
καὶ χαῖρε πόλλ᾽, ὦδελφέ.

152–53 hos vv. Aristophanem Byz. quasi alternos notasse ΣVE,
unde 152 del. et 153 ἢ π. γρΣ

40

copy out a speech by Morsimus.[20]

DIONYSUS

And by heaven, we should add anyone who learned that war dance by Cinesias.[21]

HERACLES

And next a breath of pipes will waft about you, and there'll be brilliant sunlight, just like ours, and myrtle groves, happy bands of men and women, and a great clapping of hands.

DIONYSUS

And who are those people?

HERACLES

The initiates.

XANTHIAS

And I'm the damn donkey who carries out the Mysteries! But I'm not going to put up with it any longer. (*tossing down the baggage*)

HERACLES

They'll tell you everything you need to know. They live right beside the road you'll be taking, at Pluto's palace gate. So bon voyage, my brother.

HERACLES goes inside.

[20] Son of the tragic poet Philocles and great-nephew of Aeschylus; ridiculed also in *Knights* (401) and *Peace* (803).

[21] The dance in full armor (*pyrriche*) was a prestigious competition at the quadrennial Panathenaea (held the previous summer). Cinesias was a contemporary dithyrambic poet much ridiculed in comedy for his wasted physique and airy, avant-garde music.

ΔΙΟΝΥΣΟΣ

νὴ Δία καὶ σύ γε

165 ὑγίαινε. σὺ δὲ τὰ στρώματ᾽ αὖθις λάμβανε.

ΞΑΝΘΙΑΣ

πρὶν καὶ καταθέσθαι;

ΔΙΟΝΥΣΟΣ

καὶ ταχέως μέντοι πάνυ.

ΞΑΝΘΙΑΣ

μὴ δῆθ᾽, ἱκετεύω σ᾽, ἀλλὰ μίσθωσαί τινα
τῶν ἐκφερομένων, ὅστις ἐπὶ ταῦτ᾽ ἔρχεται.

ΔΙΟΝΥΣΟΣ

ἐὰν δὲ μηὕρω;

ΞΑΝΘΙΑΣ

τότ᾽ ἔμ᾽ ἄγειν.

ΔΙΟΝΥΣΟΣ

καλῶς λέγεις.

170 καὶ γάρ τιν᾽ ἐκφέρουσι τουτονὶ νεκρόν.
οὗτος, σὲ λέγω μέντοι, σὲ τὸν τεθνηκότα.
ἄνθρωπε, βούλει σκευάρι᾽ εἰς Ἅιδου φέρειν;

ΝΕΚΡΟΣ

πόσ᾽ ἄττα;

ΔΙΟΝΥΣΟΣ

ταυτί.

ΝΕΚΡΟΣ

δύο δραχμὰς μισθὸν τελεῖς;

DIONYSUS

Sure, and you be well too. (*to Xanthias*) You there, pick up
that baggage again.

XANTHIAS

Before I've even put it down?

DIONYSUS

Yes, and make it snappy too.

XANTHIAS

No, please no! Hire someone instead, someone being laid
to rest, who's headed in the same direction.

DIONYSUS

What if I can't find one?

XANTHIAS

Then take me.

Enter Pall Bearers, bearing a CORPSE *on a bier.*

DIONYSUS

Good suggestion. And look, here's a corpse they're bearing
off now. (*approaching the bier*) You there, yes I mean you,
the deceased one. Hey buddy, want to haul some bags to
Hades?

CORPSE

How many?

DIONYSUS

These here.

CORPSE

Will you pay two drachmas?

ΔΙΟΝΥΣΟΣ

μὰ Δί᾽, ἀλλ᾽ ἔλαττον.

ΝΕΚΡΟΣ

ὑπάγεθ᾽ ὑμεῖς τῆς ὁδοῦ.

ΔΙΟΝΥΣΟΣ

175 ἀνάμεινον, ὦ δαιμόνι᾽, ἐὰν ξυμβῶ τί σοι.

ΝΕΚΡΟΣ

εἰ μὴ καταθήσεις δύο δραχμάς, μὴ διαλέγου.

ΔΙΟΝΥΣΟΣ

λάβ᾽ ἐννέ᾽ ὀβολούς.

ΝΕΚΡΟΣ

ἀναβιῴην νυν πάλιν.

ΞΑΝΘΙΑΣ

ὡς σεμνὸς ὁ κατάρατος. οὐκ οἰμώξεται;
ἐγὼ βαδιοῦμαι.

ΔΙΟΝΥΣΟΣ

χρηστὸς εἶ καὶ γεννάδας.
χωρῶμεν ἐπὶ τὸ πλοῖον.

ΧΑΡΩΝ

180   ὤόπ, παραβαλοῦ.

ΔΙΟΝΥΣΟΣ

τουτὶ τί ἐστι;

DIONYSUS
Certainly not that much.

CORPSE
Move along, bearers.

DIONYSUS
Hold on, fella, maybe we can work something out.

CORPSE
Put down two drachmas or shut up.

DIONYSUS
Here's one and a half.

CORPSE
I'd sooner live again!

CORPSE is borne away.

XANTHIAS
Pretty arrogant, the bastard. To hell with him! I'll go. (*picks up the baggage*)

DIONYSUS
You're a fine gentleman. Let's head for the boat. (*they move to the edge of the stage*)

CHARON puts a wheeled boat into the orchestra and over to the stage.

CHARON
Woo-op, lay her alongside.

DIONYSUS
(*looking out over the orchestra*) What's this?

ΞΑΝΘΙΑΣ

τοῦτο; λίμνη.

ΔΙΟΝΥΣΟΣ

νὴ Δία
αὕτή 'στὶν ἣν ἔφραζε, καὶ πλοῖόν γ' ὁρῶ.

ΞΑΝΘΙΑΣ

νὴ τὸν Ποσειδῶ κἄστι γ' ὁ Χάρων οὑτοσί.

ΔΙΟΝΥΣΟΣ

χαῖρ', ὦ Χάρων.

ΞΑΝΘΙΑΣ

χαῖρ', ὦ Χάρων.

ΔΙΟΝΥΣΟΣ καὶ ΞΑΝΘΙΑΣ

χαῖρ', ὦ Χάρων.

ΧΑΡΩΝ

185   τίς εἰς ἀναπαύλας ἐκ κακῶν καὶ πραγμάτων;
τίς εἰς τὸ Λήθης πεδίον, ἢ 'ς Ὄκνου πλοκάς,
ἢ 'ς Κερβερίους, ἢ 'ς κόρακας, ἢ 'πὶ Ταίναρον;

ΔΙΟΝΥΣΟΣ

ἐγώ.

186 Ὄκνου πλοκάς Aristarchus ap. Phot. 338.8 = S o 399:
Ὄνου πόκας a testt.

---

[22] The triple greeting of Charon parodies a scene in Achaeus'
lost satyr play, *Aethon* (*TrGF* 20 F 11).

XANTHIAS

This? A lake.

DIONYSUS

Why yes, it's the very lake that he told us about, and I see a boat too.

XANTHIAS

Yes, by Poseidon, and that's Charon himself.

DIONYSUS

Welcome Charon!

XANTHIAS

Welcome, Charon!

DIONYSUS AND XANTHIAS

Welcome Charon![22]

CHARON

Who's for release from cares and troubles? Who's for the Plain of Oblivion? For Ocnus' Twinings?[23] The Land of the Cerberians?[24] The buzzards? Taenarum?[25]

DIONYSUS

Me.

[23] A famous painting by Polygnotus at Delphi (Pausanias 10.29.1–2) depicted Ocnus in the underworld, plaiting a rope that a donkey keeps eating away; and he was known elsewhere in Athenian drama (Cratinus fr. 367, Pollux 4.142).

[24] A people mentioned in Sophocles (fr. 1060) and (variant) in *Odyssey* 11.14; here appropriately suggesting Cerberus (111 n.).

[25] The middle of the three promontories at the southern tip of the Peloponnese (now Cape Matapan), where Heracles entered the underworld to fetch Cerberus.

ΧΑΡΩΝ

ταχέως ἔμβαινε.

ΔΙΟΝΥΣΟΣ
ποῦ σχήσειν δοκεῖς;

ΧΑΡΩΝ

ἐς κόρακας.

ΔΙΟΝΥΣΟΣ
ὄντως;

ΧΑΡΩΝ
ναὶ μὰ Δία, σοῦ γ᾽ οὕνεκα.
εἴσβαινε δή.

ΔΙΟΝΥΣΟΣ
παῖ, δεῦρο.

ΧΑΡΩΝ
190   δοῦλον οὐκ ἄγω,
εἰ μὴ νεναυμάχηκε τὴν περὶ τῶν κρεῶν.

ΞΑΝΘΙΑΣ
μὰ τὸν Δί᾽ οὐ γὰρ ἀλλ᾽ ἔτυχον ὀφθαλμιῶν.

ΧΑΡΩΝ
οὔκουν περιθρέξει δῆτα τὴν λίμνην τρέχων;

ΞΑΝΘΙΑΣ
ποῦ δῆτ᾽ ἀναμενῶ;

191 κρεῶν] νεκρῶν (cj. Demetrius Ixion teste Photio 1.350) R
K γρΣRVE
193 τρέχων A K: κύκλῳ R V

CHARON

Hurry aboard.

DIONYSUS

Where are you headed?

CHARON

To the buzzards!

DIONYSUS

Really?

CHARON

Sure, just for you. Now get aboard!

DIONYSUS

(*to Xanthias*) Come on, boy.

CHARON

I'm not taking a slave, not unless he fought for his hide in the sea battle.[26]

XANTHIAS

Actually, I couldn't be there; had the pinkeye.

CHARON

Then you'd better start running around the lake, double-time.

XANTHIAS

Then where should I wait?

[26] Arginusae, cf. 33 n.

ΧΑΡΩΝ

παρὰ τὸν Αὐαίνου λίθον,
ἐπὶ ταῖς ἀναπαύλαις.

ΔΙΟΝΤΣΟΣ

μανθάνεις;

ΞΑΝΘΙΑΣ

195   πάνυ μανθάνω.
οἴμοι κακοδαίμων, τῷ ξυνέτυχον ἐξιών;

ΧΑΡΩΝ

κάθιζ᾽ ἐπὶ κώπην. εἴ τις ἔτι πλεῖ, σπευδέτω.
οὗτος, τί ποιεῖς;

ΔΙΟΝΤΣΟΣ

                 ὅ τι ποιῶ; τί δ᾽ ἄλλο γ᾽ ἢ
ἴζω ᾽πὶ κώπην, οὗπερ ἐκέλευές με σύ;

ΧΑΡΩΝ

200 οὔκουν καθεδεῖ δῆτ᾽ ἐνθαδί, γάστρων;

ΔΙΟΝΤΣΟΣ

                              ἰδού.

ΧΑΡΩΝ

οὔκουν προβαλεῖ τὼ χεῖρε κἀκτενεῖς;

ΔΙΟΝΤΣΟΣ

                              ἰδού.

ΧΑΡΩΝ

οὐ μὴ φλυαρήσεις ἔχων, ἀλλ᾽ ἀντιβὰς
ἐλᾷς προθύμως.

CHARON

By the Withering Stone; there's a rest stop there.

DIONYSUS

Did you get that?

XANTHIAS

Loud and clear. Damn my luck, what crossed my path when I left the house?

Exit XANTHIAS *by one of the parodoi.*

CHARON

(*to Dionysus*) Sit to the oar. (*Dionysus gets into the boat*) If anyone else is sailing, hurry it up. (*to Dionysus*) Hey you there, what do you think you're doing?

DIONYSUS

Who me? Just sitting on the oar, right where you told me.

CHARON

No, sit over here, fatso.

DIONYSUS

All right.

CHARON

Now put out those hands and stretch your arms.

DIONYSUS

All right.

CHARON

Quit playing around! Put your feet against the stretcher and start rowing, gung-ho.

ΔΙΟΝΥΣΟΣ

κᾆτα πῶς δυνήσομαι
ἄπειρος, ἀθαλάττευτος, ἀσαλαμίνιος
ὢν εἶτ᾽ ἐλαύνειν;

ΧΑΡΩΝ

205   ῥᾷστ᾽· ἀκούσει γὰρ μέλη
κάλλιστ᾽, ἐπειδὰν ἐμβάλῃς ἅπαξ.

ΔΙΟΝΥΣΟΣ

                    τίνων;

ΧΑΡΩΝ

βατράχων κύκνων θαυμαστά.

ΔΙΟΝΥΣΟΣ

               κατακέλευε δή.

ΧΑΡΩΝ

ὠοπόπ, ὠοπόπ.

ΒΑΤΡΑΧΟΙ

βρεκεκεκὲξ κοὰξ κοάξ,
210 βρεκεκεκὲξ κοὰξ κοάξ.
λιμναῖα κρηνῶν τέκνα,
    ξύναυλον ὕμνων βοὰν
    φθεγξώμεθ᾽, εὔγηρυν ἐμὰν
    ἀοιδάν, κοὰξ κοάξ,
215 ἣν ἀμφὶ Νυσήιον
    Διὸς Διόνυσον ἐν
    λίμναισιν ἰαχήσαμεν,
ἡνίχ᾽ ὁ κραιπαλόκωμος

DIONYSUS

Now how will I manage that? I'm green, a landlubber, no
Salaminian, and I'm supposed to row?

CHARON

It's very easy, because you'll hear some gorgeous songs as
soon as you dip your oar.

DIONYSUS

Whose songs?

CHARON

The Frog Swans; wonderful stuff.

DIONYSUS

Then give me the stroke.

CHARON

O-op-op, O-op-op.

As the boat moves across the orchestra, a CHORUS OF
FROGS *enter by the parodoi and begin to leap about, fol-
lowing the boat.*

FROGS

Brekekekex koax koax,
brekekekex koax koax!
Children of lake and stream,
let's voice a cry in concert
with the pipes, our own euphonious
song—koax koax—
that once we sounded
for the Nysean son of Zeus,
Dionysus, in the Marshes,
when the hungover throng of revellers

τοῖς ἱεροῖσι Χύτροις χω-
ρεῖ κατ᾽ ἐμὸν τέμενος λαῶν ὄχλος.
220 βρεκεκεκὲξ κοὰξ κοάξ.

ΔΙΟΝΥΣΟΣ

ἐγὼ δέ γ᾽ ἀλγεῖν ἄρχομαι
τὸν ὄρρον, ὦ κοὰξ κοάξ.

ΒΑΤΡΑΧΟΙ

βρεκεκεκὲξ κοὰξ κοάξ.

ΔΙΟΝΥΣΟΣ

ὑμῖν δ᾽ ἴσως οὐδὲν μέλει.

ΒΑΤΡΑΧΟΙ

225 βρεκεκεκὲξ κοὰξ κοάξ.

ΔΙΟΝΥΣΟΣ

ἀλλ᾽ ἐξόλοισθ᾽ αὐτῷ κοάξ·
οὐδὲν γάρ ἐστ᾽ ἀλλ᾽ ἢ κοάξ.

ΒΑΤΡΑΧΟΙ

εἰκότως γ᾽, ὦ πολλὰ πράττων.
ἐμὲ γὰρ ἔστερξαν εὔλυροί τε Μοῦσαι
230   καὶ κεροβάτας Πάν, ὁ καλαμόφθογγα παίζων·
231/2 προσεπιτέρπεται δ᾽ ὁ φορμικτὰς Ἀπόλλων,
ἕνεκα δόνακος, ὃν ὑπολύριον
ἔνυδρον ἐν λίμναις τρέφω.
235 βρεκεκεκὲξ κοὰξ κοάξ.

on holy Pot Day
reeled through my precinct. [27]
Brekekekex koax koax!

DIONYSUS

As for me, my butt's
getting sore, you koax koax.

FROGS

Brekekekex koax koax!

DIONYSUS

But I don't suppose you care.

FROGS

Brekekekex koax koax!

DIONYSUS

Blast you, and your koax too!
Yes, all you are is koax.

FROGS

Quite so, you busybody!
For the Muses skillful on the lyre cherish us,
and hornfoot Pan, who plays the tuneful reeds,
and Apollo the Harper delights in us too,
in thanks for the stalks that I grow
in lake water, as girding for his lyre.
Brekekekex koax koax!

[27] The sanctuary of Dionysus ("Nysean" refers to Nysa, the
mythical mountain of his birth) in the Marshes (located southwest
of the Acropolis) was the site of the Anthesteria festival, the sec-
ond day of which (Pitchers) featured heavy drinking, and the third
and final day (Pots) the dedication of the pitchers.

ΔΙΟΝΥΣΟΣ

ἐγὼ δὲ φλυκταίνας γ' ἔχω,
χὠ πρωκτὸς ἰδίει πάλαι,
κᾆτ' αὐτίκ' ἐκκύψας ἐρεῖ—

ΒΑΤΡΑΧΟΙ

βρεκεκεκὲξ κοὰξ κοάξ.

ΔΙΟΝΥΣΟΣ

240 ἀλλ', ὦ φιλῳδὸν γένος,
παύσασθε.

ΒΑΤΡΑΧΟΙ

μᾶλλον μὲν οὖν
φθεγξόμεσθ', εἰ δή ποτ' εὐ-
ηλίοις ἐν ἁμέραισιν
ἡλάμεσθα διὰ κυπείρου
καὶ φλέω, χαίροντες ᾠδῆς
245 πολυκολύμβοισι μέλεσιν,
ἢ Διὸς φεύγοντες ὄμβρον
ἔνυδρον ἐν βυθῷ χορείαν
αἰόλαν ἐφθεγξάμεσθα
πομφολυγοπαφλάσμασιν.

ΔΙΟΝΥΣΟΣ καὶ ΒΑΤΡΑΧΟΙ

250 βρεκεκεκὲξ κοὰξ κοάξ.

ΔΙΟΝΥΣΟΣ

τουτὶ παρ' ὑμῶν λαμβάνω.

ΒΑΤΡΑΧΟΙ

δεινὰ τἄρα πεισόμεσθα.

FROGS

DIONYSUS

But I've got blisters,
and my arsehole's been seeping,
and pretty soon it'll poke out and say—

FROGS

Brekekekex koax koax!

DIONYSUS

Ah, you songful race,
do stop!

FROGS

Oh no, we'll sound off
even louder, if ever
on sunshiny days
we hopped through sedge
and reed, rejoicing in our song's
busily diving melodies,
or if ever in flight from Zeus' rain
we chimed underwater in the depths
a chorale spangled with
bubbly ploppifications.

DIONYSUS AND FROGS

Brekekekex koax koax!

DIONYSUS

I'm borrowing this from you!

FROGS

What an awful thing to do!

---

238 ἐκ- Π2: ἐγ- a

ΔΙΟΝΥΣΟΣ

253/4   δεινότερα δ' ἔγωγ', ἐλαύνων
255   εἰ διαρραγήσομαι.

ΔΙΟΝΥΣΟΣ καὶ ΒΑΤΡΑΧΟΙ

βρεκεκεκὲξ κοὰξ κοάξ.

ΔΙΟΝΥΣΟΣ

οἰμώζετ'· οὐ γάρ μοι μέλει.

ΒΑΤΡΑΧΟΙ

ἀλλὰ μὴν κεκραξόμεσθά γ'
ὁπόσον ἡ φάρυξ ἂν ἡμῶν
χανδάνῃ δι' ἡμέρας·

ΔΙΟΝΥΣΟΣ καὶ ΒΑΤΡΑΧΟΙ

260   βρεκεκεκὲξ κοὰξ κοάξ.

ΔΙΟΝΥΣΟΣ

τούτῳ γὰρ οὐ νικήσετε.

ΒΑΤΡΑΧΟΙ

οὐδὲ μὴν ἡμᾶς σὺ πάντως.

ΔΙΟΝΥΣΟΣ

οὐδὲ μὴν ὑμεῖς γ' ἐμέ,
οὐδέποτε· κεκράξομαι γὰρ
265   κἂν με δῇ δι' ἡμέρας, ἔ-
ως ἂν ὑμῶν ἐπικρατήσω τῷ κοάξ.
βρεκεκεκὲξ κοὰξ κοάξ.

ἔμελλον ἄρα παύσειν ποθ' ὑμᾶς τοῦ κοάξ.

DIONYSUS

But more awful for me, if this rowing
makes me burst apart.

DIONYSUS AND FROGS

Brekekekex koax koax!

DIONYSUS

Wail away; what do I care?

FROGS

In fact we'll bellow
as loud as our gullets will stretch,
all the livelong day!

DIONYSUS AND FROGS

Brekekekex koax koax!

DIONYSUS

You won't beat me at this!

FROGS

And you absolutely won't beat us!

DIONYSUS

And you won't beat me either,
never, for if need be I'll bellow
all the livelong day, until
I vanquish you at koax.
Brekekekex koax koax!

Exit FROGS, *unseen by Dionysus.*

(*discovering them gone*) I knew I'd put a stop to that koax
of yours!

ΧΑΡΩΝ

ὦ παῦε, παῦε, παραβαλοῦ τῷ κωπίῳ.
ἔκβαιν᾽, ἀπόδος τὸν ναῦλον.

ΔΙΟΝΥΣΟΣ

270   ἔχε δὴ τὠβολώ.
ὁ Ξανθίας. ποῦ Ξανθίας; ἢ Ξανθία.

ΞΑΝΘΙΑΣ

ἰαῦ.

ΔΙΟΝΥΣΟΣ

βάδιζε δεῦρο.

ΞΑΝΘΙΑΣ

          χαῖρ᾽, ὦ δέσποτα.

ΔΙΟΝΥΣΟΣ

τί ἐστι τἀνταυθοῖ;

ΞΑΝΘΙΑΣ

          σκότος καὶ βόρβορος.

ΔΙΟΝΥΣΟΣ

κατεῖδες οὖν που τοὺς πατραλοίας αὐτόθι
καὶ τοὺς ἐπιόρκους, οὓς ἔλεγεν ἡμῖν;

ΞΑΝΘΙΑΣ

275   σὺ δ᾽ οὔ;

ΔΙΟΝΥΣΟΣ

νὴ τὸν Ποσειδῶ ᾽γωγε, καὶ νυνί γ᾽ ὁρῶ.
ἄγε δή, τί δρῶμεν;

FROGS

CHARON

(*as the boat reaches the stage*) Stop now, stop! Bring her alongside, with your oar. Off you go. Pay your fare!

DIONYSUS

Here's your two obols.

CHARON punts away and exits by a parodos.

Xanthias! Where's Xanthias! Hey Xanthias!

XANTHIAS

(*off*) Yo!

DIONYSUS

Get over here!

Reenter XANTHIAS by the other parodos, as having walked around the lake.

XANTHIAS

Hello, master.

DIONYSUS

What was your route like?

XANTHIAS

Darkness and mud.

DIONYSUS

So you must have seen those father beaters and perjurers that he told us about.

XANTHIAS

Didn't you?

DIONYSUS

Sure I did, by Poseidon; (*regarding the spectators*) and I can still see them. Well now, what's next?

ΞΑΝΘΙΑΣ

προϊέναι βέλτιστα νῷν,
ὡς οὗτος ὁ τόπος ἐστὶν οὗ τὰ θηρία
τὰ δείν᾽ ἔφασκ᾽ ἐκεῖνος.

ΔΙΟΝΤΣΟΣ

ὡς οἰμώξεται.

280 ἠλαζονεύεθ᾽ ἵνα φοβηθείην ἐγώ,
εἰδώς με μάχιμον ὄντα, φιλοτιμούμενος.
οὐδὲν γὰρ οὕτω γαῦρόν ἐσθ᾽ ὡς Ἡρακλῆς.
ἐγὼ δέ γ᾽ εὐξαίμην ἂν ἐντυχεῖν τινι
λαβεῖν τ᾽ ἀγώνισμ᾽ ἄξιόν τι τῆς ὁδοῦ.

ΞΑΝΘΙΑΣ

285 νὴ τὸν Δία· καὶ μὴν αἰσθάνομαι ψόφου τινός.

ΔΙΟΝΤΣΟΣ

ποῦ ποῦ 'στ᾽;

ΞΑΝΘΙΑΣ

ὄπισθεν.

ΔΙΟΝΤΣΟΣ

ἐξόπισθέ νυν ἴθι.

ΞΑΝΘΙΑΣ

ἀλλ᾽ ἔστιν ἐν τῷ πρόσθε.

ΔΙΟΝΤΣΟΣ

πρόσθε νυν ἴθι.

ΞΑΝΘΙΑΣ

καὶ μὴν ὁρῶ νὴ τὸν Δία θηρίον μέγα.

XANTHIAS

We'd best be moving along, because this is the place where he was talking about those awful beasts.

DIONYSUS

And he'll regret it! He was bluffing, trying to scare me; he knew I'm a fighter, and he wanted no rival. There's nothing as puffed up as Heracles.[28] Why, I'd like nothing better than to run across one of them and chalk up an achievement worthy of this journey.

XANTHIAS

I know you would. As a matter of fact, I can hear something.

DIONYSUS

Where? Where is it?

XANTHIAS

Behind you.

DIONYSUS

Then get behind me!

XANTHIAS

But now it's in front.

DIONYSUS

Then get in front of me!

XANTHIAS

And now, by Zeus, I see a huge beast.

[28] Sophocles, *Philoctetes* fr. 788.1 (substituting "Heracles" for "a man").

ARISTOPHANES

ΔΙΟΝΥΣΟΣ

ποῖόν τι;

ΞΑΝΘΙΑΣ

δεινόν. παντοδαπὸν γοῦν γίγνεται·
290 τοτὲ μέν γε βοῦς, νυνὶ δ᾽ ὀρεύς, τοτὲ δ᾽ αὖ γυνὴ
ὡραιοτάτη τις.

ΔΙΟΝΥΣΟΣ

ποῦ 'στι; φέρ᾽ ἐπ᾽ αὐτὴν ἴω.

ΞΑΝΘΙΑΣ

ἀλλ᾽ οὐκέτ᾽ αὖ γυνή 'στιν, ἀλλ᾽ ἤδη κύων.

ΔΙΟΝΥΣΟΣ

Ἔμπουσα τοίνυν ἐστί.

ΞΑΝΘΙΑΣ

πυρὶ γοῦν λάμπεται
ἅπαν τὸ πρόσωπον.

ΔΙΟΝΥΣΟΣ

καὶ σκέλος χαλκοῦν ἔχει;

ΞΑΝΘΙΑΣ

295 νὴ τὸν Ποσειδῶ, καὶ βολίτινον θάτερον,
σάφ᾽ ἴσθι.

ΔΙΟΝΥΣΟΣ

ποῖ δῆτ᾽ ἂν τραποίμην;

ΞΑΝΘΙΑΣ

ποῖ δ᾽ ἐγώ;

DIONYSUS

What kind?

XANTHIAS

Frightful! Anyway, it's a shape-shifter: now a cow; now a mule; and now a woman, very nice looking.

DIONYSUS

Where? Come on, let me at her!

XANTHIAS

Wait, she's not a woman any more, she's a bitch.

DIONYSUS

Then it must be Empusa!

XANTHIAS

Yes, her whole face is ablaze with fire.

DIONYSUS

And does she have a brazen leg?

XANTHIAS

Yes indeed, and the other one's made of dung, I swear.

DIONYSUS

(*running about*) Where can I run to?

XANTHIAS

Where can I?

ΔΙΟΝΤΣΟΣ

ἱερεῦ, διαφύλαξόν μ', ἵν' ὦ σοι ξυμπότης.

ΞΑΝΘΙΑΣ

ἀπολούμεθ', ὦναξ Ἡράκλεις.

ΔΙΟΝΤΣΟΣ

οὐ μὴ καλεῖς μ',
ὦνθρωφ', ἱκετεύω, μηδὲ κατερεῖς τοὔνομα.

ΞΑΝΘΙΑΣ

Διόνυσε τοίνυν.

ΔΙΟΝΤΣΟΣ

300   τοῦτ' ἔθ' ἧττον θἀτέρου.

ΞΑΝΘΙΑΣ

ἴθ' ᾗπερ ἔρχει. δεῦρο δεῦρ', ὦ δέσποτα.

ΔΙΟΝΤΣΟΣ

τί δ' ἐστί;

ΞΑΝΘΙΑΣ

θάρρει· πάντ' ἀγαθὰ πεπράγαμεν,
ἔξεστί θ' ὥσπερ Ἡγέλοχος ἡμῖν λέγειν·
"ἐκ κυμάτων γὰρ αὖθις αὖ γαλῆν ὁρῶ."
Ἔμπουσα φρούδη.

ΔΙΟΝΤΣΟΣ

305   κατόμοσον.

DIONYSUS

(*to the Priest of Dionysus in the front row of seats*) Priest, save me, so I can come to your party![29]

XANTHIAS

Lord Heracles, we're done for!

DIONYSUS

Don't invoke me, man, I beg you, and don't use my name![30]

XANTHIAS

Well then, hey Dionysus!

DIONYSUS

That's even worse!

XANTHIAS

(*to the imaginary Empusa*) Begone now! (*to Dionysus*) Come here, master; over here.

DIONYSUS

What?

XANTHIAS

Buck up; everything's working out just fine, and we can say, with Hegelochus, "After the storm how weasily we sail."[31] Empusa's gone.

DIONYSUS

Swear it.

---

[29] Party for a victorious troupe after the performance, cf. *Acharnians* 1085–94.

[30] Dionysus is still disguised as Heracles.

[31] This actor played the lead in Euripides' play *Orestes* three years earlier, and had thus mispronounced line 279; the comic poets Sannyrion (fr. 8) and Strattis (frr. 1, 63) also recall his mishap.

ΞΑΝΘΙΑΣ
νὴ τὸν Δία.

ΔΙΟΝΥΣΟΣ
καῦθις κατόμοσον.

ΞΑΝΘΙΑΣ
νὴ Δί'.

ΔΙΟΝΥΣΟΣ
ὄμοσον.

ΞΑΝΘΙΑΣ
νὴ Δία.

ΔΙΟΝΥΣΟΣ
οἴμοι τάλας, ὡς ὠχρίασ' αὐτὴν ἰδών.

ΞΑΝΘΙΑΣ
ὁδὶ δὲ δείσας ὑπερεπυρρίασέ σου.

ΔΙΟΝΥΣΟΣ
οἴμοι, πόθεν μοι τὰ κακὰ ταυτὶ προσέπεσεν;
310 τίν' αἰτιάσομαι θεῶν μ' ἀπολλύναι;
αἰθέρα Διὸς δωμάτιον ἢ χρόνου πόδα;

ΞΑΝΘΙΑΣ
οὗτος.

ΔΙΟΝΥΣΟΣ
τί ἐστιν;

308 σοῦ R: μοῦ A K: που V

XANTHIAS

So help me Zeus.

DIONYSUS

Swear it again!

XANTHIAS

By Zeus.

DIONYSUS

Swear.

XANTHIAS

By Zeus.

DIONYSUS

Good grief, how pale I went at the very sight of her!

XANTHIAS

(*indicating Dionysus' robe*) And how brown *this* went in fear for you!

DIONYSUS

Alas, whence have these woes befallen me? Whom of the gods shall I blame for my undoing? Aether, Bedchamber of Zeus? Or Time's Foot?[32]

XANTHIAS

Shhh.

DIONYSUS

What is it?

[32] Cf. line 100.

ΞΑΝΘΙΑΣ

οὐ κατήκουσας;

ΔΙΟΝΥΣΟΣ

τίνος;

ΞΑΝΘΙΑΣ

αὐλῶν πνοῆς.

ΔΙΟΝΥΣΟΣ

ἔγωγε, καὶ δᾴδων γέ με
αὔρα τις εἰσέπνευσε μυστικωτάτη.
315 ἀλλ' ἠρεμεὶ πτήξαντες ἀκροασώμεθα.

ΧΟΡΟΣ

Ἴακχ', ὦ Ἴακχε.
Ἴακχ', ὦ Ἴακχε.

ΞΑΝΘΙΑΣ

τοῦτ' ἔστ' ἐκεῖν', ὦ δέσποθ'· οἱ μεμνημένοι
ἐνταῦθά που παίζουσιν, οὓς ἔφραζε νῷν.
320 ᾄδουσι γοῦν τὸν Ἴακχον ὅνπερ Διαγόρας.

ΔΙΟΝΥΣΟΣ

κἀμοὶ δοκοῦσιν. ἡσυχίαν τοίνυν ἄγειν
βέλτιστόν ἐστιν, ὡς ἂν εἰδῶμεν σαφῶς.

---

320 Διαγόρας R A K γρV ΣR Aristarchus ap. ΣE Lex. Vindob.:
δι' ἀγορᾶς V Apollodorus Tarsensis ap. ΣE Hesych. δ 975

XANTHIAS

Didn't you hear?

DIONYSUS

Hear what?

XANTHIAS

The breath of pipes.

DIONYSUS

I did, and a most mystic whiff of torches wafted over me.
Let's hunker down here and have a listen.

CHORUS

(*off*)

    Iacchus, Iacchus![33]
    Iacchus, Iacchus!

XANTHIAS

It's just as I thought, master: the initiates he told us about
are frolicking hereabouts. Listen, they're singing the Iac-
chus Hymn, the one by Diagoras.[34]

DIONYSUS

I think so too. We'd better keep still until we know for sure.

Enter CHORUS *of male and female initiates, wearing worn
clothes and carrying torches.*

---

[33] The Eleusinian cult name of Dionysus.

[34] Diagoras of Melos was a noted atheist who by 414 had been
outlawed from Athens with a price on his head for impugning
the Mysteries in a lyric poem (*Clouds* 830, *Birds* 1073–74,
Hermippus fr. 43, [Lysias] 6.17, Craterus *FGrH* 342 F 16). The al-
ternative segmentation *di' agoras* ("the one ‹they sing when pro-
cessing› through the agora") is unlikely Greek.

ΧΟΡΟΣ

(στρ) Ἴακχ’, ὦ πολυτίμητ’ ἐν ἕδραις ἐνθάδε ναίων,
325   Ἴακχ’, ὦ Ἴακχε,
ἐλθὲ τόνδ’ ἀνὰ λειμῶνα χορεύσων
ὁσίους εἰς θιασώτας,
πολύκαρπον μὲν τινάσσων
περὶ κρατὶ σῷ βρύοντα
330/1   στέφανον μύρτων, θρασεῖ δ’ ἐγκατακρούων
ποδὶ τὴν ἀκόλαστον
φιλοπαίγμονα τιμήν,
334/5   Χαρίτων πλεῖστον ἔχουσαν μέρος, ἁγνήν, ἱερὰν
ὁσίοις μύσταις χορείαν.

ΞΑΝΘΙΑΣ

ὦ πότνια πολυτίμητε Δήμητρος κόρη,
ὡς ἡδύ μοι προσέπνευσε χοιρείων κρεῶν.

ΔΙΟΝΥΣΟΣ

οὔκουν ἀτρέμ’ ἕξεις, ἤν τι καὶ χορδῆς λάβῃς;

ΧΟΡΟΣ

(ἀντ) ἔγειρ’ ⟨ὦ⟩ φλογέας λάμπαδας ἐν χερσὶ τινάσσων,
342   Ἴακχ’, ὦ Ἴακχε,
νυκτέρου τελετῆς φωσφόρος ἀστήρ.
φλέγεται δὴ φλογὶ λειμών·
345   γόνυ πάλλεται γερόντων·
ἀποσείονται δὲ λύπας
347/8   χρονίους τ’ ἐτῶν παλαιῶν ἐνιαυτοὺς
ἱερᾶς ὑπὸ τιμῆς.
350   σὺ δὲ λαμπάδι φέγγων

CHORUS

Iacchus, dwelling exalted here in your abode,
Iacchus, Iacchus,
come to this meadow to dance
with your reverent followers,
brandishing about your brow
a fruitful, a burgeoning
garland of myrtle, and stamping
with bold foot in our licentious,
fun-loving worship,
that is richly endowed by the Graces, a dance
pure and holy to pious initiates.

XANTHIAS

Most exalted lady, daughter of Demeter, what a nice aroma
of pork wafted over me!

DIONYSUS

Then be still, and you might get some sausage too.

CHORUS

Awaken blazing torches, tossing them in your hands,
Iacchus, Iacchus,
brilliant star of our nighttime rite!
Lo, the meadow's ablaze with flame,
and old men's knees are aleap
as they shed their cares
and the longdrawn seasons of ancient years,
owing to your worship.
Now illuminate with torchlight

---

344 φλέγεται   δὴ   φλογὶ   Hermann: φλογὶ   φλέγεται
(φέγγεται Rᵖᶜ: φθέγγεταιᵃᶜ) δὲ V A U Mᵖᶜ

προβάδην ἔξαγ᾽ ἐπ᾽ ἀνθηρὸν ἕλειον δάπεδον
χοροποιόν, μάκαρ, ἥβαν.

ΚΟΡΥΦΑΙΟΣ

εὐφημεῖν χρὴ κἀξίστασθαι τοῖς ἡμετέροισι
χοροῖσιν,

355 ὅστις ἄπειρος τοιῶνδε λόγων ἢ γνώμην μὴ
καθαρεύει

ἢ γενναίων ὄργια Μουσῶν μήτ᾽ εἶδεν μήτ᾽
ἐχόρευσεν,

μηδὲ Κρατίνου τοῦ ταυροφάγου γλώττης Βακχεῖ᾽
ἐτελέσθη,

ἢ βωμολόχοις ἔπεσιν χαίρει μὴ ᾽ν καιρῷ τοῦτο
ποιούντων,

ἢ στάσιν ἐχθρὰν μὴ καταλύει μηδ᾽ εὔκολός ἐστι
πολίταις,

360 ἀλλ᾽ ἀνεγείρει καὶ ῥιπίζει κερδῶν ἰδίων ἐπιθυμῶν,

ἢ τῆς πόλεως χειμαζομένης ἄρχων
καταδωροδοκεῖται,

ἢ προδίδωσιν φρούριον ἢ ναῦς, ἢ τἀπόρρητ᾽
ἀποπέμπει

ἐξ Αἰγίνης Θωρυκίων ὢν εἰκοστολόγος κακοδαίμων,

ἀσκώματα καὶ λίνα καὶ πίτταν διαπέμπων εἰς
Ἐπίδαυρον,

365 ἢ χρήματα ταῖς τῶν ἀντιπάλων ναυσὶν παρέχειν
τινὰ πείθει,

ἢ κατατιλᾷ τῶν Ἑκατείων κυκλίοισι χοροῖσιν
ὑπᾴδων,

and lead forth to blooming meadowland
our dancing youth, o blest one!

CHORUS LEADER

All speak fair, and the following shall stand apart from
our dances: whoever is unfamiliar with such utterances as
this, or harbors unclean attitudes, or has never beheld
or danced in the rites of the first-class Muses nor been
initiated in the Bacchic rites of bull-eating Cratinus' lan-
guage,[35] or enjoys clownish words from those who deliver
them at the wrong time, or forbears to resolve hateful
factionalism and act peaceably toward other citizens,[36] but
foments and inflames it from desire for personal gain, or as
an official sells out the city when she's tossed on stormy
seas, or betrays a fortress or fleet, or is a goddamned collec-
tor of 5% duties like Thorycion[37] and ships contraband
from Aegina, sending oar pads, flax, and pitch across to
Epidaurus,[38] or talks someone into supplying money for
our adversaries' navy, or shits on the offerings for Hecate

---

[35] Cratinus, here given a Dionysiac epithet, was the leading
comic poet of the generation before Aristophanes; his last attested
play, *Pytine*, defeated *Clouds* in 423.

[36] Or, with the variant, "and act like a peaceable citizen."

[37] In 413 these harbor duties on Athens' allies had replaced
the tribute; according to the scholia, Thorycion was a taxiarch.

[38] The island of Aegina was an Athenian settlement, and
Epidaurus a contributor to the Peloponnesian navy.

---

358 ποιούντων von Velsen: ποιοῦσιν a
359 πολίταις K: πολιτ R: πολίτης V A

ἢ τοὺς μισθοὺς τῶν ποιητῶν ῥήτωρ ὢν εἶτ᾽
    ἀποτρώγει,
κωμῳδηθεὶς ἐν ταῖς πατρίοις τελεταῖς ταῖς τοῦ
    Διονύσου.
τούτοις αὐδῶ καὖθις ἐπαυδῶ καὖθις τὸ τρίτον μάλ᾽
    ἐπαυδῶ
370 ἐξίστασθαι μύσταισι χοροῖς· ὑμεῖς δ᾽ ἀνεγείρετε
    μολπὴν
καὶ παννυχίδας τὰς ἡμετέρας, αἳ τῇδε πρέπουσιν
    ἑορτῇ.

ΧΟΡΟΣ

(στρ) χώρει νυν πᾶς ἀνδρείως
    εἰς τοὺς εὐανθεῖς κόλπους
374a λειμώνων ἐγκρούων
374b κἀπισκώπτων
375 καὶ παίζων καὶ χλευάζων.
    ἠρίστηται δ᾽ ἐξαρκούντως.

(ἀντ) ἀλλ᾽ ἔμβα χὤπως ἀρεῖς
    τὴν Σώτειραν γενναίως
    τῇ φωνῇ μολπάζων,
380 ἢ τὴν χώραν
    σώσειν φήσ᾽ εἰς τὰς ὥρας,
    κἂν Θωρυκίων μὴ βούληται.

ΚΟΡΥΦΑΙΟΣ

ἄγε νυν ἑτέραν ὕμνων ἰδέαν τὴν καρποφόρον
    βασίλειαν,

while singing for dithyrambic choruses,[39] or is a politician who nibbles away the poets' honoraria after being lampooned in a comedy during the ancestral rites of Dionysus.[40] To these I proclaim, and proclaim again, and thrice proclaim: stand apart from the initiates' dances; (*to the Chorus*) but do you awaken the song and our nightlong revels, which befit this festival.

CHORUS
Move on now boldly, everyone,
to the lap of the flowery
meadows, stamping the ground
and jesting
and frolicking and mocking;
you've breakfasted well enough!

So step out and be sure you exalt
the Savior Goddess[41] in fine fashion,
hymning her with your voices,
she who vows to safeguard
our land through the ages,
despite what Thorycion wants.

CHORUS LEADER
Come now, celebrate in another form of song the queen of

---

[39] A reference to Cinesias (*Assemblywomen* 330 n.); for the offerings cf. *Wealth* 594–99.

[40] The scholia identify the author of this proposal (also mentioned in Plato com. fr. 141 and Sannyrion fr. 9) as Archinus "and possibly" (but less plausibly) "Agyrrhius."

[41] Athena.

Δήμητρα θεάν, ἐπικοσμοῦντες ζαθέοις μολπαῖς
κελαδεῖτε.

ΧΟΡΟΣ

(στρ.) Δήμητερ, ἁγνῶν ὀργίων
      ἄνασσα, συμπαραστάτει,
386   καὶ σῷζε τὸν σαυτῆς χορόν·
      καί μ' ἀσφαλῶς πανήμερον
      παῖσαί τε καὶ χορεῦσαι.

(ἀντ) καὶ πολλὰ μὲν γέλοιά μ' εἰ-
390   πεῖν, πολλὰ δὲ σπουδαῖα, καὶ
      τῆς σῆς ἑορτῆς ἀξίως
      παίσαντα καὶ σκώψαντα νι-
      κήσαντα ταινιοῦσθαι.

      ἄγ' εἷά νυν
395   καὶ τὸν ὡραῖον θεὸν παρακαλεῖτε δεῦρο
      ᾠδαῖσι, τὸν ξυνέμπορον τῆσδε τῆς χορείας.

(στρ) Ἴακχε πολυτίμητε, μέλος ἑορτῆς
      ἥδιστον εὑρών, δεῦρο συνακολούθει
400   πρὸς τὴν θεὸν
      καὶ δεῖξον ὡς ἄνευ πόνου
      πολλὴν ὁδὸν περαίνεις.
      Ἴακχε φιλοχορευτά, συμπρόπεμπέ με.

(ἀντ. α) σὺ γὰρ κατεσχίσω μὲν ἐπὶ γέλωτι

78

bounteous harvests, the goddess Demeter, adorning her
with holy hymns.

CHORUS

Demeter, lady of pure rites,
stand beside us
and keep your chorus safe;
and may I safely frolic and dance
all the livelong day.

And may I utter much that's funny,
and also much that's serious,
and may I frolic and jest
worthily of your festival
and be garlanded in victory.

Hey now,
let your song invite the youthful god as well,
our travel companion in this dance.

Exalted Iacchus, inventor of most enjoyable
festive song, come and march along with us
to the goddess,
and show us how effortlessly
you get through a long trek.[42]
Iacchus lover of choruses, escort me on my way.

For it was you who, for a joke

---

[42] From Athens to Eleusis, about twelve miles.

405 κἀπ᾽ εὐτελείᾳ τόδε τὸ σανδαλίσκον
καὶ τὸ ῥάκος,
κἀξηῦρες ὥστ᾽ ἀζημίους
παίζειν τε καὶ χορεύειν.
Ἴακχε φιλοχορευτά, συμπρόπεμπέ με.

(ἀντ. β) καὶ γὰρ παραβλέψας τι μειρακίσκης
410 νυνδὴ κατεῖδον καὶ μάλ᾽ εὐπροσώπου,
συμπαιστρίας,
χιτωνίου παραρραγέν-
τος τιτθίον προκύψαν.
Ἴακχε φιλοχορευτά, συμπρόπεμπέ με.

ΔΙΟΝΥΣΟΣ

ἐγὼ δ᾽ ἀεί πως φιλακόλου-
θός εἰμι καὶ μετ᾽ αὐτῆς
παίζων χορεύειν βούλομαι.

ΞΑΝΘΙΑΣ

415   κἄγωγε πρός.

ΧΟΡΟΣ

βούλεσθε δῆτα κοινῇ
σκώψωμεν Ἀρχέδημον;
ὃς ἑπτέτης ὢν οὐκ ἔφυσε φράτερας,

---

43 The chorus, in character as initiates, wear the customary old clothing (cf. *Wealth* 845 n.), but also call attention to the producer's cheapness in providing their costumes—no doubt a result of the Athenians' financial straits at this time: according to the scholiast, citing Aristotle (fr. 630), two producers were assigned

and for economizing, had my sandals split
and my rags tattered,[43]
and you who found a way for us
to frolic and dance without charge.
Iacchus lover of choruses, escort me on my way.

Just now in fact I stole a glance
at a young girl, a very pretty one too,
a playmate,
and where her dress was torn I saw
her titty peeking out.
Iacchus lover of choruses, escort me on my way.

DIONYSUS

I've always been an eager
follower, and want to play with her
as I dance.

XANTHIAS

Me too!

CHORUS

So what say we get together
and ridicule Archedemus?[44]
At seven he still hadn't cut his kinsdom teeth,[45]

to each competitor at the City Dionysia this year, because not
enough candidates could be found who could afford to undertake
the expense alone.

[44] Prosecutor of one of the commanders at Arginusae (Xeno-
phon *Hellenica* 1.7); known as "Bleary Eyes" (588, Lysias 14.25)
and mocked elsewhere for foreign ancestry (Eupolis fr. 80).

[45] Punning on *phrateras* ("brethren" of a phratry) and
phrasteres (permanent teeth). Enrollment of a boy in his father's
phratry normally took place in his first year, and was considered
proof of legitimate birth and citizen status.

νυνὶ δὲ δημαγωγεῖ
420 ἐν τοῖς ἄνω νεκροῖσι,
κἄστιν τὰ πρῶτα τῆς ἐκεῖ μοχθηρίας.

τὸν Κλεισθένους δ᾽ ἀκούω
ἐν ταῖς ταφαῖσι πρωκτὸν
τίλλειν ἑαυτοῦ καὶ σπαράττειν τὰς γνάθους·

425 κἀκόπτετ᾽ ἐγκεκυφώς,
κἄκλαε κἀκεκράγει
Σεβῖνον ὅστις ἐστὶν Ἀναφλύστιος.

καὶ Καλλίαν γέ φασι
τοῦτον τὸν Ἱπποκίνου
430 κύσθου λεοντῆν ναυμαχεῖν ἐνημμένον.

ΔΙΟΝΥΣΟΣ

ἔχοιτ᾽ ἂν οὖν φράσαι νῷν
Πλούτων᾽ ὅπου ᾽νθάδ᾽ οἰκεῖ;
ξένω γάρ ἐσμεν ἀρτίως ἀφιγμένω.

ΧΟΡΟΣ

μηδὲν μακρὰν ἀπέλθῃς,

422 Κλεισθένους R V A K: Κλεισθένη(ν) P20ʲ U L Aldina
429 Ἱπποκίνου Sternbach: Ἱπποβίνου a S
430 κύσθῳ Bothe

---

46 No son of Cleisthenes (48 n.) is otherwise attested; alterna-

but now he's a leading politician
among the stiffs above,
and holds the local record for rascality.

And I hear that Cleisthenes' son
is in the graveyard, plucking
his arsehole and tearing his cheeks;[46]

all bent over, he kept beating his head,
wailing and weeping
for Humpus of Wankton, whoever that may be.[47]

And Callias, we're told,
that son of Hippocoitus,[48]
fights at sea in a lionskin made of pussy.[49]

DIONYSUS

Now could you please tell us
where hereabouts Pluto dwells?
We're strangers who've just arrived.

CHORUS

You haven't very far to go

tive possibilities are "Cleisthenes' arsehole is . . . plucking and
tearing its cheeks," or (with the variant) "Cleisthenes is . . . pluck-
ing . . . his arsehole and tearing his cheeks."

[47] "Sebinus of Anaphlystus" (suggesting *se binein* "fuck you"
and *anaphlan* "masturbate") is evidently a fictitious name; it
recurs in *Assemblywomen* 979–80.   [48] Callias (*c.* 450–*c.* 366),
ridiculed in comedy for extravagance and debauchery since the
420s, by the 390s had largely squandered the fortune left him by
his father Hipponicus (cf. *Assemblywomen* 810–12), whose name
is here distorted for a pun on *kinein* "screw."

[49] Or, with Bothe's conjecture, "in a lionskin fights a pussy at
sea." Cf. also 501 n.

435 μηδ' αὖθις ἐπανέρῃ με,
ἀλλ' ἴσθ' ἐπ' αὐτὴν τὴν θύραν ἀφιγμένος.

ΔΙΟΝΥΣΟΣ

αἶροί ἂν αὖθις, ὦ παῖ.

ΞΑΝΘΙΑΣ

τουτὶ τί ἦν τὸ πρᾶγμα
ἀλλ' ἢ Διὸς Κόρινθος ἐν τοῖς στρώμασιν;

ΧΟΡΟΣ

440 χωρεῖτέ νυν
441/2 ἱερὸν ἀνὰ κύκλον θεᾶς, ἀνθοφόρον ἀν' ἄλσος
443/4 παίζοντες οἷς μετουσία θεοφιλοῦς ἑορτῆς.
445 ἐγὼ δὲ σὺν ταῖσιν κόραις εἶμι καὶ γυναιξίν,
446/7 οὗ παννυχίζουσιν θεᾷ, φέγγος ἱερὸν οἴσων.

(στρ) χωρῶμεν εἰς πολυρρόδους
λειμῶνας ἀνθεμώδεις,
450 τὸν ἡμέτερον τρόπον
τὸν καλλιχορώτατον
παίζοντες, ὃν ὄλβιαι
Μοῖραι ξυνάγουσιν.

(ἀντ) μόνοις γὰρ ἡμῖν ἥλιος
455 καὶ φέγγος ἱερόν ἐστιν,
ὅσοι μεμυήμεθ' εὐ-

455 ἱερὸν I R V K: ἱλαρὸν A

and needn't question me again:
I'll have you know you're right at his door.

DIONYSUS

Hoist it up again, boy.

XANTHIAS

This whole routine is nothing
but "Zeus' Cootie-rinthus" in the bedclothes.[50]

CHORUS

Go forward now
to the goddess' sacred circle, and in her blossoming
    grove
frolic, you who partake in the festival dear to the
    gods.
I will go with the girls and the women,
to carry the sacred flame where they revel all night
    for the goddess.

Let us go forward to the flowery
meadows full of roses,
frolicking in our own style
of beautiful dance,
which the blessed
Fates array.

For us alone is there sun
and sacred daylight,
for we are initiated

---

[50] "Zeus' son Corinthus" (here with a pun on *koreis* "bed-bugs") meant "the same old story."

σεβῆ τε διήγομεν
τρόπον περὶ τοὺς ξένους
καὶ τοὺς ἰδιώτας.

ΔΙΟΝΥΣΟΣ

460 ἄγε δὴ τίνα τρόπον τὴν θύραν κόψω; τίνα;
πῶς ἐνθάδ᾽ ἄρα κόπτουσιν οὑπιχώριοι;

ΞΑΝΘΙΑΣ

οὐ μὴ διατρίψεις, ἀλλὰ γεύσει τῆς θύρας,
καθ᾽ Ἡρακλέα τὸ σχῆμα καὶ τὸ λῆμ᾽ ἔχων.

ΔΙΟΝΥΣΟΣ

παῖ παῖ.

ΑΙΑΚΟΣ

τίς οὗτος;

ΔΙΟΝΥΣΟΣ

Ἡρακλῆς ὁ καρτερός.

ΑΙΑΚΟΣ

465 ὦ βδελυρὲ κἀναίσχυντε καὶ τολμηρὲ σὺ
καὶ μιαρὲ καὶ παμμίαρε καὶ μιαρώτατε,
ὃς τὸν κύν᾽ ἡμῶν ἐξελάσας τὸν Κέρβερον
ἀπῇξας ἄγχων κἀποδρὰς ᾤχου λαβών,
ὃν ἐγὼ ᾽φύλαττον. ἀλλὰ νῦν ἔχει μέσος·
470 τοία Στυγός σε μελανοκάρδιος πέτρα
Ἀχερόντιός τε σκόπελος αἱματοσταγὴς
φρουροῦσι, Κωκυτοῦ τε περίδρομοι κύνες,
ἔχιδνά θ᾽ ἑκατογκέφαλος, ἣ τὰ σπλάγχνα σου

and righteous was our behavior
toward strangers
and ordinary people.

DIONYSUS

Now then, how should I knock at the door? Hmm. I wonder how the locals knock here?

XANTHIAS

Stop dillydallying. Just tuck into that door; show Heracles' guts as well as his garb.

DIONYSUS

(*knocking with his club*) Boy! Boy!

AEACUS[51]

(*within*) Who's that?

DIONYSUS

The mighty Heracles.

AEACUS

(*emerging*) You loathesome, shameless, insolent scum you! Utter scum! Scum of the earth! You're the one who rustled our dog Cerberus, grabbed him by the throat and darted off and got clean away with him, the dog I was in charge of! Ah but now you're in a hammerlock, such is the black-hearted rock of Styx and such the blood-dripping crag of Acheron that hem you in, and the coursing hounds of Cocytus, and the hundred-headed Echidna, who shall lac-

---

[51] The son of Zeus and Aegina and father of Peleus, who with Minos and Rhadymanthus judges souls in Hades, but also popularly thought of, much like St. Peter later, as Pluto's gatekeeper and steward. In Critias' *Perithous* (fr. 1) he had similarly accosted and questioned Heracles on his way to rescue Theseus and Perithous from the underworld.

δισπαράξει· πλευμόνων τ' ἀνθάψεται
475 Ταρτησσία μύραινα, τὼ νεφρὼ δέ σου
αὐτοῖσιν ἐντέροισιν ἡματωμένω
διασπάσονται Γοργόνες Τειθράσιαι,
ἐφ' ἃς ἐγὼ δρομαῖον ὁρμήσω πόδα.

ΞΑΝΘΙΑΣ
οὗτος, τί δέδρακας;

ΔΙΟΝΤΣΟΣ
ἐγκέχοδα· κάλει θεόν.

ΞΑΝΘΙΑΣ
480 ὦ καταγέλαστ', οὔκουν ἀναστήσει ταχὺ
πρίν τινά σ' ἰδεῖν ἀλλότριον;

ΔΙΟΝΤΣΟΣ
ἀλλ' ὡρακιῶ.
ἀλλ' οἶσε πρὸς τὴν καρδίαν μου σπογγιάν.

ΞΑΝΘΙΑΣ
ἰδού, λαβέ· προσθοῦ. ποῦ 'στιν; ὦ χρυσοῖ θεοί,
ἐνταῦθ' ἔχεις τὴν καρδίαν;

ΔΙΟΝΤΣΟΣ
δείσασα γὰρ
485 εἰς τὴν κάτω μου κοιλίαν καθείρπυσεν.

ΞΑΝΘΙΑΣ
ὦ δειλότατε θεῶν σὺ κἀνθρώπων.

ΔΙΟΝΤΣΟΣ
ἐγώ;
πῶς δειλὸς ὅστις σπογγιὰν ᾔτησά σε;

erate your vitals, while the Tartessian moray clutches your
lungs and Teithrasian Gorgons[52] tear up your bleeding
balls, and your guts along with them! Whom I on rapid foot
shall now go fetch. (*goes back inside; Dionysus faints*)

XANTHIAS
Hey there, what's the matter?

DIONYSUS
My butt runneth over; let us pray.

XANTHIAS
Stand up right now, you clown, before somebody sees you!

DIONYSUS
But I feel faint. Please, give me a wet sponge for my heart.

XANTHIAS
Here, take this and apply it. Where is it? Ye golden gods, is
that where you keep your heart?

DIONYSUS
Yes, it got scared and sneaked down to my colon.

XANTHIAS
You're the worst coward in heaven and earth!

DIONYSUS
Who me, a coward? Me, who asked you for a sponge,

[52] Teithras was an Attic deme, presumably inhabited by some
formidable ladies.

οὐ τἂν ἕτερός γ' αὕτ' εἰργάσατ' ἀνήρ.

ΞΑΝΘΙΑΣ

ἀλλὰ τί;

ΔΙΟΝΥΣΟΣ

κατέκειτ' ἂν ὀσφραινόμενος, εἴπερ δειλὸς ἦν·
490 ἐγὼ δ' ἀνέστην καὶ προσέτ' ἀπεψησάμην.

ΞΑΝΘΙΑΣ

ἀνδρεῖά γ', ὦ Πόσειδον.

ΔΙΟΝΥΣΟΣ

οἶμαι νὴ Δία.
σὺ δ; οὐκ ἔδεισας τὸν ψόφον τῶν ῥημάτων
καὶ τὰς ἀπειλάς;

ΞΑΝΘΙΑΣ

οὐ μὰ Δί' οὐδ' ἐφρόντισα.

ΔΙΟΝΥΣΟΣ

ἴθι νυν, ἐπειδὴ λημιατίας κἀνδρεῖος εἶ,
495 σὺ μὲν γενοῦ 'γὼ τὸ ῥόπαλον τουτὶ λαβών
καὶ τὴν λεοντῆν, εἴπερ ἀφοβόσπλαγχνος εἶ·
ἐγὼ δ' ἔσομαί σοι σκευοφόρος ἐν τῷ μέρει.

ΞΑΝΘΙΑΣ

φέρε δὴ ταχέως αὕτ'· οὐ γὰρ ἀλλὰ πειστέον.
καὶ βλέψον εἰς τὸν Ἡρακλειοξανθίαν,
500 εἰ δειλὸς ἔσομαι καὶ κατὰ σὲ τὸ λῆμ' ἔχων.

ΔΙΟΝΥΣΟΣ

μὰ Δί' ἀλλ' ἀληθῶς οὐκ Μελίτης μαστιγίας.
φέρε νυν, ἐγὼ τὰ στρώματ' αἴρωμαι ταδί.

something no other man would have dared?

XANTHIAS
Well, what would he have done?

DIONYSUS
If he were a coward, he'd have lain there in his own stink.
But I got up, and wiped myself too.

XANTHIAS
Poseidon, what bravery!

DIONYSUS
Damn right. Say, weren't you scared by those noisy rants
and threats?

XANTHIAS
Nope, never even gave it a thought.

DIONYSUS
Very well, if you're such a brave he-man, take this club
here and be me, and the lionskin too, if you're such a hard-
ass. And I'll take my turn being your bellboy.

XANTHIAS
Then hand them right over; after all, an order's an order.
(*drops the baggage, dons the lionskin, and takes the club*)
Now watch Xanthio-Heracles, and see if I turn into a
yellow-belly like you.

DIONYSUS
Not a chance: you're that whip-fodder from Melite to the
life![53] Now let me hoist this baggage.

---

[53] Heracles had a temple in the deme Melite, but the scholia
see here an allusion to Callias, earlier mentioned as wearing a
lionskin (428–30 n.) and referred to also by Cratinus as a whipped
slave (fr. 81).

ΘΕΡΑΠΑΙΝΑ

ὦ φίλταθ' ἥκεις Ἡράκλεις; δεῦρ' εἴσιθι.
ἡ γὰρ θεός σ' ὡς ἐπύθεθ' ἥκοντ', εὐθέως
505 ἔπεττεν ἄρτους, ἧψε κατερικτῶν χύτρας
ἔτνους δύ' ἢ τρεῖς, βοῦν ἀπηνθράκιζ' ὅλον,
πλακοῦντας ὦπτα, κολλάβους. ἀλλ' εἴσιθι.

ΞΑΝΘΙΑΣ

κάλλιστ', ἐπαινῶ.

ΘΕΡΑΠΑΙΝΑ

μὰ τὸν Ἀπόλλω οὐ μή σ' ἐγὼ
περιόψομἀπελθόντ', ἐπεί τοι καὶ κρέα
510 ἀνέβραττεν ὀρνίθεια, καὶ τραγήματα
ἔφρυγε, κᾦνον ἀνεκέραννυ γλυκύτατον.
ἀλλ' εἴσιθ' ἅμ' ἐμοί.

ΞΑΝΘΙΑΣ

πάνυ καλῶς.

ΘΕΡΑΠΑΙΝΑ

ληρεῖς ἔχων·
οὐ γάρ σ' ἀφήσω. καὶ γὰρ αὐλητρίς τέ σοι
ἤδη 'νδον ἔσθ' ὡραιοτάτη κὠρχηστρίδες
ἕτεραι δύ' ἢ τρεῖς.

ΞΑΝΘΙΑΣ

515 πῶς λέγεις; ὀρχηστρίδες;

ΘΕΡΑΠΑΙΝΑ

ἡβυλλιῶσαι κᾆρτι παρατετιλμέναι.
ἀλλ' εἴσιθ', ὡς ὁ μάγειρος ἤδη τὰ τεμάχη

Enter MAID *from the palace.*

MAID

Heracles, sweetheart, is that you? Come right on inside.
When the goddess heard you'd come, she started baking
bread, heating two or three pots of split-pea soup, barbe-
cuing a whole ox, and putting pies in the oven, dinner rolls
too. Now come on in!

XANTHIAS

Thanks, you're too kind.

MAID

Absolutely not, I won't stand by and watch you leave! Lis-
ten, she was stewing birdmeat too, and toasting munchies,
and mixing up some very sweet wine. Now come on in
with me!

XANTHIAS

I'm quite fine.

MAID

Nonsense, I'm not letting you get away. Listen, there's a
piper girl in there already, very pretty, and two or three
dancing girls too.

XANTHIAS

What's that you say? Dancing girls?

MAID

In first flower and freshly trimmed. Now come in, because
the cook was just about to take the fish off the grill, and

ἔμελλ᾽ ἀφαιρεῖν χἠ τράπεζ᾽ εἰσῄρετο.

ΞΑΝΘΙΑΣ

ἴθι νυν, φράσον πρώτιστα ταῖς ὀρχηστρίσιν
520 ταῖς ἔνδον οὔσαις αὐτὸς ὅτι εἰσέρχομαι.
ὁ παῖς, ἀκολούθει δεῦρο τὰ σκεύη φέρων.

ΔΙΟΝΥΣΟΣ

ἐπίσχες, οὗτος. οὔ τί που σπουδὴν ποιεῖ,
ὁτιή σε παίζων Ἡρακλέα 'νεσκεύασα;
οὐ μὴ φλυαρήσεις ἔχων, ὦ Ξανθία,
525 ἀλλ᾽ ἀράμενος οἴσεις πάλιν τὰ στρώματα.

ΞΑΝΘΙΑΣ

τί δ᾽ ἐστίν; οὔ τί πού μ᾽ ἀφελέσθαι διανοεῖ
ἅδωκας αὐτός;

ΔΙΟΝΥΣΟΣ

οὐ τάχ᾽, ἀλλ᾽ ἤδη ποιῶ.
κατάθου τὸ δέρμα.

ΞΑΝΘΙΑΣ

ταῦτ᾽ ἐγὼ μαρτύρομαι
καὶ τοῖς θεοῖσιν ἐπιτρέπω.

ΔΙΟΝΥΣΟΣ

ποίοις θεοῖς;
530 τὸ δὲ προσδοκῆσαί σ᾽ οὐκ ἀνόητον καὶ κενὸν
ὡς δοῦλος ὢν καὶ θνητὸς Ἀλκμήνης ἔσει;

ΞΑΝΘΙΑΣ

ἀμέλει, καλῶς· ἔχ᾽ αὐτ᾽. ἴσως γάρ τοί ποτε
ἐμοῦ δεηθείης ἄν, εἰ θεὸς θέλοι.

they're bringing in the tables.

XANTHIAS
Then go on ahead, and tell those dancing girls that I'm coming right in, in person. (*to Dionysus*) Boy, come along here, and bring our stuff.

DIONYSUS
Hold on there, you're not really taking it seriously, my having some fun by dressing you up as Heracles? Now stop kidding around, Xanthias, and pick up that baggage again.

XANTHIAS
What? You're not really thinking about taking back what you gave me, are you?

DIONYSUS
(*grabbing the lionskin*) Not maybe, I'm doing it! Off with that lionskin.

XANTHIAS
Witnesses take note! I'm putting this in the gods' hands.

DIONYSUS
Gods indeed! And how brainless and vain of you, a mortal slave, to think that you could be Alcmene's son!

XANTHIAS
Oh all right, then, take them. There may come a time, you know, when you'll need me again, god willing.

ΧΟΡΟΣ

(στρ) ταῦτα μὲν πρὸς ἀνδρός ἐστι
νοῦν ἔχοντος καὶ φρένας
535 καὶ πολλὰ περιπεπλευκότος,
μετακυλίνδειν αὑτὸν ἀεὶ
537a πρὸς τὸν εὖ πράττοντα τοῖχον
537b μᾶλλον ἢ γεγραμμένην
εἰκόν᾽ ἑστάναι, λαβόνθ᾽ ἓν
539a σχῆμα· τὸ δὲ μεταστρέφεσθαι
539b πρὸς τὸ μαλθακώτερον
540 δεξιοῦ πρὸς ἀνδρός ἐστι
καὶ φύσει Θηραμένους.

ΔΙΟΝΥΣΟΣ

(ἀντ) οὐ γὰρ ἂν γέλοιον ἦν, εἰ
542b Ξανθίας μὲν δοῦλος ὢν ἐν
543a στρώμασιν Μιλησίοις
543b ἀνατετραμμένος κυνῶν ὀρ-
544a χηστρίδ᾽ εἶτ᾽ ᾔτησεν ἀμίδ᾽, ἐ-
544b γὼ δὲ πρὸς τοῦτον βλέπων
545 τοὐρεβίνθου ᾽δραττόμην, οὖ-
546a τος δ᾽ ἅτ᾽ ὢν καὐτὸς πανοῦργος
546b εἶδε, κᾆτ᾽ ἐκ τῆς γνάθου
πὺξ πατάξας μοὐξέκοψε
τοῦ χοροῦ τοὺς προσθίους;

FROGS

CHORUS

The mark of a man
with brains and sense,
one who's voyaged far and wide,
is ever to shift
to the comfy side of the ship
and not just stand fast
in one position, like a painted
picture; to roll over
to the softer side
is the mark of a smart man,
a born Theramenes.[54]

DIONYSUS

Wouldn't it be hilarious
if Xanthias, a mere slave,
were lying all atumble
on Milesian coverlets, and kissing
a dancing girl, then asked for a potty,
and I was looking over at him
with my weenie in hand,
and he caught me watching,
recognizing a fellow rascal, then
punched me in the mouth and knocked out
my front row of chorus men?

Enter from the side a female INNKEEPER *with her Maid.*

---

[54] A leading politician nicknamed "Buskin" (a boot that fits
either foot) for his knack of landing on his feet in any situation: in
411 he had helped both to establish and to overthrow the Four
Hundred, and after Arginusae had transferred blame for failing to
rescue Athenian shipwrecks onto his colleagues.

ΠΑΝΔΟΚΕΤΤΡΙΑ

Πλαθάνη, Πλαθάνη, δεῦρ' ἔλθ'. ὁ πανοῦργος
  οὑτοσί,
550 ὃς εἰς τὸ πανδοκεῖον εἰσελθών ποτε
  ἑκκαίδεκ' ἄρτους κατέφαγ' ἡμῶν.

ΠΛΑΘΑΝΗ

  νὴ Δία,
ἐκεῖνος αὐτὸς δῆτα.

ΞΑΝΘΙΑΣ

  κακὸν ἥκει τινί.

ΠΑΝΔΟΚΤΤΡΙΑ

καὶ κρέα γε πρὸς τούτοισιν ἀνάβραστ' εἴκοσιν
ἀνημιωβολιαῖα.

ΞΑΝΘΙΑΣ

  δώσει τις δίκην.

ΠΑΝΔΟΚΤΤΡΙΑ

καὶ τὰ σκόροδα τὰ πολλά.

ΔΙΟΝΤΣΟΣ

555   ληρεῖς, ὦ γύναι,
κοὐκ οἶσθ' ὅ τι λέγεις.

ΠΑΝΔΟΚΤΤΡΙΑ

  οὐ μὲν οὖν με προσεδόκας,
ὁτιὴ κοθόρνους εἶχες, ἀναγνῶναί σ' ἔτι.
τί δαί; τὸ πολὺ τάριχος οὐκ εἴρηκά πω.

INNKEEPER

Plathane![55] Plathane, come here! Here's that hooligan, the one who came to the inn and gobbled sixteen loaves of bread!

Enter PLATHANE with her Maid.

PLATHANE

By god, it *is* him!

XANTHIAS

Somebody's in for it.

INNKEEPER

And on top of that, twenty half-obol orders of stew at one go!

XANTHIAS

Somebody's gonna catch it.

INNKEEPER

And all that garlic!

DIONYSUS

Nonsense, madam; you don't know what you're talking about.

INNKEEPER

Hah! You didn't think I'd recognize you again with those buskins on. Well? I haven't even mentioned all that fish yet.

[55] The name (derived from *plathanon*, kneading board) was not uncommon.

ARISTOPHANES

ΠΛΑΘΑΝΗ

μὰ Δί' οὐδὲ τὸν τυρόν γε τὸν χλωρόν, τάλαν,
560 ὃν οὗτος αὐτοῖς τοῖς ταλάροις κατήσθιεν.

ΠΑΝΔΟΚΤΤΡΙΑ

κἄπειτ' ἐπειδὴ τἀργύριον ἐπραττόμην,
ἔβλεψεν εἴς με δριμὺ κἀμυκᾶτό γε—

ΞΑΝΘΙΑΣ

τούτου πάνυ τοὔργον· οὗτος ὁ τρόπος πανταχοῦ.

ΠΑΝΔΟΚΤΤΡΙΑ

καὶ τὸ ξίφος γ' ἐσπᾶτο μαίνεσθαι δοκῶν.

ΠΛΑΘΑΝΗ

νὴ Δία, τάλαινα.

ΠΑΝΔΟΚΤΤΡΙΑ

565   νὼ δὲ δεισάσα γέ που
ἐπὶ τὴν κατήλιφ' εὐθὺς ἀνεπηδήσαμεν·
ὁ δ' ᾤχετ' ἐξᾴξας γε τὰς ψιάθους λαβών.

ΞΑΝΘΙΑΣ

καὶ τοῦτο τούτου τοὔργον.

ΠΑΝΔΟΚΤΤΡΙΑ

                                   ἀλλ' ἐχρῆν τι δρᾶν.
ἴθι δὴ κάλεσον τὸν προστάτην Κλέωνά μοι.

ΠΛΑΘΑΝΗ

570 σὺ δ' ἔμοιγ', ἐάνπερ ἐπιτύχῃς, Ὑπέρβολον,
ἵν' αὐτὸν ἐπιτρίψωμεν.

PLATHANE

Right, dearie, or the fresh cheese that he ate up, baskets and all.

INNKEEPER

And when I presented the bill, he gave me a nasty look and started bellowing.

XANTHIAS

That's his style exactly; he acts that way everywhere.

INNKEEPER

And he drew his sword like a lunatic.

PLATHANE

Amen, my poor dear.

INNKEEPER

And we were so scared I guess we jumped right up to the loft, while he dashed out and got away, taking our mattresses with him.

XANTHIAS

That's his style, too.

INNKEEPER

Well, we should do something about it. (*to her Maid*) Go fetch my patron, Cleon.[56]

PLATHANE

(*to her Maid*) And you go fetch mine, Hyperbolus,[57] if you run into him, so that we can fix this guy good.

[56] The leading politician of the 420s, a champion of ordinary citizens, and notorious for prosecutory zeal (cf. *Knights* and *Wasps*); he died in 422.

[57] Cleon's successor, and also much satirized in comedy; he died in 411.

ARISTOPHANES

ΠΑΝΔΟΚΤΤΡΙΑ

ὦ μιαρὰ φάρυξ,
ὡς ἡδέως ἄν σου λίθῳ τοὺς γομφίους
κόπτοιμ' ἄν, οἷς μου κατέφαγες τὰ φορτία.

ΠΛΑΘΑΝΗ

ἐγὼ δέ γ' εἰς τὸ βάραθρον ἐμβάλοιμί σε.

ΠΑΝΔΟΚΤΤΡΙΑ

575 ἐγὼ δὲ τὸν λάρυγγ' ἂν ἐκτέμοιμί σου
δρέπανον λαβοῦσ', ᾧ τὰς χόλικας κατέσπασας.
ἀλλ' εἶμ' ἐπὶ τὸν Κλέων', ὃς αὐτοῦ τήμερον
ἐκπηνιεῖται ταῦτα προσκαλούμενος.

ΔΙΟΝΤΣΟΣ

κάκιστ' ἀπολοίμην, Ξανθίαν εἰ μὴ φιλῶ.

ΞΑΝΘΙΑΣ

580 οἶδ' οἶδα τὸν νοῦν· παῦε παῦε τοῦ λόγου.
οὐκ ἂν γενοίμην Ἡρακλῆς αὖ.

ΔΙΟΝΤΣΟΣ

μηδαμῶς,
ὦ Ξανθίδιον.

ΞΑΝΘΙΑΣ

καὶ πῶς ἂν Ἀλκμήνης ἐγὼ
υἱὸς γενοίμην δοῦλος ἅμα καὶ θνητὸς ὤν;

ΔΙΟΝΤΣΟΣ

οἶδ' οἶδ' ὅτι θυμοῖ, καὶ δικαίως αὐτὸ δρᾷς·
585 κἂν εἴ με τύπτοις, οὐκ ἂν ἀντείποιμί σοι.
ἀλλ' ἢν σε τοῦ λοιποῦ ποτ' ἀφέλωμαι χρόνου,

INNKEEPER

(*to Dionysus*) You filthy hog, I'd just love to take a rock and bash out your teeth, that gobbled my goods!

PLATHANE

And I'd love to toss you into the executioner's pit!

INNKEEPER

And I'd love to get a sickle and cut out your gizzard, that guzzled my sausages! Now I'm off to get Cleon; he'll summons this guy today and wind the stuffing out of him!

Exit INNKEEPER *and* PLATHANE.

DIONYSUS

May I die a miserable death if I don't love Xanthias!

XANTHIAS

I know what you're thinking, I know. Stop talking, stop it. I'm not going to be Heracles again.

DIONYSUS

Don't be that way, Xanthikins.

XANTHIAS

And how could I, a mere mortal slave, become Alcmene's son?

DIONYSUS

I know you're angry, I know, and you've every right to be. You could even take a punch at me and I wouldn't complain. But I swear, if ever I take it away from you again, may

πρόρριζος αὐτός, ἡ γυνή, τὰ παιδία,
κάκιστ᾽ ἀπολοίμην, κἀρχέδημος ὁ γλάμων.

ΞΑΝΘΙΑΣ
δέχομαι τὸν ὅρκον κἀπὶ τούτοις λαμβάνω.

ΧΟΡΟΣ
(στρ) νῦν σὸν ἔργον ἔστ᾽, ἐπειδὴ
591a   τὴν στολὴν εἴληφας ἥνπερ
591b   εἶχες, ἐξ ἀρχῆς πάλιν
592a   ἀνανεάζειν ⟨αὖ τὸ λῆμα⟩
592b   καὶ βλέπειν αὖθις τὸ δεινόν,
593a   τοῦ θεοῦ μεμνημένον
593b   ᾧπερ εἰκάζεις σεαυτόν.
         ἢν δὲ παραληρῶν ἁλῶς ἢ
595   κἀκβάλῃς τι μαλθακόν,
         αὖθις αἴρεσθαί σ᾽ ἀνάγκη
         'σται πάλιν τὰ στρώματα.

ΞΑΝΘΙΑΣ
(ἀντ) οὐ κακῶς, ὦνδρες, παραινεῖτ᾽,
598b   ἀλλὰ καὐτὸς τυγχάνω ταῦτ᾽
599a   ἄρτι συννοούμενος.
599b   ὅτι μὲν οὖν, ἢν χρηστὸν ᾖ τι,
600   ταῦτ᾽ ἀφαιρεῖσθαι πάλιν πει-
         ράσεταί μ᾽ εὖ οἶδ᾽ ὅτι.
602a   ἀλλ᾽ ὅμως ἐγὼ παρέξω
602b   'μαυτὸν ἀνδρεῖον τὸ λῆμα
603a   καὶ βλέποντ᾽ ὀρίγανον·
603b   δεῖν δ᾽ ἔοικεν, ὡς ἀκούω
         τῆς θύρας καὶ δὴ ψόφον.

104

I die a miserable death and be utterly eradicated, my wife
and children too, and bleary Archedemus!

XANTHIAS
I accept your oath, and will take the gear on those terms.

CHORUS
Now it's up to you,
since you've accepted the outfit
you wore before, to revive anew
your old fighting spirit,
and once more look formidable,
mindful of the god
whose guise you're taking on.
If you're caught jabbering,
if you utter anything wimpish,
you'll be forced to hoist
the baggage once again.

XANTHIAS
Gentlemen, that's not bad advice,
but just now I happened to be
thinking along those lines myself.
Yes, I'm quite aware
that if anything good's to be gained
he'll try to take this outfit back.
But all the same you'll find me
brave in spirit,
with a pungent look in my eye.
And I'd better be, because I hear,
yes, a clattering at the door.

---

592 suppl. Seidler
595 κἀκβάλῃς Π V: καὶ βάλῃς R A K

ΑΙΑΚΟΣ

605 ξυνδεῖτε ταχέως τουτονὶ τὸν κυνοκλόπον,
ἵνα δῷ δίκην· ἀνύετον.

ΔΙΟΝΤΣΟΣ
ἥκει τῳ κακόν.

ΞΑΝΘΙΑΣ
οὐκ ἐς κόρακας; μὴ πρόσιτον.

ΑΙΑΚΟΣ
εἶέν, καὶ μάχει;
ὁ Διτύλας χὠ Σκεβλύας χὠ Παρδόκας,
χωρεῖτε δευρὶ καὶ μάχεσθε τουτῳί.

ΔΙΟΝΤΣΟΣ
610 εἶτ᾽ οὐχὶ δεινὰ ταῦτα, τύπτειν τουτονὶ
κλέπτοντα πρὸς τἀλλότρια;

ΑΙΑΚΟΣ
μᾶλλ᾽ ὑπερφυᾶ.

ΔΙΟΝΤΣΟΣ
σχέτλια μὲν οὖν καὶ δεινά.

ΞΑΝΘΙΑΣ
καὶ μὴν νὴ Δία,
εἰ πώποτ᾽ ἦλθον δεῦρ᾽, ἐθέλω τεθνηκέναι,
ἢ 'κλεψα τῶν σῶν ἄξιόν τι καὶ τριχός.

AEACUS bursts out of the door, with two Slaves.

AEACUS

Tie up this dog thief here right away, so he can pay his penalty. Get a move on!

DIONYSUS

Somebody's in for it!

XANTHIAS

You two stay the hell away from me!

AEACUS

Oh, so you want to fight, eh? (*calling inside*) Ditylas! Sceblyas! Pardocas![58] Get out here and fight this guy!

Enter from the house Ditylas, Sceblyas, and Pardocas; they attack and subdue Xanthias.

DIONYSUS

Shocking, isn't it, the way this guy steals from people and then assaults them too!

AEACUS

Absolutely monstrous.

DIONYSUS

Terrible even, and shocking!

XANTHIAS

Now look here, dammit, I hope to die if I've ever been here before, or ever stole so much as a hair of your property!

---

[58] Names of (or suggesting) Scythian archers, who were used in Athens as police.

615   καί σοι ποιήσω πρᾶγμα γενναῖον πάνυ·
βασάνιζε γὰρ τὸν παῖδα τουτονὶ λαβών,
κἄν ποτέ μ᾽ ἕλῃς ἀδικοῦντ᾽, ἀπόκτεινόν μ᾽ ἄγων.

ΑΙΑΚΟΣ
καὶ πῶς βασανίσω;

ΞΑΝΘΙΑΣ
          πάντα τρόπον· ἐν κλίμακι
δήσας, κρεμάσας, ὑστριχίδι μαστιγῶν, δέρων,
620   στρεβλῶν, ἔτι δ᾽ εἰς τὰς ῥῖνας ὄξος ἐγχέων,
πλίνθους ἐπιτιθείς, πάντα τἄλλα, πλὴν πράσῳ
μὴ τύπτε τοῦτον μηδὲ γητείῳ νέῳ.

ΑΙΑΚΟΣ
δίκαιος ὁ λόγος· κἄν τι πηρώσω γέ σοι
τὸν παῖδα τύπτων, τἀργύριόν σοι κείσεται.

ΞΑΝΘΙΑΣ
625   μὴ δῆτ᾽ ἔμοιγ᾽. οὕτω δὲ βασάνιζ᾽ ἀπαγαγών.

ΑΙΑΚΟΣ
αὐτοῦ μὲν οὖν, ἵνα σοι κατ᾽ ὀφθαλμοὺς λέγῃ.
κατάθου σὺ τὰ σκεύη ταχέως, χὤπως ἐρεῖς
ἐνταῦθα μηδὲν ψεῦδος.

ΔΙΟΝΥΣΟΣ
          ἀγορεύω τινὶ
ἐμὲ μὴ βασανίζειν ἀθάνατον ὄντ᾽· εἰ δὲ μή,
αὐτὸς σεαυτὸν αἰτιῶ.

ΑΙΑΚΟΣ
630   λέγεις δὲ τί;

And I'll make you a right handsome offer: take my slave
here and torture him, and if you catch me in any wrong-
doing, then take me and put me to death.

AEACUS
And how should I torture him?

XANTHIAS
Any way you like. Bind him to the ladder. Hang him up.
Bristle-whip him. Flay him. Rack him. Pour vinegar up his
nose too. Put bricks on him. Anything at all, except don't
beat him with a stalk of leek or onion.

AEACUS
Fair enough. And of course if my beating maims your
slave, the compensation will be credited to your account.

XANTHIAS
Never mind that; just take him away and torture him.

AEACUS
No, I'll do it right here, so he can testify to your face. (*to
Dionysus*) Put that baggage down right away, and see that
you tell no lies here.

DIONYSUS
Somebody's hereby warned not to torture me, because I'm
immortal. Otherwise, you'll have only yourself to blame.

AEACUS
What are you talking about?

ΔΙΟΝΥΣΟΣ

ἀθάνατος εἶναί φημι, Διόνυσος Διός,
τοῦτον δὲ δοῦλον.

ΑΙΑΚΟΣ

ταῦτ᾽ ἀκούεις;

ΞΑΝΘΙΑΣ

φήμ᾽ ἐγώ.

καὶ πολύ γε μᾶλλόν ἐστι μαστιγωτέος·
εἴπερ θεὸς γάρ ἐστιν, οὐκ αἰσθήσεται.

ΔΙΟΝΥΣΟΣ

635   τί δῆτ᾽, ἐπειδὴ καὶ σὺ φῂς εἶναι θεός,
οὐ καὶ σὺ τύπτει τὰς ἴσας πληγὰς ἐμοί;

ΞΑΝΘΙΑΣ

δίκαιος ὁ λόγος· χὠπότερόν γ᾽ ἂν νῷν ἴδῃς
κλαύσαντα πρότερον ἢ προτιμήσαντά τι
τυπτόμενον, εἶναι τοῦτον ἡγοῦ μὴ θεόν.

ΑΙΑΚΟΣ

640   οὐκ ἔσθ᾽ ὅπως οὐκ εἶ σὺ γεννάδας ἀνήρ·
χωρεῖς γὰρ εἰς τὸ δίκαιον. ἀποδύεσθε δή.

ΞΑΝΘΙΑΣ

πῶς οὖν βασανιεῖς νὼ δικαίως;

ΑΙΑΚΟΣ

ῥᾳδίως·

πληγὴν παρὰ πληγὴν ἑκάτερον.

DIONYSUS

I'm saying that I'm immortal, Dionysus son of Zeus, and
he's the slave.

AEACUS

(*to Xanthias*) Do you hear that?

XANTHIAS

I do. And all the more reason for a flogging; if he's really a
god, he won't feel it.

DIONYSUS

All right, since you claim to be a god too, why shouldn't you
be beaten along with me, stroke for stroke?

XANTHIAS

Fair enough. (*to Aeacus*) And whichever of us you catch
yelping first, or caring at all that he's getting flogged, him
you can consider no god.

AEACUS

You're beyond question a gentleman, the way you take the
high road. Now both of you strip.

XANTHIAS

So how are you going to test us fairly?

AEACUS

Simple: stroke for stroke.

ΞΑΝΘΙΑΣ

καλῶς λέγεις.

ἰδού· σκόπει νυν ἤν μ' ὑποκινήσαντ' ἴδῃς.
ἤδη 'πάταξας;

ΑΙΑΚΟΣ

οὐ μὰ Δί'.

ΞΑΝΘΙΑΣ

645   οὐδ' ἐμοὶ δοκεῖς.

ΑΙΑΚΟΣ

ἀλλ' εἶμ' ἐπὶ τονδὶ καὶ πατάξω.

ΔΙΟΝΥΣΟΣ

πηνίκα;

ΑΙΑΚΟΣ

καὶ δὴ 'πάταξα.

ΔΙΟΝΥΣΟΣ

κᾆτα πῶς οὐκ ἔπταρον;

ΑΙΑΚΟΣ

οὐκ οἶδα· τουδὶ δ' αὖθις ἀποπειράσομαι.

ΞΑΝΘΙΑΣ

οὔκουν ἀνύσεις; ἰατταταῖ.

ΑΙΑΚΟΣ

τί τἀτταταῖ;

μῶν ὠδυνήθης;

ΞΑΝΘΙΑΣ

650   οὐ μὰ Δί', ἀλλ' ἐφρόντισα
ὁπόθ' Ἡράκλεια τἀν Διομείοις γίγνεται.

XANTHIAS

That's fine. (*presents his back*) OK, now see if you catch me
flinching. Have you hit me yet?

AEACUS

Zeus no. (*strikes Xanthias*)

XANTHIAS

That's what I thought.

AEACUS

All right, now I'll go hit this other one. (*strikes Dionysus*)

DIONYSUS

Say when.

AEACUS

I just hit you!

DIONYSUS

Then why didn't I sneeze?

AEACUS

No idea. I'll try the other one again.

XANTHIAS

Then hurry up! (*struck*) Ow!

AEACUS

Why the "ow"? Did that hurt?

XANTHIAS

Hell no, I was just thinking of when the Heracles festival at
Diomeia is scheduled.

ΑΙΑΚΟΣ

ἄνθρωπος ἱερός. δεῦρο πάλιν βαδιστέον.

ΔΙΟΝΤΣΟΣ

ἰοὺ ἰού.

ΑΙΑΚΟΣ

τί ἐστιν;

ΔΙΟΝΤΣΟΣ

ἱππέας ὁρῶ.

ΑΙΑΚΟΣ

τί δῆτα κλάεις;

ΔΙΟΝΤΣΟΣ

κρομμύων ὀσφραίνομαι.

ΑΙΑΚΟΣ

ἐπεὶ προτιμᾷς γ᾽ οὐδέν;

ΔΙΟΝΤΣΟΣ

655   οὐδέν μοι μέλει.

ΑΙΑΚΟΣ

βαδιστέον τἄρ᾽ ἐστὶν ἐπὶ τονδὶ πάλιν.

ΞΑΝΘΙΑΣ

οἴμοι.

ΑΙΑΚΟΣ

τί ἐστι;

ΞΑΝΘΙΑΣ

τὴν ἄκανθαν ἔξελε.

FROGS

AEACUS

The man's sanctified. Let's go back the other way. (*strikes Dionysus*)

DIONYSUS

Hi yo!

AEACUS

What's the matter?

DIONYSUS

I see horsemen.

AEACUS

So why are you crying?

DIONYSUS

I can smell onions![59]

AEACUS

Meaning you didn't feel anything?

DIONYSUS

Couldn't care less!

AEACUS

Then I'd better go back over to the other one. (*strikes Xanthias*)

XANTHIAS

Ahh!

AEACUS

What's the matter?

XANTHIAS

(*lifting a foot*) Do take out this thorn.

[59] Typical cavalry rations.

ΑΙΑΚΟΣ

τί τὸ πρᾶγμα τουτί; δεῦρο πάλιν βαδιστέον.

ΔΙΟΝΥΣΟΣ

Ἄπολλον,—ὅς που Δῆλον ἢ Πυθῶν᾽ ἔχεις.

ΞΑΝΘΙΑΣ

ἤλγησεν· οὐκ ἤκουσας;

ΔΙΟΝΥΣΟΣ

660   οὐκ ἔγωγ᾽, ἐπεὶ
ἴαμβον Ἱππώνακτος ἀνεμιμνησκόμην.

ΞΑΝΘΙΑΣ

οὐδὲν ποιεῖς γάρ· ἀλλὰ τὰς λαγόνας σπόδει.

ΑΙΑΚΟΣ

μὰ τὸν Δί᾽, ἀλλ᾽ ἤδη πάρεχε τὴν γαστέρα.

ΔΙΟΝΥΣΟΣ

Πόσειδον.

ΞΑΝΘΙΑΣ

      ἤλγησέν τις.

ΔΙΟΝΥΣΟΣ

664/5   —ὃς Αἰγαίου
πρωνὸς ἢ γλαυκᾶς μέδεις
ἁλὸς ἐν βένθεσιν.

AEACUS

What's going on here? Got to go back over here. (*strikes Dionysus*)

DIONYSUS

Apollo!—who abides perchance on Delos or in Pytho.

XANTHIAS

That hurt him, didn't you hear?

DIONYSUS

No it didn't! I was just recollecting a line of Hipponax.[60]

XANTHIAS

(*to Aeacus*) Look, you're getting nowhere: go ahead and bash him in the ribs.

AEACUS

God no; (*to Dionysus*) stick out your belly now. (*strikes Dionysus*)

DIONYSUS

Poseidon!

XANTHIAS

Somebody felt that!

DIONYSUS

   —who hold sway
on the cape of Aegae or in
the depths of the deep blue sea.[61]

[60] The renowned sixth-century iambic poet from Ephesus; but this verse is ascribed by a scholiast to Hipponax's contemporary, Ananius.

[61] From Sophocles' *Laocoon* (fr. 371).

ΑΙΑΚΟΣ

οὔ τοι μὰ τὴν Δήμητρα δύναμαι 'γὼ μαθεῖν
ὁπότερος ὑμῶν ἐστι θεός. ἀλλ' εἴσιτον·
670 ὁ δεσπότης γὰρ αὐτὸς ὑμᾶς γνώσεται
χἠ Φερρέφατθ', ἅτ' ὄντε κἀκείνω θεώ.

ΔΙΟΝΥΣΟΣ

ὀρθῶς λέγεις· ἐβουλόμην δ' ἂν τοῦτό σε
πρότερον νοῆσαι, πρὶν ἐμὲ τὰς πληγὰς λαβεῖν.

ΧΟΡΟΣ

(στρ) Μοῦσα, χορῶν ἱερῶν ἐπίβηθι καὶ
675 ἔλθ' ἐπὶ τέρψιν ἀοιδᾶς ἐμᾶς,
τὸν πολὺν ὀψομένη λαῶν ὄχλον, οὗ σοφίαι
μυρίαι κάθηνται
φιλοτιμότεραι Κλεοφῶντος, ἐφ' οὗ
δὴ χείλεσιν ἀμφιλάλοις
680 δεινὸν ἐπιβρέμεταί τις
Θρηκία χελιδὼν
ἐπὶ βάρβαρον ἑζομένη πέταλον·
κελαδεῖ δ' ἐπίκλαυτον ἀηδόνιον
νόμον, ὡς ἀπολεῖται,
685 κἂν ἴσαι γένωνται.

ΚΟΡΥΦΑΙΟΣ

τὸν ἱερὸν χορὸν δίκαιόν ἐστι χρηστὰ τῇ πόλει
ξυμπαραινεῖν καὶ διδάσκειν. πρῶτον οὖν ἡμῖν δοκεῖ

---

62 Persephone's Attic name.
63 The most influential popular politician in the period after

FROGS

AEACUS

By Demeter, I can't make out which of you is a god. But go
along inside; the master himself and Pherrephatta[62] will
recognize you, because they're gods too.

DIONYSUS

That's right. But I wish you'd thought of that before I took
those blows!

*Exit AEACUS, DIONYSUS, XANTHIAS, and Slaves into
the palace.*

CHORUS

Embark, Muse, on the sacred dance,
and come to inspire joy in my song,
beholding the great multitude of people,
where thousands of wits are in session
more high-reaching than Cleophon,[63]
on whose bilingual lips
some Thracian swallow
roars terribly,
perched on an alien petal,
and bellows the nightingale's weepy
song, that he's done for,
even if the jury's hung.

CHORUS LEADER

It's right and proper for the sacred chorus to help give good
advice and instruction to the city. First then, we think that

the restoration of democracy in 410, and executed in 404 (af-
ter the second performance of *Frogs*: cf. 1504) on trumped-up
charges brought by anti-democratic forces; he was the titular
character in the play by Plato that competed against the first
Frogs.

ARISTOPHANES

ἐξισῶσαι τοὺς πολίτας κἀφελεῖν τὰ δείματα.
κεἴ τις ἥμαρτε σφαλείς τι Φρυνίχου παλαίσμασιν,
690 ἐγγενέσθαι φημὶ χρῆναι τοῖς ὀλισθοῦσιν τότε
αἰτίαν ἐκθεῖσι λῦσαι τὰς πρότερον ἁμαρτίας.
εἶτ᾽ ἄτιμόν φημι χρῆναι μηδέν᾽ εἶν᾽ ἐν τῇ πόλει·
καὶ γὰρ αἰσχρόν ἐστι τοὺς μὲν ναυμαχήσαντας
    μίαν
καὶ Πλαταιᾶς εὐθὺς εἶναι κἀντὶ δούλων δεσπότας·
695 κοὐδὲ ταῦτ᾽ ἔγωγ᾽ ἔχοιμ᾽ ἂν μὴ οὐ καλῶς φάσκειν
    ἔχειν,
ἀλλ᾽ ἐπαινῶ· μόνα γὰρ αὐτὰ νοῦν ἔχοντ᾽ ἐδράσατε·
πρὸς δὲ τούτοις εἰκὸς ὑμᾶς, οἳ μεθ᾽ ὑμῶν πολλὰ δὴ
χοἱ πατέρες ἐναυμάχησαν καὶ προσήκουσιν γένει
τὴν μίαν ταύτην παρεῖναι ξυμφορὰν αἰτουμένοις.
700 ἀλλὰ τῆς ὀργῆς ἀνέντες, ὦ σοφώτατοι φύσει,
πάντας ἀνθρώπους ἑκόντες ξυγγενεῖς κτησώμεθα
κἀπιτίμους καὶ πολίτας, ὅστις ἂν ξυνναυμαχῇ.
εἰ δὲ ταῦτ᾽ ὀγκωσόμεσθα κἀποσεμνυνούμεθα,
τὴν πόλιν καὶ ταῦτ᾽ ἔχοντες κυμάτων ἐν ἀγκάλαις,
705 ὑστέρῳ χρόνῳ ποτ᾽ αὖθις εὖ φρονεῖν οὐ δόξομεν.

ΧΟΡΟΣ
(ἀντ) εἰ δ᾽ ἐγὼ ὀρθὸς ἰδεῖν βίον ἀνέρος

697 ὑμῶν R A K: ἡμῶν V
699 αἰτουμένοις R A K: -μένους V

---

[64] I.e., fears of prosecution or attack for offenses they had

all the citizens should be made equal, and their fears removed,[64] and if anyone was tripped up by Phrynichus' holds,[65] I say that those who slipped up at that time should be permitted to dispose of their liability and put right their earlier mistakes. Next I say that no one in the city should be disenfranchised, for it's a disgrace that veterans of a single sea battle should forthwith become Plataeans, turning from slaves into masters;[66] not that I have any criticism to voice about that—indeed I applaud it as being your only intelligent action—but in addition to that it's fitting, in the case of people[67] who have fought many a sea battle at your side, as have their fathers, and who are your blood relations, that you pardon this one misadventure when they ask you to. Now relax your anger, you people most naturally sage, and let's readily accept as kinsmen and as citizens in good standing everyone who fights on our ships. If we puff ourselves up about this and are too proud to do it, especially now that we have a city "embraced by high seas,"[68] there will come a time when we'll seem to have acted thoughtlessly.

CHORUS
"If I read aright the life or character

committed under the oligarchy of 411, in spite of the amnesty of 410.

[65] One of the leaders of the Four Hundred, whose assassination in summer 411 accelerated the fall of their regime.

[66] Refugees of the Spartan massacre at Plataea in 427 were given Athenian citizenship (Thucydides 3.68, Demosthenes 59.104–6), just as had the slaves who rowed in the battle of Arginusae.   [67] I.e., those disenfranchised in 411.

[68] Archilochus fr. 213.

ἢ τρόπον ὅστις ἔτ᾽ οἰμώξεται,
οὐ πολὺν οὐδ᾽ ὁ πίθηκος οὗτος ὁ νῦν ἐνοχλῶν,
Κλειγένης ὁ μικρός,
710 ὁ πονηρότατος βαλανεὺς ὁπόσοι
κρατοῦσι κυκησίτεφροι
ψευδολίτρου τε κονίας
καὶ Κιμωλίας γῆς,
χρόνον ἐνδιατρίψει· ἰδὼν δὲ τάδ᾽ οὐκ
715 εἰρηνικὸς ἔσθ᾽, ἵνα μή ποτε κά-
ποδυθῇ μεθύων ἄ-
νευ ξύλου βαδίζων.

ΚΟΡΥΦΑΙΟΣ

πολλάκις γ᾽ ἡμῖν ἔδοξεν ἡ πόλις πεπονθέναι
ταὐτὸν εἴς τε τῶν πολιτῶν τοὺς καλούς τε κἀγαθοὺς
720 εἴς τε τἀρχαῖον νόμισμα καὶ τὸ καινὸν χρυσίον.
οὔτε γὰρ τούτοισιν οὖσιν οὐ κεκιβδηλευμένοις,
ἀλλὰ καλλίστοις ἁπάντων, ὡς δοκεῖ, νομισμάτων
καὶ μόνοις ὀρθῶς κοπεῖσι καὶ κεκωδωνισμένοις
ἔν τε τοῖς Ἕλλησι καὶ τοῖς βαρβάροισι πανταχοῦ
725 χρώμεθ᾽ οὐδέν, ἀλλὰ τούτοις τοῖς πονηροῖς χαλκίοις
χθές τε καὶ πρώην κοπεῖσι τῷ κακίστῳ κόμματι.
τῶν πολιτῶν θ᾽ οὓς μὲν ἴσμεν εὐγενεῖς καὶ
σώφρονας

711 -τεφροι Radermacher: -τέφρου a S

---

69 Adapted from a tragedy by Ion of Chios (*TrGF* 19 F 1).
70 The only Cleigenes attested at this time served as Council

of a man"[69] who's sure to be sorry yet,
then this monkey who's so annoying now—
pint-sized Cleigenes,[70]
the basest bathman of all
the ash-mixers who lord it over
fake washing soda
and fuller's earth—
he won't be around much longer, and knows it,
so he's unpeaceable, for fear that some night
on a drunken stroll without his stick
he'll be mugged.

CHORUS LEADER

It's often struck us that the city deals with its fine upstanding citizens just as with the old coinage and the new gold.[71] Though both of these are unalloyed, indeed considered the finest of all coins, the only ones minted true and tested everywhere among Greeks and barbarians alike, we make no use of them;[72] instead we use these crummy coppers, struck just yesterday or the day before with a stamp of the lowest quality.[73] Just so with our citizens: the ones we ac-

Secretary in 410/9 (*IG* i[3] 375.1, Andocides1.96), and is perhaps the predatory litigator of Lysias 25.25 (where his name was conjectured by Schwartz for the mss' Cleisthenes).   [71] The "old" was the traditional coinage made of silver from the Laureium mines, largely incapacitated since the enemy occupation of Deceleia, and the "new," issued in 407/6, was made from the dedications to Victory on the Acropolis.   [72] Because they were earmarked for external payments, e.g. for imports and mercenaries.

[73] Silver-plated bronze coins issued along with the new gold coins; they were removed from circulation at some time between 403 and 392 (cf. *Assemblywomen* 815–22).

ἄνδρας ὄντας καὶ δικαίους καὶ καλούς τε κἀγαθοὺς
καὶ τραφέντας ἐν παλαίστραις καὶ χοροῖς καὶ
μουσικῇ,
730 προυσελοῦμεν, τοῖς δὲ χαλκοῖς καὶ ξένοις καὶ
πυρρίαις
καὶ πονηροῖς κἀκ πονηρῶν εἰς ἅπαντα χρώμεθα
ὑστάτοις ἀφιγμένοισιν, οἷσιν ἡ πόλις πρὸ τοῦ
οὐδὲ φαρμακοῖσιν εἰκῇ ῥᾳδίως ἐχρήσατ᾽ ἄν.
ἀλλὰ καὶ νῦν, ὦνόητοι, μεταβαλόντες τοὺς τρόπους
735 χρῆσθε τοῖς χρηστοῖσιν αὖθις· καὶ κατορθώσασι
γὰρ
εὔλογον, κἄν τι σφαλῆτ᾽, ἐξ ἀξίου γοῦν τοῦ ξύλου,
ἤν τι καὶ πάσχητε, πάσχειν τοῖς σοφοῖς δοκήσετε.

OIKETHΣ
νὴ τὸν Δία τὸν σωτῆρα, γεννάδας ἀνὴρ
ὁ δεσπότης σου.

ΞΑΝΘΙΑΣ
πῶς γὰρ οὐχὶ γεννάδας,
740 ὅστις γε πίνειν οἶδε καὶ βινεῖν μόνον;

OIKETHΣ
τὸ δὲ μὴ πατάξαι σ᾽ ἐξελεγχθέντ᾽ ἀντικρυς,
ὅτι δοῦλος ὢν ἔφασκες εἶναι δεσπότης.

ΞΑΝΘΙΑΣ
ᾤμωξε μεντἄν.

OIKETHΣ
τοῦτο μέντοι δουλικὸν
εὐθὺς πεποίηκας, ὅπερ ἐγὼ χαίρω ποιῶν.

124

knowledge to be well-born, well-behaved, just, fine, and outstanding men, men brought up in wrestling schools, choruses, and the arts, we treat them shabbily, while for all purposes we choose the coppers, the aliens, the red-heads,[74] bad people with bad ancestors, the latest arrivals, whom formerly the city wouldn't readily have used even as scapegoats. But even at this late hour, you fools, do change your ways and once again choose the good people. You'll be congratulated for it if you're successful, and if you take a fall, at least the intelligent will say that if something does happen to you, you're hanging from a worthy tree.

Enter from the palace XANTHIAS *and a* SLAVE *of Pluto*.

SLAVE
By Zeus the Savior, that master of yours is a gentleman.

XANTHIAS
Of course he's a gentleman; all he knows is boozing and balling.

SLAVE
But not to have beaten you as soon as you, the slave, were caught pretending to be the master!

XANTHIAS
He'd have regretted that!

SLAVE
Spoken like a true slave! I like talking that way myself.

---

[74] Conventional of Thracians (cf. 681), and in later comedy of slaves.

ΞΑΝΘΙΑΣ

χαίρεις, ἱκετεύω;

ΟΙΚΕΤΗΣ

745   μάλλ᾽ ἐποπτεύειν δοκῶ,
ὅταν καταράσωμαι λάθρᾳ τῷ δεσπότῃ.

ΞΑΝΘΙΑΣ

τί δὲ τονθορύζων, ἡνίκ᾽ ἂν πληγὰς λαβὼν
πολλὰς ἀπίῃς θύραζε;

ΟΙΚΕΤΗΣ

καὶ τοῦθ᾽ ἥδομαι.

ΞΑΝΘΙΑΣ

τί δὲ πολλὰ πράττων;

ΟΙΚΕΤΗΣ

ὡς μὰ Δί᾽ οὐδὲν οἶδ᾽ ἐγώ.

ΞΑΝΘΙΑΣ

750   ὁμόγνιε Ζεῦ· καὶ παρακούων δεσποτῶν
ἅττ᾽ ἂν λαλῶσι;

ΟΙΚΕΤΗΣ

μάλλὰ πλεῖν ἢ μαίνομαι.

ΞΑΝΘΙΑΣ

τί δὲ τοῖς θύραζε ταῦτα καταλαλῶν;

ΟΙΚΕΤΗΣ

ἐγώ;
μὰ Δί᾽ ἀλλ᾽ ὅταν δρῶ τοῦτο, κἀκμιαίνομαι.

XANTHIAS

You like it? I'm interested.

SLAVE

Why, it's like nirvana when I curse my master behind his back!

XANTHIAS

What about muttering when you leave the house after getting a good beating?

SLAVE

I love it.

XANTHIAS

What about meddling?

SLAVE

Positively nonpareil!

XANTHIAS

Zeus of True Kin! And eavesdropping on masters when they're gossiping?

SLAVE

I'm simply mad about it!

XANTHIAS

And what about blabbing what you've heard to outsiders?

SLAVE

Who, me? Why, doing that gives me an actual orgasm!

ΞΑΝΘΙΑΣ

ὦ Φοῖβ᾽ Ἄπολλον, ἔμβαλέ μοι τὴν δεξιάν,
755 καὶ δὸς κύσαι καὐτὸς κύσον. καί μοι φράσον
πρὸς Διός, ὃς ἡμῖν ἐστιν ὁμομαστιγίας,
τίς οὗτος οὕνδον ἐστὶ θόρυβος καὶ βοὴ
χὠ λοιδορησμός;

ΟΙΚΕΤΗΣ

Αἰσχύλου κεὐριπίδου.

ΞΑΝΘΙΑΣ

ᾶ.

ΟΙΚΕΤΗΣ

πρᾶγμα, πρᾶγμα μέγα κεκίνηται, μέγα
760 ἐν τοῖς νεκροῖσι καὶ στάσις πολλὴ πάνυ.

ΞΑΝΘΙΑΣ

ἐκ τοῦ;

ΟΙΚΕΤΗΣ

νόμος τις ἐνθάδ᾽ ἐστὶ κείμενος·
ἀπὸ τῶν τεχνῶν, ὅσαι μεγάλαι καὶ δεξιαί,
τὸν ἄριστον ὄντα τῶν ἑαυτοῦ συντέχνων
σίτησιν αὐτὸν ἐν πρυτανείῳ λαμβάνειν
765 θρόνον τε τοῦ Πλούτωνος ἑξῆς—

ΞΑΝΘΙΑΣ

μανθάνω.

ΟΙΚΕΤΗΣ

ἕως ἀφίκοιτο τὴν τέχνην σοφώτερος
ἕτερός τις αὐτοῦ· τότε δὲ παραχωρεῖν ἔδει.

XANTHIAS

Phoebus Apollo, put 'er there, and let's exchange kisses! (*sounds of wrangling are heard inside*) Now tell me, by Zeus, our mutual god of floggings, what's all this commotion and yelling and name-calling inside the palace?

SLAVE

It's Aeschylus and Euripides.

XANTHIAS

Aha.

SLAVE

An event's underway, a big event among the dead, and very intense factionalism.

XANTHIAS

About what?

SLAVE

There's a traditional custom down here: in each of the most important and skilled professions, the one who's best of all his fellow professionals is entitled to maintenance in the Prytaneum and a seat next to Pluto[75]—

XANTHIAS

I get the picture.

SLAVE

—until someone more competent in the same craft arrives, at which point he has to step down.

[75] At Athens, free meals in the Prytaneum (the official building housing the sacred hearth) and privileged seating at public events were awarded for outstanding athletic, military, or political achievement.

ΞΑΝΘΙΑΣ

τί δῆτα τουτὶ τεθορύβηκεν Αἰσχύλον;

ΟΙΚΕΤΗΣ

ἐκεῖνος εἶχε τὸν τραγῳδικὸν θρόνον,
770 ὡς ὢν κράτιστος τὴν τέχνην.

ΞΑΝΘΙΑΣ

νυνὶ δὲ τίς;

ΟΙΚΕΤΗΣ

ὅτε δὴ κατῆλθ᾽ Εὐριπίδης, ἐπεδείκνυτο
τοῖς λωποδύταις καὶ τοῖσι βαλλαντιοτόμοις
καὶ τοῖσι πατραλοίαισι καὶ τοιχωρύχοις,
ὅπερ ἔστ᾽ ἐν Ἅιδου πλῆθος, οἱ δ᾽ ἀκροώμενοι
775 τῶν ἀντιλογιῶν καὶ λυγισμῶν καὶ στροφῶν
ὑπερεμάνησαν κἀνόμισαν σοφώτατον·
κἄπειτ᾽ ἐπαρθεὶς ἀντελάβετο τοῦ θρόνου,
ἵν᾽ Αἰσχύλος καθῆστο.

ΞΑΝΘΙΑΣ

κοὐκ ἐβάλλετο;

ΟΙΚΕΤΗΣ

μὰ Δί᾽, ἀλλ᾽ ὁ δῆμος ἀνεβόα κρίσιν ποιεῖν
780 ὁπότερος εἴη τὴν τέχνην σοφώτερος.

ΞΑΝΘΙΑΣ

ὁ τῶν πανούργων;

ΟΙΚΕΤΗΣ

νὴ Δί᾽, οὐράνιόν γ᾽ ὅσον.

XANTHIAS

So why has this flustered Aeschylus?

SLAVE

He was the one who held the Chair of Tragedy, for being dominant in that art.

XANTHIAS

And who holds it now?

SLAVE

When Euripides came down here, he started giving recitals for the muggers and purse-snatchers and father-beaters and burglars (there's a lot of them in Hades), and when they heard his disputations and twists and dodges, they went crazy for him and considered him the best, and that inspired him to claim the chair that Aeschylus was occupying.

XANTHIAS

And wasn't he pelted?

SLAVE

He was not; the public clamored to hold a trial of who's best in that art.

XANTHIAS

The criminal public clamored?

SLAVE

That's right, to high heaven.

ΞΑΝΘΙΑΣ

μετ᾽ Αἰσχύλου δ᾽ οὐκ ἦσαν ἕτεροι σύμμαχοι;

ΟΙΚΕΤΗΣ

ὀλίγον τὸ χρηστόν ἐστιν, ὥσπερ ἐνθάδε.

ΞΑΝΘΙΑΣ

τί δῆθ᾽ ὁ Πλούτων δρᾶν παρασκευάζεται;

ΟΙΚΕΤΗΣ

785 ἀγῶνα ποιεῖν αὐτίκα μάλα καὶ κρίσιν
κἄλεγχον αὐτοῖν τῆς τέχνης.

ΞΑΝΘΙΑΣ

κἄπειτα πῶς
οὐ καὶ Σοφοκλέης ἀντελάβετο τοῦ θρόνου;

ΟΙΚΕΤΗΣ

μὰ Δί᾽ οὐκ ἐκεῖνος, ἀλλ᾽ ἔκυσε μὲν Αἰσχύλος,
ὅτε δὴ κατῆλθε, κἀνέβαλε τὴν δεξιάν·
790 κἄνεικος ὑπεχώρησεν αὐτῷ τοῦ θρόνου.
νυνὶ δ᾽ ἔμελλεν, ὡς ἔφη Κλειδημίδης,
ἔφεδρος καθεδεῖσθαι· κἂν μὲν Αἰσχύλος κρατῇ,
ἕξειν κατὰ χώραν· εἰ δὲ μή, περὶ τῆς τέχνης
διαγωνιεῖσθ᾽ ἔφασκε πρός γ᾽ Εὐριπίδην.

ΞΑΝΘΙΑΣ

795 τὸ χρῆμ᾽ ἄρ᾽ ἔσται;

788 Αἰσχύλος Naber: Αἰσχύλον a

XANTHIAS

But weren't there others who sided with Aeschylus?

SLAVE

The good are the minority, (*indicating the spectators*) just like up here.

XANTHIAS

So what does Pluto intend to do?

SLAVE

To hold a contest immediately, a test and trial of the artistry of both.

XANTHIAS

Then how come Sophocles didn't stake a claim to the chair?

SLAVE

Not him! When he came down here Aeschylus gave him a kiss and grasped his hand, and he withdrew any rival claim on the chair.[76] And now he's ready, in the words of Cleidemides,[77] to take a bye and sit it out, and if Aeschylus wins, he'll stay where he is; otherwise, he's promised to challenge Euripides for his art's sake.

XANTHIAS

So it's going to happen?

[76] Or, with the mss., "when he came . . . he kissed Aeschylus and grasped his hand, and *he* [in contrast with Euripides] withdrew . . . "

[77] Unknown.

ΟΙΚΕΤΗΣ

νὴ Δί᾽ ὀλίγον ὕστερον.
κἀνταῦθα δὴ τὰ δεινὰ κινηθήσεται.
καὶ γὰρ ταλάντῳ μουσικὴ σταθμήσεται—

ΞΑΝΘΙΑΣ

τί δέ; μειαγωγήσουσι τὴν τραγῳδίαν;

ΟΙΚΕΤΗΣ

καὶ κανόνας ἐξοίσουσι καὶ πήχεις ἐπῶν
800 καὶ πλαίσια ξύμπτυκτα—

ΞΑΝΘΙΑΣ

πλινθεύσουσι γάρ;

ΟΙΚΕΤΗΣ

καὶ διαμέτρους καὶ σφῆνας. ὁ γὰρ Εὐριπίδης
κατ᾽ ἔπος βασανιεῖν φησι τὰς τραγῳδίας.

ΞΑΝΘΙΑΣ

ἦ που βαρέως οἶμαι τὸν Αἰσχύλον φέρειν.

ΟΙΚΕΤΗΣ

ἔβλεψε γοῦν ταυρηδὸν ἐγκύψας κάτω.

ΞΑΝΘΙΑΣ

κρινεῖ δὲ δὴ τίς ταῦτα;

ΟΙΚΕΤΗΣ

τοῦτ᾽ ἦν δύσκολον·
805 σοφῶν γὰρ ἀνδρῶν ἀπορίαν ηὑρισκέτην.
οὔτε γὰρ Ἀθηναίοισι συνέβαιν᾽ Αἰσχύλος—

SLAVE

Yes, and pretty soon. And then we'll see great events set in motion. Poetic art will be weighed in a balance—

XANTHIAS

You mean they'll be weighing tragedy like Apaturia cutlets?[78]

SLAVE

—and they'll be bringing out rulers, and measuring tapes for words, and folding frames—

XANTHIAS

You mean they'll be making bricks?

SLAVE

—and set squares and wedges; because Euripides says he's going to examine the tragedies word for word.

XANTHIAS

I'd guess that Aeschylus is pretty sore about that.

SLAVE

Well, he did put his head down and glowered like a bull.

XANTHIAS

And who's to be the judge?

SLAVE

That was a tough one, because both discovered a shortage of competent people. You see, Aeschylus wouldn't agree to use Athenians—

[78] A phratry festival (cf. 418 n.) to which fathers brought sacrificial meat to celebrate their sons' coming of age; an element of the ritual was the weighing of the meat.

ARISTOPHANES

ΞΑΝΘΙΑΣ

πολλοὺς ἴσως ἐνόμιζε τοὺς τοιχωρύχους.

ΟΙΚΕΤΗΣ

λῆρόν τε τἄλλ᾽ ἡγεῖτο τοῦ γνῶναι πέρι
810 φύσεις ποιητῶν. εἶτα τῷ σῷ δεσπότῃ
ἐπέτρεψαν, ὁτιὴ τῆς τέχνης ἔμπειρος ἦν.
ἀλλ᾽ εἰσίωμεν· ὡς ὅταν γ᾽ οἱ δεσπόται
ἐσπουδάκωσι, κλαύμαθ᾽ ἡμῖν γίγνεται.

ΧΟΡΟΣ

ἦ που δεινὸν ἐριβρεμέτας χόλον ἔνδοθεν ἕξει,
815 ἡνίκ᾽ ἂν ὀξύλαλόν περ ἴδῃ θήγοντος ὀδόντα
ἀντιτέχνου· τότε δὴ μανίας ὑπὸ δεινῆς
ὄμματα στροβήσεται.

ἔσται δ᾽ ὑψιλόφων τε λόγων κορυθαίολα νείκη
σχινδάλαμοί τε παραξονίων σμιλεύματά τ᾽ ἔργων
820 φωτὸς ἀμυνομένου φρενοτέκτονος ἀνδρὸς
ῥήμαθ᾽ ἱπποβάμονα.

φρίξας δ᾽ αὐτοκόμου λοφιᾶς λασιαύχενα χαίταν,
δεινὸν ἐπισκύνιον ξυνάγων, βρυχώμενος ἥσει
ῥήματα γομφοπαγῆ, πινακηδὸν ἀποσπῶν
825 γηγενεῖ φυσήματι.

818 ὑψι- U γρΣ: ἱππο- R V A K
819 σχινδάλαμοί Dover: σκινδαλάμων vel sim. a S παραξονίων Stanford: παραξόνια a

XANTHIAS

Maybe he considered too many of them crooks.

SLAVE

—and the rest of them he thought were pure piffle when it comes to judging what poets really are. Then they turned it over to your master, because he's familiar with the art. Now let's go inside, because serious business for our masters means afflictions for us.

XANTHIAS and SLAVE go inside; various measuring instruments are brought onstage.

CHORUS

Surely fearful wrath will fill the heart of the mighty
    thunderer
when he sees the sharp-talking tusk of his rival in art
being whetted; then with fearful fury
will his eyes whirl about.

We'll have helmet-glinting struggles of tall-crested
    words,
we'll have linchpin-shavings and chisel-parings of
    artworks
as a man fends off a thought-building hero's
galloping utterances.

Bristling the shaggy-necked shock of his hirsute ridge
    of mane,
his formidable brow frowning, with a roar he will hurl
utterances bolted together, tearing off timbers
with his gigantic blast.

ARISTOPHANES

ἔνθεν δὴ στοματουργὸς ἐπῶν βασανίστρια λίσπη
γλῶσσ' ἀνελισσομένη, φθονεροὺς κινοῦσα
  χαλινούς,
ῥήματα δαιομένη καταλεπτολογήσει
πλευμόνων πολὺν πόνον.

ΕΤΡΙΠΙΔΗΣ

830 οὐκ ἂν μεθείμην τοῦ θρόνου, μὴ νουθέτει·
κρείττων γὰρ εἶναί φημι τούτου τὴν τέχνην.

ΔΙΟΝΥΣΟΣ

Αἰσχύλε, τί σιγᾷς; αἰσθάνει γὰρ τοῦ λόγου.

ΕΤΡΙΠΙΔΗΣ

ἀποσεμνυνεῖται πρῶτον, ἅπερ ἑκάστοτε
ἐν ταῖς τραγῳδίαισιν ἐτερατεύετο.

ΔΙΟΝΥΣΟΣ

835 ὦ δαιμόνι' ἀνδρῶν, μὴ μεγάλα λίαν λέγε.

ΕΤΡΙΠΙΔΗΣ

ἐγᾦδα τοῦτον καὶ διέσκεμμαι πάλαι,
ἄνθρωπον ἀγριοποιόν, αὐθαδόστομον,
ἔχοντ' ἀχάλινον, ἀκρατές, ἀπύλωτον στόμα,
ἀπεριλάλητον, κομποφακελορρήμονα.

838 ἀπύλωτον V A K: ἀθύρωτον R

138

Then the smooth tongue unfurling, mouth-working
tester of words, slipping the reins of envy
will sort out those utterances and parse clean away
much labor of lungs.

Three chairs are brought out; then enter PLUTO, *who takes
the center chair, and* DIONYSUS *(now normally costumed),
who takes the left-hand chair; then enter* AESCHYLUS, *who
takes the right-hand chair, followed by* EURIPIDES, *who
lays hands on it; alternatively, the whole tableau may be
rolled out on the eccyclema.*

EURIPIDES

Don't give me any lectures, I won't let go the chair! I say
I'm better at the art than he is.

DIONYSUS

Why so quiet, Aeschylus? You hear what he says.

EURIPIDES

He'll be haughtily aloof at first, just the way he tried to
mystify us in his tragedies.

DIONYSUS

Careful, my friend, don't speak too confidently!

EURIPIDES

I know this fellow, and have long had him pegged: he's
a creator of savages, a boorish talker, with an unbridled,
unruly, ungated mouth, uncircumlocutory, a big bom-
bastolocutor.

ARISTOPHANES

ΑΙΣΧΥΛΟΣ

840　ἄληθες, ὦ παῖ τῆς ἀρουραίας θεοῦ;
σὺ δὴ 'μὲ ταῦτ', ὦ στωμυλιοσυλλεκτάδη
καὶ πτωχοποιὲ καὶ ῥακιοσυρραπτάδη;
ἀλλ' οὔ τι χαίρων αὔτ' ἐρεῖς.

ΔΙΟΝΥΣΟΣ

παῦ', Αἰσχύλε,
καὶ μὴ πρὸς ὀργὴν σπλάγχνα θερμήνῃς κότῳ.

ΑΙΣΧΥΛΟΣ

845　οὐ δῆτα, πρίν γ' ἂν τοῦτον ἀποφήνω σαφῶς
τὸν χωλοποιὸν οἷος ὢν θρασύνεται.

ΔΙΟΝΥΣΟΣ

ἄρν' ἄρνα μέλανα, παῖδες, ἐξενέγκατε·
τυφὼς γὰρ ἐκβαίνειν παρασκευάζεται.

ΑΙΣΧΥΛΟΣ

ὦ Κρητικὰς μὲν συλλέγων μονῳδίας,
850　γάμους δ' ἀνοσίους εἰσφέρων εἰς τὴν τέχνην—

ΔΙΟΝΥΣΟΣ

ἐπίσχες οὗτος, ὦ πολυτίμητ' Αἰσχύλε.
ἀπὸ τῶν χαλαζῶν δ', ὦ πόνηρ' Εὐριπίδη,
ἄναγε σεαυτὸν ἐκποδών, εἰ σωφρονεῖς,
ἵνα μὴ κεφαλαίῳ τὸν κρόταφόν σου ῥήματι
855　θενὼν ὑπ' ὀργῆς ἐκχέῃ τὸν Τήλεφον.

---

79 Adapted from Euripides fr. 885 ("you scion of the sea goddess"); the origin of Aristophanes' allusions to Euripides' mother

FROGS

AESCHYLUS

Is that so, you scion of the greenery goddess?[79] This about me from you? You babble-collector, you creator of beggars,[80] you rag stitcher! Oh, you'll be sorry you said it!

DIONYSUS

Stop it, Aeschylus; heat not your innards with wrathful rage.[81]

AESCHYLUS

No, not till I've manifestly shown up this creator of cripples for what he is, for all his impudence.

DIONYSUS

A lamb, boys, bring out a black lamb! Here's a hurricane hurtling our way!

AESCHYLUS

You collector of Cretan arias,[82] who brought unholy couplings into out art—

DIONYSUS

Hold on there, my exalted Aeschylus! And you, rascally Euripides, if you have any sense you'll move out of this hailstorm, or in his anger he may bash your skull with a crushing comeback and dash out your *Telephus*.[83] And

---

as a seller of wild herbs (*Acharnians* 457, 478, *Knights* 19, *Women at the Thesmophoria* 387, 456) is obscure.

[80] Cf. *Acharnians* 410–79, *Peace* 146–48.

[81] Probably quoting or adapting an Aeschylean line.

[82] Referring perhaps to their setting (cf. 1356–60), choreographic accompaniment, or mythical content (e.g. Pasiphae and Phaedra).   [83] Produced in 438 and featuring the classic Euripidean beggar-hero; parodied by Aristophanes in *Acharnians* and *Women at the Thesmophoria*.

σὺ δὲ μὴ πρὸς ὀργήν, Αἰσχύλ᾽, ἀλλὰ πραόνως
ἔλεγχ᾽, ἐλέγχου· λοιδορεῖσθαι δ᾽ οὐ πρέπει
ἄνδρας ποιητὰς ὥσπερ ἀρτοπώλιδας·
σὺ δ᾽ εὐθὺς ὥσπερ πρῖνος ἐμπρησθεὶς βοᾷς.

ΕΥΡΙΠΙΔΗΣ

860 ἕτοιμός εἰμ᾽ ἔγωγε, κοὐκ ἀναδύομαι,
δάκνειν, δάκνεσθαι πρότερος, εἰ τούτῳ δοκεῖ,
τἄπη, τὰ μέλη, τὰ νεῦρα τῆς τραγῳδίας,
καὶ νὴ Δία τὸν Πηλέα γε καὶ τὸν Αἴολον
καὶ τὸν Μελέαγρον κἄτι μάλα τὸν Τήλεφον.

ΔΙΟΝΥΣΟΣ

865 σὺ δὲ δὴ τί βουλεύει ποιεῖν; λέγ᾽, Αἰσχύλε.

ΑΙΣΧΥΛΟΣ

ἐβουλόμην μὲν οὐκ ἐρίζειν ἐνθάδε·
οὐκ ἐξ ἴσου γάρ ἐστιν ἀγὼν νῷν.

ΔΙΟΝΥΣΟΣ

                              τί δαί;

ΑΙΣΧΥΛΟΣ

ὅτι ἡ ποίησις οὐχὶ συντέθηκέ μοι,
τούτῳ δὲ συντέθηκεν, ὥσθ᾽ ἕξει λέγειν.
870 ὅμως δ᾽ ἐπειδή σοι δοκεῖ, δρᾶν ταῦτα χρή.

ΔΙΟΝΥΣΟΣ

ἴθι νυν λιβανωτὸν δεῦρό τις καὶ πῦρ δότω,
ὅπως ἂν εὔξωμαι πρὸ τῶν σοφισμάτων
ἀγῶνα κρῖναι τόνδε μουσικώτατα·
ὑμεῖς δὲ ταῖς Μούσαις τι μέλος ὑπᾴσατε.

you, Aeschylus, give and take arguments not angrily but calmly; it's unseemly for upstanding poets to squabble like bread women, but right away you start roaring like an oak tree on fire.

EURIPIDES

I'm ready if he is—and I won't back out—to go first in an exchange of pecks at my words, my songs, the sinews of my tragedies, including, yes, my *Peleus*, my *Aeolus*, my *Meleager*, and even my *Telephus*.

DIONYSUS

And what do you want to do, Aeschylus? Do say.

AESCHYLUS

I'd have preferred not to wrangle here, since the contest isn't equal.

DIONYSUS

How so?

AESCHYLUS

Because my poetry hasn't died with me, while his is as dead as he is, so he'll have it here to recite.[84] Still, if that's your decision, so be it.

DIONYSUS

Then someone bring me incense and fire here, and I'll preface the intellectualisms with a prayer that I may judge this contest with the utmost artistic integrity; (*to Chorus*) meanwhile, invoke the Muses with a song.

[84] Sometime after Aeschylus' death and before 425 (cf. *Acharnians* 10), a decree was passed permitting his plays to be entered in competition against new plays.

ARISTOPHANES

ΧΟΡΟΣ

875 ὦ Διὸς ἐννέα παρθένοι ἁγναὶ
Μοῦσαι, λεπτολόγους ξυνετὰς φρένας αἳ καθορᾶτε
ἀνδρῶν γνωμοτύπων, ὅταν εἰς ἔριν ὀξυμερίμνοις
ἔλθωσι στρεβλοῖσι παλαίσμασιν ἀντιλογοῦντες,
ἔλθετ᾽ ἐποψόμεναι δύναμιν
880 δεινοτάτοιν στομάτοιν πορίσασθαι
ῥή‹γ›ματα καὶ παραπρίσματ᾽ ἐπῶν.
882/3 νῦν γὰρ ἀγὼν σοφίας ὁ μέγας
χωρεῖ πρὸς ἔργον ἤδη.

ΔΙΟΝΥΣΟΣ

885 εὔχεσθε δὴ καὶ σφώ τι πρὶν τἄπη λέγειν.

ΑΙΣΧΥΛΟΣ

Δήμητερ ἡ θρέψασα τὴν ἐμὴν φρένα,
εἶναί με τῶν σῶν ἄξιον μυστηρίων.

ΔΙΟΝΥΣΟΣ

ἐπίθες λιβανωτὸν καὶ σὺ δὴ λαβών.

ΕΥΡΙΠΙΔΗΣ

καλῶς·
ἕτεροι γάρ εἰσιν οἷσιν εὔχομαι θεοῖς.

ΔΙΟΝΥΣΟΣ

ἴδιοί τινές σου, κόμμα καινόν;

ΕΥΡΙΠΙΔΗΣ

890 καὶ μάλα.

881 suppl. Fraenkel

The Chorus performs while Dionysus lights incense and silently prays.

CHORUS

Zeus' nine maiden daughters immaculate,
o Muses, who oversee the keen and subtly reasoning
    minds
of men who mint ideas, when they come into conflict,
debating each other with knotty and precisely plotted
    ploys,
come and behold the power
of two mouths most formidable at purveying
hewn chunks and whittlings of words.
Yes, now the great intellectual contest
at last goes into action.

DIONYSUS

Now each of you say a prayer before you say your piece.

AESCHYLUS

Demeter, who nourished my mind, may I be worthy of
your Mysteries!

DIONYSUS

(*to Euripides*) You take some incense too, and put it on the
fire.

EURIPIDES

No thanks; the gods I pray to are different.

DIONYSUS

Some private gods of your own, a novel coinage?

EURIPIDES

Precisely.

ΔΙΟΝΥΣΟΣ

ἴθι δὴ προσεύχου τοῖσιν ἰδιώταις θεοῖς.

ΕΥΡΙΠΙΔΗΣ

Αἰθήρ, ἐμὸν βόσκημα, καὶ Γλώττης Στρόφιγξ
καὶ Ξύνεσι καὶ Μυκτῆρες Ὀσφραντήριοι,
ὀρθῶς μ᾽ ἐλέγχειν ὧν ἂν ἅπτωμαι λόγων.

ΧΟΡΟΣ

(στρ) καὶ μὴν ἡμεῖς ἐπιθυμοῦμεν
896a   παρὰ σοφοῖν ἀνδροῖν ἀκοῦσαί
896b   τινα λόγων ἐμμέλειαν·
   ἔπιτε δαΐαν ὁδόν.
   γλῶσσα μὲν γὰρ ἠγρίωται,
899a   λῆμα δ᾽ οὐκ ἄτολμον ἀμφοῖν,
899b   οὐδ᾽ ἀκίνητοι φρένες.
900   προσδοκᾶν οὖν εἰκός ἐστι
901a   τὸν μὲν ἀστεῖόν τι λέξειν
901b   καὶ κατερρινημένον,
   τὸν δ᾽ ἀνασπῶντ᾽ αὐτοπρέμνοις
   τοῖς λόγοισιν ἐμπεσόντα
   συσκεδᾶν πολλὰς ἀλινδήθρας ἐπῶν.

ΚΟΡΥΦΑΙΟΣ

905 ἀλλ᾽ ὡς τάχιστα χρὴ λέγειν· οὕτω δ᾽ ὅπως ἐρεῖτον
ἀστεῖα καὶ μήτ᾽ εἰκόνας μήθ᾽ οἷ᾽ ἂν ἄλλος εἴποι.

ΕΥΡΙΠΙΔΗΣ

καὶ μὴν ἐμαυτὸν μέν γε, τὴν ποίησιν οἷός εἰμι,
ἐν τοῖσιν ὑστάτοις φράσω· τοῦτον δὲ πρῶτ᾽ ἐλέγξω,
ὡς ἦν ἀλαζὼν καὶ φέναξ οἵοις τε τοὺς θεατὰς

DIONYSUS

Then go ahead and pray to these unofficial gods.

EURIPIDES

Sky, my nourisher, and Pivot of Tongue, and Smarts, and Keen Nostrils, may I correctly refute any arguments I get hold of!

CHORUS

And now we're eager
to hear from two smart men
a real ballet of words.
Embark on the warpath!
Their tongues have gone wild,
their spirit lacks no boldness,
nor are their minds unmoved.
So it makes sense to expect
that this one will say something sophisticated
and finely honed,
while that one will launch his attack
with arguments torn up by the roots,
and scatter great dustclouds of words.

CHORUS LEADER

Now you must begin speaking at once, and be sure to come out with sophisticated material, not riddles or the sort of stuff just anyone could think up.

EURIPIDES

Very well, as for myself, the kind of poet I am, I will tell you in my final remarks; but first I'll expose my opponent for the charlatan and quack that he was, and by what means he hoodwinked his audiences, whom he took over from

910 ἐξηπάτα μώρους λαβὼν παρὰ Φρυνίχῳ τραφέντας.
πρώτιστα μὲν γὰρ ἕνα τιν' ἂν καθῖσεν ἐγκαλύψας,
Ἀχιλλέα τιν' ἢ Νιόβην, τὸ πρόσωπον οὐχὶ δεικνύς,
πρόσχημα τῆς τραγῳδίας, γρύζοντας οὐδὲ τουτί.

ΔΙΟΝΤΣΟΣ

μὰ τὸν Δί' οὐ δῆθ'.

ΕΤΡΙΠΙΔΗΣ

ὁ δὲ χορός γ' ἤρειδεν ὁρμαθοὺς ἂν
915 μελῶν ἐφεξῆς τέτταρας ξυνεχῶς ἄν· οἱ δ' ἐσίγων.

ΔΙΟΝΤΣΟΣ

ἐγὼ δ' ἔχαιρον τῇ σιωπῇ, καί με τοῦτ' ἔτερπεν
οὐχ ἧττον ἢ νῦν οἱ λαλοῦντες.

ΕΤΡΙΠΙΔΗΣ

ἠλίθιος γὰρ ἦσθα,
σάφ' ἴσθι.

ΔΙΟΝΤΣΟΣ

κἀμαυτῷ δοκῶ. τί δὲ ταῦτ' ἔδρασ' ὁ δεῖνα;

ΕΤΡΙΠΙΔΗΣ

ὑπ' ἀλαζονείας, ἵν' ὁ θεατὴς προσδοκῶν καθῆτο,
920 ὁπόθ' ἡ Νιόβη τι φθέγξεται· τὸ δρᾶμα δ' ἂν διῄει.

ΔΙΟΝΤΣΟΣ

ὦ παμπόνηρος, οἷ' ἄρ' ἐφενακιζόμην ὑπ' αὐτοῦ.
τί σκορδινᾷ καὶ δυσφορεῖς;

ΕΤΡΙΠΙΔΗΣ

ὅτι αὐτὸν ἐξελέγχω.
κἄπειτ' ἐπειδὴ ταῦτα ληρήσειε καὶ τὸ δρᾶμα

148

Phrynichus[85] already trained to be morons. He'd always start by having some solitary character sit there muffled up, say Achilles or Niobe, not letting us see their face (a poor excuse for tragic drama!) or hear even *this* much of a peep.

DIONYSUS
That's true, he didn't.

EURIPIDES
And while they sat there in silence, his chorus would rattle off four suites of choral lyric one after another without a break.

DIONYSUS
I enjoyed those silences, and found them no less pleasant than the chatterboxes we get nowadays.

EURIPIDES
That's because you were naive.

DIONYSUS
I think so too. But what was the guy up to?

EURIPIDES
Pure charlatanism. He wanted the spectator to sit there waiting for the moment when his Niobe would make a sound; meanwhile the play went on and on.

DIONYSUS
What a devil! The way he took me in! (*to Aeschylus*) Why are you fussing and fidgeting?

EURIPIDES
Because I'm exposing him. And then, when he'd hum-

---

[85] An older contemporary of Aeschylus.

ἤδη μεσοίη, ῥήματ᾽ ἂν βόεια δώδεκ᾽ εἶπεν,
925 ὀφρῦς ἔχοντα καὶ λόφους, δείν᾽ ἄττα μορμορωπά,
ἄγνωτα τοῖς θεωμένοις.

ΑΙΣΧΥΛΟΣ
οἴμοι τάλας.

ΔΙΟΝΥΣΟΣ
σιώπα.

ΕΥΡΙΠΙΔΗΣ
σαφὲς δ᾽ ἂν εἶπεν οὐδὲ ἕν—

ΔΙΟΝΥΣΟΣ
μὴ πρῖε τοὺς ὀδόντας.

ΕΥΡΙΠΙΔΗΣ
ἀλλ᾽ ἢ Σκαμάνδρους ἢ τάφρους ἢ ᾽π᾽ ἀσπίδων
ἐπόντας
γρυπαιέτους χαλκηλάτους καὶ ῥήμαθ᾽ ἱππόκρημνα,
930 ἃ ξυμβαλεῖν οὐ ῥᾴδι᾽ ἦν.

ΔΙΟΝΥΣΟΣ
νὴ τοὺς θεούς, ἐγὼ γοῦν
ἤδη ποτ᾽ ἐν μακρῷ χρόνῳ νυκτὸς διηγρύπνησα
τὸν ξουθὸν ἱππαλεκτρυόνα ζητῶν τίς ἐστιν ὄρνις.

ΑΙΣΧΥΛΟΣ
σημεῖον ἐν ταῖς ναυσίν, ὠμαθέστατ᾽, ἐνεγέγραπτο.

ΔΙΟΝΥΣΟΣ
ἐγὼ δὲ τὸν Φιλοξένου γ᾽ ᾤμην Ἔρυξιν εἶναι.

---

86 Adapted from Euripides, *Hippolytus* 375–76.

bugged along like that and the play was half over, he'd come out with a dozen words as big as an ox with crests and beetling brows, formidable bogey-faced things unfamiliar to the spectators.

AESCHYLUS
Good grief!

DIONYSUS
Be quiet!

EURIPIDES
And he wouldn't say a single intelligible word—

DIONYSUS
(*to Aeschylus*) Stop gnashing your teeth!

EURIPIDES
—but only Scamanders, or moats, or shields bronze-bossed and blazoned with griffin-eagles, and huge craggy utterances that weren't easy to decipher.

DIONYSUS
By heaven, I myself "have lain awake through long stretches of night trying to figure out"[86] what kind of bird a zooming horsecock is.

AESCHYLUS
It was carved on the ships[87] as a figurehead, you ignoramus!

DIONYSUS
And here I thought it was Philoxenus' son, Eryxis![88]

---

[87] I.e. the ships at Troy, cf. Aeschylus' *Myrmidons* fr. 134, Euripides' *Iphigeneia at Aulis* 231 ff. [88] Probably Eryxis of Cephisia (*PA* 5191), who had recently had a seat on the Council and (to infer from this context) a naval command.

ΕΥΡΙΠΙΔΗΣ

935 εἶτ᾽ ἐν τραγῳδίαις ἐχρῆν κἀλεκτρυόνα ποιῆσαι;

ΑΙΣΧΥΛΟΣ

σὺ δ᾽, ὦ θεοῖσιν ἐχθρέ, ποῖ᾽ ἄττ᾽ ἐστὶν ἄττ᾽ ἐποίεις;

ΕΥΡΙΠΙΔΗΣ

οὐχ ἱππαλεκτρυόνας μὰ Δί᾽ οὐδὲ τραγελάφους, ἅπερ
    σύ,
ἂν τοῖσι παραπετάσμασιν τοῖς Μηδικοῖς
    γράφουσιν·
ἀλλ᾽ ὡς παρέλαβον τὴν τέχνην παρὰ σοῦ τὸ
    πρῶτον εὐθὺς
940 οἰδοῦσαν ὑπὸ κομπασμάτων καὶ ῥημάτων ἐπαχθῶν,
ἴσχνανα μὲν πρώτιστον αὐτὴν καὶ τὸ βάρος
    ἀφεῖλον
ἐπυλλίοις καὶ περιπάτοις καὶ τευτλίοισι λευκοῖς,
χυλὸν διδοὺς στωμυλμάτων ἀπὸ βιβλίων ἀπηθῶν·
εἶτ᾽ ἀνέτρεφον μονῳδίαις Κηφισοφῶντα μειγνύς.
945 εἶτ᾽ οὐκ ἐλήρουν ὅ τι τύχοιμ᾽ οὐδ᾽ ἐμπεσὼν ἔφυρον,
ἀλλ᾽ οὑξιὼν πρώτιστα μέν μοι τὸ γένος εἶπ᾽ ἂν
    εὐθὺς
τοῦ δράματος.

ΑΙΣΧΥΛΟΣ

    κρεῖττον γὰρ ἦν σοι νὴ Δί᾽ ἢ τὸ σαυτοῦ.

ΕΥΡΙΠΙΔΗΣ

ἔπειτ᾽ ἀπὸ τῶν πρώτων ἐπῶν παρῆκ᾽ ἂν οὐδέν᾽
    ἀργόν,
ἀλλ᾽ ἔλεγεν ἡ γυνή τέ μοι χὠ δοῦλος οὐδὲν ἧττον,

EURIPIDES

But really, should one write about a *rooster* in tragedy?

AESCHYLUS

And what about you, you enemy of the gods, what sort of things did you write about?

EURIPIDES

Certainly not horsecocks or goatstags, like you, the sort of things they embroider on Persian tapestries. No, as soon as I first inherited the art from you, bloated with bombast and obese vocabulary, I immediately put it on a diet and took off the weight with a regimen of wordlets and strolls and little white beets, administering chatter-juice pressed from books; then I built up its strength with an admixture of Cephisophon's arias.[89] And I didn't write any old humbug that came into my head, or charge in and make a mess, but the very first character who walked onto my stage started by explaining the origins of the play.

AESCHYLUS

Because they were a damn sight better than your own!

EURIPIDES

Again, from the very first lines I wouldn't leave any character idle; I'd have the wife speak, and the slave just as much,

[89] Cephisophon was evidently a close friend of Euripides; the later tradition that he helped write Euripides' plays and seduced his wife (*Life* 92–96, cf. below, 1046–48) was probably derived from comedy.

χὠ δεσπότης χἠ παρθένος χἠ γραῦς ἄν.

ΑΙΣΧΥΛΟΣ

950
        εἶτα δῆτα
οὐκ ἀποθανεῖν σε ταῦτ᾽ ἐχρῆν τολμῶντα;

ΕΤΡΙΠΙΔΗΣ

        μὰ τὸν Ἀπόλλω·
δημοκρατικὸν γὰρ αὔτ᾽ ἔδρων.

ΔΙΟΝΤΣΟΣ

      τοῦτο μὲν ἔασον, ὦ τᾶν·
οὐ σοὶ γάρ ἐστι περίπατος κάλλιστα περί γε
  τούτου.

ΕΤΡΙΠΙΔΗΣ

ἔπειτα τουτουσὶ λαλεῖν ἐδίδαξα—

ΑΙΣΧΥΛΟΣ

       φημὶ κἀγώ.
955 ὡς πρὶν διδάξαι γ᾽ ὤφελες μέσος διαρραγῆναι.

ΕΤΡΙΠΙΔΗΣ

λεπτῶν τε κανόνων εἰσβολὰς ἐπῶν τε γωνιασμούς,
νοεῖν, ὁρᾶν, ξυνιέναι, στρέφειν ἕδραν, τεχνάζειν,
κἄχ᾽ ὑποτοπεῖσθαι, περινοεῖν ἅπαντα—

ΑΙΣΧΥΛΟΣ

       φημὶ κἀγώ.

ΕΤΡΙΠΙΔΗΣ

οἰκεῖα πράγματ᾽ εἰσάγων, οἷς χρώμεθ᾽, οἷς
  ξύνεσμεν,
960 ἐξ ὧν γ᾽ ἂν ἐξηλεγχόμην· ξυνειδότες γὰρ οὗτοι

and the master, and the maiden, and the old lady.

AESCHYLUS
And for such audacity you surely deserved the death penalty!

EURIPIDES
No, by Apollo: it was a democratic act.

DIONYSUS
Better change the subject, my friend; that's not the best theme for a sermon from *you*!

EURIPIDES
(*indicating the spectators*) Then I taught these people how to talk—

AESCHYLUS
I'll say you did! If only you'd split in two before you had the chance!

EURIPIDES
—and how to apply subtle rules and square off their words, to think, to see, to understand, to be quick on their feet, to scheme, to see the bad in others, to think of all aspects of everything—

AESCHYLUS
I'll say!

EURIPIDES
—by staging everyday scenes, things we're used to, things that we live with, things that I wouldn't have got away with falsifying, because these spectators knew them as well as I

---

957 ἕδραν Ussher: ἐρᾶν a

ἤλεγχον ἄν μου τὴν τέχνην· ἀλλ᾽ οὐκ ἐκομπολάκουν
ἀπὸ τοῦ φρονεῖν ἀποσπάσας, οὐδ᾽ ἐξέπληττον
   αὐτούς,
Κύκνους ποιῶν καὶ Μέμνονας
   κωδωνοφαλαροπώλους.
γνώσει δὲ τοὺς τούτου τε κἀμοὺς ἑκατέρου μαθητάς.
965 τουτουμενὶ Φορμίσιος Μεγαίνετός θ᾽ ὁ Μανῆς,
σαλπιγγολογχυπηνάδαι, σαρκασμοπιτυοκάμπται,
οὑμοὶ δὲ Κλειτοφῶν τε καὶ Θηραμένης ὁ κομψός.

ΔΙΟΝΥΣΟΣ

Θηραμένης; σοφός γ᾽ ἀνὴρ καὶ δεινὸς εἰς τὰ πάντα,
ὃς ἢν κακοῖς που περιπέσῃ καὶ πλησίον παραστῇ,
970 πέπτωκεν ἔξω τῶν κακῶν, οὐ Χῖος, ἀλλὰ Κεῖος.

ΕΥΡΙΠΙΔΗΣ

τοιαῦτα μέντοὐγὼ φρονεῖν
τούτοισιν εἰσηγησάμην,
λογισμὸν ἐνθεὶς τῇ τέχνῃ
καὶ σκέψιν, ὥστ᾽ ἤδη νοεῖν
975 ἅπαντα καὶ διειδέναι
τά τ᾽ ἄλλα καὶ τὰς οἰκίας
οἰκεῖν ἄμεινον ἢ πρὸ τοῦ
κἀνασκοπεῖν· "πῶς τοῦτ᾽ ἔχει;
ποῦ μοι τοδί; τίς τόδ᾽ ἔλαβεν;"

965 Μάγνης A, cf. Pollux 7.204–5
970 Κεῖος V A S λΣV: Κῖος R K ΣRVE: Κῷος Aristarchus ap.
ΣVE

and could have exposed my faulty art. I never distracted their minds with bombastic bluster, and never tried to shock them by creating Cycnuses and Memnons with bells on their horses' cheek plates.[90] You can judge by comparing his followers and mine: his are Phormisius[91] and Megaenetus the Stooge,[92] bugle boys with long beards and lances, flesh-ripping pine-benders, while mine are Cleitophon[93] and the sharp Theramenes.

DIONYSUS

Theramanes? That man's formidably intelligent across the board: if he happens to get into trouble or even comes close to it, he gives that trouble the slip, not a bust after all but a blackjack![94]

EURIPIDES

That's how I encouraged these people to think, by putting rationality and critical thinking into my art, so that now they grasp and really understand everything, especially how to run their households better than they used to, and how to keep an eye on things: "How's this going?" "Where'd that get to?" "Who took that?"

---

[90] Trojan allies slain by Achilles; Memnon was a character in *Memnon* and *Weighing of Souls*, but Cycnus cannot be assigned to any Aeschylean play on present evidence.

[91] A moderate democrat whose beard suggested female genitalia (cf. *Assemblywomen* 97).   [92] Otherwise unknown.

[93] A supporter and then an enemy of the Four Hundred; Plato portrays him as an associate of the sophist Thrasymachus (*Cleitophon* 406a, 410c, *Republic* 328b, 340a).

[94] Lit. "not a Chian [the lowest throw at dice] but a Cean [punning on 'Coan,' the highest throw, and suggesting foreign ancestry or a connection with the Cean philosopher Prodicus]."

ΔΙΟΝΥΣΟΣ

980 νὴ τοὺς θεούς, νῦν γοῦν Ἀθη-
ναίων ἅπας τις εἰσιὼν
κέκραγε πρὸς τοὺς οἰκέτας
ζητεῖ τε· "ποῦ 'στιν ἡ χύτρα;
τίς τὴν κεφαλὴν ἀπεδήδοκεν
985 τῆς μαινίδος; τὸ τρύβλιον
τὸ περυσινὸν τέθνηκέ μοι.
ποῦ τὸ σκόροδον τὸ χθιζινόν;
τίς τῆς ἐλάας παρέτραγεν;"
τέως δ' ἀβελτερώτατοι
990 κεχηνότες μαμμάκυθοι,
Μελιτίδαι καθῆντο.

ΧΟΡΟΣ

(ἀντ) τάδε μὲν λεύσσεις, φαίδιμ' Ἀχιλλεῦ·
993a σὺ δὲ τί, φέρε, πρὸς ταῦτα λέξεις;
993b μόνον ὅπως
μή σ' ὁ θυμὸς ἁρπάσας
995 ἐκτὸς οἴσει τῶν ἐλαῶν·
δεινὰ γὰρ κατηγόρηκεν.
ἀλλ' ὅπως, ὦ γεννάδα,
μὴ πρὸς ὀργὴν ἀντιλέξεις,
ἀλλὰ συστείλας ἄκροισι
1000 χρώμενος τοῖς ἱστίοις,
εἶτα μᾶλλον μᾶλλον ἄξεις
καὶ φυλάξεις, ἡνίκ' ἂν τὸ
πνεῦμα λεῖον καὶ καθεστηκὸς λάβῃς.

DIONYSUS

Heavens yes, these days each and every Athenian comes
home and starts yelling at the slaves, demanding to know
"Where's the pot? Who chewed the head off this sprat?
The bowl I bought last year is shot! Where's that garlic
from yesterday? Who's been nibbling olives?" They used to
sit there like dummies, gaping boobies, Simple Simons.

CHORUS

"You behold all this, glorious Achilles!"[95]
But what will you say in reply?
Only take care
that your anger doesn't seize you
and drive you off the track,
for his accusations are formidable.
Yes, take care, good sir,
that you don't reply in a rage,
but shorten your sails
and cruise with them furled,
then little by little make headway
and keep watch for the moment
when you get a soft, smooth breeze.

[95] The opening line of Aeschylus' *Myrmidons* (fr. 131).

ΚΟΡΥΦΑΙΟΣ

ἀλλ᾽ ὦ πρῶτος τῶν Ἑλλήνων πυργώσας ῥήματα
  σεμνὰ
1005 καὶ κοσμήσας τραγικὸν λῆρον, θαρρῶν τὸν κρουνὸν
  ἀφίει.

ΑΙΣΧΥΛΟΣ

θυμοῦμαι μὲν τῇ ξυντυχίᾳ, καί μου τὰ σπλάγχν᾽
  ἀγανακτεῖ,
εἰ πρὸς τοῦτον δεῖ μ᾽ ἀντιλέγειν· ἵνα μὴ φάσκῃ δ᾽
  ἀπορεῖν με,
ἀπόκριναί μοι, τίνος οὕνεκα χρὴ θαυμάζειν ἄνδρα
  ποιητήν;

ΕΥΡΙΠΙΔΗΣ

δεξιότητος καὶ νουθεσίας, ὅτι βελτίους τε ποιοῦμεν
τοὺς ἀνθρώπους ἐν ταῖς πόλεσιν.

ΑΙΣΧΥΛΟΣ

1010   ταῦτ᾽ οὖν εἰ μὴ πεποίηκας,
ἀλλ᾽ ἐκ χρηστῶν καὶ γενναίων μοχθηροτέρους
  ἀπέδειξας,
τί παθεῖν φήσεις ἄξιος εἶναι;

ΔΙΟΝΥΣΟΣ

                 τεθνάναι· μὴ τοῦτον ἐρώτα.

ΑΙΣΧΥΛΟΣ

σκέψαι τοίνυν οἵους αὐτοὺς παρ᾽ ἐμοῦ παρεδέξατο
  πρῶτον,

CHORUS LEADER

Now then, you who were the first of the Greeks to rear towers of majestic utterance and adorn tragic rant, take heart and open the floodgates!

AESCHYLUS

I'm enraged at this turn of events, and it sours my stomach that I have to debate this man, but I don't want him claiming that I'm at a loss, so answer me this: for what qualities should a poet be admired?

EURIPIDES

Skill and good counsel, and because we make people better members of their communities.

AESCHYLUS

And if you haven't done this, but rather turned good, upstanding people into obvious scoundrels, what punishment would you say you deserve?

DIONYSUS

Death; you needn't ask *him*!

AESCHYLUS

Then just consider what they were like when he took them

εἰ γενναίους καὶ τετραπήχεις, καὶ μὴ
    διαδρασιπολίτας,
1015 μηδ᾽ ἀγοραίους μηδὲ κοβάλους, ὥσπερ νῦν, μηδὲ
    πανούργους,
ἀλλὰ πνέοντας δόρυ καὶ λόγχας καὶ λευκολόφους
    τρυφαλείας
καὶ πήληκας καὶ κνημῖδας καὶ θυμοὺς ἑπταβοείους.

ΔΙΟΝΥΣΟΣ
καὶ δὴ χωρεῖ τουτὶ τὸ κακόν· κρανοποιῶν αὖ μ᾽
    ἐπιτρίψει.

ΕΥΡΙΠΙΔΗΣ
καὶ τί σὺ δράσας οὕτως αὐτοὺς γενναίους
    ἐξεδίδαξας;

ΔΙΟΝΥΣΟΣ
1020 Αἰσχύλε, λέξον, μηδ᾽ αὐθάδως σεμνυνόμενος
    χαλέπαινε.

ΑΙΣΧΥΛΟΣ
δρᾶμα ποιήσας Ἄρεως μεστόν.

ΔΙΟΝΥΣΟΣ
                 ποῖον;

ΑΙΣΧΥΛΟΣ
                     τοὺς Ἕπτ᾽ ἐπὶ Θήβας·
ὃ θεασάμενος πᾶς ἄν τις ἀνὴρ ἠράσθη δάιος εἶναι.

ΔΙΟΝΥΣΟΣ
τουτὶ μέν σοι κακὸν εἴργασται· Θηβαίους γὰρ
    πεποίηκας

over from me, noble six-footers and not the civic shirkers,
vulgarians, imps, and criminals they are now, but men with
an aura of spears, lances, white-crested helmets, green
berets, greaves, and seven-ply oxhide hearts.

DIONYSUS

This is going from bad to worse: making helmets now—
he'll wear me out!

EURIPIDES

And just how did you train them to be so noble?

DIONYSUS

Speak up, Aeschylus, and don't be willfully prideful and
difficult.

AESCHYLUS

By composing a play chock-full of Ares.

DIONYSUS

Namely?

AESCHYLUS

My *Seven Against Thebes*; every single man who watched
it was hot to be warlike.

DIONYSUS

Well, that was an evil accomplishment, because you've

1018 -τρίψει R A: -τρίψεις V K
1019 γενναίους R: ἀνδρείους V A K

ἀνδρειοτέρους εἰς τὸν πόλεμον· καὶ τούτου γ᾽ οὕνεκα
τύπτου.

ΑΙΣΧΥΛΟΣ

1025 ἀλλ᾽ ὑμῖν αὔτ᾽ ἐξῆν ἀσκεῖν, ἀλλ᾽ οὐκ ἐπὶ τοῦτ᾽
ἐτράπεσθε.
εἶτα διδάξας Πέρσας μετὰ τοῦτ᾽ ἐπιθυμεῖν
ἐξεδίδαξα
νικᾶν ἀεὶ τοὺς ἀντιπάλους, κοσμήσας ἔργον
ἄριστον.

ΔΙΟΝΥΣΟΣ

ἐχάρην γοῦν, ἡνίκ᾽ ἐπήκουσαν τοῦ Δαρείου
τεθνεῶτος,
ὁ χορὸς δ᾽ εὐθὺς τὼ χεῖρ᾽ ὡδὶ συγκρούσας εἶπεν·
"ἰαυοῖ."

ΑΙΣΧΥΛΟΣ

1030 ταῦτα γὰρ ἄνδρας χρὴ ποιητὰς ἀσκεῖν. σκέψαι γὰρ
ἀπ᾽ ἀρχῆς
ὡς ὠφέλιμοι τῶν ποιητῶν οἱ γενναῖοι γεγένηνται.
Ὀρφεὺς μὲν γὰρ τελετάς θ᾽ ἡμῖν κατέδειξε φόνων τ᾽
ἀπέχεσθαι,
Μουσαῖος δ᾽ ἐξακέσεις τε νόσων καὶ χρησμούς,
Ἡσίοδος δὲ
γῆς ἐργασίας, καρπῶν ὥρας, ἀρότους· ὁ δὲ θεῖος
Ὅμηρος
1035 ἀπὸ τοῦ τιμὴν καὶ κλέος ἔσχεν πλὴν τοῦδ᾽, ὅτι
χρήστ᾽ ἐδίδαξεν,
τάξεις, ἀρετάς, ὁπλίσεις ἀνδρῶν;

made the Thebans[96] more valiant in battle, and you deserve a beating for it.

AESCHYLUS

No, you could all have had the same training, but you didn't go in that direction. Thereafter I produced my *Persians*, which taught them to yearn always to defeat the enemy, and thus I adorned an excellent achievement.[97]

DIONYSUS

I certainly enjoyed it when they listened to the dead Darius, and right away the chorus clapped their hands together like this and cried "aiee!"

AESCHYLUS

That's the sort of thing that poets should practice. Just consider how beneficial the noble poets have been from the earliest times. Orpheus revealed mystic rites to us, and taught us to abstain from killings; Musaeus instructed us on oracles and cures for diseases; Hesiod on agriculture, the seasons for crops, and ploughing. And where did the godlike Homer get respect and renown if not by giving good instruction in the tactics, virtues, and weaponry of men?

---

96 The Thebans were bitter enemies of Athens in the Peloponnesian War.

97 The defeat of the Persians at Salamis (in 480) and Plataea (479).

1028 ἐπήκουσαν τοῦ Sommerstein praeeunte Dover: ἤκουσα περὶ a

ΔΙΟΝΥΣΟΣ

καὶ μὴν οὐ Παντακλέα γε

ἐδίδαξεν ὅμως τὸν σκαιότατον. πρώην γοῦν, ἡνίκ'
ἔπεμπεν,

τὸ κράνος πρῶτον περιδησάμενος τὸν λόφον ἤμελλ'
ἐπιδήσειν.

ΑΙΣΧΥΛΟΣ

ἀλλ' ἄλλους τοι πολλοὺς ἀγαθούς, ὧν ἦν καὶ
Λάμαχος ἥρως·

1040 ὅθεν ἡμὴ φρὴν ἀπομαξαμένη πολλὰς ἀρετὰς
ἐποίησεν,

Πατρόκλων, Τεύκρων θυμολεόντων, ἵν' ἐπαίροιμ'
ἄνδρα πολίτην

ἀντεκτείνειν αὑτὸν τούτοις, ὁπόταν σάλπιγγος
ἀκούσῃ.

ἀλλ' οὐ μὰ Δί' οὐ Φαίδρας ἐποίουν πόρνας οὐδὲ
Σθενεβοίας,

οὐδ' οἶδ' οὐδεὶς ἥντιν' ἐρῶσαν πώποτ' ἐποίησα
γυναῖκα.

ΕΥΡΙΠΙΔΗΣ

μὰ Δί', οὐ γὰρ ἐπῆν τῆς Ἀφροδίτης οὐδέν σοι.

ΑΙΣΧΥΛΟΣ

1045   μηδέ γ' ἐπείη·

ἀλλ' ἐπὶ σοί τοι καὶ τοῖς σοῖσιν πολλὴ πολλοῦ
'πικαθῆτο,

ὥστε γε καὐτόν σε κατ' οὖν ἔβαλεν.

FROGS

DIONYSUS

Yes, but all the same he didn't succeed with that lummox
Pantacles,[98] who just the other day, in a parade, was trying
to fasten the crest to his helmet after he'd put it on!

AESCHYLUS

But surely he did succeed with many other brave men, one
of whom was the hero Lamachus;[99] from that mold my
imagination created many profiles in courage, men like
Patroclus and the lionhearted Teucer, in hopes of inspiring
every citizen to measure himself against them every time
he heard the bugle. But I certainly created no whores like
Phaedra and Stheneboea,[100] and no one can find a lustful
woman in anything I ever composed.

EURIPIDES

Certainly not, since Aphrodite had absolutely nothing to
do with you.

AESCHYLUS

And I hope she never does! Whereas she plunked herself
down plenty hard on you and yours, and yes, even flattened
you personally.

[98] Ridiculed in the same terms by Eupolis in the 420s (fr. 318).

[99] His distinguished military career began in the 430s and
ended with a courageous death in action in 414 (Thucydides
6.101); though Aristophanes portrayed him as a braggart soldier
in *Acharnians*, he praised him after his death (*Women at the
Thesmophoria* 841).

[100] Both heroines (of Euripides' *Hippolytus* and *Stheneboea*
resp.) propositioned a stepson (Hippolytus, Bellerophon) and
then accused him of rape when rejected.

ΔΙΟΝΥΣΟΣ

νὴ τὸν Δία τοῦτό γέ τοι δή.
ἃ γὰρ εἰς τὰς ἀλλοτρίας ἐποίεις, αὐτὸς τούτοισιν
ἐπλήγης.

ΕΥΡΙΠΙΔΗΣ

καὶ τί βλάπτουσ᾽, ὦ σχέτλι᾽ ἀνδρῶν, τὴν πόλιν
ἁμαὶ Σθενέβοιαι;

ΑΙΣΧΥΛΟΣ

1050 ὅτι γενναίας καὶ γενναίων ἀνδρῶν ἀλόχους
ἀνέπεισας
κώνεια πίνειν αἰσχυνθείσας διὰ τοὺς σοὺς
Βελλεροφόντας.

ΕΥΡΙΠΙΔΗΣ

πότερον δ᾽ οὐκ ὄντα λόγον τοῦτον περὶ τῆς Φαίδρας
ξυνέθηκα;

ΑΙΣΧΥΛΟΣ

μὰ Δί᾽, ἀλλ᾽ ὄντ᾽· ἀλλ᾽ ἀποκρύπτειν χρὴ τὸ πονηρὸν
τόν γε ποιητήν,
καὶ μὴ παράγειν μηδὲ διδάσκειν. τοῖς μὲν γὰρ
παιδαρίοισιν
1055 ἐστὶ διδάσκαλος ὅστις φράζει, τοῖσιν δ᾽ ἡβῶσι
ποιηταί.
πάνυ δὴ δεῖ χρηστὰ λέγειν ἡμᾶς.

ΕΥΡΙΠΙΔΗΣ

ἢν οὖν σὺ λέγῃς Λυκαβηττοὺς

DIONYSUS

That's the truth, all right! You yourself got hit by the same stuff you wrote about other people's wives.

EURIPIDES

And what harm did my Stheneboeas do to the community, you bastard?

AESCHYLUS

You motivated respectable women, the spouses of respectable men, to take hemlock in their shame over your Bellerophons.

EURIPIDES

But the story I told about Phaedra was already established, wasn't it?

AESCHYLUS

Of course it was. But the poet has a special duty to conceal what's wicked, not stage it or teach it. For children the teacher is the one who instructs, but grownups have the poet. It's very important that we tell them things that are good.

EURIPIDES

So if you give us stuff like Lycabettus and massy Parnas-

καὶ Παρνασσῶν ἡμῖν μεγέθη, τοῦτ᾽ ἐστὶ τὸ χρηστὰ
   διδάσκειν,
ὃν χρῆν φράζειν ἀνθρωπείως;

ΑΙΣΧΥΛΟΣ
             ἀλλ᾽, ὦ κακόδαιμον, ἀνάγκη
μεγάλων γνωμῶν καὶ διανοιῶν ἴσα καὶ τὰ ῥήματα
   τίκτειν.

1060 κἄλλως εἰκὸς τοὺς ἡμιθέους τοῖς ῥήμασι μείζοσι
   χρῆσθαι·
καὶ γὰρ τοῖς ἱματίοις ἡμῶν χρῶνται πολὺ
   σεμνοτέροισιν·
ἁμοῦ χρηστῶς καταδείξαντος διελυμήνω σύ.

ΕΥΡΙΠΙΔΗΣ
             τί δράσας;

ΑΙΣΧΥΛΟΣ
πρῶτον μὲν τοὺς βασιλεύοντας ῥάκι᾽ ἀμπισχών, ἵν᾽
   ἐλεινοὶ
τοῖς ἀνθρώποις φαίνοιντ᾽ εἶναι.

ΕΥΡΙΠΙΔΗΣ
        τοῦτ᾽ οὖν ἔβλαψα τί δράσας;

ΑΙΣΧΥΛΟΣ
1065 οὔκουν ἐθέλει γε τριηραρχεῖν πλουτῶν οὐδεὶς διὰ
   ταῦτα,
ἀλλὰ ῥακίοις περιιλάμενος κλάει καὶ φησὶ
   πένεσθαι.

170

sus,[101] that's supposed to teach what's good? You should
have done your instructing in plain human language.

AESCHYLUS

Look, you wretch, great thoughts and ideas force us to pro-
duce expressions that are equal to them. And anyway, it
suits the demigods to use exalted expressions, just as they
wear much more impressive clothing than we do; that's
where I set a good example that you completely corrupted.

EURIPIDES

How so?

AESCHYLUS

First, you made your royals wear rags, so that they'd strike
people as being piteous.

EURIPIDES

So what harm did I do there?

AESCHYLUS

Well, for one thing, that's why no rich man is willing to
command a warship, but instead wraps himself in rags and
whines, claiming to be poor.[102]

---

[101] Mountains.

[102] A trierarchy was a service levied on the rich, who could sue
for exemption by demonstrating insufficient wealth to a jury.

ΔΙΟΝΥΣΟΣ

νὴ τὴν Δήμητρα χιτῶνά γ᾽ ἔχων οὔλων ἐρίων
ὑπένερθεν.
κἂν ταῦτα λέγων ἐξαπατήσῃ, περὶ τοὺς ἰχθῦς
ἀνέκυψεν.

ΑΙΣΧΥΛΟΣ

εἶτ᾽ αὖ λαλιὰν ἐπιτηδεῦσαι καὶ στωμυλίαν ἐδίδαξας,
1070 ἣ ᾽ξεκένωσεν τάς τε παλαίστρας καὶ τὰς πυγὰς
ἐνέτριψεν
τῶν μειρακίων στωμυλλομένων, καὶ τοὺς Παράλους
ἀνέπεισεν
ἀνταγορεύειν τοῖς ἄρχουσιν. καίτοι τότε γ᾽, ἡνίκ᾽
ἐγὼ ᾽ζων,
οὐκ ἠπίσταντ᾽ ἀλλ᾽ ἢ μᾶζαν καλέσαι καὶ
"ῥυππαπαῖ" εἰπεῖν.

ΔΙΟΝΥΣΟΣ

νὴ τὸν Ἀπόλλω, καὶ προσπαρδεῖν γ᾽ εἰς τὸ στόμα
τῷ θαλάμακι,
1075 καὶ μινθῶσαι τὸν ξύσσιτον κἀκβάς τινα
λωποδυτῆσαι·
1076/7 νῦν δ᾽ ἀντιλέγει κοὐκέτ᾽ ἐλαύνει· πλεῖ δευρὶ καὖθις
ἐκεῖσε.

ΑΙΣΧΥΛΟΣ

ποίων δὲ κακῶν οὐκ αἴτιός ἐστ᾽;
οὐ προαγωγοὺς κατέδειξ᾽ οὗτος,
1080 καὶ τικτούσας ἐν τοῖς ἱεροῖς,
καὶ μειγνυμένας τοῖσιν ἀδελφοῖς,

DIONYSUS

When he's actually wearing a soft woollen shirt underneath, by Demeter! And if he pulls that lie off, he pops up in the fish market!

AESCHYLUS

Then you taught people to cultivate chitchat and gab, which has emptied the wrestling schools and worn down the butts of the young men as they gab away, and prompted the crew of the *Paralus* to talk back to their officers.[103] Yet in the old days, when I was alive, all they knew how to do was shout for their rations and cry "heave ho!"

DIONYSUS

God yes, and fart in the bottom bencher's face, and smear shit on their messmates, and steal people's clothes when on shore leave! Now they talk back and refuse to row, and the ship sails this way and that.

AESCHYLUS

And what evils can't be laid at his door? Didn't he show women procuring,[104] and having babies in temples,[105] and sleeping with their brothers,[106] and claiming that "life is

---

[103] One of two triremes used for state business, whose all-citizen crew were strongly democratic (cf. Thucydides 8.73.5).

[104] Phaedra's nurse in *Hippolytus*.

[105] The heroine in *Auge*.

[106] Canace with Macareus in *Aeolus*, though this was probably a rape.

καὶ φασκούσας οὐ ζῆν τὸ ζῆν;
κᾆτ᾽ ἐκ τούτων ἡ πόλις ἡμῶν
ὑπογραμματέων ἀνεμεστώθη
1085 καὶ βωμολόχων δημοπιθήκων
ἐξαπατώντων τὸν δῆμον ἀεί,
λαμπάδα δ᾽ οὐδεὶς οἷός τε φέρειν
ὑπ᾽ ἀγυμνασίας ἔτι νυνί.

ΔΙΟΝΥΣΟΣ

μὰ Δί᾽ οὐ δῆθ᾽, ὥστ᾽ ἐπαφηυάνθην
1090 Παναθηναίοισι γελῶν, ὅτε δὴ
βραδὺς ἄνθρωπός τις ἔθει κύψας
λευκός, πίων, ὑπολειπόμενος
καὶ δεινὰ ποιῶν· κᾆθ᾽ οἱ Κεραμῆς
ἐν ταῖσι πύλαις παίουσ᾽ αὐτοῦ
1095 γαστέρα, πλευράς, λαγόνας, πυγήν,
ὁ δὲ τυπτόμενος ταῖσι πλατείαις
ὑποπερδόμενος
φυσῶν τὴν λαμπάδ᾽ ἔφευγεν.

ΧΟΡΟΣ

(στρ) μέγα τὸ πρᾶγμα, πολὺ τὸ νεῖκος,
          ἁδρὸς ὁ πόλεμος ἔρχεται.
1100 χαλεπὸν οὖν ἔργον διαιρεῖν,
          ὅταν ὁ μὲν τείνῃ βιαίως,
          ὁ δ᾽ ἐπαναστρέφειν δύνηται
          κἀπερείδεσθαι τορῶς.
          ἀλλὰ μὴ 'ν ταὐτῷ κάθησθον·
          εἰσβολαὶ γάρ εἰσι πολλαὶ

not life"?[107] As a result, our community's filled with assistant secretaries and clownish monkeys of politicians forever lying to the people, and from lack of physical fitness there's nobody left who can run with a torch.

DIONYSUS

Amen to that! I about died laughing at the Panathenaea when some laggard was running, all pale-faced, stooped over, and fat, falling behind and struggling badly; and then at the Gates the Potter's Field people whacked his stomach, ribs, flanks, and butt, and at their flat-handed slaps he started farting, and ran away blowing on his torch!

CHORUS

It's a great affair, a great quarrel,
a stern war that's in progress!
So it's a tough task to decide the issue,
when one strives forcefully
and the other can wheel around
and sharply counterattack.
Now don't just sit tight, you two:
there are plenty more thrusts to come,

---

[107] Perhaps Pasiphae in *Polyidus*.

χἄτεραι σοφισμάτων.
1105 ὅ τι περ οὖν ἔχετον ἐρίζειν,
λέγετον, ἔπιτον, ἀνὰ δὲ δέρετον
τά τε παλαιὰ καὶ τὰ καινά,
κἀποκινδυνεύετον λεπ-
τόν τι καὶ σοφὸν λέγειν.

(ἀντ) εἰ δὲ τοῦτο καταφοβεῖσθον,
μή τις ἀμαθία προσῇ
1110 τοῖς θεωμένοισιν, ὡς τὰ
λεπτὰ μὴ γνῶναι λεγόντοιν,
μηδὲν ὀρρωδεῖτε τοῦθ᾽· ὡς
οὐκέθ᾽ οὕτω ταῦτ᾽ ἔχει.
ἐστρατευμένοι γάρ εἰσι,
βιβλίον τ᾽ ἔχων ἕκαστος
μανθάνει τὰ δεξιά·
1115 αἱ φύσεις τ᾽ ἄλλως κράτισται,
νῦν δὲ καὶ παρηκόνηνται.
μηδὲν οὖν δείσητον, ἀλλὰ
πάντ᾽ ἐπέξιτον, θεατῶν γ᾽
οὕνεχ᾽, ὡς ὄντων σοφῶν.

ΕΥΡΙΠΙΔΗΣ

καὶ μὴν ἐπ᾽ αὐτοὺς τοὺς προλόγους σοι τρέψομαι,
1120 ὅπως τὸ πρῶτον τῆς τραγῳδίας μέρος
πρώτιστον αὐτοῦ βασανιῶ τοῦ δεξιοῦ·
ἀσαφὴς γὰρ ἦν ἐν τῇ φράσει τῶν πραγμάτων.

176

and more intellectualities.
So whatever your grounds of dispute,
argue out, attack, and lay bare
the old and the new,
and take a chance on saying
something subtle and sage.

And if you're afraid
of any ignorance among
the spectators, that they won't
appreciate your subtleties of argument,
don't worry about that, because
things are no longer that way.
For they're veterans,
and each one has a book
and knows the fine points;
their natural endowments are masterful too,
and now sharpened up.
So have no fear,
but tackle it all, resting assured
that the spectators are sage.

EURIPIDES

Now then, let me turn just to your prologues, so as first off
to examine the first section of this competent man's tragic
drama, because he was obscure in the exposition of his
plots.

ΔΙΟΝΥΣΟΣ

καὶ ποῖον αὐτοῦ βασανιεῖς;

ΕΥΡΙΠΙΔΗΣ

πολλοὺς πάνυ.

πρῶτον δέ μοι τὸν ἐξ Ὀρεστείας λέγε.

ΔΙΟΝΥΣΟΣ

1125 ἄγε δὴ σιώπα πᾶς ἀνήρ. λέγ᾽, Αἰσχύλε.

ΑΙΣΧΥΛΟΣ

"Ἑρμῆ χθόνιε, πατρῷ᾽ ἐποπτεύων κράτη
σωτὴρ γενοῦ μοι σύμμαχός τ᾽ αἰτουμένῳ·
ἥκω γὰρ εἰς γῆν τήνδε καὶ κατέρχομαι."

ΔΙΟΝΥΣΟΣ

τούτων ἔχεις ψέγειν τι;

ΕΥΡΙΠΙΔΗΣ

πλεῖν ἢ δώδεκα.

ΔΙΟΝΥΣΟΣ

1130 ἀλλ᾽ οὐδὲ πάντα ταῦτά γ᾽ ἔστ᾽ ἀλλ᾽ ἢ τρία.

ΕΥΡΙΠΙΔΗΣ

ἔχει δ᾽ ἕκαστον εἴκοσίν γ᾽ ἁμαρτίας.

ΔΙΟΝΥΣΟΣ

Αἰσχύλε, παραινῶ σοι σιωπᾶν· εἰ δὲ μή,
πρὸς τρισὶν ἰαμβείοισι προσοφείλων φανεῖ.

ΑΙΣΧΥΛΟΣ

ἐγὼ σιωπῶ τῷδ᾽;

DIONYSUS

And what prologue of his do you mean to examine?

EURIPIDES

A great many. First, recite me the one from the *Oresteia*.

DIONYSUS

Come on, everyone, be quiet! Go ahead, Aeschylus.

AESCHYLUS

"Underworld Hermes, who keeps watch over the paternal domain, be now, I pray, my ally and savior, for I've come back to this land and return."

DIONYSUS

Do you have any criticism of that?

EURIPIDES

A dozen or so.

DIONYSUS

But the whole quote is only three lines long!

EURIPIDES

And each one contains twenty mistakes.

DIONYSUS

Aeschylus, I advise you to keep quiet, or else you'll be shown up as liable for even more than three iambics!

AESCHYLUS

Me keep quiet for him?

ΔΙΟΝΥΣΟΣ
ἐὰν πείθῃ γ᾽ ἐμοί.

ΕΥΡΙΠΙΔΗΣ
1135 εὐθὺς γὰρ ἡμάρτηκεν οὐράνιον ὅσον.

ΑΙΣΧΥΛΟΣ
ὁρᾷς ὅτι ληρεῖς.

ΔΙΟΝΥΣΟΣ
ἀλλ᾽ ὀλίγον γέ μοι μέλει.

ΑΙΣΧΥΛΟΣ
πῶς φῄς μ᾽ ἁμαρτεῖν;

ΕΥΡΙΠΙΔΗΣ
αὖθις ἐξ ἀρχῆς λέγε.

ΑΙΣΧΥΛΟΣ
"Ἑρμῆ χθόνιε, πατρῷ᾽ ἐποπτεύων κράτη."

ΕΥΡΙΠΙΔΗΣ
οὔκουν Ὀρέστης τοῦτ᾽ ἐπὶ τῷ τύμβῳ λέγει
τῷ τοῦ πατρὸς τεθνεῶτος;

ΑΙΣΧΥΛΟΣ
1140 οὐκ ἄλλως λέγω.

ΕΥΡΙΠΙΔΗΣ
πότερ᾽ οὖν τὸν Ἑρμῆν, ὡς ὁ πατὴρ ἀπώλετο
αὐτοῦ βιαίως ἐκ γυναικείας χερὸς
δόλοις λαθραίοις, ταῦτ᾽ ἐποπτεύειν ἔφη;

ΑΙΣΧΥΛΟΣ
οὐ δῆτ᾽ ἐκεῖνος, ἀλλὰ τὸν Ἐριούνιον

DIONYSUS

If you take my advice.

EURIPIDES

I say he's made a mistake of cosmic scale.

AESCHYLUS

Listen to you rant!

DIONYSUS

(*to Aeschylus*) Go ahead then, it doesn't matter to me.

AESCHYLUS

What mistake are you referring to?

EURIPIDES

Recite it again.

AESCHYLUS

"Underworld Hermes, who keeps watch over the paternal domain."

EURIPIDES

Now doesn't Orestes say this at the tomb of his dead father?

AESCHYLUS

That's exactly right.

EURIPIDES

So let me get this right: after his father had died violently at his wife's hands in a secret plot, he was saying that Hermes "kept watch" while this happened?

AESCHYLUS

He was not! He called on Nether Hermes as "Underworld

1145 Ἑρμῆν χθόνιον προσεῖπε, κἀδήλου λέγων
    ὁτιὴ πατρῷον τοῦτο κέκτηται γέρας.

ΕΥΡΙΠΙΔΗΣ

ἔτι μεῖζον ἐξήμαρτες ἢ ’γὼ ’βουλόμην·
εἰ γὰρ πατρῷον τὸ χθόνιον ἔχει γέρας—

ΔΙΟΝΥΣΟΣ

οὕτω γ’ ἂν εἴη πρὸς πατρὸς τυμβωρύχος.

ΑΙΣΧΥΛΟΣ

1150 Διόνυσε, πίνεις οἶνον οὐκ ἀνθοσμίαν.

ΔΙΟΝΥΣΟΣ

λέγ’ ἕτερον αὐτῷ· σὺ δ’ ἐπιτήρει τὸ βλάβος.

ΑΙΣΧΥΛΟΣ

"σωτὴρ γενοῦ μοι σύμμαχός τ’ αἰτουμένῳ.
ἥκω γὰρ εἰς γῆν τήνδε καὶ κατέρχομαι."

ΕΥΡΙΠΙΔΗΣ

δὶς ταὐτὸν ἡμῖν εἶπεν ὁ σοφὸς Αἰσχύλος.

ΔΙΟΝΥΣΟΣ

πῶς δίς;

ΕΥΡΙΠΙΔΗΣ

1155   σκόπει τὸ ῥῆμ’· ἐγὼ δέ σοι φράσω.
    "ἥκω γὰρ εἰς γῆν," φησί, "καὶ κατέρχομαι"·
    ἥκειν δὲ ταὐτόν ἐστι τῷ κατέρχομαι.

ΔΙΟΝΥΣΟΣ

νὴ τὸν Δί’, ὥσπερ γ’ εἴ τις εἴποι γείτονι·
"χρῆσον σὺ μάκτραν, εἰ δὲ βούλει, κάρδοπον."

182

Hermes," and made it clear that Hermes possesses this function as a paternal inheritance.

EURIPIDES

That's an even bigger mistake than I was looking for! Because if he possesses the underworld as a paternal inheritance—

DIONYSUS

That would make him a graverobber on his father's side!

AESCHYLUS

Dionysus, the wine you're drinking has gone sour.

DIONYSUS

Recite him another one, and you watch for the mistake.

AESCHYLUS

"Be now, I pray, my ally and savior, for I've come back to this land and return."

EURIPIDES

The sage Aeschylus has told us the same thing twice.

DIONYSUS

How twice?

EURIPIDES

Look at the expression, and I'll show you. "I've come back to this land," he says, "and return"; but "coming back to" is the same as "returning."

DIONYSUS

Of course! It's like asking your neighbor, "Lend me a kneading trough, or else a trough to knead in."

ΑΙΣΧΥΛΟΣ

1160 οὐ δῆτα τοῦτό γ', ὦ κατεστωμυλμένε
ἄνθρωπε, ταῦτ' ἔστ', ἀλλ' ἄριστ' ἐπῶν ἔχον.

ΔΙΟΝΥΣΟΣ

πῶς δή; δίδαξον γάρ με καθ' ὅτι δὴ λέγεις.

ΑΙΣΧΥΛΟΣ

ἐλθεῖν μὲν εἰς γῆν ἔσθ' ὅτῳ μετῇ πάτρας·
χωρὶς γὰρ ἄλλης συμφορᾶς ἐλήλυθεν·
1165 φεύγων δ' ἀνὴρ ἥκει τε καὶ κατέρχεται.

ΔΙΟΝΥΣΟΣ

εὖ νὴ τὸν Ἀπόλλω. τί σὺ λέγεις, Εὐριπίδη;

ΕΥΡΙΠΙΔΗΣ

οὔ φημι τὸν Ὀρέστην κατελθεῖν οἴκαδε·
λάθρᾳ γὰρ ἦλθεν οὐ πιθὼν τοὺς κυρίους.

ΔΙΟΝΥΣΟΣ

εὖ νὴ τὸν Ἑρμῆν· ὅ τι λέγεις δ' οὐ μανθάνω.

ΕΥΡΙΠΙΔΗΣ

πέραινε τοίνυν ἕτερον.

ΔΙΟΝΥΣΟΣ

1170   ἴθι πέραινε σύ,
Αἰσχύλ', ἀνύσας· σὺ δ' εἰς τὸ κακὸν ἀπόβλεπε.

ΑΙΣΧΥΛΟΣ

"τύμβου δ' ἐπ' ὄχθῳ τῷδε κηρύσσω πατρὶ
κλύειν, ἀκοῦσαι"—

AESCHYLUS

That is not the same thing, you fool for folderol! The wording is excellent.

DIONYSUS

How so? Explain to me what you mean by that.

AESCHYLUS

Anyone who belongs to a country can "come back" to it; he just arrives without any further circumstance. But an exile both "comes back" and "returns."

DIONYSUS

Very good, by Apollo! What do you say, Euripides?

EURIPIDES

I deny that Orestes was coming home; he arrived secretly and without informing the authorities.

DIONYSUS

Very good, by Hermes, though I don't know what you mean.

EURIPIDES

Well, go ahead with another line.

DIONYSUS

Yes, hurry up and go ahead, Aeschylus; and you keep an eye out for the mistake.

AESCHYLUS

"And at this burial mound I invoke my father, to hearken and hear—"

ARISTOPHANES

ΕΥΡΙΠΙΔΗΣ
τοῦθ᾽ ἕτερον αὖθις λέγει,
κλύειν, ἀκοῦσαι, ταὐτὸν ὂν σαφέστατα.

ΔΙΟΝΥΣΟΣ
1175 τεθνηκόσιν γὰρ ἔλεγεν, ὦ μόχθηρε σύ,
οἷς οὐδὲ τρὶς λέγοντες ἐξικνούμεθα.
σὺ δὲ πῶς ἐποίεις τοὺς προλόγους;

ΕΥΡΙΠΙΔΗΣ
ἐγὼ φράσω.
κἄν που δὶς εἴπω ταὐτόν, ἢ στοιβὴν ἴδῃς
ἐνοῦσαν ἔξω τοῦ λόγου, κατάπτυσον.

ΔΙΟΝΥΣΟΣ
1180 ἴθι δὴ λέγ᾽· οὐ γὰρ μοὐστὶν ἀλλ᾽ ἀκουστέα
σῶν προλόγων τῆς ὀρθότητος τῶν ἐπῶν.

ΕΥΡΙΠΙΔΗΣ
"ἦν Οἰδίπους τὸ πρῶτον εὐδαίμων ἀνήρ,"—

ΑΙΣΧΥΛΟΣ
μὰ τὸν Δί᾽ οὐ δῆτ᾽, ἀλλὰ κακοδαίμων φύσει.
ὅντινά γε, πρὶν φῦναι μέν, Ἀπόλλων ἔφη
1185 ἀποκτενεῖν τὸν πατέρα, πρὶν καὶ γεγονέναι.
πῶς οὗτος ἦν τὸ πρῶτον εὐτυχὴς ἀνήρ;

ΕΥΡΙΠΙΔΗΣ
"εἶτ᾽ ἐγένετ᾽ αὖθις ἀθλιώτατος βροτῶν."

ΑΙΣΧΥΛΟΣ
μὰ τὸν Δί᾽ οὐ δῆτ᾽, οὐ μὲν οὖν ἐπαύσατο.
πῶς γάρ; ὅτε δὴ πρῶτον μὲν αὐτὸν γενόμενον

EURIPIDES

There again he says the same thing twice: "hearkening" and "hearing" are quite obviously identical.

DIONYSUS

Yes, but he was addressing the dead, my poor fellow, and we can't reach them even if we speak three times! Now how did you compose your own prologues?

EURIPIDES

I'll show you. And if anywhere I say the same thing twice, or you spot any irrelevant padding, why go ahead and spit on me.

DIONYSUS

Go ahead then, recite one. I'm more than eager to hear the verbal precision of your prologues.

EURIPIDES

"At first was Oedipus a lucky man—"

AESCHYLUS

He certainly was not; he was born unfortunate, seeing that he's the one who, even before his birth, Apollo said would kill his father—before he was even conceived! So how could he be "at first a lucky man"?

EURIPIDES

"—but then he became the wretchedest of mortals."

AESCHYLUS

Certainly not "became," by heaven, because he never stopped being that, did he? Considering that as a newborn

187

1190 χειμῶνος ὄντος ἐξέθεσαν ἐν ὀστράκῳ,
ἵνα μὴ ʼκτραφεὶς γένοιτο τοῦ πατρὸς φονεύς·
εἶθ' ὡς Πόλυβον ἤρρησεν οἰδῶν τὼ πόδε·
ἔπειτα γραῦν ἔγημεν αὐτὸς ὢν νέος
καὶ πρός γε τούτοις τὴν ἑαυτοῦ μητέρα·
εἶτ' ἐξετύφλωσεν αὐτόν.

ΔΙΟΝΥΣΟΣ

1195   εὐδαίμων ἄρ' ἦν,
εἰ κἀστρατήγησέν γε μετ' Ἐρασινίδου.

ΕΥΡΙΠΙΔΗΣ

ληρεῖς· ἐγὼ δὲ τοὺς προλόγους καλῶς ποιῶ.

ΑΙΣΧΥΛΟΣ

καὶ μὴν μὰ τὸν Δί' οὐ κατ' ἔπος γέ σου κνίσω
τὸ ῥῆμ' ἕκαστον, ἀλλὰ σὺν τοῖσιν θεοῖς
1200 ἀπὸ ληκυθίου σου τοὺς προλόγους διαφθερῶ.

ΕΥΡΙΠΙΔΗΣ

ἀπὸ ληκυθίου σὺ τοὺς ἐμούς;

ΑΙΣΧΥΛΟΣ

                              ἑνὸς μόνου.
ποιεῖς γὰρ οὕτως ὥστ' ἐναρμόζειν ἅπαν,
καὶ κῳδάριον καὶ ληκύθιον καὶ θυλάκιον,
ἐν τοῖς ἰαμβείοισι. δείξω δ' αὐτίκα.

ΕΥΡΙΠΙΔΗΣ

ἰδού, σὺ δείξεις;

ΑΙΣΧΥΛΟΣ

                     φημί.

FROGS

they put him in a pot and exposed him in the dead of win-
ter, so he wouldn't become his father's murderer when he
grew up; then he wandered off on two swollen feet to
Polybus; then as a young man he married an old lady; and
on top of that she was his own mother; and then he blinded
himself.

DIONYSUS
Yes, a lucky man, provided he also shared command with
Erasinides![108]

EURIPIDES
Hogwash. I compose prologues very well.

AESCHYLUS
Look here, I certainly don't intend to pick away at your
expressions word by word; instead, the gods willing, I'll
demolish those prologues of yours with an oil bottle.

EURIPIDES
My prologues with an oil bottle?

AESCHYLUS
With only one. The way you compose, any such object can
be tagged on to your iambics: "tuft of wool," "oil bottle,"
"little sack." I'll show you right now.

EURIPIDES
You'll show me, will you?

AESCHYLUS
I will.

[108] Among the admirals at Arginusae who were put to death
for failing to rescue the shipwrecked sailors.

189

ΕΥΡΙΠΙΔΗΣ

1205   καὶ δὴ χρὴ λέγειν.
"Αἴγυπτος, ὡς ὁ πλεῖστος ἔσπαρται λόγος,
ξὺν παισὶ πεντήκοντα ναυτίλῳ πλάτῃ
Ἄργος κατασχών"—

ΑΙΣΧΥΛΟΣ

ληκύθιον ἀπώλεσεν.

ΔΙΟΝΥΣΟΣ

τουτὶ τί ἦν τὸ ληκύθιον; οὐ κλαύσεται;
1210 λέγ' ἕτερον αὐτῷ πρόλογον, ἵνα καὶ γνῶ πάλιν.

ΕΥΡΙΠΙΔΗΣ

"Διόνυσος, ὃς θύρσοισι καὶ νεβρῶν δοραῖς
καθαπτὸς ἐν πεύκῃσι Παρνασσὸν κάτα
πηδᾷ χορεύων"—

ΑΙΣΧΥΛΟΣ

ληκύθιον ἀπώλεσεν.

ΔΙΟΝΥΣΟΣ

οἴμοι πεπλήγμεθ' αὖθις ὑπὸ τῆς ληκύθου.

ΕΥΡΙΠΙΔΗΣ

1215 ἀλλ' οὐδὲν ἔσται πρᾶγμα· πρὸς γὰρ τουτονὶ
τὸν πρόλογον οὐχ ἕξει προσάψαι λήκυθον.
"οὐκ ἔστιν ὅστις πάντ' ἀνὴρ εὐδαιμονεῖ·
ἢ γὰρ πεφυκὼς ἐσθλὸς οὐκ ἔχει βίον,
ἢ δυσγενὴς ὤν"—

ΑΙΣΧΥΛΟΣ

ληκύθιον ἀπώλεσεν.

EURIPIDES

All right, I'd better recite one. "Aegyptus, as the story is most widely disseminated, by sailor's oar together with his fifty sons, made for Argos and—"[109]

AESCHYLUS

Lost his oil bottle.

DIONYSUS

What's with this oil bottle? To hell with it! Recite him another prologue, so I can hear that again.

EURIPIDES

"Dionysus, decked out with wands and fawnskins midst the pines of Parnassus, leaping in the dance—"[110]

AESCHYLUS

Lost his oil bottle.

DIONYSUS

Ouch, we're struck again by that oil bottle!

EURIPIDES

Well, no big deal. Here's a prologue that he can't attach an oil bottle to: "No man exists who's blessed in every way; he may have been noble born yet lacking livelihood, he may have been lowborn and—"[111]

AESCHYLUS

Lost his oil bottle.

---

[109] From *Archelaus*, according to the scholia, but ancient scholars could not locate these lines in the version available to them; presumably the opening in their text had been revised, either by Euripides or (more likely, since this was among Euripides' last plays) by later performers. [110] From *Hypsipyle* (fr. 752).
[111] From *Stheneboea* (fr. 661).

ARISTOPHANES

ΔΙΟΝΥΣΟΣ

Εὐριπίδη.

ΕΥΡΙΠΙΔΗΣ

τί ἐστιν;

ΔΙΟΝΥΣΟΣ

1220   ὑφέσθαι μοι δοκεῖ·
τὸ ληκύθιον γὰρ τοῦτο πνευσεῖται πολύ.

ΕΥΡΙΠΙΔΗΣ

οὐδ᾽ ἂν μὰ τὴν Δήμητρα φροντίσαιμί γε·
νυνὶ γὰρ αὐτοῦ τοῦτό γ᾽ ἐκκεκόψεται.

ΔΙΟΝΥΣΟΣ

ἴθι δὴ λέγ᾽ ἕτερον κἀπέχου τῆς ληκύθου.

ΕΥΡΙΠΙΔΗΣ

1225 "Σιδώνιόν ποτ᾽ ἄστυ Κάδμος ἐκλιπὼν
Ἀγήνορος παῖς"—

ΑΙΣΧΥΛΟΣ

ληκύθιον ἀπώλεσεν.

ΔΙΟΝΥΣΟΣ

ὦ δαιμόνι᾽ ἀνδρῶν, ἀποπρίω τὴν λήκυθον,
ἵνα μὴ διακναίσῃ τοὺς προλόγους ἡμῶν.

ΕΥΡΙΠΙΔΗΣ

                τὸ τί;
ἐγὼ πρίωμαι τῷδ᾽;

ΔΙΟΝΥΣΟΣ

ἐὰν πείθῃ γ᾽ ἐμοί.

FROGS

DIONYSUS

Euripides?

EURIPIDES

What?

DIONYSUS

I think you should reef your sails; that oil bottle's blowing up a gale.

EURIPIDES

Quite the contrary, I'm not at all worried. This time it'll be knocked right out of his hand.

DIONYSUS

Then go ahead and recite another one, and dodge the oil bottle.

EURIPIDES

"Cadmus, Agenor's son, departed Sidon's citadel, and—"[112]

AESCHYLUS

Lost his oil bottle.

DIONYSUS

Listen, my friend, do buy that oil bottle, so he won't mangle our prologues.

EURIPIDES

What's that? Me buy from him?

DIONYSUS

If you take my advice.

[112] From the second *Phrixus* (fr. 819).

193

ΕΤΡΙΠΙΔΗΣ

1230 οὐ δῆτ᾽, ἐπεὶ πολλοὺς προλόγους ἔξω λέγειν
ἵν᾽ οὗτος οὐχ ἕξει προσάψαι λήκυθον.
"Πέλοψ ὁ Ταντάλειος εἰς Πῖσαν μολὼν
θοαῖσιν ἵπποις"—

ΑΙΣΧΥΛΟΣ
ληκύθιον ἀπώλεσεν.

ΔΙΟΝΥΣΟΣ
ὁρᾷς, προσῆψεν αὖθις αὖ τὴν λήκυθον.
1235 ἀλλ᾽, ὦγάθ᾽, ἔτι καὶ νῦν ἀπόδος πάσῃ τέχνῃ·
λήψει γὰρ ὀβολοῦ πάνυ καλήν τε κἀγαθήν.

ΕΤΡΙΠΙΔΗΣ
μὰ τὸν Δί᾽ οὔπω γ᾽· ἔτι γάρ εἰσί μοι συχνοί.
"Οἰνεύς ποτ᾽ ἐκ γῆς"—

ΑΙΣΧΥΛΟΣ
ληκύθιον ἀπώλεσεν.

ΕΤΡΙΠΙΔΗΣ
ἔασον εἰπεῖν πρῶθ᾽ ὅλον με τὸν στίχον.
1240 "Οἰνεύς ποτ᾽ ἐκ γῆς πολύμετρον λαβὼν στάχυν
θύων ἀπαρχάς"—

ΑΙΣΧΥΛΟΣ
ληκύθιον ἀπώλεσεν.

ΔΙΟΝΥΣΟΣ
μεταξὺ θύων; καὶ τίς αὔθ᾽ ὑφείλετο;

ΕΤΡΙΠΙΔΗΣ
ἔασον, ὦ τᾶν· πρὸς τοδὶ γὰρ εἰπάτω.

FROGS

EURIPIDES

I will not, because I can recite plenty of prologues where
he won't be able to attach an oil bottle. "Pelops, son of
Tantalus, came to Pisa on swift steeds and—"[113]

AESCHYLUS

Lost his oil bottle.

DIONYSUS

There, he attached that oil bottle again! My man, there's
still time: please make him an offer. You'll get it for an obol,
and it's fine quality.

EURIPIDES

No indeed, not yet; I've still got heaps. "Once Oeneus from
his land—"[114]

AESCHYLUS

Lost his oil bottle.

EURIPIDES

At least let me finish the whole line first! "Once Oeneus
from his land reaped a bounteous harvest, and while
sacrificing the first fruits—"

AESCHYLUS

Lost his oil bottle.

DIONYSUS

In the middle of his sacrifice? And who swiped it?

EURIPIDES

Never mind, my man; let him respond to this: "Zeus, as the

---

[113] From *Iphigeneia among the Taurians* (1–2).
[114] From *Meleager*, but not the opening lines (fr. 515), which
do not allow the tag.

"Ζεύς, ὡς λέλεκται τῆς ἀληθείας ὕπο"—

ΔΙΟΝΥΣΟΣ

1245 ἀπολεῖς· ἐρεῖ γὰρ "ληκύθιον ἀπώλεσεν."
τὸ ληκύθιον γὰρ τοῦτ᾽ ἐπὶ τοῖς προλόγοισί σου
ὥσπερ τὰ σῦκ᾽ ἐπὶ τοῖσιν ὀφθαλμοῖς ἔφυ.
ἀλλ᾽ εἰς τὰ μέλη πρὸς τῶν θεῶν αὐτοῦ τραποῦ.

ΕΥΡΙΠΙΔΗΣ

καὶ μὴν ἔχω γ᾽ οἷς αὐτὸν ἀποδείξω κακὸν
1250 μελοποιὸν ὄντα καὶ ποιοῦντα ταῦτ᾽ ἀεί.

ΧΟΡΟΣ

τί ποτε πρᾶγμα γενήσεται;
φροντίζειν γὰρ ἐγὼ οὐκ ἔχω,
    τίν᾽ ἄρα μέμψιν ἐποίσει
    ἀνδρὶ τῷ πολὺ πλεῖστα δὴ
1255   καὶ κάλλιστα μέλη ποιή-
    σαντι τῶν μέχρι νυνί.

θαυμάζω γὰρ ἔγωγ᾽ ὅπη
    μέμψεταί ποτε τοῦτον
τὸν Βακχεῖον ἄνακτα,
1260 καὶ δέδοιχ᾽ ὑπὲρ αὐτοῦ.

ΕΥΡΙΠΙΔΗΣ

πάνυ γε μέλη θαυμαστά· δείξει δὴ τάχα·
εἰς ἓν γὰρ αὐτοῦ πάντα τὰ μέλη ξυντεμῶ.

true story goes—"[115]

DIONYSUS

You'll be the death of me,[116] because he's going to say "lost
his oil bottle." Yes, that oil bottle grows on your prologues
like sties on eyes. For heaven's sake turn to his choral lyrics
now.

EURIPIDES

Very well, I've got the evidence to show that he's a bad lyri-
cist and writes the same thing over and over.

CHORUS[117]

How will this affair proceed?
I simply can't imagine
what criticism he aims to make
of a man who composed
more lyrics of the finest quality
than anyone else to this day.

I simply can't help wondering
how he aims to criticize
this Bacchic lord,
and I'm afraid for him.

EURIPIDES

A great many wonderful lyrics, eh? We'll soon find out, be-
cause I'm going to trim all his lyrics to a single pattern.

[115] From *Wise Melanippe* (fr. 481).

[116] Alternatively, "he'll be the death of you . . . "

[117] (1) 1252–56 and (2) 1257–60 are apparently authorial vari-
ants, probably composed for the first (2) and the revised (1) ver-
sions of the play; (2) has perhaps lost one or more lines at the end.

ΔΙΟΝΥΣΟΣ

καὶ μὴν λογιοῦμαι ταῦτα τῶν ψήφων λαβών.

ΕΥΡΙΠΙΔΗΣ

Φθιῶτ᾽ Ἀχιλλεῦ, τί ποτ᾽ ἀνδροδάικτον ἀκούων

1265   ἰὴ κόπον οὐ πελάθεις ἐπ᾽ ἀρωγάν;

Ἑρμᾶν μὲν πρόγονον τίομεν γένος οἱ περὶ λίμναν.

ἰὴ κόπον οὐ πελάθεις ἐπ᾽ ἀρωγάν;

ΔΙΟΝΥΣΟΣ

δύο σοι κόπω, Αἰσχύλε, τούτω.

ΕΥΡΙΠΙΔΗΣ

κύδιστ᾽ Ἀχαιῶν, Ἀτρέως πολυκοίρανε

1269/70   μάνθανέ μου παῖ.

ἰὴ κόπον οὐ πελάθεις ἐπ᾽ ἀρωγάν;

ΔΙΟΝΥΣΟΣ

τρίτος, Αἰσχύλε, σοι κόπος οὗτος.

ΕΥΡΙΠΙΔΗΣ

εὐφαμεῖτε. Μελισσονόμοι δόμον Ἀρτέμι-

1273/4   δος πέλας οἴγειν.

1275   ἰὴ κόπον οὐ πελάθεις ἐπ᾽ ἀρωγάν;

κύριός εἰμι θροεῖν ὅδιον κράτος αἴσιον ἀνδρῶν.

ἰὴ κόπον οὐ πελάθεις ἐπ᾽ ἀρωγάν;

---

118 From *Myrmidons* (fr. 132).
119 From *Ghost Raisers* (fr. 273).

DIONYSUS

Very well, and I'll pick up some pebbles to count them off.

EURIPIDES

Phthian Achilles, why, when you hear the slaughter of
heroes,—
    Aiee the strike!—draw you not near to the
      rescue?[118]
We, the people of the lake shore, honor Hermes our
forebear—[119]
    Aiee the strike!—draw you not near to the rescue?

DIONYSUS

That's two strikes against you, Aeschylus.

EURIPIDES

Most reknowned of Achaeans, puissant child of
Atreus,
hearken to me when I say—[120]
    Aiee the strike!—draw you not near to the rescue?

DIONYSUS

That's strike three, Aeschylus!

EURIPIDES

Keep holy silence! The Bee Governesses are nigh
to open the temple of Artemis—[121]
    Aiee the strike!—draw you not near to the rescue?
I've mastery yet to declare the propitious drive of
wayfaring heroes.[122]
    Aiee the strike!—draw you not near to the rescue?

---

[120] Ancient scholars could not identify the source.

[121] From *Priestesses* (fr. 87).

[122] *Agamemnon* 104.

ΔΙΟΝΥΣΟΣ

ὦ Ζεῦ βασιλεῦ, τὸ χρῆμα τῶν κόπων ὅσον.
ἐγὼ μὲν οὖν εἰς τὸ βαλανεῖον βούλομαι·
1280 ὑπὸ τῶν κόπων γὰρ τὼ νεφρὼ βουβωνιῶ.

ΕΥΡΙΠΙΔΗΣ

μή, πρίν γ᾽ ἀκούσῃς χἀτέραν στάσιν μελῶν
ἐκ τῶν κιθαρῳδικῶν νόμων εἰργασμένην.

ΔΙΟΝΥΣΟΣ

ἴθι δὴ πέραινε, καὶ κόπον μὴ προστίθει.

ΕΥΡΙΠΙΔΗΣ

ὅπως Ἀχαιῶν δίθρονον κράτος,
1284/5 Ἑλλάδος ἥβας,
φλαττοθραττοφλαττοθρατ,
Σφίγγα, δυσαμεριᾶν πρύτανιν κύνα, πέμπει,
φλαττοθραττοφλαττοθρατ,
ξὺν δορὶ καὶ χερὶ πράκτορι θούριος ὄρνις,
1290 φλαττοθραττοφλαττοθρατ,
κυρεῖν παρασχὼν ἰταμαῖς κυσὶν
1291/2 ἀεροφοίτοις,
φλαττοθραττοφλαττοθρατ,
τὸ συγκλινές τ᾽ ἐπ᾽ Αἴαντι,
1295 φλαττοθραττοφλαττοθρατ.

ΔΙΟΝΥΣΟΣ

τί τὸ φλαττοθρατ τοῦτ᾽ ἐστίν; ἐκ Μαραθῶνος ἢ
πόθεν συνέλεξας ἱμονιοστρόφου μέλη;

---

123 Based on *Agamemnon* 108–11, with phrases inserted from

DIONYSUS

Lord Zeus, what a volley of strikes! I'd like to get to the bathhouse, because these strikes have made my kidneys sore!

EURIPIDES

No, not till you've heard the next set of choral lyrics, made from tunes for the lyre.

DIONYSUS

Go ahead with it then, but don't put in any strikes.

EURIPIDES

How the twin-throned command of the Achaeans,
the flower of Greece—
    brumda brumda brumda brum
sends the Sphinx, Head Bitch of Bad Days—
    brumda brumda brumda brum
with avenging spear and arm, did the warlike bird of
    omen—
    brumda brumda brumda brum
that gave her into the hands of the nasty hounds
that roam the sky—
    brumda brumda brumda brum
and the company clinging to Ajax—
    brumda brumda brumda brum.[123]

DIONYSUS

What's this brumda brumda brumda brum? Did you collect these rope-winders' songs from Marathon or someplace?

Sphinx (fr. 236), *Thracian Women* (fr. 84), and perhaps *Memnon* (cf. the scholia on 1291–92).

ARISTOPHANES

ΑΙΣΧΥΛΟΣ

ἀλλ' οὖν ἐγὼ μὲν εἰς τὸ καλὸν ἐκ τοῦ καλοῦ
ἤνεγκον αὔθ', ἵνα μὴ τὸν αὐτὸν Φρυνίχῳ
1300 λειμῶνα Μουσῶν ἱερὸν ὀφθείην δρέπων·
οὗτος δ' ἀπὸ πάντων μὲν φέρει, πορνῳδιῶν,
σκολίων Μελήτου, Καρικῶν αὐλημάτων,
θρήνων, χορειῶν. τάχα δὲ δηλωθήσεται.
ἐνεγκάτω τις τὸ λύριον. καίτοι τί δεῖ
1305 λύρας ἐπὶ τοῦτο; ποῦ 'στιν ἡ τοῖς ὀστράκοις
αὕτη κροτοῦσα; δεῦρο, Μοῦσ' Εὐριπίδου,
πρὸς ἥνπερ ἐπιτήδεια ταῦτ' ᾄδειν μέλη.

ΔΙΟΝΥΣΟΣ

αὕτη ποθ' ἡ Μοῦσ' οὐκ ἐλεσβίαζεν, οὔ.

ΑΙΣΧΥΛΟΣ

ἀλκυόνες, αἳ παρ' ἀενάοις θαλάσ-
1310 σης κύμασι στωμύλλετε,
τέγγουσαι νοτίοις πτερῶν
ῥανίσι χρόα δροσιζόμεναι·
αἵ θ' ὑπωρόφιοι κατὰ γωνίας
εἰειειειειλίσσετε δακτύλοις φάλαγγες
1315 ἱστότονα πηνίσματα,
κερκίδος ἀοιδοῦ μελέτας,
ἵν' ὁ φίλαυλος ἔπαλλε δελ-

1305 τοῦτο Sommerstein: τοῦτον a

AESCHYLUS

Never mind that; I took them from a good source for a
good purpose: so I wouldn't be caught culling the same
sacred meadow of the Muses as Phrynichus, whereas this
one takes material from everywhere: whore songs, drink-
ing songs by Meletus,[124] Carian pipe tunes, dirges, and
dances. Someone hand me my lyre! Then again, who needs
a lyre for this job? Where's that female percussionist who
plays potsherds? Oh Muse of Euripides, come out here;
you're the proper accompanist for a recital of these songs.

Enter Muse of Euripides.

DIONYSUS

This Muse once, well, she never gave throat to a Lesbian
tune![125]

AESCHYLUS

You halcyons, who chatter by the everflowing
waves of the sea,
wetting and bedewing the skin
of your wings with rainy drops;
and you spiders in crannies beneath the roof
who with your fingers wi-i-i-i-i-nd
loom-taut spoolings,
a recital by the minstrel loom,
where the pipe-loving dolphin leaped

---

[124] A sixth- (possibly early 5th-) century erotic poet, cf.
Epicrates fr. 4.2.

[125] A reference to the Lesbian musical tradition (e.g. Sappho)
and to fellatio (associated by the Athenians with Lesbos) and
implying both musical and sexual unattractiveness.

φὶς πρῴραις κυανεμβόλοις
μαντεῖα καὶ σταδίους.
1320 οἰνάνθας γάνος ἀμπέλου,
βότρυος ἕλικα παυσίπονον,
περίβαλλ᾽, ὦ τέκνον, ὠλένας.

ὁρᾷς τὸν πόδα τοῦτον;

ΕΥΡΙΠΙΔΗΣ
ὁρῶ.

ΑΙΣΧΥΛΟΣ
τί δαί; τοῦτον ὁρᾷς;

ΕΥΡΙΠΙΔΗΣ
ὁρῶ.

ΑΙΣΧΥΛΟΣ
1325 τοιαυτὶ μέντοι σὺ ποιῶν
τολμᾷς τἀμὰ μέλη ψέγειν,
ἀνὰ τὸ δωδεκαμήχανον
Κυρήνης μελοποιῶν;

τὰ μὲν μέλη σου ταῦτα· βούλομαι δ᾽ ἔτι
1330 τὸν τῶν μονῳδιῶν διεξελθεῖν τρόπον.

ὦ Νυκτὸς κελαινοφαὴς ὄρφνα,
τίνα μοι δύστανον ὄνειρον
πέμπεις, ἀφανοῦς Ἀίδα πρόμολον,

¹³³³ πρόμολον R V K: πρόπολον A^{ac}: πρόπυλον A^{pc}

at the prows with their dark rams
for oracles and race tracks.
Sparkle of the vine's winey blossom,
anodyne tendril of the grape cluster,
throw your arms around me, child![126]
Notice that foot?

EURIPIDES
I do.

AESCHYLUS
And this one, see that?

EURIPIDES
I do.

AESCHYLUS
And you who compose such stuff
have the nerve to criticize my songs,
you who turn out lays à la Cyrene's
Twelve Tricks?[127]

That will do for your choral lyrics; now I want to have a
close look at the style of your arias.

O darkness of Night gloomily gleaming,
what baleful dream do you send me,
an emanation from obscure Hades,

---

[126] A pastiche from *Hypsipyle*, with snippets from *Meleager*
and *Electra* (435–37).

[127] Cyrene was a famous courtesan, cf. *Women at the Thesmo-phoria* 98.

ARISTOPHANES

ψυχὰν ἄψυχον ἔχοντα,
1335a Νυκτὸς παῖδα μελαίνας
1335b φρικώδη δεινὰν ὄψιν
1336a μελανονεκυείμονα
1336b φόνια φόνια δερκόμενον,
μεγάλους ὄνυχας ἔχοντα.
ἀλλά μοι, ἀμφίπολοι, λύχνον ἅψατε
1339a κάλπισί τ᾽ ἐκ ποταμῶν δρόσον ἄρατε,
1339b θέρμετε δ᾽ ὕδωρ,
1340 ὡς ἂν θεῖον ὄνειρον ἀποκλύσω.
ἰὼ πόντιε δαῖμον,
τοῦτ᾽ ἐκεῖν᾽· ἰὼ ξύνοικοι,
1343a τάδε τέρα θεάσασθε· τὸν ἀλεκτρυόνα
1343b μου ξυναρπάσασα φρούδη Γλύκη.
Νύμφαι ὀρεσσίγονοι,
1345 ὦ Μανία, ξύλλαβε.
ἐγὼ δ᾽ ἁ τάλαινα
προσέχουσ᾽ ἔτυχον ἐμαυτῆς
ἔργοισι, λίνου μεστὸν ἄτρακτον
εἰειειλίσσουσα χεροῖν
1350a κλωστῆρα ποιοῦσ᾽, ὅπως
1350b κνεφαῖος εἰς ἀγορὰν
φέρουσ᾽ ἀποδοίμαν.
1352a ὁ δ᾽ ἀνέπτατ᾽ ἀνέπτατ᾽ ἐς αἰθέρα
1352b κουφοτάταις πτερύγων ἀκμαῖς,
ἐμοὶ δ᾽ ἄχε᾽ ἄχεα κατέλιπε,
δάκρυα δάκρυά τ᾽ ἀπ᾽ ὀμμάτων

206

a thing of lifeless life,
ghastly child of black Night,
a fearful sight,
shrouded in cadaverous black,
with murderous murderous stare
and big claws?
Now handmaidens, light me a lamp,
fetch river dew in buckets,
and heat the water,
that I may wash away the god-sent dream.
Oho god of the deep,
it's come to pass! Oho my fellow lodgers,
behold these marvels: my rooster
Glyce has snatched, and vanished!
Nymphs of the mountains,
and you, Mania,[128] help me!
I, poor thing,
happened to be seeing to my own
chores, wi-i-i-inding in my hands
a full spindle of flax
as I made my cloth, so I could get
to the market before sunup
and sell it.
But he flew up flew up to the sky
on the lightest of wingtips,
leaving to me but woes woes,
and tears tears from my eyes

[128] A typical name for a slave or freedwoman.

1355 ἔβαλον ἔβαλον ἁ τλάμων.
1356a ἀλλ᾽, ὦ Κρῆτες, Ἴδας τέκνα,
1356b τὰ τόξα λαβόντες ἐπαμύνατε,
1357a τὰ κῶλά τ᾽ ἀμπάλλετε
1357b κυκλούμενοι τὴν οἰκίαν.
    ἅμα δὲ Δίκτυννα παῖς ἁ καλὰ
    τὰς κυνίσκας ἔχουσ᾽ ἐλθέτω
1360 διὰ δόμων πανταχῇ.
1361a σὺ δ᾽, ὦ Διός, διπύρους ἀνέχουσα
1361b λαμπάδας ὀξυτάτας χεροῖν,
    Ἑκάτα, παράφηνον εἰς Γλύκης,
    ὅπως ἂν εἰσελθοῦσα φωράσω.

ΔΙΟΝΥΣΟΣ
    παύσασθον ἤδη τῶν μελῶν.

ΑΙΣΧΥΛΟΣ
                κἄμοιγ᾽ ἅλις·
1365 ἐπὶ τὸν σταθμὸν γὰρ αὐτὸν ἀγαγεῖν βούλομαι,
    ὅπερ ἐξελέγξει τὴν ποίησιν νῷν μόνον·
    τὸ γὰρ βάρος νὼ βασανιεῖ τῶν ῥημάτων.

ΔΙΟΝΥΣΟΣ
    ἴτε δεῦρό νυν, εἴπερ γε δεῖ καὶ τοῦτό με,
    ἀνδρῶν ποιητῶν τυροπωλῆσαι τέχνην.

ΧΟΡΟΣ
1370 ἐπίπονοί γ᾽ οἱ δεξιοί·
    τόδε γὰρ ἕτερον αὖ τέρας

1358 ἁ Kock: Ἄρτεμις a

did I shed shed in my misery.
Now you Cretans, children of Ida,
snatch up your bows and assist me!
Shake a leg aleap
and surround her house!
And with you let the fair maid Dictynna[129]
take her pack of bitches and run
all throughout her halls.
And you, Hecate, daughter of Zeus,
brandishing in your hands the most searing
flame of your twin torches,
light my way to Glyce's,
so I can go in and search!

DIONYSUS

Now both of you stop the songs.

AESCHYLUS

I've had enough too; what I'd like to do is take him to the scales.[130] That's the only real test of our poetry; the weight of our utterances will be the decisive proof.

DIONYSUS

(*at the scales*) Come over here then, if that's what I really must do, weighing the art of poets like a cheese monger.

CHORUS

Experts are indefatigable,
for here is another marvel,

---

[129] A Cretan goddess similar to Artemis.

[130] This weighing scene is probably modelled on the scene in Aeschylus' *Weighing of Souls* where Zeus weighs the souls of Achilles and Memnon as they fight.

νεοχμόν, ἀτοπίας πλέων,
ὃ τίς ἂν ἐπενόησεν ἄλλος;
μὰ τόν, ἐγὼ μὲν οὐδ' ἂν εἴ τις
1375 ἔλεγέ μοι τῶν ἐπιτυχόντων,
ἐπιθόμην, ἀλλ' ᾠόμην ἂν
αὐτὸν αὐτὰ ληρεῖν.

ΔΙΟΝΥΣΟΣ
ἴθι δὴ παρίστασθον παρὰ τὼ πλάστιγγ'.

ΑΙΣΧΥΛΟΣ καὶ ΕΥΡΙΠΙΔΗΣ
ἰδού.

ΔΙΟΝΥΣΟΣ
καὶ λαβομένω τὸ ῥῆμ' ἑκάτερος εἴπατον,
1380 καὶ μὴ μεθῆσθον, πρὶν ἂν ἐγὼ σφῷν κοκκύσω.

ΑΙΣΧΥΛΟΣ καὶ ΕΥΡΙΠΙΔΗΣ
ἐχόμεθα.

ΔΙΟΝΥΣΟΣ
τοὔπος νυν λέγετον εἰς τὸν σταθμόν.

ΕΥΡΙΠΙΔΗΣ
"εἴθ' ὤφελ' Ἀργοῦς μὴ διαπτάσθαι σκάφος."

ΑΙΣΧΥΛΟΣ
"Σπερχειὲ ποταμὲ βούνομοί τ' ἐπιστροφαί."

ΔΙΟΝΥΣΟΣ
κόκκυ.

startling and altogether eccentric;
who else could have thought it up?
Gee, even if some chance passerby
had told me about this,
I wouldn't have believed him,
I'd have thought he was drivelling.

DIONYSUS

All right now, both of you stand by the scale pans.

AESCHYLUS AND EURIPIDES

Here we are!

DIONYSUS

Now each take hold of your pan and speak a line into it, and don't let go until I give a cuckoo call.

AESCHYLUS AND EURIPIDES

Ready!

DIONYSUS

Now speak your lines into the scales.

EURIPIDES

"Ah would the good ship *Argo* ne'er had winged her way."[131]

AESCHYLUS

"O river Spercheius and the haunts where oxen graze."[132]

DIONYSUS

Cuckoo!

[131] *Medea* 1.
[132] From *Philoctetes* (fr. 249).

211

ΑΙΣΧΥΛΟΣ καὶ ΕΥΡΙΠΙΔΗΣ
μεθεῖται.

ΔΙΟΝΥΣΟΣ
καὶ πολύ γε κατωτέρω
χωρεῖ τὸ τοῦδε.

ΕΥΡΙΠΙΔΗΣ
1385   καὶ τί ποτ᾽ ἐστὶ ταἴτιον;

ΔΙΟΝΥΣΟΣ
ὅ τι; εἰσέθηκε ποταμόν, ἐριοπωλικῶς
ὑγρὸν ποιήσας τοὔπος ὥσπερ τἄρια,
σὺ δ᾽ εἰσέθηκας τοὔπος ἐπτερωμένον.

ΕΥΡΙΠΙΔΗΣ
ἀλλ᾽ ἕτερον εἰπάτω τι κἀντιστησάτω.

ΔΙΟΝΥΣΟΣ
λάβεσθε τοίνυν αὖθις.

ΑΙΣΧΥΛΟΣ καὶ ΕΥΡΙΠΙΔΗΣ
ἢν ἰδού.

ΔΙΟΝΥΣΟΣ
1390   λέγε.

ΕΥΡΙΠΙΔΗΣ
"οὐκ ἔστι Πειθοῦς ἱερὸν ἄλλο πλὴν λόγος."

ΑΙΣΧΥΛΟΣ
"μόνος θεῶν γὰρ Θάνατος οὐ δώρων ἐρᾷ."

[1384] μεθεῖται Radermacher: μεθεῖτε a

AESCHYLUS AND EURIPIDES

There they go!

DIONYSUS

Look, this one's going much lower!

EURIPIDES

And just why is that?

DIONYSUS

Why? He put in a river, wetting his line like a wool merchant wetting wool, while you put in a line with wings on it.

EURIPIDES

Well, let him speak another one and weigh it against mine.

DIONYSUS

Then take hold again.

AESCHYLUS AND EURIPIDES

Ready!

DIONYSUS

Speak.

EURIPIDES

"Persuasion's only temple is the spoken word."[133]

AESCHYLUS

"For the only god who covets no gifts is Death."[134]

[133] From *Antigone* (fr. 170).
[134] From *Niobe* (fr. 161).

ΔΙΟΝΥΣΟΣ

μέθετε.

ΑΙΣΧΥΛΟΣ καὶ ΕΥΡΙΠΙΔΗΣ
μεθεῖται.

ΔΙΟΝΥΣΟΣ
 καὶ τὸ τοῦδέ γ᾽ αὖ ῥέπει·
θάνατον γὰρ εἰσέθηκε, βαρύτατον κακόν.

ΕΥΡΙΠΙΔΗΣ
1395 ἐγὼ δὲ πειθώ γ᾽, ἔπος ἄριστ᾽ εἰρημένον.

ΔΙΟΝΥΣΟΣ
πειθὼ δὲ κοῦφόν ἐστι καὶ νοῦν οὐκ ἔχον.
ἀλλ᾽ ἕτερον αὖ ζήτει τι τῶν βαρυστάθμων,
ὅ τι σοι καθέλξει, καρτερόν τι καὶ μέγα.

ΕΥΡΙΠΙΔΗΣ
φέρε ποῦ τοιοῦτον δῆτα μοὐστί; ποῦ;

ΔΙΟΝΥΣΟΣ
     φράσω·
1400 "βέβληκ᾽ Ἀχιλλεὺς δύο κύβω καὶ τέτταρα."
λέγοιτ᾽ ἄν, ὡς αὕτη ᾽στὶ λοιπὴ σφῷν στάσις.

ΕΥΡΙΠΙΔΗΣ
"σιδηροβριθές τ᾽ ἔλαβε δεξιᾷ ξύλον."

1393 μέθετε | μεθεῖται Blass et Radermacher: μεθεῖτε μεθεῖτε a

DIONYSUS

Let 'em go!

AESCHYLUS AND EURIPIDES

There they go!

DIONYSUS

His went down farther again, because he put in Death, the heaviest blow.

EURIPIDES

But I put in Persuasion, a word that's always à propos.

DIONYSUS

Persuasion is a lightweight thing and has no mind of its own. Try to come up with something else this time, something heavyweight, big and strong enough to depress your pan.

EURIPIDES

Hmm, where have I got something like that? Hmm.

DIONYSUS

I suggest "Achilles cast two ones and a four."[135] Each speak your lines, please, because this is your final weighing.

EURIPIDES

"He took in hand the handle heavy with iron."[136]

---

[135] A poor throw in dice; the line is adapted from an unknown play.

[136] From *Meleager* (fr. 531).

ARISTOPHANES

ΑΙΣΧΥΛΟΣ

"ἐφ' ἅρματος γὰρ ἅρμα καὶ νεκρῷ νεκρός."

ΔΙΟΝΥΣΟΣ

ἐξηπάτηκεν αὖ σε καὶ νῦν.

ΕΥΡΙΠΙΔΗΣ

τῷ τρόπῳ;

ΔΙΟΝΥΣΟΣ

1405   δύ' ἅρματ' εἰσέθηκε καὶ νεκρὼ δύο,
οὓς οὐκ ἂν ἄραιντ' οὐδ' ἑκατὸν Αἰγύπτιοι.

ΑΙΣΧΥΛΟΣ

καὶ μηκέτ' ἔμοιγε κατ' ἔπος, ἀλλ' εἰς τὸν σταθμὸν
αὐτός, τὰ παιδί', ἡ γυνή, Κηφισοφῶν,
ἐμβὰς καθήσθω, ξυλλαβὼν τὰ βιβλία·
1410   ἐγὼ δὲ δύ' ἔπη τῶν ἐμῶν ἐρῶ μόνον.

ΔΙΟΝΥΣΟΣ

ἄνδρες φίλοι, κἀγὼ μὲν αὐτοὺς οὐ κρινῶ.
οὐ γὰρ δι' ἔχθρας οὐδετέρῳ γενήσομαι·
τὸν μὲν γὰρ ἡγοῦμαι σοφόν, τῷ δ' ἥδομαι.

ΠΛΟΥΤΩΝ

οὐδὲν ἄρα πράξεις ὧνπερ ἦλθες οὕνεκα.

ΔΙΟΝΥΣΟΣ

ἐὰν δὲ κρίνω τὸν ἕτερον;

ΠΛΟΥΤΩΝ

λαβὼν ἄπει
1415   ὁπότερον ἂν κρίνῃς, ἵν' ἔλθῃς μὴ μάτην.

216

FROGS

AESCHYLUS

"Chariot upon chariot, corpse upon corpse."[137]

DIONYSUS

He's got the better of you once again!

EURIPIDES

How did he do it?

DIONYSUS

He put in two chariots and two corpses: even a hundred Egyptians couldn't lift that!

AESCHYLUS

No more of this line-by-line for me; he could get in that pan himself, with his wife and kids and Cephisophon, and take his books along too, and I'd have only to recite two of my lines.

DIONYSUS

(*to Pluto*) These men are my friends, and I'll not judge between them; I don't want to get on the bad side of either of them. One I consider a master, the other I enjoy!

PLUTO

Then you won't accomplish your mission here at all.

DIONYSUS

And what if I do reach a verdict?

PLUTO

The one you choose you may take back with you; that way you won't have come for nothing.

---

[137] From *Glaucus of Potniae* (fr. 38).

ΔΙΟΝΤΣΟΣ

εὐδαιμονοίης. φέρε, πύθεσθέ μου ταδί.
ἐγὼ κατῆλθον ἐπὶ ποιητήν. τοῦ χάριν;
ἵν᾽ ἡ πόλις σωθεῖσα τοὺς χοροὺς ἄγῃ.
1420 ὁπότερος οὖν ἂν τῇ πόλει παραινέσειν
μέλλῃ τι χρηστόν, τοῦτον ἄξειν μοι δοκῶ.
πρῶτον μὲν οὖν περὶ Ἀλκιβιάδου τίν᾽ ἔχετον
γνώμην ἑκάτερος; ἡ πόλις γὰρ δυστοκεῖ.

ΑΙΣΧΤΛΟΣ

ἔχει δὲ περὶ αὐτοῦ τίνα γνώμην;

ΔΙΟΝΤΣΟΣ

                              τίνα;
1425 ποθεῖ μέν, ἐχθαίρει δέ, βούλεται δ᾽ ἔχειν.
ἀλλ᾽ ὅ τι νοεῖτον εἴπατον τούτου πέρι.

ΕΤΡΙΠΙΔΗΣ

μισῶ πολίτην, ὅστις ὠφελεῖν πάτραν
βραδὺς φανεῖται, μεγάλα δὲ βλάπτειν ταχύς,
καὶ πόριμον αὑτῷ, τῇ πόλει δ᾽ ἀμήχανον.

ΔΙΟΝΤΣΟΣ

1430 εὖ γ᾽, ὦ Πόσειδον. σὺ δὲ τίνα γνώμην ἔχεις;

1428 φανεῖται R S: πέφυκε V A K

---

138 This brilliant, aristocratic, and notorious leader was
elected to the command of the Sicilian Expedition in 415 but,
soon after it sailed, fled to Sparta to avoid prosecution in the scan-

DIONYSUS

Bless you! (*to Aeschylus and Euripides*) Now listen to me.
I came down here for a poet. Why? So our city could sur-
vive and continue her choral festivals. So whichever of you
is prepared to offer the city some good advice, he's the one
I've decided to take back with me. So for starters, which of
you has an opinion about Alcibiades?[138] The city's in travail
about him.

AESCHYLUS

And what does the city think of him?

DIONYSUS

Well: it yearns for him, detests him, and wants to have
him.[139] Now both of you tell me what you think about him.

EURIPIDES

I detest the citizen who will prove to be slow to aid his
country, quick to do her great harm, resourceful for him-
self, incompetent for the city.

DIONYSUS

Well said, by Poseidon! Now what's your opinion?

---

dal of the Mysteries; in 411 he broke with the Spartans and was
elected commander by the Athenian fleet, and enjoyed consider-
able success during the next four years; in 407 he triumphantly
returned to Athens and was elected Supreme Commander, but af-
ter the naval defeat at Notium a few months later was dismissed
and retired to an estate on the Hellespont (Xenophon *Hellenica*
1.5.16–17), where in 404 he was assassinated on the orders of
Lysander. Our passage shows that the issue of his recall was still a
live one in the aftermath of Arginusae.

139 Adapted from a line in Ion's *Guards* (fr. 44).

ΑΙΣΧΥΛΟΣ

1431a   οὐ χρὴ λέοντος σκύμνον ἐν πόλει τρέφειν.
1431b   μάλιστα μὲν λέοντα μὴ 'ν πόλει τρέφειν·
    ἢν δ' ἐκτραφῇ τις, τοῖς τρόποις ὑπηρετεῖν.

ΔΙΟΝΥΣΟΣ

    νὴ τὸν Δία τὸν σωτῆρα, δυσκρίτως γ' ἔχω·
    ὁ μὲν σοφῶς γὰρ εἶπεν, ὁ δ' ἕτερος σαφῶς.
1435   ἀλλ' ἔτι μίαν γνώμην ἑκάτερος εἴπατον
    περὶ τῆς πόλεως ἥντιν' ἔχετον σωτηρίαν.

(A)

ΕΥΡΙΠΙΔΗΣ

    εἴ τις πτερώσας Κλεόκριτον Κινησίᾳ,
    ἄρειεν αὔρας πελαγίαν ὑπὲρ πλάκα—

ΔΙΟΝΥΣΟΣ

    γέλοιον ἂν φαίνοιτο. νοῦν δ' ἔχει τίνα;

ΕΥΡΙΠΙΔΗΣ

1440   εἰ ναυμαχοῖεν, κᾆτ' ἔχοντες ὀξίδας
1441   ῥαίνοιεν εἰς τὰ βλέφαρα τῶν ἐναντίων.

1437–50 sic disposuit Sommerstein, alii aliter
  1438 ἄρειεν αὔρας Sommerstein praeeunte MacDowell:
αἴροιεν αὖραι (αὔραις Μ^{pc}) a

AESCHYLUS

(A)

It's not good to rear a lion cub in the city.

(B)

It's best to rear no lion in the city.[140]
If you do raise one to maturity, then cater to its ways.

DIONYSUS

By Zeus the Savior, I can't decide! One spoke sagely, the other clearly. So each of you tell me one more idea that you have about the city's salvation.[141]

(A)

EURIPIDES

If someone were to wing Cleocritus[142] with Cinesias, and send him aloft on the breezes o'er the watery plain—

DIONYSUS

That would be a funny sight! But what's the point?

EURIPIDES

If there were a naval battle in progress, and they carried vinegar cruets, they could spray it in the enemy's eyes.

---

[140] Apparently authorial variants, though we cannot tell which belonged to the original and which to the revision. Oracular references to the lion often point to tyrants or political strongmen, e.g. *Knights* 1037–44, Aeschylus, *Agamemnon* 717–36.

[141] Lines 1437–50 contain authorial variants whose priority and line order are controversial; for this arrangement see Sommerstein ad loc.

[142] In *Birds* 877 a fat man with an ostrich for a mother.

ΔΙΟΝΥΣΟΣ

1451 εὖ γ᾽, ὦ Παλάμηδες, ὦ σοφωτάτη φύσις.
1452 ταυτὶ πότερ᾽ αὐτὸς ηὗρες ἢ Κηφισοφῶν;

ΕΥΡΙΠΙΔΗΣ

1453 ἐγὼ μόνος· τὰς δ᾽ ὀξίδας Κηφισοφῶν.

(B)

ΕΥΡΙΠΙΔΗΣ

ἐγὼ μὲν οἶδα καὶ θέλω φράζειν.

ΔΙΟΝΥΣΟΣ

1442   λέγε.

ΕΥΡΙΠΙΔΗΣ

1443 ὅταν τὰ νῦν ἄπιστα πίσθ᾽ ἡγώμεθα,
τὰ δ᾽ ὄντα πίστ᾽ ἄπιστα—

ΔΙΟΝΥΣΟΣ

1444   πῶς; οὐ μανθάνω.
1445 ἀμαθέστερόν πως εἰπὲ καὶ σαφέστερον.

ΕΥΡΙΠΙΔΗΣ

1446 εἰ τῶν πολιτῶν οἷσι νῦν πιστεύομεν,
1447 τούτοις ἀπιστήσαιμεν, οἷς δ᾽ οὐ χρώμεθα,
τούτοισι χρησαίμεσθα—

ΔΙΟΝΥΣΟΣ

1448   σωθεῖημεν ἄν;

1448 σωθεῖημεν ἄν R S: ἴσως σωθεῖημεν (σωθεῖμεν Dawes)
ἄν fere cett.

DIONYSUS

By Palamedes,[143] that's good; you're a genius! Did you
think that up yourself, or was it Cephisophon?

EURIPIDES

All by myself, but Cephisophon thought up the cruets.

(B)

EURIPIDES

I've got one that I'd like to tell you.

DIONYSUS

Go ahead.

EURIPIDES

When we put our trust in what's untrusted, and what's
trustworthy is untrusted—

DIONYSUS

How's that? I don't follow. Try to speak somewhat less
cleverly and more clearly.

EURIPIDES

If we stopped trusting the citizens we now trust, and
start making use of the citizens we now don't use—

DIONYSUS

Then we'd find salvation?

[143] The cleverest hero at Troy and a legendary inventor; sub-
ject of a play by Euripides parodied in *Women at the Thesmo-
phoria* 768–84.

ΕΥΡΙΠΙΔΗΣ

1449 εἰ νῦν γε δυστυχοῦμεν ἐν τούτοισι, πῶς
1450 τἀναντί᾽ ἂν πράξαντες οὐ σῳζοίμεθ᾽ ἄν;

ΔΙΟΝΥΣΟΣ

τί δαὶ σύ; τί λέγεις;

ΑΙΣΧΥΛΟΣ

1454   τὴν πόλιν νῦν μοι φράσον
πρῶτον τίσι χρῆται· πότερα τοῖς χρηστοῖς;

ΔΙΟΝΥΣΟΣ

1455   πόθεν;
μισεῖ κάκιστα.

ΑΙΣΧΥΛΟΣ

           τοῖς πονηροῖς δ᾽ ἥδεται;

ΔΙΟΝΥΣΟΣ

οὐ δῆτ᾽ ἐκείνη γ᾽, ἀλλὰ χρῆται πρὸς βίαν.

ΑΙΣΧΥΛΟΣ

πῶς οὖν τις ἂν σώσειε τοιαύτην πόλιν,
ᾗ μήτε χλαῖνα μήτε σισύρα ξυμφέρει;

ΔΙΟΝΥΣΟΣ

1460 εὕρισκε νὴ Δί᾽, εἴπερ ἀναδύσει πάλιν.

ΑΙΣΧΥΛΟΣ

ἐκεῖ φράσαιμ᾽ ἄν, ἐνθαδὶ δ᾽ οὐ βούλομαι.

ΔΙΟΝΥΣΟΣ

μὴ δῆτα σύ γ᾽, ἀλλ᾽ ἐνθένδ᾽ ἀνίει τἀγαθά.

EURIPIDES
If we're faring poorly with the current bunch, how
wouldn't we find salvation if we did the opposite?

DIONYSUS
And what about you? What have you got to say?

AESCHYLUS
Tell me who the city's making use of now: the good people?

DIONYSUS
Of course not! She absolutely hates them.

AESCHYLUS
And she delights in the bad people?

DIONYSUS
No, she doesn't; she makes use of them perforce.

AESCHYLUS
Then how could anyone save a city like that, if she won't
wear either a cloak or a goatskin?

DIONYSUS
By god, think of something, if you want to go back up there.

AESCHYLUS
I'll tell you up there, but here I don't want to.

DIONYSUS
Oh no you don't; you send up your blessings from here.

1450 πράξαντες R S: πράττοντες V A K

ΑΙΣΧΥΛΟΣ

τὴν γῆν ὅταν νομίσωσι τὴν τῶν πολεμίων
εἶναι σφετέραν, τὴν δὲ σφετέραν τῶν πολεμίων,
1465 πόρον δὲ τὰς ναῦς, ἀπορίαν δὲ τὸν πόρον.

ΔΙΟΝΥΣΟΣ

εὖ, πλήν γ᾽ ὁ δικαστὴς αὐτὰ καταπίνει μόνος.

ΠΛΟΥΤΩΝ

κρίνοις ἄν.

ΔΙΟΝΥΣΟΣ

αὕτη σφῷν κρίσις γενήσεται.
αἱρήσομαι γὰρ ὅνπερ ἡ ψυχὴ θέλει.

ΕΥΡΙΠΙΔΗΣ

μεμνημένος νυν τῶν θεῶν οὓς ὤμοσας
1470 ἦ μὴν ἀπάξειν μ᾽ οἴκαδ᾽, αἱροῦ τοὺς φίλους.

ΔΙΟΝΥΣΟΣ

ἡ γλῶττ᾽ ὀμώμοκ᾽, Αἰσχύλον δ᾽ αἱρήσομαι.

ΕΥΡΙΠΙΔΗΣ

τί δέδρακας, ὦ μιαρώτατ᾽ ἀνθρώπων;

ΔΙΟΝΥΣΟΣ

                                    ἐγώ;
ἔκρινα νικᾶν Αἰσχύλον. τιὴ γὰρ οὔ;

ΕΥΡΙΠΙΔΗΣ

αἴσχιστον ἔργον προσβλέπεις μ᾽ εἰργασμένος;

FROGS

AESCHYLUS

When they think of the enemy's country as their own, and
their own as the enemy's; and the fleet as their wealth; and
their wealth as despair.

DIONYSUS

Good, except that the juryman will gobble that down all by
himself![144]

PLUTO

Please render your verdict.

DIONYSUS

This will be my decision between you: I will choose the one
that my soul wishes to choose.

EURIPIDES

Now remember the gods by whom you swore that you'd
take me back home, and choose your friends.

DIONYSUS

It was my tongue that swore:[145] I'm choosing Aeschylus.

EURIPIDES

What have you done, you absolute scum of the earth?

DIONYSUS

Me? I've judged Aeschylus the winner; why shouldn't I?

EURIPIDES

How can you look me in the eye after doing something so
utterly disgraceful?

[144] Referring to state pay for public services.
[145] Cf. line 101–2, above.

ΔΙΟΝΥΣΟΣ

1475 τί δ' αἰσχρόν, ἢν μὴ τοῖς θεωμένοις δοκῇ;

ΕΥΡΙΠΙΔΗΣ

ὦ σχέτλιε, περιόψει με δὴ τεθνηκότα;

ΔΙΟΝΥΣΟΣ

τίς δ' οἶδεν εἰ τὸ ζῆν μέν ἐστι κατθανεῖν,
τὸ πνεῖν δὲ δειπνεῖν, τὸ δὲ καθεύδειν κῴδιον;

ΠΛΟΥΤΩΝ

χωρεῖτε τοίνυν, ὦ Διόνυσ', εἴσω.

ΔΙΟΝΥΣΟΣ

τί δαί;

ΠΛΟΥΤΩΝ

ἵνα ξενίσω⟨μεν⟩ σφὼ πρὶν ἀποπλεῖν.

ΔΙΟΝΥΣΟΣ

1480   εὖ λέγεις
νὴ τὸν Δί'· οὐ γὰρ ἄχθομαι τῷ πράγματι.

ΧΟΡΟΣ

(στρ) μακάριός γ' ἀνὴρ ἔχων
ξύνεσιν ἠκριβωμένην.
πάρα δὲ πολλοῖσιν μαθεῖν·
1485 ὅδε γὰρ εὖ φρονεῖν δοκήσας

1480 suppl. Rogers

---

146 Euripides' *Aeolus*, fr. 19, with "the spectators" substituted for "those who do it."

147 The first phrase is from Euripides' *Polyidus* (fr. 638).

DIONYSUS

What's disgraceful, if it doesn't seem so to the specta-
tors?[146]

EURIPIDES

You bastard, are you going to stand by and watch me stay
dead?

DIONYSUS

Who knows if life be really death, and breath be dinner,
and sleep a fleecy blanket?[147]

Exit EURIPIDES.[148]

PLUTO

Dionysus, you two go along inside now.

DIONYSUS

Why?

PLUTO

So we can entertain you before you depart.

DIONYSUS

Good suggestion, by Zeus; I can't complain about that!

PLUTO escorts DIONYSUS and AESCHYLUS into the palace.

CHORUS

Happy the man who has
keen intelligence,
as is abundantly clear:
this man, for his eminent good sense,

[148] Either he runs off or is wheeled back inside on the
eccyclema, if it was used (cf. entrance at 830).

πάλιν ἄπεισιν οἴκαδ᾽ αὖθις,
ἐπ᾽ ἀγαθῷ μὲν τοῖς πολίταις,
ἐπ᾽ ἀγαθῷ δὲ τοῖς ἑαυτοῦ
ξυγγενέσι τε καὶ φίλοισι,
1490 διὰ τὸ συνετὸς εἶναι.

(ἀντ) χαρίεν οὖν μὴ Σωκράτει
παρακαθήμενον λαλεῖν,
ἀποβαλόντα μουσικὴν
τά τε μέγιστα παραλιπόντα
1495 τῆς τραγῳδικῆς τέχνης.
τὸ δ᾽ ἐπὶ σεμνοῖσιν λόγοισι
καὶ σκαριφησμοῖσι λήρων
διατριβὴν ἀργὸν ποιεῖσθαι,
παραφρονοῦντος ἀνδρός.

ΠΛΟΥΤΩΝ
1500 ἄγε δὴ χαίρων, Αἰσχύλε, χώρει,
καὶ σῷζε πόλιν τὴν ἡμετέραν
γνώμαις ἀγαθαῖς, καὶ παίδευσον
τοὺς ἀνοήτους· πολλοὶ δ᾽ εἰσίν·
καὶ δὸς τουτὶ Κλεοφῶντι φέρων
1505 καὶ τουτουσὶ τοῖσι πορισταῖς
Μύρμηκί θ᾽ ὁμοῦ καὶ Νικομάχῳ

1501 ὑμετέραν Scaliger

---

149 It is likely, though not indicated in the text, that
Persephone enters as well, in view of her prominent Eleusinian
associations.   150 Cf. 678 n. The objects given by Pluto (and

is going back home again,
a boon to his fellow citizens,
a boon as well
to his family and friends,
through being intelligent.

So what's stylish is not to sit
beside Socrates and chatter,
casting the arts aside
and ignoring the best
of the tragedian's craft.
To hang around killing time
in pretentious conversation
and hairsplitting twaddle
is the mark of a man who's lost his mind.

Enter PLUTO *with* AESCHYLUS, DIONYSUS, *and* XAN-
THIAS.[149]

PLUTO

Fare you well then, Aeschylus. Save our city with your fine
counsels, and educate the thoughtless people; there are
many of them. And take this and give it to Cleophon;[150]
and this to the Commissioners of Revenue,[151] together
with Myrmex[152] and Nicomachus;[153] and this to Archeno-

more fittingly carried by Xanthias than by Aeschylus, who will de-
part carrying a torch) are instruments of suicide, probably a
sword, a noose, and a mortar of hemlock (cf. 121–34).
   151 Nothing is known of their particular functions.
   152 Otherwise unknown.   153 Probably the defendant in
Lysias 30 (399/98), who currently held an appointment to review,
consolidate, and supervise the public inscription of the laws.

231

τόδε δ' Ἀρχενόμῳ· καὶ φράζ' αὐτοῖς
ταχέως ἥκειν ὡς ἐμὲ δευρὶ
καὶ μὴ μέλλειν· κἂν μὴ ταχέως
1510 ἥκωσιν, ἐγὼ νὴ τὸν Ἀπόλλω
στίξας αὐτοὺς καὶ ξυμποδίσας
μετ' Ἀδειμάντου τοῦ Λευκολόφου
1513/4 κατὰ γῆς ταχέως ἀποπέμψω.

ΑΙΣΧΥΛΟΣ

1515 ταῦτα ποιήσω· σὺ δὲ τὸν θᾶκον
τὸν ἐμὸν παράδος Σοφοκλεῖ τηρεῖν
καὶ διασῴζειν, ἢν ἄρ' ἐγώ ποτε
δεῦρ' ἀφίκωμαι. τοῦτον γὰρ ἐγὼ
σοφίᾳ κρίνω δεύτερον εἶναι.
1520 μέμνησο δ' ὅπως ὁ πανοῦργος ἀνὴρ
καὶ ψευδολόγος καὶ βωμολόχος
μηδέποτ' εἰς τὸν θᾶκον τὸν ἐμὸν
μηδ' ἄκων ἐγκαθεδεῖται.

ΠΛΟΥΤΩΝ

φαίνετε τοίνυν ὑμεῖς τούτῳ
1525 λαμπάδας ἱεράς, χἄμα προπέμπετε
τοῖσιν τούτου τοῦτον μέλεσιν
καὶ μολπαῖσιν κελαδοῦντες.

ΧΟΡΟΣ

πρῶτα μὲν εὐοδίαν ἀγαθὴν ἀπιόντι ποιητῇ
εἰς φάος ὀρνυμένῳ δότε, δαίμονες οἱ κατὰ γαίας,
1530 τῇ δὲ πόλει μεγάλων ἀγαθῶν ἀγαθὰς ἐπινοίας·

mus;[154] and tell them hurry on down here to me, without delay; and if they don't come quickly, by Apollo I'll tattoo them, clap them in leg irons, and dispatch them below ground right quick,[155] along with Leucolophus' son, Adeimantus![156]

AESCHYLUS

That I shall do. And you hand over my chair to Sophocles to look after and preserve, for I rank him second to me in the art. And remember to see to it that that criminal, that liar, that buffoon, never sits down on my chair, not even accidentally.

PLUTO

(*to the Chorus*) Now display your sacred torches in this man's honor and escort him forth, hymning his praises with his own songs and melodies.

CHORUS

First, you gods below earth, grant to the departing poet a fine journey as he ascends to the sunlight, and to the city grant fine ideas that will bring fine blessings. For that way

[154] Otherwise unknown.

[155] These punishments were available to masters or overseers with misbehaved slaves.

[156] Alcibiades' cousin, who fled Athens after implication in the scandal of the Mysteries in 415, returned in 407, and then served as a general. He was the only Athenian prisoner not executed by the Spartans after Aegospotami, where he was widely believed to have behaved treasonously (Xenophon, *Hellenica* 2.1.32, cf. *Assemblywomen* 644–45), so that the reference here was probably added for the revised production. It may be relevant to Pluto's threat that he had unsuccessfully opposed an Assembly motion to mutilate all enemy prisoners (Xenophon ibid.).

ARISTOPHANES

πάγχυ γὰρ ἐκ μεγάλων ἀχέων παυσαίμεθ᾽ ἂν οὕτως
ἀργαλέων τ᾽ ἐν ὅπλοις ξυνόδων. Κλεοφῶν δὲ
  μαχέσθω
κάλλος ὁ βουλόμενος τούτων πατρίοις ἐν ἀρούραις.

234

we may have an end of great griefs and painful encounters in arms. Let Cleophon do the fighting, and any of those others who wants to fight on his own native soil![157]

[157] Implying non-Athenian ancestry, cf. 678–82, 730–33.

ASSEMBLYWOMEN

INTRODUCTORY NOTE

No precise information about the production of *Assemblywomen* survives,[1] but internal evidence dates it to the period of the "Corinthian War" (395–387/6), evidently between 392, the earliest the Athenians could be said to have had "a fleeting glimpse of salvation" (202–3), and the production of *Wealth* in 388; references to proposals to launch a fleet (197–98) and to collect large revenues by levying a new tax (823–29) best suit 391 (after the arrest and dismissal of Conon had cost Athens both his fleet and Persian money), or possibly 390 (after a fleet had actually been launched). Greater precision is impossible, for in *Assemblywomen* allusions to the political status quo are few, and serve mainly to motivate its abolition in favor of a radically new system, a communal utopia under female governance.

As in *Lysistrata* a heroine, Praxagora ("Woman Effective in Public"), leads her fellow Athenian women in a plot to save Athens from male misgovernance: the women disguise themselves as men, pack the Assembly, vote to transfer power to themselves, and elect Praxagora to be their commander. But unlike Lysistrata, whose plot was a tem-

---

[1] A scholium on line 193, citing Philochorus (*FGrH* 328 F 148), preserves discussion about the date, but is vaguely worded and probably corrupt.

porary intervention designed to force the men to stop the war and return Greece to normality, Praxagora enacts a permanent economic, social, and sexual revolution. Private property is abolished: every citizen is to surrender his possessions to the common store, from which the women will provision all citizens equally, civic buildings having been turned into communal dining halls. Household and family are abolished too: dividing walls are to be removed, and any man may copulate with, and have children by, any woman, provided that the young and the beautiful of both sexes copulate with the old and the ugly first. As for slaves and other non-citizens, they will do the farming and (presumably) all other manual labor, and are debarred from sexual competition with citizens. In the new order, social inequalities based on wealth, age, and beauty are thus eliminated, and with them the principal motives for civic selfishness.

A pair of episodes illustrate the two main elements of the plan and the main problem that threatens their implementation: the desire of some to take unfair advantage of the new system by holding onto the privileges that they had enjoyed under the old. The first is a conversation between a law-abiding citizen, who is preparing to surrender his property, and a selfish sceptic, who hesitates to surrender his own. At the end of the scene the sceptic goes off to claim his place at the communal dinner while still hoping keep his property. We never learn whether his cheating succeeds, but Praxagora has already explained that under the new regime the desire to own property makes no sense, since everyone will be amply supplied from the common store. The second episode illustrates the new equality of sexual opportunity, which gives priority to the old and the ugly. In this more elaborate scene, a young man who has enjoyed the communal feast nevertheless tries to visit his young girlfriend, but is frustrated by the intervention of three hags, each one older and uglier than the last, who stake their legal claim to his services. In the end the young man is dragged off by the last two hags together, since in their case it proves impossible to resolve the question of priority.

The final scene illustrates the benefits enjoyed by men who cooperate with the new regime. Praxagora's husband Blepyrus, earlier counted among the old and ugly and the last to come to dinner, now arrives in the embrace of two young girls, his virility apparently recovered. All that remains is for a tipsy maid to invite Blepyrus and the Chorus, representing all the women, to dance off to the feast, which she describes in opulent terms in a lively song.

In creating the comic utopia of *Assemblywomen* Aristophanes does not set up a true gynecocracy, where women usurp male roles,[2] but rather takes an old idea (at work also in *Lysistrata*), that polis management should be like household management, to its logical conclusion: the household actually replaces the polis, with the women playing their traditional roles as managers and caregivers. And since the polis is abolished, the men have no duties other than to put on their new clothes, eat, drink, and

[2] Mythical models included the Amazons (dramatized in an earlier comedy by Cephisodorus) and the Lemnian Women (comedies by Aristophanes and Nicochares); Pherecrates' *Tyrannis* (cf. frs. 152, 269) and Theopompus' *Lady Soldiers* probably featured gynecocracies as well.

copulate. In effect, the men will enjoy a life of carefree boyhood, with women doing all the chores—not unlike Hesiod's Golden Age, when men "lived like gods, with carefree heart, free and apart from trouble and pain," or the Silver Age, when "a boy was raised by his dear mother for a hundred years, a large infant playing in his house."[3] But by relieving men of their responsibilities the women realize important gains too: liberated from confinement in their husbands' households, they may openly associate, enjoy the sexual freedom hitherto reserved for men without need of deception, and rest assured that their household will not be damaged by the men's foolish policies.

Assemblywomen also satirizes contemporary Athenian fondness for political experimentation and theorizing. The political crisis and constitutional reforms precipitated by the loss of their empire in 404, in combination with an Assembly revitalized by the introduction of pay for attendees,[4] had prompted the Athenians to discuss and debate their democratic system afresh, and also stimulated speculation about ideal systems of government, including women's potential for participation in civic affairs.[5] The best known of these ideal states, Plato's *Republic*, indeed envisions a regime for elite Guardians that is essentially the same as Praxagora's, save for its abolition of the tradi-

[3] *Works and Days* 112–13, 130–31.

[4] In *Acharnians* of 425 Aristophanes had complained that assemblies were poorly attended and that ordinary citizens were discouraged from speaking up.

[5] Socrates, for example, reportedly believed in the natural equality of women: Xenophon *Symposium* 2.9.

tional distinction between men's and women's work, and its system of eugenic breeding.[6] Since *Assemblywomen* cannot on chronological grounds have caricatured *Republic*, Plato may in fact have been inspired by the play; if both authors drew on a common source, it is unlikely to have been a written one, since Aristotle tells us that Plato's system had no antecedents.[7]

Assemblywomen follows the pattern of Aristophanes' fifth-century comedies in its plot but shows significant changes in formal structure, particularly in its handling of the chorus. Though the chorus plays a prominent role at the beginning and end of the play, its silent and gradual entry, subsequent absences, and minimal involvement in the central scenes are paralleled only in tragedy; there is no parabasis and only a truncated agon; and the choral songs separating episodes are absent from the script, the lacuna sometimes indicated by the note *chorou* ("place for a chorus"), as would become the norm by Menander's time.

Text

One papyrus contains parts of 32 lines of *Assemblywomen*, and four independent medieval MSS preserve the play in whole (R Λ) or in part (A Γ). The MSS divide into two families, with R on one side, and on the other A Γ, which have a common ancestor, and Λ, which derives from a close relative of Γ that was thoroughly corrected from R or a copy of R. Another MS (B), though derived from a

---

[6] See especially *Republic*, books 3 and 5.

[7] *Politics* 1266a31–36, 1274b9–10; he would hardly have mentioned a comic antecedent.

copy of Γ, contains a number of good conjectures. The Aldine *editio princeps* (1498) was based on a MS (no longer extant) stemming from an ancestor of Λ that incorporated a number of corrections and emendations, some of which are found also in B.

Sigla

Π   *PMich*. inv. 6649 (IV/V), lines 600–16, 638–54
R   Ravennas 429 (*c*. 950)
S   Readings found in the Suda
A   Parisinus Regius 2712 (XIV), lines 1–282
Γ   Laurentianus 31.15 (*c*. 1325), lines 1–1135
Λ   (= Pe1) Perusinus H 56 (XV[in])
B   Parisinus Regius 2715 (XV), lines 1–1135
a   the consensus of R A Γ Λ (1–282), R Γ Λ (283–1135), R Λ (1136–end)

Annotated Editions

F. H. M. Blaydes (Halle 1881).
J. van Leeuwen (Leiden 1905).
B. B. Rogers (London 1902), with English translation.
R. G. Ussher (Oxford 1973).
G. Paduano (Milan 1983), with Italian translation.
M. Vetta (Milan 1989), with Italian translation.
A. H. Sommerstein (Warminster 1998), with English translation.

ΤΑ ΤΟΥ ΔΡΑΜΑΤΟΣ ΠΡΟΣΩΠΑ

ΠΡΑΞΑΓΟΡΑ, γυνὴ
  Ἀττική
ΓΥΝΗ Α, γείτων
  Πραξαγόρας
ΓΥΝΗ Β
ΒΛΕΠΥΡΟΣ, ἀνὴρ
  Πραξαγόρας
ΓΕΙΤΩΝ Βλεπύρου
ΧΡΕΜΗΣ
ΑΝΗΡ φειδωλός
ΚΗΡΥΚΑΙΝΑ
ΓΡΑΥΣ Α
ΝΕΑΝΙΣ
ΕΠΙΓΕΝΗΣ, μειράκιον
ΓΡΑΥΣ Β
ΓΡΑΥΣ Γ
ΘΕΡΑΠΑΙΝΑ
  Πραξαγόρας

ΧΟΡΟΣ γυναικῶν
  Ἀττικῶν

ΚΩΦΑ ΠΡΟΣΩΠΑ
ΣΙΚΩΝ καὶ
  ΠΑΡΜΕΝΩΝ, οἰκέται
  τοῦ Γείτονος
ΜΕΙΡΑΚΕΣ δύο

244

DRAMATIS PERSONAE

PRAXAGORA, an
  Athenian wife
FIRST WOMAN, a
  neighbor of Praxagora
SECOND WOMAN,
  Praxagora's neighbor
BLEPYRUS, Praxagora's
  husband
NEIGHBOR of Blepyrus
CHREMES
SELFISH MAN
HERALD, a woman
  appointed by Praxagora
FIRST OLD WOMAN
GIRL
EPIGENES, a young man
SECOND OLD WOMAN
THIRD OLD WOMAN
MAID of Praxagora

CHORUS of Athenian
  women

SILENT CHARACTERS
SICON and
  PARMENON,
  Neighbor's slaves
TWO GIRLS

ΕΚΚΛΗΣΙΑΖΟΥΣΑΙ

ΠΡΑΞΑΓΟΡΑ
ὦ λαμπρὸν ὄμμα τοῦ τροχηλάτου λύχνου,
κάλλιστ' ἐν εὐστόχοισιν ἐξηυρημένον—
γονάς τε γὰρ σὰς καὶ τύχας δηλώσομεν·
τροχῷ γὰρ ἐλαθεὶς κεραμικῆς ῥύμης ὕπο
μυκτῆρσι λαμπρὰς ἡλίου τιμὰς ἔχεις—   5
ὅρμα φλογὸς σημεῖα τὰ ξυγκείμενα.
σοὶ γὰρ μόνῳ δηλοῦμεν εἰκότως, ἐπεὶ
κἂν τοῖσι δωματίοισιν Ἀφροδίτης τρόπων
πειρωμέναισι πλησίος παραστατεῖς,
λορδουμένων τε σωμάτων ἐπιστάτην   10
ὀφθαλμὸν οὐδεὶς τὸν σὸν ἐξείργει δόμων.
μόνος δὲ μηρῶν εἰς ἀπορρήτους μυχοὺς
λάμπεις ἀφεύων τὴν ἐπανθοῦσαν τρίχα·
στοὰς δὲ καρποῦ Βακχίου τε νάματος
πλήρεις ὑποιγνύσαισι συμπαραστατεῖς·   15
καὶ ταῦτα συνδρῶν οὐ λαλεῖς τοῖς πλησίον.
ἀνθ' ὧν συνείσει καὶ τὰ νῦν βουλεύματα

ASSEMBLYWOMEN

*An Athenian street before daybreak; the stage building
represents three houses. From the central house emerges a
young figure wearing men's clothing but a woman's mask,
and carrying a walking stick and lighted lamp.*

PRAXAGORA[1]
O radiant eye of the wheel-whirled lamp, fairest invention
of skilled artisans (yes, I shall reveal your pedigree and
fortunes, for whirled on the wheel by the potter's impetus,
you bear the sun's radiant offices in your nozzles): broad-
cast now the fiery signal as arranged. (*she swings the lamp
to and fro*) You alone we make privy to our plot, and rightly,
for also in our bedrooms you stand close by as we essay
Aphrodite's maneuvers; and when our bodies are flexed,
no one banishes from the room your supervisory eye. You
alone illuminate the ineffable nooks between our thighs,
when you singe away the hair that sprouts there; and you
stand by us when stealthily we open pantries stocked with
bread and the liquor of Bacchus; and you're an accomplice
that never blabs to the neighbors. So you'll be in on our

---

[1] Praxagora's name means "Woman Effective in Public"; her
opening lines parody an unknown tragic source or sources.

ὅσα Σκίροις ἔδοξε ταῖς ἐμαῖς φίλαις.
ἀλλ᾿ οὐδεμία πάρεστιν ἃς ἥκειν ἐχρῆν.
20 καίτοι πρὸς ὄρθρον γ᾿ ἐστίν, ἡ δ᾿ ἐκκλησία
αὐτίκα μάλ᾿ ἔσται· καταλαβεῖν δ᾿ ἡμᾶς ἕδρας
23 δεῖ τὰς ἑταίρας κἀγκαθιζομένας λαθεῖν,
22 ἃς Φυρόμαχός ποτ᾿ εἶπεν, εἰ μέμνησθ᾿ ἔτι.
τί δῆτ᾿ ἂν εἴη; πότερον οὐκ ἐρραμμένους
25 ἔχουσι τοὺς πώγωνας, οὓς εἴρητ᾿ ἔχειν;
ἢ θαἰμάτια τἀνδρεῖα κλεψάσαις λαθεῖν
ἦν χαλεπὸν αὐταῖς; ἀλλ᾿ ὁρῶ τονδὶ λύχνον
προσιόντα. φέρε νυν ἐπαναχωρήσω πάλιν,
μὴ καί τις ὢν ἀνὴρ ὁ προσιὼν τυγχάνει.

ΚΟΡΥΦΑΙΑ

30 ὥρα βαδίζειν, ὡς ὁ κῆρυξ ἀρτίως
ἡμῶν προσιουσῶν δεύτερον κεκόκκυκεν.

ΠΡΑΞΑΓΟΡΑ

ἐγὼ δέ γ᾿ ὑμᾶς προσδοκῶσ᾿ ἐγρήγορα
τὴν νύκτα πᾶσαν. ἀλλὰ φέρε τὴν γείτονα
τήνδ᾿ ἐκκαλέσωμαι θρυγανῶσα τὴν θύραν.
δεῖ γὰρ τὸν ἄνδρ᾿ αὐτῆς λαθεῖν.

22–23 transp. Dover
22 Φυρόμαχός R: Σφυρόμαχός A Γ Λ S Σ(i)[R]: Κλεόμαχός γρΛ Σ(ii)[R] γρSΓA
31 -ουσῶν LeFebvre: -όντων a

---

2 A women's festival for Demeter.

present plans too, all that my friends agreed on at the Scira.[2]

But not one of the women who are supposed to meet here has shown up, though it's almost light and the Assembly begins any minute. We wenchmen must grab our seats, as Phyromachus once put it, if you still remember,[3] and settle ourselves without attracting attention. What can be keeping them? Don't they have the false beards they were told to get? Was it hard for them to swipe their husbands' clothes without getting caught?

A figure dressed like a man and carrying a lamp and bundle enters the orchestra through a wing, leading several other figures, similarly dressed; these and the women soon to follow form the Chorus.

But I see a lamp over there, coming this way. I'll duck aside in case it happens to be a man.

CHORUS LEADER

Time to move! Just now, as we were on our way, the Herald crowed a second time.

PRAXAGORA

And I was up the whole night waiting for you. Now let me call this neighbor of mine out of the house; I'll scratch softly at her door, since her husband mustn't notice.

FIRST WOMAN emerges from the door, dressed in men's clothing.

---

[3] Evidently this Phyromachus (otherwise unknown) had somehow mispronounced *hetairoi* "associates" as *hetairai* "courtesans"; and *hedras* "seats" can also mean "rear ends."

ΓΥΝΗ Α

35   ἤκουσά τοι
ὑποδουμένη τὸ κνῦμά σου τῶν δακτύλων,
ἅτ᾿ οὐ καταδαρθοῦσ᾿. ὁ γὰρ ἀνήρ, ὦ φιλτάτη,
Σαλαμίνιος γάρ ἐστιν ᾧ ξύνειμ᾿ ἐγώ,
τὴν νύχθ᾿ ὅλην ἤλαυνέ μ᾿ ἐν τοῖς στρώμασιν,
40 ὥστ᾿ ἄρτι τουτὶ θοἰμάτιον αὐτοῦ 'λαβον.

ΠΡΑΞΑΓΟΡΑ

καὶ μὴν ὁρῶ καὶ Κλειναρέτην καὶ Σωστράτην
προσιοῦσαν ἤδη τήνδε καὶ Φιλαινέτην.

ΚΟΡΥΦΑΙΑ

οὔκουν ἐπείξεσθ᾿; ὡς Γλύκη κατώμοσεν
τὴν ὑστάτην ἥκουσαν οἴνου τρεῖς χοᾶς
45 ἦ μὴν ἀποτείσειν κἀρεβίνθων χοίνικα.

ΠΡΑΞΑΓΟΡΑ

τὴν Σμικυθίωνος δ᾿ οὐχ ὁρᾷς Μελιστίχην
σπεύδουσαν ἐν ταῖς ἐμβάσιν; καί μοι δοκεῖ
κατὰ σχολὴν παρὰ τἀνδρὸς ἐξελθεῖν μόνη.

ΓΥΝΗ Α

τὴν τοῦ καπήλου δ᾿ οὐχ ὁρᾷς Γευσιστράτην
50 ἔχουσαν ἐν τῇ δεξιᾷ τὴν λαμπάδα;

ΠΡΑΞΑΓΟΡΑ

καὶ τὴν Φιλοδωρήτου τε καὶ Χαιρητάδου
ὁρῶ προσιούσας χἀτέρας πολλὰς πάνυ
γυναῖκας, ὅ τι πέρ ἐστ᾿ ὄφελος ἐν τῇ πόλει.

FIRST WOMAN

I was just getting dressed when I heard you give the secret knock: see, I wasn't asleep. You know, my dear, the man I live with is from Salamis,[4] and all night long he was sailing me under the sheets, so I just now got the chance to grab his cloak.

PRAXAGORA

Hey, I see Cleinarete and Sostrate coming, and there's Philainete.[5]

CHORUS LEADER

Get a move on; Glyce[6] solemnly swore that the last woman here will be fined ten quarts of wine and a bag of chickpeas!

PRAXAGORA

Look, there's Smicythion's wife Melistiche trying to run in her old man's boots![7] And I think she's the only one who had no trouble getting away from her husband.

FIRST WOMAN

And there's the barkeep's wife Geusistrate.[8] See her, with the torch in her hand?

PRAXAGORA

And there's Philodoretus' wife, and Chaeretades',[9] and a lot more women besides, anyone who's anybody in town!

---

[4] These islanders were noted oarsmen.

[5] Typical names.   [6] An ordinary name.

[7] Perhaps this Smicythion (identity unknown) was negligent or impotent.   [8] A comic version of women's names ending in -*strate*: *Geusi-* suggests wine drinking.

[9] Identities unknown.

ΓΥΝΗ Β

καὶ πάνυ ταλαιπώρως ἔγωγ᾽, ὦ φιλτάτη,
55 ἐκδρᾶσα παρέδυν· ὁ γὰρ ἀνὴρ τὴν νύχθ᾽ ὅλην
ἔβηττε τριχίδων ἑσπέρας ἐμπλήμενος.

ΠΡΑΞΑΓΟΡΑ

κάθησθε τοίνυν, ὡς ἂν ἀνέρωμαι τάδε
ὑμᾶς, ἐπειδὴ συλλελεγμένας ὁρῶ,
ὅσα Σκίροις ἔδοξεν εἰ δεδράκατε.

ΓΥΝΗ Α

60 ἔγωγε. πρῶτον μέν γ᾽ ἔχω τὰς μασχάλας
λόχμης δασυτέρας, καθάπερ ἦν ξυγκείμενον.
ἔπειθ᾽, ὁπόθ᾽ ἀνὴρ εἰς ἀγορὰν οἴχοιτό μου,
ἀλειψαμένη τὸ σῶμ᾽ ὅλον δι᾽ ἡμέρας
ἐχραινόμην ἑστῶσα πρὸς τὸν ἥλιον.

ΓΥΝΗ Β

65 κἄγωγε· τὸ ξυρὸν δέ γ᾽ ἐκ τῆς οἰκίας
ἔρριψα πρῶτον, ἵνα δασυνθείην ὅλη
καὶ μηδὲν εἴην ἔτι γυναικὶ προσφερής.

ΠΡΑΞΑΓΟΡΑ

ἔχετε δὲ τοὺς πώγονας, οὓς εἴρητ᾽ ἔχειν
πάσαισιν ὑμῖν, ὁπότε συλλεγοίμεθα;

ΓΥΝΗ Α

70 νὴ τὴν Ἑκάτην, καλόν γ᾽ ἔγωγε τουτονί.

69 ὑμῖν R Λ: ἡμῖν A Γ

252

ASSEMBLYWOMEN

Enter SECOND WOMAN on the run.

SECOND WOMAN
I had an awful time, my dear, making my escape and getting over here quietly. My husband stuffed himself with anchovies at dinner last night and was up all night coughing.

PRAXAGORA
(*to Women and Chorus*) Now then, please be seated, so I can put a question to you, now that I see you're all here: have you done everything we agreed on at the Scira?

FIRST WOMAN
I have. First, I've got armpits bushier than underbrush, just as we agreed; then, whenever my husband went off to the agora, I oiled myself and stood in the sun all day getting a tan.

SECOND WOMAN
Me too. I threw my razor out of the house right away, so that I'd get hairy all over and not look female at all.

PRAXAGORA
And you've all got the beards you were told to bring with you when next we met?

FIRST WOMAN
Sure, by Hecate; isn't this one a beauty?

ARISTOPHANES

ΓΥΝΗ Β
κἄγωγ' Ἐπικράτους οὐκ ὀλίγῳ καλλίονα.

ΠΡΑΞΑΓΟΡΑ
ὑμεῖς δὲ τί φατε;

ΓΥΝΗ Α
φασί· κατανεύουσι γοῦν.

ΠΡΑΞΑΓΟΡΑ
καὶ μὴν τά γ' ἄλλ' ὑμῖν ὁρῶ πεπραγμένα·
Λακωνικὰς γὰρ ἔχετε καὶ βακτηρίας
75 καὶ θαἰμάτια τἀνδρεῖα, καθάπερ εἴπομεν.

ΓΥΝΗ Α
ἔγωγέ τοι τὸ σκύταλον ἐξηνεγκάμην
τὸ τοῦ Λαμίου τουτὶ καθεύδοντος λάθρᾳ.

ΓΥΝΗ Β
τοῦτ' ἔστ' ἐκεῖνο τὸ σκύταλον ᾧ πέρδεται.

ΠΡΑΞΑΓΟΡΑ
νὴ τὸν Δία τὸν σωτῆρ' ἐπιτήδειός γ' ἂν ἦν
80 τὴν τοῦ πανόπτου διφθέραν ἐνημμένος
εἴπερ τις ἄλλος βουκολεῖν τὸν δήμιον.
ἀλλ' ἄγεθ' ὅπως καὶ τἀπὶ τούτοις δράσομεν,
ἕως ἔτ' ἐστὶν ἄστρα κατὰ τὸν οὐρανόν·
ἠκκλησία δ', εἰς ἣν παρεσκευάσμεθα
85 ἡμεῖς βαδίζειν, ἐξ ἕω γενήσεται.

78 ἐκεῖνο τὸ σκύταλον ᾧ Bothe: ἐκεῖνο (ἐκείνων S) τῶν
σκυτάλων ὧν a S

254

ASSEMBLYWOMEN

SECOND WOMAN
And mine's a far piece nicer than Epicrates'![10]

PRAXAGORA
And what about the rest of you?

FIRST WOMAN
They've got them; see, they're nodding yes.

PRAXAGORA
And I see you've taken care of everything else: you've got Spartan boots and walking sticks and men's cloaks, just as we said.

FIRST WOMAN
I've brought Lamius' shillelagh; I took it as he slept.

SECOND WOMAN
That must be the shillelagh he uses to fart![11]

PRAXAGORA
By Zeus the Savior, if he wore old All-Eyes' leather jacket he'd be the very man to provide fodder for the public executioner.[12] But let's get on with the next items of business, while there are still stars in the sky. The Assembly we're prepared to attend begins at dawn.

[10] A populist politician nicknamed "shield-bearer" because of his imposing beard (Platon fr. 130).

[11] Presumably this unidentifiable Lamius (according to the scholia, a nickname for one Mnesitheus) was likened to the fabled ogre Lamia, who carried a stick and "farted when captured" (*Wasps* 1177).

[12] Argus was the many-eyed giant sent by Hera to stand guard over Zeus' human favorite, Io, whom she had turned into a heifer.

ΓΥΝΗ Α

νὴ τὸν Δί', ὥστε δεῖ γε καταλαβεῖν ἕδρας
ὑπὸ τῷ λίθῳ τῶν πρυτάνεων καταντικρύ.

ΓΥΝΗ Β

ταυτί γέ τοι νὴ τὸν Δί' ἐφερόμην, ἵνα
πληρουμένης ξαίνοιμι τῆς ἐκκλησίας.

ΠΡΑΞΑΓΟΡΑ

πληρουμένης, τάλαινα;

ΓΥΝΗ Β

90   νὴ τὴν Ἄρτεμιν
ἔγωγε. τί γὰρ ἂν χεῖρον ἀκροώμην ἄρα
ξαίνουσα; γυμνὰ δ' ἐστί μου τὰ παιδία.

ΠΡΑΞΑΓΟΡΑ

ἰδού γέ σε ξαίνουσαν, ἣν τοῦ σώματος
οὐδὲν παραφῆναι τοῖς καθημένοις ἔδει.
95 οὐκοῦν καλά γ' ἂν πάθοιμεν, εἰ πλήρης τύχοι
ὁ δῆμος ὢν κἄπειθ' ὑπερβαίνουσά τις
ἀναβαλλομένη δείξειε τὸν Φορμίσιον.
ἢν δ' ἐγκαθεζώμεσθα πρότεραι, λήσομεν
ξυστειλάμεναι θαἰμάτια· τὸν πώγονά τε
100 ὅταν καθῶμεν ὃν περιδησόμεσθ' ἐκεῖ,
τίς οὐκ ἂν ἡμᾶς ἄνδρας ἡγήσαιθ' ὁρῶν;
Ἀγύρριος γοῦν τὸν Προνόμου πώγων' ἔχων
λέληθε· καίτοι πρότερον ἦν οὗτος γυνή.
νυνὶ δ', ὁρᾷς, πράττει τὰ μέγιστ' ἐν τῇ πόλει.
105 τούτου γέ τοι, νὴ τὴν ἐπιοῦσαν ἡμέραν,
τόλμημα τολμῶμεν τοσοῦτον οὕνεκα,

FIRST WOMAN

Right you are, so we've got to grab some seats under the rock,[13] right in front of the Chairmen.

SECOND WOMAN

(*producing a knitting basket*) That's exactly why I brought this along, to get some knitting done while the Assembly's filling up.

PRAXAGORA

Filling up, stupid?

SECOND WOMAN

Sure, by Artemis. Won't I be able to listen just as well while I knit? And my kids have nothing to wear.

PRAXAGORA

Listen to you: knitting! When you shouldn't be showing any part of your body to the men. Wouldn't we be in a fine fix if the citizenry's all there and then some woman has to climb over them, hitching up her clothes and flashing her—Phormisius![14] If we're the first to take our seats, no one will notice that we're wearing our cloaks wrapped tight. And when we unfurl the beards we'll tie on over there, what onlooker will think we're not men? Take Agyrrhius: now that he's wearing Pronomus' beard he passes for a man; and yet this very man used to be a woman.[15] And now look at him, he's top cock in the city. And it's because of him, I swear by this dawning day, that we must dare such

13 I.e. the speaker's platform.

14 See *Frogs* 965.

15 Agyrrhius was a wealthy politician who recently had successfully proposed the introduction of Assembly pay; Pronomus is otherwise unknown.

ἤν πως παραλαβεῖν τῆς πόλεως τὰ πράγματα
δυνώμεθ᾽ ὥστ᾽ ἀγαθόν τι πρᾶξαι τὴν πόλιν.
νῦν μὲν γὰρ οὔτε θέομεν οὔτ᾽ ἐλαύνομεν.

ΓΥΝΗ Α

110 καὶ πῶς γυναικῶν θηλύφρων ξυνουσία
δημηγορήσει;

ΠΡΑΞΑΓΟΡΑ

πολὺ μὲν οὖν ἄριστά που.
λέγουσι γὰρ καὶ τῶν νεανίσκων ὅσοι
πλεῖστα σποδοῦνται, δεινοτάτους εἶναι λέγειν·
ἡμῖν δ᾽ ὑπάρχει τοῦτο κατὰ τύχην τινά.

ΓΥΝΗ Α

115 οὐκ οἶδα· δεινὸν δ᾽ ἐστὶν ἡ μὴ ᾽μπειρία.

ΠΡΑΞΑΓΟΡΑ

οὔκουν ἐπίτηδες ξυνελέγημεν ἐνθάδε,
ὅπως προμελετήσωμεν ἀκεῖ δεῖ λέγειν;
οὐκ ἂν φθάνοις τὸ γένειον ἂν περιδουμένη
ἄλλαι θ᾽ ὅσαι λαλεῖν μεμελετήκασί που.

ΓΥΝΗ Α

120 τίς δ᾽, ὦ μέλ᾽, ἡμῶν οὐ λαλεῖν ἐπίσταται;

ΠΡΑΞΑΓΟΡΑ

ἴθι δὴ σὺ περιδοῦ καὶ ταχέως ἀνὴρ γενοῦ.
ἐγὼ δὲ θεῖσα τοὺς στεφάνους περιδήσομαι
καὐτὴ μεθ᾽ ὑμῶν, ἤν τί μοι δόξῃ λέγειν.

ΓΥΝΗ Β

δεῦρ᾽ ὦ γλυκυτάτη Πραξαγόρα· σκέψαι, τάλαν,

258

a daring deed, hopeful that somehow we can take over the
government and do something good for the city. As it is,
our city is oarless and becalmed.

FIRST WOMAN
But how can a congregation of women, with women's
minds, expect to address the people?

PRAXAGORA
Much better than anybody, that's how. They say that the
young men who've been reamed the most are also the most
effective orators. And as luck would have it, that's exactly
what nature suits us for!

FIRST WOMAN
I'm not so sure: inexperience is a dangerous thing.

PRAXAGORA
Well, isn't that why we've gathered here, to practice what
we're going to say over there? You can't attach your beard
too soon; and the same goes for the others who I'm sure
have been practicing how to gab.

FIRST WOMAN
Is there anyone here, my friend, who hasn't got the gift
of gab?

PRAXAGORA
All right then, you attach your beard and be a man; I'll put
these garlands aside and attach my own, in case I decide to
do some speaking too.

SECOND WOMAN
(*holding a mirror*) Come here, darling Praxagora. Look,

125 ὡς καὶ καταγέλαστον τὸ πρᾶγμα φαίνεται.

ΠΡΑΞΑΓΟΡΑ
πῶς καταγέλαστον;

ΓΥΝΗ Β
ὥσπερ εἴ τις σηπίαις
πώγωνα περιδήσειεν ἐσταθευμέναις.

ΠΡΑΞΑΓΟΡΑ
ὁ περιστίαρχος, περιφέρειν χρὴ τὴν γαλῆν.
πάριτ᾽ ἐς τὸ πρόσθεν. Ἀρίφραδες, παῦσαι λαλῶν·
130 κάθιζε παριών. τίς ἀγορεύειν βούλεται;

ΓΥΝΗ Α
ἐγώ.

ΠΡΑΞΑΓΟΡΑ
περίθου δὴ τὸν στέφανον τύχἀγαθῇ.

ΓΥΝΗ Α
ἰδού.

ΠΡΑΞΑΓΟΡΑ
λέγοις ἄν.

ΓΥΝΓ Α
εἶτα πρὶν πιεῖν λέγω;

ΠΡΑΞΑΓΟΡΑ
ἰδοὺ πιεῖν.

---

16 Pointing up the incongruity of beards against the pale (and here insufficiently tanned) complexions of the women.

my dear, how ridiculous this is.

PRAXAGORA

Why ridiculous?

SECOND WOMAN

It's like somebody bearded a grilled squid![16]

PRAXAGORA

(*moving to the platform and speaking as Herald*) Purifier, please make your rounds with the sacrificial cat.[17] All move into the sanctified area. Ariphrades,[18] stop chattering; move forward and take your seat. Who wishes to address the Assembly?

FIRST WOMAN

I do.

PRAXAGORA

Then put on the garland, and may your speech be propitious.

FIRST WOMAN

Ready.

PRAXAGORA

You may speak.

FIRST WOMAN

Don't I get a drink first?

PRAXAGORA

Drink?

---

[17] Actually the Assembly was purified with a piglet; the women, normally confined to the house, think of a housepet.

[18] Otherwise unknown.

ΓΥΝΗ Α

τί γάρ, ὦ μέλ᾽, ἐστεφανωσάμην;

ΠΡΑΞΑΓΟΡΑ

ἄπιθ᾽ ἐκποδών· τοιαῦτ᾽ ἂν ἡμᾶς ἠργάσω
κἀκεῖ.

ΓΥΝΗ Α

135   τί δ᾽; οὐ πίνουσι κἀν τἠκκλησίᾳ;

ΠΡΑΞΑΓΟΡΑ

ἰδού γε σοὶ πίνουσι.

ΓΥΝΗ Α

νὴ τὴν Ἄρτεμιν,
καὶ ταῦτά γ᾽ εὔζωρον. τὰ γοῦν βουλεύματα
αὐτῶν, ὅσ᾽ ἂν πράξωσιν ἐνθυμουμένοις,
ὥσπερ μεθυόντων ἐστὶ παραπεπληγμένα.
140 καὶ νὴ Δία σπένδουσί γ᾽· ἢ τίνος χάριν
τοσαῦτ᾽ ἂν ηὔχοντ᾽, εἴπερ οἶνος μὴ παρῆν;
καὶ λοιδοροῦνταί γ᾽ ὥσπερ ἐμπεπωκότες,
καὶ τὸν παροινοῦντ᾽ ἐκφέρουσ᾽ οἱ τοξόται.

ΠΡΑΞΑΓΟΡΑ

σὺ μὲν βάδιζε καὶ κάθησ᾽· οὐδὲν γὰρ εἶ.

ΓΥΝΗ Α

145 νὴ τὸν Δί᾽, ἦ μοι μὴ γενειᾶν κρεῖττον ἦν·
δίψῃ γάρ, ὡς ἔοικ᾽, ἀφανανθήσομαι.

ΠΡΑΞΑΓΟΡΑ

ἔσθ᾽ ἥτις ἑτέρα βούλεται λέγειν;

ASSEMBLYWOMEN

FIRST WOMAN

Well, sir, why else did I put on a garland?[19]

PRAXAGORA

Get off of there! You would have done the same thing to us in the real Assembly.

FIRST WOMAN

What? Don't they drink in the real Assembly?

PRAXAGORA

Listen to you, "don't they drink"!

FIRST WOMAN

They do, by Artemis, and straight shots at that! When you think about what they get up to, their decrees are like the ravings of drunkards. And they certainly pour libations too: why else would they make those long prayers, if they didn't have wine? And they yell at each other like drunks, and the police remove the guy who's had too much.

PRAXAGORA

You go and sit down. You're worthless!

FIRST WOMAN

I swear I would have been better off without this beard— I'm absolutely parched with thirst!

PRAXAGORA

Is there anyone else who wishes to speak?

[19] Garlands were worn not only by speakers in assembly but also at symposia.

ΓΤΝΗ Β

ἐγώ.

ΠΡΑΞΑΓΟΡΑ

ἴθι δὴ στεφανοῦ· καὶ γὰρ τὸ χρῆμ᾿ ἐργάζεται.
ἄγε νυν ὅπως ἀνδριστὶ καὶ καλῶς ἐρεῖς
150 διερεισαμένη τὸ σχῆμα τῇ βακτηρίᾳ.

ΓΤΝΗ Β

ἐβουλόμην μὲν ἕτερον ἂν τῶν ἠθάδων
λέγειν τὰ βέλτισθ᾿, ἵν᾿ ἐκαθήμην ἥσυχος.
νῦν δ᾿ οὐκ ἐάσω, κατά γε τὴν ἐμὴν μίαν,
ἐν τοῖς καπηλείοισι λάκκους ἐμποιεῖν
155 ὕδατος. ἐμοὶ μὲν οὐ δοκεῖ, μὰ τὼ θεώ.

ΠΡΑΞΑΓΟΡΑ

μὰ τὼ θεώ, τάλαινα; ποῦ τὸν νοῦν ἔχεις;

ΓΤΝΗ Β

τί δ᾿ ἔστιν; οὐ γὰρ δὴ πιεῖν γ᾿ ᾔτησά σε.

ΠΡΑΞΑΓΟΡΑ

μὰ Δί᾿ ἀλλ᾿ ἀνὴρ ὢν τὼ θεὼ κατώμοσας,
καίτοι τά γ᾿ ἄλλ᾿ εἰποῦσα δεξιώτατα.

ΓΤΝΗ Β

ὢ νὴ τὸν Ἀπόλλω—

ΠΡΑΞΑΓΟΡΑ

160   παῦε τοίνυν, ὡς ἐγὼ
ἐκκλησιάσουσ᾿ οὐκ ἂν προβαίην τὸν πόδα
τὸν ἕτερον, εἰ μὴ ταῦτ᾿ ἀκριβωθήσεται.

SECOND WOMAN

Me!

PRAXAGORA

Then don the garland; the plan's under way now. All right then, speak like a man and be cogent; lean hard on your stick.

SECOND WOMAN

I would have preferred that one of the usual speakers had offered the best counsel, so that I could have sat still. But as it is, my vote says we outlaw the installation in barrooms of kegs to hold water. I think it's bad policy, by the Two Goddesses.[20]

PRAXAGORA

By the Two Goddesses, you bungler? Where is your mind?

SECOND WOMAN

What's the matter? I didn't ask for a drink.

PRAXAGORA

That's true, but you did swear by the Two Goddesses when you were supposed to be a man. And the rest was so good, too.

SECOND WOMAN

Oh! By Apollo—

PRAXAGORA

No, stop. (*taking the garland herself*) I won't take another step on the road to being an assemblywoman until everything's exactly right.

---

[20] I.e. Demeter and Persephone, a woman's oath.

ΓΥΝΗ Β

φέρε τὸν στέφανον· ἐγὼ γὰρ αὖ λέξω πάλιν·
οἶμαι γὰρ ἤδη μεμελετηκέναι καλῶς.
165 ἐμοὶ γάρ, ὦ γυναῖκες αἱ καθήμεναι,—

ΠΡΑΞΑΓΟΡΑ

γυναῖκας αὖ, δύστηνε, τοὺς ἄνδρας λέγεις;

ΓΥΝΗ Β

δι᾽ Ἐπίγονόν γ᾽ ἐκεῖνον· ἐπιβλέψασα γὰρ
ἐκεῖσε πρὸς γυναῖκας ᾠόμην λέγειν.

ΠΡΑΞΑΓΟΡΑ

ἄπερρε καὶ σὺ καὶ κάθησ᾽ ἐντευθενί·
170 αὐτὴ γὰρ ὑμῶν γ᾽ ἕνεκά μοι λέξειν δοκῶ
τονδὶ λαβοῦσα. τοῖς θεοῖς μὲν εὔχομαι
τυχεῖν κατορθώσασα τὰ βεβουλευμένα.
ἐμοὶ δ᾽ ἴσον μὲν τῆσδε τῆς χώρας μέτα
ὅσονπερ ὑμῖν· ἄχθομαι δὲ καὶ φέρω
175 τὰ τῆς πόλεως ἅπαντα βαρέως πράγματα.
ὁρῶ γὰρ αὐτὴν προστάταισι χρωμένην
ἀεὶ πονηροῖς. κἄν τις ἡμέραν μίαν
χρηστὸς γένηται, δέκα πονηρὸς γίγνεται.
ἐπέτρεψας ἑτέρῳ· πλείον᾽ ἔτι δράσει κακά.
180 χαλεπὸν μὲν οὖν ἄνδρας δυσαρέστους νουθετεῖν,
οἳ τοὺς φιλεῖν μὲν βουλομένους δεδοίκατε,
τοὺς δ᾽ οὐκ ἐθέλοντας ἀντιβολεῖθ᾽ ἑκάστοτε.
ἐκκλησίαισιν ἦν ὅτ᾽ οὐκ ἐχρώμεθα
οὐδὲν τὸ παράπαν· ἀλλὰ τόν γ᾽ Ἀγύρριον
185 πονηρὸν ἡγούμεσθα. νῦν δὲ χρωμένων

SECOND WOMAN

Give me back the garland; I want to try my speech again. I think I've got it down nicely now. In my view, assembled ladies—

PRAXAGORA

Again, you loser? You're calling men ladies!

SECOND WOMAN

It's that Epigonus[21] over there: I caught sight of him and thought I was addressing ladies!

PRAXAGORA

(*taking the platform*) Shoo, you go back to your seat over there too. (*to the seated women*) To judge from what I've seen of your abilities it seems best that I put on this garland and make a speech myself. I beseech the gods to grant success to today's deliberations. My own stake in this country is equal to your own, and I am annoyed and depressed at all the city's affairs. For I see that she constantly employs scoundrels as her leaders. Even if one of them turns virtuous for one day, he'll turn out wicked for ten. You look to another one? He'll make even worse trouble. I realize how hard it is to talk sense to men as cantankerous as you, who fear those who want to befriend you and consistently court those who do not. There was a time when we convened no assemblies at all, but at least we knew Agyrrhius for a scoundrel. Nowadays we do convene them, and the people

---

[21] Otherwise unknown, although a man with this rare name was listed among the female members of a cult association in the early fourth century (*IG* ii² 2346.109).

ὁ μὲν λαβὼν ἀργύριον ὑπερεπήνεσεν,
ὁ δ᾽ οὐ λαβὼν εἶναι θανάτου φήσ᾽ ἀξίους
τοὺς μισθοφορεῖν ζητοῦντας ἐν τἠκκλησίᾳ.

ΓΥΝΗ Α
νὴ τὴν Ἀφροδίτην εὖ γε ταυταγὶ λέγεις.

ΠΡΑΞΑΓΟΡΑ
190   τάλαιν᾽, Ἀφροδίτην ὤμοσας; χαρίεντά γ᾽ ἂν
ἔδρασας, εἰ τοῦτ᾽ εἶπας ἐν τἠκκλησίᾳ.

ΓΥΝΗ Α
ἀλλ᾽ οὐκ ἂν εἶπον.

ΠΡΑΞΑΓΟΡΑ
μηδ᾽ ἐθίζου νῦν λέγειν.
τὸ συμμαχικὸν αὖ τοῦθ᾽, ὅτ᾽ ἐσκοπούμεθα,
εἰ μὴ γένοιτ᾽, ἀπολεῖν ἔφασκον τὴν πόλιν.
195   ὅτε δὴ δ᾽ ἐγένετ᾽, ἤχθοντο, τῶν δὲ ῥητόρων
ὁ τοῦτ᾽ ἀναπείσας εὐθὺς ἀποδρὰς ᾤχετο.
ναῦς δεῖ καθέλκειν· τῷ πένητι μὲν δοκεῖ,
τοῖς πλουσίοις δὲ καὶ γεωργοῖς οὐ δοκεῖ.
Κορινθίοις ἄχθεσθε, κἀκεῖνοί γέ σοι·
200   νῦν εἰσὶ χρηστοί, καὶ σύ νυν χρηστὸς γενοῦ.
ἀργεῖος ἀμαθής, ἀλλ᾽ Ἱερώνυμος σοφός.

²² Probably conflating the Theban alliance of 395 (Lysias
16.13, Andocides 3.25; for the debate cf. Xenophon *Hellenica*
3.5.7–17) with its wider successor (Diodorus Siculus 14.82; for the
recriminations cf. Xenophon *Hellenica* 4.2.18–23, 4.3.17–23); the
discredited "supporter" is not certainly identifiable.

who draw pay praise him to the skies, while those who draw none say that the people who attend for the pay deserve the death penalty.

FIRST WOMAN

Well said, by Aphrodite!

PRAXAGORA

Pitiful: you swore by Aphrodite. Wouldn't it be charming if you spoke that way in the Assembly?

FIRST WOMAN

But I wouldn't have.

PRAXAGORA

Well, don't get into the habit now. (*resuming her speech*) And about this alliance: when we were examining the issue, the people insisted that the city would perish if we did not ratify it. But when it finally was ratified, the people were unhappy, and its staunchest supporter had to leave town in a hurry.[22] We need to launch a fleet: the poor man votes yes, the wealthy and the farmers vote no. You get angry with the Corinthians, and they with you;[23] now they're nice people, "so you be nice too."[24] The Argives are morons, but Hieronymus is sage.[25] And occasionally we get a

[23] Probably referring to the aftermath of the battle of Nemea in 394, when the allies feared that Corinth, which had not assisted their retreat, might join the Spartans.

[24] After its democratic revolution of 393/2 Corinth formed a union with Argos and in 392/1 rejected Spartan peace proposals that would have dissolved the union; Athens followed suit.

[25] Hieronymus was a prominent general in this period; the reference here is uncertain.

σωτηρία παρέκυψεν, ἀλλ᾽ ὀργίζεται
Θρασύβουλος αὐτὸς οὐχὶ παρακαλούμενος.

ΓΥΝΗ Α

ὡς ξυνετὸς ἀνήρ.

ΠΡΑΞΑΓΟΡΑ

νῦν καλῶς ἐπήνεσας.

205 ὑμεῖς γάρ ἐστ᾽, ὦ δῆμε, τούτων αἴτιοι.
τὰ δημόσια γὰρ μισθοφοροῦντες χρήματα
ἰδίᾳ σκοπεῖσθ᾽ ἕκαστος ὅ τι τις κερδανεῖ,
τὸ δὲ κοινὸν ὥσπερ Αἴσιμος κυλίνδεται.
ἢν οὖν ἐμοὶ πείθησθε, σωθήσεσθ᾽ ἔτι·
210 ταῖς γὰρ γυναιξὶ φημὶ χρῆναι τὴν πόλιν
ἡμᾶς παραδοῦναι. καὶ γὰρ ἐν ταῖς οἰκίαις
ταύταις ἐπιτρόποις καὶ ταμίαισι χρώμεθα.

ΓΥΝΗ Β

εὖ γ᾽ εὖ γε νὴ Δί᾽, εὖ γε.

ΓΥΝΗ Α

λέγε, λέγ᾽ ὦγαθέ.

ΠΡΑΞΑΓΟΡΑ

ὡς δ᾽ εἰσὶν ἡμῶν τοὺς τρόπους βελτίονες
215 ἐγὼ διδάξω. πρῶτα μὲν γὰρ τἄρια
βάπτουσι θερμῷ κατὰ τὸν ἀρχαῖον νόμον
ἁπαξάπασαι, κοὐχὶ μεταπειρωμένας
ἴδοις ἂν αὐτάς. ἡ δ᾽ Ἀθηναίων πόλις,

---

202 ὀργίζεται Hermann: ορείζεται R: ὁρίζεται Λ: οὐκ
ὁρίζεται Α Γ

fleeting glimpse of salvation, but Thrasybulus gets angry that you're not inviting him to take charge.[26]

FIRST WOMAN

This man's intelligent!

PRAXAGORA

Now that's the way to applaud! And you, the sovereign people, are responsible for this mess. For while drawing your civic pay from public funds, each of you angles for a personal profit. Meanwhile the public interest flounders like Aesimus.[27] But listen to my advice and you shall escape from your muddle. I propose that we turn over governance of the city to the women; after all, we employ them as stewards and treasurers in our own households.

SECOND WOMAN

Hear hear! Well said!

FIRST WOMAN

Pray continue, sir!

PRAXAGORA

And their character is superior to ours, as I will demonstrate. First, they dye their wool in hot water according to their ancient custom, each and every one of them; you'll never see them try anything new. But the Athenian state

---

[26] The "fleeting glimpse of salvation" probably refers to Spartan peace terms recently offered, only to be rejected by the Athenians; apparently it was Thrasybulus, the venerable general and stalwart democrat, who had decisively argued against peace (cf. also line 356–57). Praxagora portrays his opposition as selfish (desire for personal credit) rather than patriotic.   [27] Prominent since 403, when he had commanded the democratic forces in the civil war (Lysias 13.80), but perhaps currently in eclipse.

εἰ τοῦτο χρηστῶς εἶχεν, οὐκ ἂν ἐσῴζετο,
220 εἰ μή τι καινόν ⟨γ᾽⟩ ἄλλο περιηργάζετο.
καθήμεναι φρύγουσιν ὥσπερ καὶ πρὸ τοῦ·
ἐπὶ τῆς κεφαλῆς φέρουσιν ὥσπερ καὶ πρὸ τοῦ·
223a τὰ Θεσμοφόρι᾽ ἄγουσιν ὥσπερ καὶ πρὸ τοῦ·
223b πέττουσι τοὺς πλακοῦντας ὥσπερ καὶ πρὸ τοῦ·
τοὺς ἄνδρας ἐπιτρίβουσιν ὥσπερ καὶ πρὸ τοῦ·
225 μοιχοὺς ἔχουσιν ἔνδον ὥσπερ καὶ πρὸ τοῦ·
αὑταῖς παροψωνοῦσιν ὥσπερ καὶ πρὸ τοῦ·
οἶνον φιλοῦσ᾽ εὔζωρον ὥσπερ καὶ πρὸ τοῦ·
βινούμεναι χαίρουσιν ὥσπερ καὶ πρὸ τοῦ.
ταύταισιν οὖν, ὦνδρες, παραδόντες τὴν πόλιν
230 μὴ περιλαλῶμεν, μηδὲ πυνθανώμεθα
τί ποτ᾽ ἄρα δρᾶν μέλλουσιν, ἀλλ᾽ ἁπλῷ τρόπῳ
ἐῶμεν ἄρχειν, σκεψάμενοι ταυτὶ μόνα,
ὡς τοὺς στρατιώτας πρῶτον οὖσαι μητέρες
σῴζειν ἐπιθυμήσουσιν· εἶτα σιτία
235 τίς τῆς τεκούσης θᾶττον ἐπιπέμψειεν ἄν;
χρήματα πορίζειν εὐπορώτατον γυνή,
ἄρχουσά τ᾽ οὐκ ἂν ἐξαπατηθείη ποτέ·
αὑταὶ γάρ εἰσιν ἐξαπατᾶν εἰθισμέναι.
τὰ δ᾽ ἄλλ᾽ ἐάσω. ταῦτ᾽ ἐὰν πείθησθέ μοι,
240 εὐδαιμονοῦντες τὸν βίον διάξετε.

ΓΥΝΗ Β

εὖ γ᾽ ὦ γλυκυτάτη Πραξαγόρα, καὶ δεξιῶς.
πόθεν, ὦ τάλαινα, ταῦτ᾽ ἔμαθες οὕτω καλῶς;

220 suppl. Wilson

wouldn't hold on to that custom if it worked just fine; no, they'd be fiddling around with some innovation. Meanwhile the women settle down to their cooking, as they always have. They carry burdens on their heads, as they always have. They celebrate the Thesmophoria, as they always have. They bake cookies, as they always have. They drive their husbands nuts, as they always have. They hide their lovers in the house, as they always have. They buy themselves extra treats, as they always have. They like their wine neat, as they always have. They like a fucking, as they always have. And so, gentlemen, let us hand over governance of the city to the women, and let's not beat around the bush or ask what they plan to accomplish. Let's simply let them govern. Consider only these points: first, as mothers they'll want to protect our soldiers; and second, who would be quicker to send extra rations than the one who bore you? There's nobody more inventive at getting funds than a woman, and when in power she'll never get cheated, since women themselves are past masters at cheating. I'll pass over my other points. Adopt my resolution and you'll lead happy lives.

SECOND WOMAN

Well said, Praxagora my sweet! What skill! Where did you learn such fine talk, my dear?

ΠΡΑΞΑΓΟΡΑ

ἐν ταῖς φυγαῖς μετὰ τἀνδρὸς ᾤκησ᾽ ἐν πυκνί.
ἔπειτ᾽ ἀκούουσ᾽ ἐξέμαθον τῶν ῥητόρων.

ΓΥΝΗ Α

245 οὐκ ἐτὸς ἄρ᾽, ὦ μέλ᾽, ἦσθα δεινὴ καὶ σοφή.
καί σε στρατηγὸν αἱ γυναῖκες αὐτόθεν
αἱρούμεθ᾽, ἢν ταῦθ᾽ ἁπινοεῖς κατεργάσῃ.
ἀτὰρ ἢν Κέφαλός σοι λοιδορῆται προσφθαρείς,
πῶς ἀντερεῖς πρὸς αὐτὸν ἐν τἠκκλησίᾳ;

ΠΡΑΞΑΓΟΡΑ

φήσω παραφρονεῖν αὐτόν.

ΓΥΝΗ Α

250   ἀλλὰ τοῦτό γε
ἴσασι πάντες.

ΠΡΑΞΑΓΟΡΑ

         ἀλλὰ καὶ μελαγχολᾶν.

ΓΥΝΗ Α

καὶ τοῦτ᾽ ἴσασιν.

ΠΡΑΞΑΓΟΡΑ

         ἀλλὰ καὶ τὰ τρύβλια
κακῶς κεραμεύειν, τὴν δὲ πόλιν εὖ καὶ καλῶς.

ΓΥΝΗ Α

τί δ᾽ ἢν Νεοκλείδης ὁ γλάμων σε λοιδορῇ;

ΠΡΑΞΑΓΟΡΑ

255 τούτῳ μὲν εἶπον ἐς κυνὸς πυγὴν ὁρᾶν.

PRAXAGORA

During the displacements[28] I lived with my husband on the Pnyx,[29] and learned by listening to the orators.

FIRST WOMAN

Then it's no wonder, madam, that you were so impressive and sage. Furthermore, your fellow women hereby elect you general if you succeed with this plan of yours. But what if Cephalus[30] confronts you abusively? How do you plan to handle him in the Assembly?

PRAXAGORA

I'll say he's crazy.

FIRST WOMAN

But everyone knows that.

PRAXAGORA

Well, I'll say he's a dangerous psychopath.

FIRST WOMAN

Everyone knows that too.

PRAXAGORA

Then I'll say that a man who makes such crummy crockery will do a terrific job making the city go to pot.

FIRST WOMAN

But what if Neocleides the squinter abuses you?[31]

PRAXAGORA

To him I say, go squint up a dog's butt.

---

[28] I.e. after the Spartan investment of 413 or the battle of Aegospotami in 405.   [29] Where the Athenian Assembly was convened.   [30] A distinguished orator who ran a pottery business.   [31] A politician known for using rough tactics.

ARISTOPHANES

ΓΥΝΗ Α

τί δ᾽ ἢν ὑποκρούωσίν σε;

ΠΡΑΞΑΓΟΡΑ

προσκινήσομαι
ἅτ᾽ οὐκ ἄπειρος οὖσα πολλῶν κρουμάτων.

ΓΥΝΗ Α

ἐκεῖνο μόνον ἄσκεπτον, ἤν σ᾽ οἱ τοξόται
ἕλκωσιν, ὅ τι δράσεις ποτ᾽.

ΠΡΑΞΑΓΟΡΑ

ἐξαγκωνιῶ
260 ὡδί· μέση γὰρ οὐδέποτε ληφθήσομαι.

ΚΟΡΥΦΑΙΑ

ἡμεῖς δέ γ᾽, ἢν αἴρωσ᾽, ἐᾶν κελεύσομεν.

ΓΥΝΗ Α

ταυτὶ μὲν ἡμῖν ἐντεθύμηται καλῶς.
ἐκεῖνο δ᾽ οὐ πεφροντίκαμεν, ὅτῳ τρόπῳ
τὰς χεῖρας αἴρειν μνημονεύσομεν τότε·
265 εἰθισμέναι γάρ ἐσμεν αἴρειν τὼ σκέλει.

ΠΡΑΞΑΓΟΡΑ

χαλεπὸν τὸ πρᾶγμ᾽· ὅμως δὲ χειροτονητέον
ἐξωμισάσαις τὸν ἕτερον βραχίονα.
ἄγε νυν ἀναστέλλεσθ᾽ ἄνω τὰ χιτώνια·
ὑποδεῖσθε δ᾽ ὡς τάχιστα τὰς Λακωνικάς,
270 ὥσπερ τὸν ἄνδρ᾽ ἐθεᾶσθ᾽, ὅτ᾽ εἰς ἐκκλησίαν
μέλλοι βαδίζειν ἢ θύραζ᾽ ἑκάστοτε.
ἔπειτ᾽, ἐπειδὰν ταῦτα πάντ᾽ ἔχῃ καλῶς,

FIRST WOMAN

And what if they try to screw you?

PRAXAGORA

I'll screw them right back: I know a good many tricks myself.

FIRST WOMAN

There's only one danger we haven't discussed: if the police jump you, what will you do then?

PRAXAGORA

I'll give them the elbow, like this; they'll never get me in a clinch.

CHORUS LEADER

And if they do hoist you, we'll, well, ask them to put you down.

FIRST WOMAN

Then we've got all of that planned out. But one thing we haven't considered is how we'll remind ourselves to put up our hands when we vote; we're so used to putting up our legs!

PRAXAGORA

That's a tough one; just remember that you vote by undraping your right arm and raising that hand. Now come on, hitch up your slips and put on those boots as quick as you can, just as you saw your husband do when he was off to an Assembly or some errand. Then when you're all dressed

περιδεῖσθε τοὺς πώγωνας. ἡνίκ᾿ ἂν δέ γε
τούτους ἀκριβώσητε περιηρμοσμέναι,
275 καὶ θαἰμάτια τἀνδρεῖ᾿, ἅπερ γ᾿ ἐκλέψατε,
ἐπαναβάλεσθε, κᾆτα ταῖς βακτηρίαις
ἐπερειδόμεναι βαδίζετ᾿ ᾄδουσαι μέλος
πρεσβυτικόν τι, τὸν τρόπον μιμούμεναι
τὸν τῶν ἀγροίκων.

KORYΦAIA

εὖ λέγεις.

ΠΡΑΞΑΓΟΡΑ

ἡμεῖς δέ γε
280 προΐωμεν αὐτῶν· καὶ γὰρ ἑτέρας οἴομαι
ἐκ τῶν ἀγρῶν ἐς τὴν πύκν᾿ ἥξειν ἄντικρυς
γυναῖκας. ἀλλὰ σπεύσαθ᾿, ὡς εἴωθ᾿ ἐκεῖ
τοῖς μὴ παροῦσιν ὀρθρίοις ἐς τὴν πύκνα
ὑπαποτρέχειν ἔχουσι μηδὲ πάτταλον.

KORYΦAIA

285 ὥρα προβαίνειν ὦνδρες ἡμῖν ἐστι· τοῦτο γὰρ χρὴ
μεμνημένας ἀεὶ λέγειν, ὡς μήποτ᾿ ἐξολίσθῃ
ἡμᾶς. ὁ κίνδυνος γὰρ οὐχὶ μικρός, ἢν ἁλῶμεν
ἐνδυόμεναι κατὰ σκότον τόλμημα τηλικοῦτον.

XOPOΣ

(στρ.) χωρῶμεν εἰς ἐκκλησίαν ὦνδρες· ἠπείλησε γὰρ
291a ὁ θεσμοθέτης, ὃς ἂν
291b   μὴ πρῲ πάνυ τοῦ κνέφους
291c   ἥκῃ κεκονιμένος,
292a   στέργων σκοροδάλμῃ,

278

up, tie on your beards. And when you've attached them exactly right, put on the men's cloaks that you stole and drape them correctly. Now lean on those walking sticks as you set off, and sing an old men's song, country-style.

CHORUS LEADER
Great instructions!

PRAXAGORA
Let's go on ahead of them, because I expect some other women from the country will come directly to the Pnyx. Now hurry, because the drill on the Pnyx is, in by dawn or go home with nary a clothespin.[32]

Exit PRAXAGORA, FIRST *and* SECOND WOMAN.

CHORUS LEADER
Gentlemen, it's time for us to march; and gentlemen is what we must always remember to say, and never let it slip our minds. We run no small risk if we're caught dressed up for so dark a deed of daring.

CHORUS
It's off to the Assembly, gentlemen! The magistrate
has sounded his warning:
anyone who isn't there bright and early,
covered with dust,
happy with garlic soup for breakfast,

[32] Only the first 6000 assemblymen in attendance were paid.

292b βλέπων ὑπότριμμα, μὴ
292c δώσειν τὸ τριώβολον.
293a ἀλλ᾽, ὦ Χαριτιμίδη
293b καὶ Σμίκυθε καὶ Δράκης,
      ἕπου κατεπείγων,
295a σαυτῷ προσέχων ὅπως
295b μηδὲν παραχορδιεῖς
295c ὧν δεῖ σ᾽ ἀποδεῖξαι·
      ὅπως δὲ τὸ σύμβολον
297a λαβόντες ἔπειτα πλη-
297b σίοι καθεδούμεθ᾽, ὡς
297c ἂν χειροτονῶμεν
      ἅπανθ᾽ ὁπόσ᾽ ἂν δέῃ
299a τὰς ἡμετέρας φίλας—
299b καίτοι τί λέγω; φίλους
299c γὰρ χρῆν μ᾽ ὀνομάζειν.

(ἀντ.) ὅρα δ᾽ ὅπως ὠθήσομεν τούσδε τοὺς ἐξ ἄστεως
302a ἥκοντας, ὅσοι πρὸ τοῦ
302b μέν, ἡνίκ᾽ ἔδει λαβεῖν
302c ἐλθόντ᾽ ὀβολὸν μόνον,
303a καθῆντο λαλοῦντες
303b ἐν τοῖς στεφανώμασιν,
303c νυνὶ δ᾽ ἐνοχλοῦσ᾽ ἄγαν.
304a ἀλλ᾽ οὐχί, Μυρωνίδης
304b ὅτ᾽ ἦρχεν ὁ γεννάδας,
305a οὐδεὶς ἂν ἐτόλμα
305b τὰ τῆς πόλεως διοι-

with a salsa look in his eye,
will not get his three-obol pay.
Hey Charitimides,
Smicythus, and Draces,[33]
get a move on,
see to it you don't
strike a false note
in the role you've got to play.
And when we've got
our tickets, let's be sure
to sit close together,
so as to raise our hands in favor
of whatever proposals
our womenfolk may want.
But what am I saying? Menfolk
is the word I ought to have used.

Let's be sure to jostle the assemblymen from town,
who before now
never used to attend,
when their pay was only one obol,
but would sit gossiping
in the garland shops.
Now they fight hard for seats.
Never in the good old days,
with noble Myronides in charge,[34]
would anyone have dared
to husband the city's affairs

[33] Generic men's names.
[34] A highly successful general during the Persian invasions and into the mid-450s.

305c   κεῖν ἀργύριον φέρων·
         ἀλλ᾽ ἧκεν ἕκαστος
         ἐν ἀσκιδίῳ φέρων

308a   πιεῖν ἅμα τ᾽ ἄρτον αὐ-
308b   <τὸς> καὶ δύο κρομμύω
308c   καὶ τρεῖς ἂν ἐλάας.
         νυνὶ δὲ τριώβολον

310a   ζητοῦσι λαβεῖν, ὅταν
310b   πράττωσί τι κοινόν, ὥσ-
310c   περ πηλοφοροῦντες.

ΒΛΕΠΤΡΟΣ

     τί τὸ πρᾶγμα; ποῖ ποθ᾽ ἡ γυνὴ φρούδη ᾽στί μοι;
     ἐπεὶ πρὸς ἔω νῦν γ᾽ ἔστιν, ἡ δ᾽ οὐ φαίνεται.
     ἐγὼ δὲ κατάκειμαι πάλαι χεζητιῶν,
     τὰς ἐμβάδας ζητῶν λαβεῖν ἐν τῷ σκότῳ

315   καὶ θοἰμάτιον. ὅτε δὴ δ᾽ ἐκεῖνο ψηλαφῶν
     οὐκ ἐδυνάμην εὑρεῖν, ὁ δ᾽ ἤδη τὴν θύραν
     ἐπεῖχε κρούων ὁ κοπρεαῖος, λαμβάνω
     τουτὶ τὸ τῆς γυναικὸς ἡμιδιπλοίδιον
     καὶ τὰς ἐκείνης Περσικὰς ὑφέλκομαι.

320   ἀλλ᾽ ἐν καθαρῷ ποῦ ποῦ τις ἂν χέσας τύχοι;
     ἢ πανταχοῦ τοι νυκτός ἐστιν ἐν καλῷ;
     οὐ γάρ με νῦν χέζοντά γ᾽ οὐδεὶς ὄψεται.
     οἴμοι κακοδαίμων, ὅτι γέρων ὢν ἠγόμην
     γυναῖχ᾽· ὅσας εἴμ᾽ ἄξιος πληγὰς λαβεῖν.

325   οὐ γάρ ποθ᾽ ὑγιὲς οὐδὲν ἐξελήλυθεν
     δράσουσ᾽. ὅμως δ᾽ οὖν ἐστιν ἀποπατητέον.

for a handful of money.
No, everyone would come
bringing his own little bag lunch,
something to drink, some bread,
a couple of onions,
and three olives.
Now what they want
is three obols
for doing a public service,
like common laborers.

Exit Chorus.

Enter from Praxagora's doorway BLEPYRUS, *an old man dressed in women's slippers and slip.*

BLEPYRUS[35]

What's going on? Where has my wife got to? It's getting near dawn and she's nowhere to be seen. I've been lying awake for ages, needing to shit, trying to grab my shoes and cloak in the dark. I've groped everywhere but couldn't find it, and all the while the dung man kept pounding at my back door, so finally I grabbed my wife's slip here and put on her Persian slippers. Now where oh where could a fellow shit in privacy? Well, anywhere is fine at night; at this hour no one's going to see me shitting. God what a fool I was, getting married at my age! I deserve a good flogging. She surely didn't go out on any decent errand. Anyway, I've got to do my business. (*squats down*)

[35] The name means "Peeper."

---

[308] suppl. Sommerstein

ARISTOPHANES

ΓΕΙΤΩΝ

τίς ἔστιν; οὐ δήπου Βλέπυρος ὁ γειτνιῶν;
νὴ τὸν Δί᾿ αὐτὸς δῆτ᾿ ἐκεῖνος. εἰπέ μοι,
τί τοῦτό σοι τὸ πυρρόν ἐστιν; οὔτι που
330 Κινησίας σου κατατετίληκέν ποθεν;

ΒΛΕΠΤΡΟΣ

οὔκ, ἀλλὰ τῆς γυναικὸς ἐξελήλυθα
τὸ κροκωτίδιον ἀμπισχόμενος οὐνδύεται.

ΓΕΙΤΩΝ

τὸ δ᾿ ἱμάτιόν σου ποῦ ᾿στιν;

ΒΛΕΠΤΡΟΣ

οὐκ ἔχω φράσαι·
ζητῶν γὰρ αὔτ᾿ οὐχ ηὗρον ἐν τοῖς στρώμασιν.

ΓΕΙΤΩΝ

335 εἶτ᾿ οὐδὲ τὴν γυναῖκ᾿ ἐκέλευσάς σοι φράσαι;

ΒΛΕΠΤΡΟΣ

μὰ τὸν Δί᾿· οὐ γὰρ ἔνδον οὖσα τυγχάνει,
ἀλλ᾿ ἐκτετρύπηκεν λαθοῦσά μ᾿ ἔνδοθεν·
ὃ καὶ δέδοικα μή τι δρᾷ νεώτερον.

ΓΕΙΤΩΝ

νὴ τὸν Ποσειδῶ ταὐτὰ τοίνυν ἄντικρυς
340 ἐμοὶ πέπονθας· καὶ γὰρ ᾗ ξύνειμ᾿ ἐγὼ
φρούδη 'στ᾿ ἔχουσα θοἰμάτιον οὑγὼ 'φόρουν.
κοὐ τοῦτο λυπεῖ μ᾿, ἀλλὰ καὶ τὰς ἐμβάδας.
οὔκουν λαβεῖν γ᾿ αὐτὰς ἐδυνάμην οὐδαμοῦ.

NEIGHBOR, *holding a lamp, appears at Second Woman's window.*

NEIGHBOR

Who's that? Surely not my neighbor Blepyrus? By god, that *is* him. Say, what's that yellow all over you? Maybe Cinesias has hit you with his droppings?[36]

BLEPYRUS

No. I'm out here wearing my wife's little yellow slip that she likes to put on.

NEIGHBOR

Where's your cloak?

BLEPYRUS

I can't say. I looked for it in the bedclothes and couldn't find it.

NEIGHBOR

And you didn't ask your wife to tell you where it is?

BLEPYRUS

I really couldn't. She doesn't happen to be in; she slipped out of the house on me, so I'm worried that she's up to no good.

NEIGHBOR

By Poseidon, exactly the same thing just happened to me. The woman I live with has gone off with the cloak I always wear. That wouldn't be so annoying, but she's taken my boots too; I couldn't lay my hands on them anywhere.

---

[36] A contemporary dithyrambic poet, teased elsewhere for some defecatory incident (cf. *Frogs* 366, with scholiast).

ΒΛΕΠΤΡΟΣ

μὰ τὸν Διόνυσον, οὐδ' ἐγὼ γὰρ τὰς ἐμὰς
345 Λακωνικάς, ἀλλ' ὡς ἔτυχον χεζητιῶν,
ἐς τὼ κοθόρνω τὼ πόδ' ἐνθεὶς ἵεμαι,
ἵνα μὴ 'γχέσαιμ' ἐς τὴν σισύραν· φανὴ γὰρ ἦν.

ΓΕΙΤΩΝ

τί δῆτ' ἂν εἴη; μῶν ἐπ' ἄριστον γυνὴ
κέκληκεν αὐτὴν τῶν φίλων;

ΒΛΕΠΤΡΟΣ

γνώμην γ' ἐμήν.
350 οὔκουν πονηρά γ' ἐστὶν ὅ τι κἄμ' εἰδέναι.

ΓΕΙΤΩΝ

ἀλλὰ σὺ μὲν ἱμονιάν τιν' ἀποπατεῖς, ἐμοὶ δ'
ὥρα βαδίζειν ἐστὶν εἰς ἐκκλησίαν,
ἤνπερ λάβω θοἰμάτιον, ὅπερ ἦν μοι μόνον.

ΒΛΕΠΤΡΟΣ

κἄγωγ', ἐπειδὰν ἀποπατήσω· νῦν δέ μοι
355 ἀχράς τις ἐγκλήσασ' ἔχει τὰ σιτία.

ΓΕΙΤΩΝ

μῶν ἦν Θρασύβουλος εἶπε τοῖς Λακωνικοῖς;

ΒΛΕΠΤΡΟΣ

νὴ τὸν Διόνυσον ἐνέχεται γοῦν μοι σφόδρα.
ἀτὰρ τί δράσω; καὶ γὰρ οὐδὲ τοῦτό με
μόνον τὸ λυποῦν ἐστιν, ἀλλ' ὅταν φάγω,
360 ὅποι βαδιεῖταί μοι τὸ λοιπὸν ἡ κόπρος.
νῦν μὲν γὰρ οὗτος βεβαλάνωκε τὴν θύραν,

BLEPYRUS

By Dionysus, I couldn't find my Spartan boots either. But as luck would have it I had to shit, so I put my feet into these pumps and dashed out. I didn't want to shit on the comforter; just had it cleaned.

NEIGHBOR

What can it be? Maybe one of her lady friends invited her out for breakfast?

BLEPYRUS

That's probably it. She's not a tramp, as far as I know.

NEIGHBOR

Well, you must be pooping a ship's cable; me, I've got to be getting along to the Assembly, if, that is, I can get hold of my cloak; it's the only one I've got.

BLEPYRUS

Me too, as soon as I finish by business; at the moment some sort of choke pear's got my food blockaded inside.

NEIGHBOR

(*disappearing from the window*) Like the one Thrasybulus mentioned to the Spartans?[37]

BLEPYRUS

By Dionysus yes; it's got me pretty uptight, anyway. (*to himself*) What am I going to do? This present predicament isn't my only anxiety: what's going to happen when I eat something? Where will the poop go? As it is, he's got my

---

[37] Or "against the Spartans;" the allusion is unclear.

ARISTOPHANES

ὅστις ποτ᾽ ἔσθ᾽ ἄνθρωπος ἀχραδούσιος.
τίς ἂν οὖν ἰατρόν μοι μετέλθοι, καὶ τίνα;
τίς τῶν καταπρώκτων δεινός ἐστι τὴν τέχνην;
365 ἆρ᾽ οἶδ᾽ Ἀμύνων; ἀλλ᾽ ἴσως ἀρνήσεται.
Ἀντισθένη τις καλεσάτω πάσῃ τέχνῃ·
οὗτος γὰρ ἀνὴρ ἕνεκά γε στεναγμάτων
οἶδεν τί πρωκτὸς βούλεται χεζητιῶν.
ὦ πότνι᾽ Ἰλείθυα μή με περιίδῃς
370 διαρραγέντα μηδὲ βεβαλανωμένον,
ἵνα μὴ γένωμαι σκωραμὶς κωμῳδική.

ΧΡΕΜΗΣ

οὗτος, τί ποιεῖς; οὔτι που χέζεις;

ΒΛΕΠΤΡΟΣ

ἐγώ;
οὐ δῆτ᾽ ἔτι γε μὰ τὸν Δί᾽, ἀλλ᾽ ἀνίσταμαι.

ΧΡΕΜΗΣ

τὸ τῆς γυναικὸς δ᾽ ἀμπέχει χιτώνιον;

ΒΛΕΠΤΡΟΣ

375 ἐν τῷ σκότῳ γὰρ τοῦτ᾽ ἔτυχον ἔνδον λαβών.
ἀτὰρ πόθεν ἥκεις ἐτεόν;

ΧΡΕΜΗΣ

ἐξ ἐκκλησίας.

ΒΛΕΠΤΡΟΣ

ἤδη λέλυται γάρ;

364 κατὰ πρωκτὸν B
369 Ἰλείθυα Coulon cl. titulis: Εἰλείθυ(ι)α a a S

288

back door bolted, this fellow from Cul-de-Sac. Who will go for a doctor, and what kind? Any of you arsehole experts out there knowledgeable about my condition? Does Amynon know? But maybe he'll say no. Somebody call Antisthenes at any cost! When it comes to grunting, he's the man to diagnose an arsehole that needs to shit.[38] Mistress Hileithya,[39] don't let me down when I'm bursting and bolted; I don't want the role of comic potty!

Enter CHREMES.

CHREMES
Hey there, what are you doing? Not taking a shit, are you?

BLEPYRUS
Who, me? No indeed, not any longer anyway. I'm on my feet again.

CHREMES
Is that your wife's slip you're wearing?

BLEPYRUS
Yes, it was dark in the house and I grabbed it by mistake. But tell me, where have you been?

CHREMES
At the Assembly.

BLEPYRUS
You mean it's adjourned already?

---

[38] The identity of these men is uncertain, but an ancient commentator says that Amynon was not a doctor but a "prostituted politician."

[39] The goddess of childbirth.

ΧΡΕΜΗΣ

νὴ Δί᾽ ὄρθριον μὲν οὖν.
καὶ δῆτα πολὺν ἡ μίλτος, ὦ Ζεῦ φίλτατε,
γέλων παρέσχεν, ἣν προσέρραινον κύκλῳ.

ΒΛΕΠΤΡΟΣ

τὸ τριώβολον δῆτ᾽ ἔλαβες;

ΧΡΕΜΗΣ

380   εἰ γὰρ ὤφελον.
ἀλλ᾽ ὕστερος νῦν ἦλθον, ὥστ᾽ αἰσχύνομαι
<κεναῖς ἀπελθὼν χερσίν.

ΒΛΕΠΤΡΟΣ

381a   οὐδὲν οὖν ἔχεις;>

ΧΡΕΜΗΣ

μὰ τὸν Δί᾽ οὐδὲν ἄλλο γ᾽ ἢ τὸν θύλακον.

ΒΛΕΠΤΡΟΣ

τὸ δ᾽ αἴτιον τί;

ΧΡΕΜΗΣ

           πλεῖστος ἀνθρώπων ὄχλος,
ὅσος οὐδεπώποτ᾽, ἦλθ᾽ ἀθρόος ἐς τὴν πύκνα.
385 καὶ δῆτα πάντας σκυτοτόμοις ἠκάζομεν
ὁρῶντες αὐτούς· οὐ γὰρ ἀλλ᾽ ὑπερφυῶς
ὡς λευκοπληθὴς ἦν ἰδεῖν ἡκκλησία.
ὥστ᾽ οὐκ ἔλαβον οὔτ᾽ αὐτὸς οὔτ᾽ ἄλλοι συχνοί.

ΒΛΕΠΤΡΟΣ

οὐδ᾽ ἄρ᾽ ἂν ἐγὼ λάβοιμι νῦν ἐλθών;

CHREMES

Yes indeed, and before daylight too. And dear Zeus, the
ruddle got quite a laugh when they flung it around![40]

BLEPYRUS

Then you got your three obols?

CHREMES

I wish I had. But this time I was too late, so I'm ashamed to
say ‹I've come away empty handed.

BLEPYRUS

So you've got nothing?›

CHREMES

Nope, absolutely nothing but my shopping bag.

BLEPYRUS

But what made you late?

CHREMES

A huge crowd of people showed up en masse at the Pnyx,
an all-time record. And you know, we thought they all
looked like shoemakers; really, the Assembly was awfully
pale faced to behold. So I didn't get anything, and a bunch
of others didn't either.

BLEPYRUS

So if I went there now I wouldn't get anything either?

---

[40] Vermilion dye was used to mark those late for Assembly.

381a lacunam susp. Elmsley, suppl. van Leeuwen et Hen-
derson

ΧΡΕΜΗΣ

πόθεν;

390 οὐδ' ἂν μὰ Δί' εἰ τότ' ἦλθες, ὅτε τὸ δεύτερον
ἀλεκτρυὼν ἐφθέγγετ'.

ΒΛΕΠΤΡΟΣ

οἴμοι δείλαιος.

Ἀντίλοχ', ἀποίμωξόν με τοῦ τριωβόλου
τὸν ζῶντα μᾶλλον· τἀμὰ γὰρ διοίχεται.
ἀτὰρ τί τὸ πρᾶγμ' ἦν, ὅτι τοσοῦτον χρῆμ' ὄχλου
οὕτως ἐν ὥρᾳ ξυνελέγη;

ΧΡΕΜΗΣ

τί δ' ἄλλο γ' ἢ

395 ἔδοξε τοῖς πρυτάνεσι περὶ σωτηρίας
γνώμας καθεῖναι τῆς πόλεως; κᾆτ' εὐθέως
πρῶτος Νεοκλείδης ὁ γλάμων παρείρπυσεν.
κἄπειθ' ὁ δῆμος ἀναβοᾷ πόσον δοκεῖς,
400 "οὐ δεινὰ τολμᾶν τουτονὶ δημηγορεῖν,
καὶ ταῦτα περὶ σωτηρίας προκειμένου,
ὃς αὐτὸς αὑτῷ βλεφαρίδ' οὐκ ἐσώσατο;"
ὁ δ' ἀναβοήσας καὶ περιβλέψας ἔφη,
"τί δαί με χρὴ δρᾶν;"

ΒΛΕΠΤΡΟΣ

"σκόροδ' ὁμοῦ τρίψαντ' ὀπῷ,

405 τιθύμαλλον ἐμβαλόντα τοῦ Λακωνικοῦ,
σαυτοῦ παραλείφειν τὰ βλέφαρα τῆς ἑσπέρας,"
ἔγωγ' ἂν εἶπον, εἰ παρὼν ἐτύγχανον.

ASSEMBLYWOMEN

CHREMES

Hah! Not even if you'd got there before the cock stopped
crowing!

BLEPYRUS

Oh my, what a blow!
    Antilochus, raise not the dirge for those three obols
    but for me who yet live: for all I had is gone.[41]
But what business could have fetched such a mob together
so early?

CHREMES

It could only be that the Chairmen decided to schedule de-
liberation about the salvation of the city. And right away
Neocleides the squinter groped his way to the podium to
speak first, but the people started to yell as loud as you
please, "Isn't it dreadful that this guy dares to address us on
the subject of our salvation no less, when he can't even save
his own eyelids?" And he squints around and yells back,
"Well, how can I help it?"

BLEPYRUS

If I'd been there I'd have said, "Grind up garlic and figs
and add Spartan spurge, and rub it on your eyelids at bed-
time."

---

[41] Parodying Achilles' lament for Patroclus in Aeschylus'
Myrmidons (fr. 138), substituting "those three obols" for "the
deceased."

---

397 προθεῖναι Schömann

ΧΡΕΜΗΣ

μετὰ τοῦτον Εὐαίων ὁ δεξιώτατος
παρῆλθε γυμνός, ὡς ἐδόκει τοῖς πλείοσιν·
410 αὐτός γε μέντοὔφασκεν ἱμάτιον ἔχειν.
κἄπειτ᾽ ἔλεξε δημοτικωτάτους λόγους·
"ὁρᾶτε μέν με δεόμενον σωτηρίας
τετρασταστήρου καὐτόν· ἀλλ᾽ ὅμως ἐρῶ
ὡς τὴν πόλιν καὶ τοὺς πολίτας σώσετε.
415 ἢν γὰρ παρέχωσι τοῖς δεομένοις οἱ κναφῆς
χλαίνας, ἐπειδὰν πρῶτον ἥλιος τραπῇ,
πλευρῖτις ἡμῶν οὐδέν᾽ ἂν λάβοι ποτέ.
ὅσοις δὲ κλίνη μή ᾽στι μηδὲ στρώματα,
ἰέναι καθευδήσοντας ἀπονενιμμένους
420 εἰς τῶν σκυλοδεψῶν· ἢν δ᾽ ἀποκλήῃ τῇ θύρᾳ
χειμῶνος ὄντος, τρεῖς σισύρας ὀφειλέτω."

ΒΛΕΠΥΡΟΣ

νὴ τὸν Διόνυσον χρηστά γ᾽. εἰ δ᾽ ἐκεῖνά γε
προσέθηκεν, οὐδεὶς ἀντεχειροτόνησεν ἄν,
τοὺς ἀλφιταμοιβοὺς τοῖς ἀπόροις τρεῖς χοίνικας
425 δεῖπνον παρέχειν ἅπασιν ἢ κλάειν μακρά,
ἵνα τοῦτ᾽ ἀπέλαυσαν Ναυσικύδους τἀγαθόν.

ΧΡΕΜΗΣ

μετὰ τοῦτο τοίνυν εὐπρεπὴς νεανίας
λευκός τις ἀνεπήδησ᾽ ὅμοιος Νικίᾳ
δημηγορήσων, κἀπεχείρησεν λέγειν
430 ὡς χρὴ παραδοῦναι ταῖς γυναιξὶ τὴν πόλιν.

CHREMES

After him, that success story Euaeon[42] stepped forward,
wearing only a shirt, most people thought, though he in-
sisted he was wearing a cloak. His speech appealed mainly
to the masses: "You see that I'm in need of salvation my-
self—about four bits would do it—but nevertheless I'll tell
you how to save the city and its citizens. If the clothiers do-
nate cloaks at the winter solstice to those who need them,
none of us would ever again catch pneumonia. And you
should allow anyone who hasn't got a bed or a blanket to
sleep in the tanneries after they've washed up; if a tanner
won't open his doors in wintertime, fine him three com-
forters."

BLEPYRUS

By Dionysus, what a noble thought! He'd have won unani-
mous approval if he'd added that grain dealers should
give the needy three quarts for their dinner or face harsh
punishment. They could have collected that benefit from
Nausicydes![43]

CHREMES

Well, after that a pale, good-looking young man sprang to
his feet to address the people; he looked like Nicias.[44]
He made a case for handing the city over to the women.

[42] Identity unknown, but evidently a poor man.

[43] A grain magnate mentioned also in Xenophon, *Memorabilia*
2.7.6 and Plato, *Gorgias* 487c.

[44] Probably the grandson of Nicias the statesman and general,
now barely twenty years old (cf. Lysias 18.10).

417 ὑμῶν S

εἶτ᾽ ἐθορύβησαν κἀνέκραγον ὡς εὖ λέγοι,
τὸ σκυτοτομικὸν πλῆθος, οἱ δ᾽ ἐκ τῶν ἀγρῶν
ἀνεβορβόρυξαν.

ΒΛΕΠΤΡΟΣ
νοῦν γὰρ εἶχον, νὴ Δία.

ΧΡΕΜΗΣ
ἀλλ᾽ ἦσαν ἥττους· ὁ δὲ κατεῖχε τῇ βοῇ,
435   τὰς μὲν γυναῖκας πόλλ᾽ ἀγαθὰ λέγων, σὲ δὲ
πολλὰ κακά.

ΒΛΕΠΤΡΟΣ
καὶ τί εἶπε;

ΧΡΕΜΗΣ
πρῶτον μέν σ᾽ ἔφη
εἶναι πανοῦργον.

ΒΛΕΠΤΡΟΣ
καὶ σέ;

ΧΡΕΜΗΣ
μή πω τοῦτ᾽ ἔρῃ.
κἄπειτα κλέπτην.

ΒΛΕΠΤΡΟΣ
ἐμὲ μόνον;

ΧΡΕΜΗΣ
καὶ νὴ Δία
καὶ συκοφάντην.

And they all cheered and yelled "well said," this mass of
cobblers, while the people from the country made deep
rumbles.

CHREMES

BLEPYRUS

That's because they were using their brains, by heaven.

CHREMES

But they were the minority, and the speaker shouted them
down. In his view, women could do no wrong, and you no
right.

BLEPYRUS

And what did he say?

CHREMES

First, he called you a criminal.

BLEPYRUS

And what did he call you?

CHREMES

I'll get to that. Then he called you a crook.

BLEPYRUS

Only me?

CHREMES

That's right, and an informer too.

ΒΛΕΠΥΡΟΣ
ἐμὲ μόνον;

ΧΡΕΜΗΣ
καὶ νὴ Δία
τωνδὶ τὸ πλῆθος.

ΒΛΕΠΥΡΟΣ
440   τίς δὲ τοῦτ᾽ ἄλλως λέγει;

ΧΡΕΜΗΣ
γυναῖκα δ᾽ εἶναι πρᾶγμ᾽ ἔφη νουβυστικὸν
καὶ χρηματοποιόν. κοὔτε τἀπόρρητ᾽ ἔφη
ἐκ Θεσμοφόροιν ἑκάστοτ᾽ αὐτὰς ἐκφέρειν,
σὲ δὲ κἀμὲ βουλεύοντε τοῦτο δρᾶν ἀεί.

ΒΛΕΠΥΡΟΣ
445 καὶ νὴ τὸν Ἑρμῆν τοῦτό γ᾽ οὐκ ἐψεύσατο.

ΧΡΕΜΗΣ
ἔπειτα συμβάλλειν πρὸς ἀλλήλας ἔφη
ἱμάτια χρυσί᾽ ἀργύριον ἐκπώματα
μόνας μόναις, οὐ μαρτύρων ἐναντίον,
καὶ ταῦτ᾽ ἀποφέρειν πάντα κοὐκ ἀποστερεῖν,
450 ἡμῶν δὲ τοὺς πολλοὺς ἔφασκε τοῦτο δρᾶν.

ΒΛΕΠΥΡΟΣ
451 νὴ τὸν Ποσειδῶ μαρτύρων γ᾽ ἐναντίον.

ΧΡΕΜΗΣ
454 ἕτερά τε πλεῖστα τὰς γυναῖκας ηὐλόγει·
452 οὐ συκοφαντεῖν, οὐ διώκειν, οὐδὲ τὸν
453 δῆμον καταλύειν, ἀλλὰ πολλὰ κἀγαθά.

298

BLEPYRUS

Only me?

CHREMES

That's right, you and most of this crowd here as well!

BLEPYRUS

Well, who'd deny that?

CHREMES

He went on to say that a woman is a creature bursting with brains, and a moneymaker, and that women never divulge the secrets of the Thesmophoria, by contrast with you and me, who leak what we say in Council all the time.

BLEPYRUS

By Hermes, that last point's no lie.

CHREMES

Then he said that women lend each other dresses, jewelry, money, drinking cups, privately and without witnesses, and always return everything and don't cheat, as most of us men, he claimed, do.

BLEPYRUS

By Poseidon, we cheat even when there *are* witnesses.

CHREMES

And he went on at great length in praise of the women, that they don't inform on people, don't sue them, don't try to overthrow the democracy, and lots of other virtues.

---

454 transp. Bachmann

ΒΛΕΠΤΡΟΣ

τί δῆτ᾽ ἔδοξεν;

ΧΡΕΜΗΣ

455   ἐπιτρέπειν γε τὴν πόλιν
ταύταις· ἐδόκει γὰρ τοῦτο μόνον ἐν τῇ πόλει
οὔπω γεγενῆσθαι.

ΒΛΕΠΤΡΟΣ
καὶ δέδοκται;

ΧΡΕΜΗΣ
φήμ᾽ ἐγώ.

ΒΛΕΠΤΡΟΣ

ἅπαντά τ᾽ αὐταῖς ἐστι προστεταγμένα
ἃ τοῖσιν ἀστοῖς ἔμελεν;

ΧΡΕΜΗΣ
οὕτω ταῦτ᾽ ἔχει.

ΒΛΕΠΤΡΟΣ

460 οὐδ᾽ εἰς δικαστήριον ἄρ᾽ εἶμ᾽, ἀλλ᾽ ἡ γυνή;

ΧΡΕΜΗΣ
οὐδ᾽ ἔτι σὺ θρέψεις οὓς ἔχεις, ἀλλ᾽ ἡ γυνή.

ΒΛΕΠΤΡΟΣ
οὐδὲ στένειν τὸν ὄρθρον ἔτι πρᾶγμ᾽ ἆρά μοι;

ΧΡΕΜΗΣ
μὰ Δί᾽ ἀλλὰ ταῖς γυναιξὶ ταῦτ᾽ ἤδη μέλει·
σὺ δ᾽ ἀστενακτὶ περδόμενος οἴκοι μενεῖς.

BLEPYRUS

And what was voted?

CHREMES

To turn the city over to them. That seemed to be the only thing that hasn't been tried.

BLEPYRUS

And this passed?

CHREMES

That's what I'm telling you.

BLEPYRUS

And they've been put in charge of everything that used to be the business of the citizens?

CHREMES

That's the way it is.

BLEPYRUS

So I won't be going to court anymore, my wife will?

CHREMES

And you won't be caring for your dependents anymore, your wife will.

BLEPYRUS

And I'll have no more need to groan myself awake at dawn?

CHREMES

God no, all that's the women's concern now; you can stop groaning and stay at home farting all day.

ΒΛΕΠΥΡΟΣ

465 ἐκεῖνο δεινὸν τοῖσιν ἡλίκοισι νῶν,
μὴ παραλαβοῦσαι τῆς πόλεως τὰς ἡνίας
ἔπειτ' ἀναγκάζωσι πρὸς βίαν—

ΧΡΕΜΗΣ

τί δρᾶν;

ΒΛΕΠΥΡΟΣ

κινεῖν ἑαυτάς. ἢν δὲ μὴ δυνώμεθα,
ἄριστον οὐ δώσουσι.

ΧΡΕΜΗΣ

σὺ δέ γε νὴ Δία

470 δρᾶ ταῦθ', ἵν' ἀριστᾷς τε καὶ κινῇς ἅμα.

ΒΛΕΠΥΡΟΣ

τὸ πρὸς βίαν δεινότατον.

ΧΡΕΜΗΣ

ἀλλ' εἰ τῇ πόλει

τοῦτο ξυνοίσει, ταῦτα χρὴ πάντ' ἄνδρα δρᾶν.

ΒΛΕΠΥΡΟΣ

λόγος γέ τοί τις ἔστι τῶν γεραιτέρων,
ὅσ' ἂν ἀνόητ' ἢ μῶρα βουλευσώμεθα,
475 ἅπαντ' ἐπὶ τὸ βέλτιον ἡμῖν ξυμφέρειν.

ΧΡΕΜΗΣ

καὶ ξυμφέροι γ', ὦ πότνια Παλλὰς καὶ θεοί.
ἀλλ' εἶμι· σὺ δ' ὑγίαινε.

ΒΛΕΠΥΡΟΣ

καὶ σύ γ', ὦ Χρέμης.

BLEPYRUS

But there lies the danger for men our age: once they've
taken the reins of power they'll force us against our will
to—

CHREMES

To what?

BLEPYRUS

To screw them! And if we can't perform, they won't make
us breakfast.

CHREMES

By god, you'd better do *this* then,[45] so you can eat breakfast
and screw at the same time.

BLEPYRUS

But it's absolutely terrible when you're forced!

CHREMES

But if this is state policy, every true man's got to do his part.

BLEPYRUS

Well, there *is* an ancestral saying, that however brainless or
foolish our policies, all our affairs will turn out for the best.

CHREMES

And I hope they do turn out for the best, Lady Pallas and
all you gods. Well, I must be off. Be well, friend.

BLEPYRUS

You too, Chremes.

Exit *CHREMES offstage, BLEPYRUS into his house.*

[45] The gesture and its significance are obscure.

ΚΟΡΥΦΑΙΑ

ἔμβα χώρει.
ἆρ' ἔστι τῶν ἀνδρῶν τις ἡμῖν ὅστις ἐπακολουθεῖ;
480   στρέφου, σκόπει,
φύλαττε σαυτὴν ἀσφαλῶς, πολλοὶ γὰρ οἱ
πανοῦργοι,
μή πού τις ἐκ τοὔπισθεν ὢν τὸ σχῆμα καταφυλάξῃ.

ΧΟΡΟΣ

(στρ)   ἀλλ' ὡς μάλιστα τοῖν ποδοῖν ἐπικτυπῶν βάδιζε.
ἡμῖν δ' ἂν αἰσχύνην φέροι
485   πάσαισι παρὰ τοῖς ἀνδράσιν
τὸ πρᾶγμα τοῦτ' ἐλεγχθέν.
πρὸς ταῦτα συστέλλου σεαυ-
τὴν καὶ περισκοπουμένη
⟨ἄθρει κύκλῳ⟩ κἀκεῖσε καὶ
488a   τἀκ δεξιᾶς, μὴ ξυμφορὰ
488b   γενήσεται τὸ πρᾶγμα.

ΚΟΡΥΦΑΙΑ

ἀλλ' ἐγκονῶμεν· τοῦ τόπου γὰρ ἐγγύς ἐσμεν ἤδη,
490   ὅθενπερ εἰς ἐκκλησίαν ὡρμώμεθ' ἡνίκ' ἦμεν.
τὴν δ' οἰκίαν ἔξεσθ' ὁρᾶν, ὅθενπερ ἡ στρατηγὸς
ἔσθ' ἡ τὸ πρᾶγμ' εὑροῦσ' ὃ νῦν ἔδοξε τοῖς πολίταις.

487 suppl. Ussher

Enter CHORUS.

CHORUS LEADER

Forward march!
Are any of the men following us?
Turn around, take a look,
watch yourselves carefully: there are lots of no-good
    men about,
and one of them might be at our rear, inspecting our
    deportment.

CHORUS

Right! As you march along stomp your feet as loud as
    you can.
We would be in disgrace
before all our husbands
if this business were exposed.
And so stay closely wrapped,
and look all around you
watching this way and that,
both left and right, lest catastrophe
befall our operation.

CHORUS LEADER

Now let's make the dust fly: we're already near the
    place
where we first set forth for Assembly.
We can see the house now where our commander
    lives,
who thought up the plan that the citizens have now
    enacted.

ΧΟΡΟΣ

(ἀντ) ὥστ᾽ εἰκὸς ἡμᾶς μὴ βραδύνειν ἔστ᾽ ἐπαναμενούσας
πώγωνας ἐξηρτημένας,
495a μὴ καί τις ὄψεθ᾽ ἡμέρας
495b χἠμῶν ἴσως κατείπῃ.
ἀλλ᾽ εἶα δεῦρ᾽ ἐπὶ σκιᾶς
ἐλθοῦσα πρὸς τὸ τειχίον,
παραβλέπουσα θατέρῳ,
499a πάλιν μετασκεύαζε σαυ-
499b τὴν αὖθις ἥπερ ἦσθα.

ΚΟΡΥΦΑΙΑ

500 καὶ μὴ βράδυν᾽· ὡς τήνδε καὶ δὴ τὴν στρατηγὸν
ἡμῶν
χωροῦσαν ἐξ ἐκκλησίας ὁρῶμεν. ἀλλ᾽ ἐπείγου
ἅπασα καὶ μίσει σάκον πρὸς ταῖν γνάθοιν ἔχουσα·
καὐταὶ γὰρ ἄκουσαι πάλαι τὸ σχῆμα τοῦτ᾽ ἔχουσιν.

ΠΡΑΞΑΓΟΡΑ

ταυτὶ μὲν ἡμῖν, ὦ γυναῖκες, εὐτυχῶς
505 τὰ πράγματ᾽ ἐκβέβηκεν ἀβουλεύσαμεν.
ἀλλ᾽ ὡς τάχιστα, πρίν τιν᾽ ἀνθρώπων ἰδεῖν,
ῥιπτεῖτε χλαίνας, ἐμβὰς ἐκποδὼν ἴτω,
χάλα συναπτοὺς ἡνίας Λακωνικάς,
βακτηρίας ἄφεσθε. καὶ μέντοι σὺ μὲν
510 ταύτας κατευτρέπιζ᾽, ἐγὼ δὲ βούλομαι,

495 ὄψεθ᾽ ἡμέρας von Blumenthal: ὄψετ᾽ ἡμᾶς R Λ: ὄψαιτο
ἡμᾶς Γ   503 καὐταὶ van Leeuwen: χαῦται a   ἄκουσαι . . .
ἔχουσιν Agar: ἤκουσιν . . . ἔχουσαι a

CHORUS

So we've no further need to waste time and hang
    around
with these beards hanging off us;
someone might see us in the daylight
and maybe turn us in.
So come this way, into the shade
by the house wall,
keeping an eye peeled,
and change yourselves
back to the way you were.

CHORUS LEADER

And don't dally, for here we can see our commander
making her way from Assembly. Now get a move on
everyone, and lose those hateful hairbags on your
    cheeks,
which have grudgingly worn this gear a long time
    now.

Enter PRAXAGORA.

PRAXAGORA

We're in luck, ladies: this business has turned out as we
planned. Now before anybody sees you, get rid of those
cloaks as quick as you can; shoes out from underfoot; you,
undo the knotted Spartan reins;[46] toss away the walking
sticks. (*to Chorus Leader*) And you, get these women into
some kind of order. I'd like to sneak back into the house

---

[46] I.e. the laces of Spartan boots, cf. 74.

ARISTOPHANES

εἴσω παρερπύσασα πρὶν τὸν ἄνδρα με
ἰδεῖν, καταθέσθαι θοἰμάτιον αὐτοῦ πάλιν
ὅθενπερ ἔλαβον, τἄλλα θ' ἀξηνεγκάμην.

ΚΟΡΥΦΑΙΑ

⟨διά⟩κειται δὴ πάνθ' ἅπερ εἶπας, σὸν δ' ἔργον
    τἄλλα διδάσκειν,
515 ὅ τί σοι δρῶσαι ξύμφορον ἡμεῖς δόξομεν ὀρθῶς
    ὑπακούειν.
οὐδεμιᾷ γὰρ δεινοτέρᾳ σου ξυμμείξασ' οἶδα
    γυναικί.

ΠΡΑΞΑΓΟΡΑ

περιμείνατέ νυν, ἵνα τῆς ἀρχῆς, ἣν ἄρτι
    κεχειροτόνημαι,
ξυμβούλοισιν πάσαις ὑμῖν χρήσωμαι. καὶ γὰρ ἐκεῖ
    μοι
ἐν τῷ θορύβῳ καὶ τοῖς δεινοῖς ἀνδρειόταται
    γεγένησθε.

ΒΛΕΠΤΡΟΣ

αὕτη, πόθεν ἥκεις, Πραξαγόρα;

ΠΡΑΞΑΓΟΡΑ

                    τί δ', ὦ μέλε,
520
σοὶ τοῦθ';

ΒΛΕΠΤΡΟΣ

        ὅ τί μοι τοῦτ' ἔστιν; ὡς εὐηθικῶς.

ΠΡΑΞΑΓΟΡΑ

οὔτοι παρά του μοιχοῦ γε φήσεις.

before my husband sees me and put his cloak back where I got it, and all this other stuff I borrowed.

CHORUS LEADER

Everything's disposed just as you ordered. Now it's up to you to continue our training: by what useful service will we pass muster in your eyes? For I know that I've never encountered a woman more impressive than you.

PRAXAGORA

Then stick around: I'll use all of you as counsellors in running the office I've been elected to, because back there, amid the hubbub and danger, you proved very manly!

Enter BLEPYRUS *from his house.*

BLEPYRUS

It's you! Where have you been, Praxagora?

PRAXAGORA

Is that any of your business, sir?

BLEPYRUS

Any of my business? What innocence!

PRAXAGORA

Now don't start saying I've been at some lover's house.

---

[514] suppl. D'Angour in *BMCR* 11.17 2000

ΒΛΕΠΤΡΟΣ

οὐκ ἴσως

ἑνός γε.

ΠΡΑΞΑΓΟΡΑ
καὶ μὴν βασανίσαι τουτί γέ σοι
ἔξεστι.

ΒΛΕΠΤΡΟΣ

πῶς;

ΠΡΑΞΑΓΟΡΑ
εἰ τῆς κεφαλῆς ὄζω μύρου.

ΒΛΕΠΤΡΟΣ
525 τί δ᾽; οὐχὶ βινεῖται γυνὴ κἄνευ μύρου;

ΠΡΑΞΑΓΟΡΑ
οὐ δὴ τάλαιν᾽ ἔγωγε.

ΒΛΕΠΤΡΟΣ
πῶς οὖν ὄρθριον
ᾤχου σιωπῇ θοἰμάτιον λαβοῦσά μου;

ΠΡΑΞΑΓΟΡΑ
γυνή μέ τις νύκτωρ ἑταίρα καὶ φίλη
μετεπέμψατ᾽ ὠδίνουσα.

ΒΛΕΠΤΡΟΣ
κᾷτ᾽ οὐκ ἦν ἐμοὶ
φράσασαν ἰέναι;

ΠΡΑΞΑΓΟΡΑ
530 τῆς λεχοῦς δ᾽ οὐ φροντίσαι
οὕτως ἐχούσης, ὦνερ;

BLEPYRUS

Maybe more than one!

PRAXAGORA

Very well, you can check it out.

BLEPYRUS

How?

PRAXAGORA

See if you can smell perfume on my head.

BLEPYRUS

What? Can't a woman get fucked even without perfume?

PRAXAGORA

Not I, more's the pity.

BLEPYRUS

Then why did you leave the house so early, without telling me, and taking my cloak with you?

PRAXAGORA

A woman I know, a dear friend, was in labor and asked me to attend her.

BLEPYRUS

So couldn't you have told me you were leaving?

PRAXAGORA

And not give a thought, husband, to a woman brought to bed in her condition?

ARISTOPHANES

ΒΛΕΠΤΡΟΣ

εἰποῦσάν γ᾽ ἐμοί.
ἀλλ᾽ ἔστιν ἐνταῦθά τι κακόν.

ΠΡΑΞΑΓΟΡΑ

μὰ τὼ θεὼ
ἀλλ᾽ ὥσπερ εἶχον ᾠχόμην· ἐδεῖτο δὲ
ἥπερ μεθῆκέ μ᾽ ἐξιέναι πάσῃ τέχνῃ.

ΒΛΕΠΤΡΟΣ

535 εἶτ᾽ οὐ τὸ σαυτῆς ἱμάτιον ἐχρῆν σ᾽ ἔχειν;
ἀλλ᾽ ἔμ᾽ ἀποδύσασ᾽, ἐπιβαλοῦσα τοὐγκυκλον,
ᾤχου καταλιποῦσ᾽ ὡσπερεὶ προκείμενον,
μόνον οὐ στεφανώσασ᾽ οὐδ᾽ ἐπιθεῖσα λήκυθον.

ΠΡΑΞΑΓΟΡΑ

ψῦχος γὰρ ἦν, ἐγὼ δὲ λεπτὴ κἀσθενής·
540 ἔπειθ᾽ ἵν᾽ ἀλεαίνοιμι, τοῦτ᾽ ἠμπεσχόμην.
σὲ δ᾽ ἐν ἀλέᾳ κατακείμενον καὶ στρώμασιν
κατέλιπον, ὦνερ.

ΒΛΕΠΤΡΟΣ

αἱ δὲ δὴ Λακωνικαὶ
ᾤχοντο μετὰ σοῦ κατὰ τί χἠ βακτηρία;

ΠΡΑΞΑΓΟΡΑ

ἵνα θοἰμάτιον σώσαιμι, μεθυπεδησάμην
545 μιμουμένη σε καὶ κτυποῦσα τοῖν ποδοῖν
καὶ τοὺς λίθους παίουσα τῇ βακτηρίᾳ.

ΒΛΕΠΤΡΟΣ

οἶσθ᾽ οὖν ἀπολωλεκυῖα πυρῶν ἑκτέα,

BLEPYRUS

Yes, but after telling me. There's something fishy here.

PRAXAGORA

Not at all, by the Two Goddesses. I went just as I was. The maid who came asked me to leave right away.

BLEPYRUS

Then shouldn't you have worn your own slip? Instead, you swiped my cloak and threw your slip over me, leaving me there like a corpse at the undertaker's; you all but laid me out with a wreath and urn!

PRAXAGORA

It was cold outside, and I'm thin and delicate, so I put this on to keep warm. And I left you lying snugly blanketed, husband.

BLEPYRUS

And why did my Spartan boots go with you, and my walking stick?

PRAXAGORA

I didn't want your cloak to get stolen, so I put these on to sound like you, stomping my feet and poking at stones with the stick.

BLEPYRUS

Do you realize that you've cost us eight quarts of wheat,

ὃν χρῆν ἔμ᾽ ἐξ ἐκκλησίας εἰληφέναι;

ΠΡΑΞΑΓΟΡΑ
μὴ φροντίσῃς· ἄρρεν γὰρ ἔτεκε παιδίον.

ΒΛΕΠΤΡΟΣ
ἡκκλησία;

ΠΡΑΞΑΓΟΡΑ
550   μὰ Δί᾽, ἀλλ᾽ ἐφ᾽ ἣν ἐγῷχόμην.
ἀτὰρ γεγένηται;

ΒΛΕΠΤΡΟΣ
ναὶ μὰ Δί᾽. οὐκ ᾔδησθά με
φράσαντά σοι χθές;

ΠΡΑΞΑΓΟΡΑ
ἄρτι γ᾽ ἀναμιμνῄσκομαι.

ΒΛΕΠΤΡΟΣ
οὐδ᾽ ἄρα τὰ δόξαντ᾽ οἶσθα;

ΠΡΑΞΑΓΟΡΑ
μὰ Δί᾽ ἐγὼ μὲν οὔ.

ΒΛΕΠΤΡΟΣ
κάθησο τοίνυν σηπίας μασωμένη.
555 ὑμῖν δέ φασι παραδεδόσθαι τὴν πόλιν.

ΠΡΑΞΑΓΟΡΑ
τί δρᾶν; ὑφαίνειν;

ΒΛΕΠΤΡΟΣ
οὐ μὰ Δί᾽, ἀλλ᾽ ἄρχειν.

what I'd have gotten by attending Assembly?

PRAXAGORA

Don't worry, she had a boy.[47]

BLEPYRUS

Who, the Assembly?

PRAXAGORA

No no, the woman I attended. So, an Assembly was held?

BLEPYRUS

God yes. Don't you remember my telling you about it yesterday?

PRAXAGORA

Yes, now I remember.

BLEPYRUS

So you don't even know what was decided?

PRAXAGORA

I sure don't.

BLEPYRUS

Well, sit down and chew some cuttlefish: they say the city's been turned over to you women.

PRAXAGORA

For what job? Some sewing?

BLEPYRUS

God no, for governing!

---

[47] In which case Praxagora, as midwife, could expect to receive a gift worth more than the 3-obol Assembly payment.

ARISTOPHANES

ΠΡΑΞΑΓΟΡΑ
τίνων;

ΒΛΕΠΤΡΟΣ
ἁπαξαπάντων τῶν κατὰ πόλιν πραγμάτων.

ΠΡΑΞΑΓΟΡΑ
νὴ τὴν Ἀφροδίτην μακαρία γ᾽ ἄρ᾽ ἡ πόλις
ἔσται τὸ λοιπόν.

ΒΛΕΠΤΡΟΣ
κατὰ τί;

ΠΡΑΞΑΓΟΡΑ
πολλῶν οὕνεκα.
560 οὐ γὰρ ἔτι τοῖς τολμῶσιν αὐτὴν αἰσχρὰ δρᾶν
ἔσται τὸ λοιπὸν οὐδάμ᾽, οὐδὲ μαρτυρεῖν,
οὐ συκοφαντεῖν—

ΒΛΕΠΤΡΟΣ
μηδαμῶς πρὸς τῶν θεῶν
τουτὶ ποιήσῃς μηδ᾽ ἀφέλῃ μου τὸν βίον.

ΓΕΙΤΩΝ
ὦ δαιμόνι᾽ ἀνδρῶν, τὴν γυναῖκ᾽ ἔα λέγειν.

ΠΡΑΞΑΓΟΡΑ
565 μὴ λωποδυτῆσαι, μὴ φθονεῖν τοῖς πλησίον,
μὴ γυμνὸν εἶναι μὴ πένητα μηδένα,
μὴ λοιδορεῖσθαι, μὴ 'νεχυραζόμενον φέρειν.

ΓΕΙΤΩΝ
νὴ τὸν Ποσειδῶ μεγάλα γ᾽, εἰ μὴ ψεύσεται.

PRAXAGORA

Governing whom?

BLEPYRUS

Absolutely all the city's affairs.

PRAXAGORA

Then, by Aphrodite, the city has a rosy future in store!

BLEPYRUS

How do you figure?

PRAXAGORA

For lots of reasons. You see, from now on aggressive people will be in no position to treat the city shamefully in any way, or to testify or trump up charges—

BLEPYRUS

Good heavens, don't do that, don't take away my livelihood!

NEIGHBOR *has come out of his house to listen.*

NEIGHBOR

Please, friend, let your wife talk.

PRAXAGORA

—no more mugging, no more envying the next guy, no more wearing rags, no more poor people, no more wrangling, no more dunning and repossessing.

NEIGHBOR

That would be great, by Poseidon, if she's not just making it up.

ΠΡΑΞΑΓΟΡΑ

ἀλλ᾽ ἀποφανῶ τοῦθ᾽, ὥστε σέ τέ μοι μαρτυρεῖν
570 καὶ τοῦτον αὐτὸν μηδὲν ἀντειπεῖν ἐμοί.

ΧΟΡΟΣ

νῦν δὴ δεῖ σε πυκνὴν φρένα
    καὶ φιλόσοφον ἐγείρειν
φροντίδ᾽ ἐπισταμένην
    ταῖσι φίλαισιν ἀμύνειν.
κοινῇ γὰρ ἐπ᾽ εὐτυχίαισιν
ἔρχεται γλώττης ἐπίνοια πολίτην
575   δῆμον ἐπαγλαΐοῦσα
576a μυρίαισιν ὠφελίαισι βίου·
576b δηλοῦν δ᾽ ὅ τί περ δύναται καιρός.
δεῖται γάρ τι σοφοῦ τινος ἐξ-
    ευρήματος ἡ πόλις ἡμῶν.
ἀλλὰ πέραινε μόνον
μήτε δεδραμένα μήτ᾽
    εἰρημένα πω πρότερον.
μισοῦσι γὰρ ἢν τὰ παλαιὰ
580   πολλάκις θεῶνται.

ΚΟΡΥΦΑΙΑ

ἀλλ᾽ οὐ μέλλειν, ἀλλ᾽ ἅπτεσθαι καὶ δὴ χρὴ τῆς
    διανοίας,
ὡς τὸ ταχύνειν χαρίτων μετέχει πλεῖστον παρὰ
    τοῖσι θεαταῖς.

PRAXAGORA

Let me explain it; you'll have to side with me, and even my
mister here will have no rebuttal to *me*.

CHORUS

Now you must summon up
a shrewd intelligence
and a philosophic mind
that knows how to fight for your comrades.
For it's to the prosperity of all alike
that from your lips comes a bright idea
to gladden the lives of the city's people
with countless benefits;
now's the time to reveal its potential.
Yes, our city needs
some kind of sage scheme;
describe it in full, making sure only
that none of it's ever been
said or done before:
they hate to watch the same old stuff
over and over again!

CHORUS LEADER

No more delay! Here and now you must put your idea in
play: what spectators most appreciate is speed.

ΠΡΑΞΑΓΟΡΑ

καὶ μὴν ὅτι μὲν χρηστὰ διδάξω πιστεύω· τοὺς δὲ
  θεατάς,
εἰ καινοτομεῖν ἐθελήσουσιν καὶ μὴ τοῖς ἠθάσι λίαν
585 τοῖς τ᾽ ἀρχαίοις ἐνδιατρίβειν, τοῦτ᾽ ἔσθ᾽ ὃ μάλιστα
  δέδοικα.

ΓΕΙΤΩΝ

περὶ μὲν τοίνυν τοῦ καινοτομεῖν μὴ δείσῃς· τοῦτο
  γὰρ ἡμῖν
δρᾶν ἀντ᾽ ἄλλης ἀρχῆς ἐστιν, τῶν δ᾽ ἀρχαίων
  ἀμελῆσαι.

ΠΡΑΞΑΓΟΡΑ

μή νυν πρότερον μηδεὶς ὑμῶν ἀντείπῃ μηδ᾽
  ὑποκρούσῃ,
πρὶν ἐπίστασθαι τὴν ἐπίνοιαν καὶ τοῦ φράζοντος
  ἀκοῦσαι.
590 κοινωνεῖν γὰρ πάντας φήσω χρῆναι πάντων
  μετέχοντας
κἀκ ταὐτοῦ ζῆν, καὶ μὴ τὸν μὲν πλουτεῖν, τὸν δ᾽
  ἄθλιον εἶναι,
μηδὲ γεωργεῖν τὸν μὲν πολλήν, τῷ δ᾽ εἶναι μηδὲ
  ταφῆναι,
μηδ᾽ ἀνδραπόδοις τὸν μὲν χρῆσθαι πολλοῖς, τὸν δ᾽
  οὐδ᾽ ἀκολούθῳ.
ἀλλ᾽ ἕνα ποιῶ κοινὸν πᾶσιν βίοτον, καὶ τοῦτον
  ὅμοιον.

PRAXAGORA

Well, I'm sure my proposals are worthwhile, but I'm aw-
fully worried about the spectators: are they ready to quarry
a new vein and not stick with what's hoary and conven-
tional?

NEIGHBOR

Don't worry about quarrying new veins: for us, indiffer-
ence to precedent takes precedence over any other princi-
ple of government.

PRAXAGORA

Then let no one object or interrupt until you've heard the
speaker out and understand the plan. Very well: I propose
that everyone should own everything in common, and
draw an equal living. No more rich man here, poor man
there, or a man with a big farm and a man without land
enough for his own grave, or a man with many slaves and a
man without even an attendant. No, I will establish one
and the same standard of life for everyone.

ΒΛΕΠΥΡΟΣ

πῶς οὖν ἔσται κοινὸς ἅπασιν;

ΠΡΑΞΑΓΟΡΑ

595   κατέδει πέλεθον πρότερός μου.

ΒΛΕΠΥΡΟΣ

καὶ τῶν πελέθων κοινωνοῦμεν;

ΠΡΑΞΑΓΟΡΑ

         μὰ Δί', ἀλλ' ἔφθης μ' ὑποκρούσας·
τοῦτο γὰρ ἤμελλον ἐγὼ λέξειν. τὴν γῆν πρώτιστα
    ποιήσω
κοινὴν πάντων καὶ τἀργύριον καὶ τἄλλ' ὁπόσ' ἐστὶν
    ἑκάστῳ.
εἶτ' ἀπὸ τούτων κοινῶν ὄντων ἡμεῖς βοσκήσομεν
    ὑμᾶς
600 ταμιευόμεναι καὶ φειδόμεναι καὶ τὴν γνώμην
    προσέχουσαι.

ΓΕΙΤΩΝ

πῶς οὖν ὅστις μὴ κέκτηται γῆν ἡμῶν, ἀργύριον δὲ
καὶ Δαρεικούς, ἀφανῆ πλοῦτον;

ΠΡΑΞΑΓΟΡΑ

         τοῦτ' ἐς τὸ μέσον καταθήσει.

ΒΛΕΠΥΡΟΣ

καὶ μὴ καταθεὶς ψευδορκήσει· κἀκτήσατο γὰρ διὰ
    τοῦτο.

ΠΡΑΞΑΓΟΡΑ

ἀλλ' οὐδέν τοι χρήσιμον ἔσται πάντως αὐτῷ.

BLEPYRUS

How will it be the same for everyone?

PRAXAGORA

If we were eating dung you'd want the first bite!

BLEPYRUS

We'll be sharing the dung too?

PRAXAGORA

God no, I mean you cut me off by interrupting; I was just about to explain that point. My first act will be to communize all the land, money, and other property that's now individually owned. We women will manage this common fund with thrift and good judgment, and take good care of you.

NEIGHBOR

And what about the man who owns no land but has invisible wealth, like silver coin and gold darics?[48]

PRAXAGORA

He'll contribute it to the common fund.

BLEPYRUS

And if he doesn't, he'll perjure himself; after all, that's how he got it in the first place!

PRAXAGORA

But see, it won't be of any use to him anyway.

---

[48] A widely circulated Persian coin worth 20 drachmas.

ΒΛΕΠΤΡΟΣ

κατὰ δὴ τί;

ΠΡΑΞΑΓΟΡΑ

605 οὐδεὶς οὐδὲν πενίᾳ δράσει· πάντα γὰρ ἕξουσιν
ἅπαντες,
ἄρτους, τεμάχη, μάζας, χλαίνας, οἶνον, στεφάνους,
ἐρεβίνθους.
ὥστε τί κέρδος μὴ καταθεῖναι; σὺ γὰρ ἐξευρὼν
ἀπόδειξον.

ΒΛΕΠΤΡΟΣ

οὔκουν καὶ νῦν οὗτοι μᾶλλον κλέπτουσ᾽ οἷς ταῦτα
πάρεστιν;

ΓΕΙΤΩΝ

πρότερόν γ᾽, ὦταῖρ᾽, ὅτε τοῖσι νόμοις διεχρώμεθα
τοῖς προτέροισιν·
610 νῦν δ᾽, ἔσται γὰρ βίος ἐκ κοινοῦ, τί τὸ κέρδος μὴ
καταθεῖναι;

ΒΛΕΠΤΡΟΣ

ἢν μείρακ᾽ ἰδὼν ἐπιθυμήσῃ καὶ βούληται
σκαλαθῦραι,
ἕξει τούτων ἀφελὼν δοῦναι, τῶν ἐκ κοινοῦ δὲ
μεθέξει
ξυγκαταδαρθών.

ΠΡΑΞΑΓΟΡΑ

ἀλλ᾽ ἐξέσται προῖκ᾽ αὐτῷ ξυγκαταδαρθεῖν.

BLEPYRUS

What do you mean?

PRAXAGORA

No one will be doing *anything* as a result of poverty, be-
cause everyone will have all the necessities: bread, salt
fish, barley cakes, cloaks, wine, garlands, chickpeas. So
where's his profit in not contributing? If you can find it, do
tell me.

BLEPYRUS

But even now, aren't the people who have all this the
bigger thieves?

NEIGHBOR

That was before, my friend, when we lived under the pre-
vious system. But now that everyone will be living from a
common fund, where's his profit in not contributing?

BLEPYRUS

If he spots a girl and fancies her and wants a poke, he'll be
able to take her price from this common fund and have all
that's commonly wanted, when he's slept with her.

PRAXAGORA

No, he'll be able to sleep with her free of charge. I'm mak-

καὶ ταύτας γὰρ κοινὰς ποιῶ τοῖς ἀνδράσι
συγκατακεῖσθαι
καὶ παιδοποιεῖν τῷ βουλομένῳ.

ΒΛΕΠΤΡΟΣ
615   πῶς οὖν οὐ πάντες ἴασιν
ἐπὶ τὴν ὡραιοτάτην αὐτῶν καὶ ζητήσουσιν ἐρείδειν;

ΠΡΑΞΑΓΟΡΑ
αἱ φαυλότεραι καὶ σιμότεραι παρὰ τὰς σεμνὰς
    καθεδοῦνται·
κᾆτ᾽ ἢν ταύτης ἐπιθυμήσῃ, τὴν αἰσχρὰν πρῶθ᾽
    ὑποκρούσει.

ΒΛΕΠΤΡΟΣ
καὶ πῶς ἡμᾶς τοὺς πρεσβύτας, ἢν ταῖς αἰσχραῖσι
    συνῶμεν,
620 οὐκ ἐπιλείψει τὸ πέος πρότερον πρὶν ἐκεῖσ᾽ οἷ φῂς
    ἀφικέσθαι;

ΠΡΑΞΑΓΟΡΑ
οὐχὶ μαχοῦνται περὶ σοῦ· θάρρει, μὴ δείσῃς· οὐχὶ
    μαχοῦνται.

ΒΛΕΠΤΡΟΣ
περὶ τοῦ;

ΠΡΑΞΑΓΟΡΑ
        τοῦ μὴ ξυγκαταδαρθεῖν. καὶ σοὶ τοιοῦτον
    ὑπάρχει.

ing these girls common property too, for the men to sleep
with and make babies with as they please.

BLEPYRUS

Then won't everyone head for the prettiest girl and try to
bang her?

PRAXAGORA

The homely and bob-nosed women will sit right beside the
classy ones, and if a man wants the latter he'll have to ball
the ugly one first.

BLEPYRUS

But what about us older men? If we go with the ugly ones
first, our cocks won't have anything left when we get where
you said.

PRAXAGORA

They won't fight about you, don't worry. Never fear, they
won't fight.

BLEPYRUS

Fight about what?

PRAXAGORA

About not getting to sleep with you! Anyway, you've got
that problem as it is.

ΒΛΕΠΤΡΟΣ

τὸ μὲν ὑμέτερον γνώμην τιν' ἔχει· προβεβούλευται
    γὰρ ὅπως ἂν
μηδεμιᾶς ᾖ τρύπημα κενόν· τὸ δὲ τῶν ἀνδρῶν τί
    ποιήσει;
625 φεύξονται γὰρ τοὺς αἰσχίους, ἐπὶ τοὺς δὲ καλοὺς
    βαδιοῦνται.

ΠΡΑΞΑΓΟΡΑ

ἀλλὰ φυλάξουσ' οἱ φαυλότεροι τοὺς καλλίους
    ἀπιόντας
ἀπὸ τοῦ δείπνου καὶ τηρήσουσ' ἐπὶ τοῖσιν
    δημοσίοισιν.
κοὐκ ἐξέσται παρὰ τοῖσι καλοῖς <καὶ τοῖς
    μεγάλοις> καταδαρθεῖν
ταῖσι γυναιξὶν πρὶν τοῖς αἰσχροῖς καὶ τοῖς μικροῖς
    χαρίσωνται.

ΒΛΕΠΤΡΟΣ

630 ἡ Λυσικράτους ἄρα νυνὶ ῥὶς ἴσα τοῖσι καλοῖσι
    φρονήσει;

ΓΕΙΤΩΝ

νὴ τὸν Ἀπόλλω· καὶ δημοτική γ' ἡ γνώμη καὶ
    καταχήνη
τῶν σεμνοτέρων ἔσται πολλὴ καὶ τῶν σφραγῖδας
    ἐχόντων,
ὅταν ἐμβάδ' ἔχων εἴπῃ πρότερος, "παραχώρει κᾆτ'
    ἐπιτήρει,

BLEPYRUS

Your side of the equation makes a certain sense; you've planned it that no woman's hole will go unplugged. But what do you mean to do for the men's side? Because the women will shun the ugly men and go for the handsome ones.

PRAXAGORA

Well, the homely men will tail the handsomer ones as they leave their dinner parties, and keep an eye on them in the public places, for it won't be lawful for handsome and tall men to sleep with any women who haven't first accommodated the uglies and the runts.

BLEPYRUS

So now Lysicrates'[49] nose will be up there with the beautiful people's!

NEIGHBOR

Absolutely. What's more, it's an idea that favors ordinary people, and it'll be a great joke on the big shots with signet rings when a guy wearing clogs speaks up and says, "Step

[49] Unidentifiable.

---

[628] οἱ φαυλότεροι ante κοὐκ R Λ (v. om. Γ) del. et suppl. Tyrwhitt

ὅταν ἤδη 'γὼ διαπραξάμενος παραδῶ σοι
δευτεριάζειν."

ΒΛΕΠΤΡΟΣ

635 πῶς οὖν οὕτω ζώντων ἡμῶν τοὺς αὑτοῦ παῖδας
ἕκαστος
ἔσται δυνατὸς διαγιγνώσκειν;

ΠΡΑΞΑΓΟΡΑ
τί δὲ δεῖ; πατέρας γὰρ ἅπαντας
τοὺς πρεσβυτέρους αὐτῶν εἶναι τοῖσι χρόνοισιν
νομιοῦσιν.

ΒΛΕΠΤΡΟΣ
οὔκουν ἄγξουσ' εὖ καὶ χρηστῶς ἑξῆς πάντ' ἄνδρα
γέροντα
διὰ τὴν ἄγνοιαν; ἐπεὶ καὶ νῦν γιγνώσκοντες πατέρ'
ὄντα
640 ἄγχουσι· τί δῆθ' ὅταν ἀγνὼς ᾖ; πῶς οὐ τότε
κἀπιχεσοῦνται;

ΠΡΑΞΑΓΟΡΑ
ἀλλ' ὁ παρεστὼς οὐκ ἐπιτρέψει· τότε δ' αὐτοῖς οὐκ
ἔμελ' οὐδὲν
τῶν ἀλλοτρίων, ὅστις τύπτοι, νῦν δ' ἢν πληγέντος
ἀκούσῃ,
μὴ αὐτὸν ἐκεῖνον τύπτει δεδιὼς τοῖς δρῶσιν τοῦτο
μαχεῖται.

638 πάντ' ἄνδρα van Leeuwen: τὸν πάντα a

aside and wait till I'm finished; then I'll give you seconds!"

BLEPYRUS

Well, if we live this way, how will any man be able to recognize his own children?[50]

PRAXAGORA

Why should he? They'll regard all older men of a certain age to be their fathers.

BLEPYRUS

Then from now on won't sons methodically strangle each and every older man? Because even now they strangle their acknowledged father; what will happen when he's unacknowledged? Won't they'll shit on him as well?

PRAXAGORA

No, the bystanders won't allow it. They didn't used to care who was beating other people's fathers, but now if they hear a man getting beaten they'll worry that the victim is their own dad, and fight the attackers.

[50] Compare Plato, *Republic* 460–65.

ARISTOPHANES

ΒΛΕΠΤΡΟΣ

τὰ μὲν ἄλλα λέγεις οὐδὲν σκαιῶς· εἰ δὲ προσελθὼν
Ἐπίκουρος
645 ἢ Λευκόλοφος "πάππαν" με καλεῖ, τοῦτ᾽ ἤδη δεινὸν
ἀκοῦσαι.

ΓΕΙΤΩΝ

πολὺ μέντοι δεινότερον τούτου τοῦ πράγματός
ἐστι—

ΒΛΕΠΤΡΟΣ

τὸ ποῖον;

ΓΕΙΤΩΝ

εἴ σε φιλήσειεν Ἀρίστυλλος φάσκων αὑτοῦ πατέρ᾽
εἶναι.

ΒΛΕΠΤΡΟΣ

οἰμώζοι γ᾽ ἂν καὶ κωκύοι.

ΓΕΙΤΩΝ

σὺ δέ γ᾽ ὄζοις ἂν καλαμίνθης.

ΠΡΑΞΑΓΟΡΑ

ἀλλ᾽ οὗτος μὲν πρότερον γέγονεν πρὶν τὸ ψήφισμα
γενέσθαι,
ὥστ᾽ οὐχὶ δέος μή σε φιλήσῃ.

ΒΛΕΠΤΡΟΣ

650   δεινὸν μεντἂν ἐπεπόνθειν.
τὴν γῆν δὲ τίς ἔσθ᾽ ὁ γεωργήσων;

650 -θη (-θην Λ) Bentley

BLEPYRUS

There's nothing wrong with your analysis, but if Epicurus[51] or Leucolophus[52] start hanging around and calling me "daddy," it's going to be frightful to listen to.

NEIGHBOR

Well, I can think of something a lot more frightful.

BLEPYRUS

Such as?

NEIGHBOR

If Aristyllus[53] claims you're his father and kisses you!

BLEPYRUS

If he does he'll sorely regret it!

NEIGHBOR

And you'd smell of *eau d'ordure*!

PRAXAGORA

But he was born before our decree, so there's no need to worry that he'll kiss you.

BLEPYRUS

He'd still have been sorry if he did. But who will there be to farm the land?

---

[51] Unidentifiable.

[52] Presumably Leucolophides, the son of Adeimantus of Scambonidae, considered a traitor at Aegospotami and prosecuted in 393 (Dem. 19.191); cf. *Frogs* 1512 n.

[53] Apparently a coprophiliac, cf. *Wealth* 313–14, fr. 551.

ΠΡΑΞΑΓΟΡΑ

οἱ δοῦλοι. σοὶ δὲ μελήσει,
ὅταν ᾖ δεκάπουν τὸ στοιχεῖον, λιπαρῷ χωρεῖν ἐπὶ
δεῖπνον.

ΒΛΕΠΤΡΟΣ

περὶ δ᾽ ἱματίων τίς πόρος ἔσται; καὶ γὰρ τοῦτ᾽
ἔστιν ἐρέσθαι.

ΠΡΑΞΑΓΟΡΑ

τὰ μὲν ὄνθ᾽ ὑμῖν πρῶτον ὑπάρξει, τὰ δὲ λοίφ᾽ ἡμεῖς
ὑφανοῦμεν.

ΒΛΕΠΤΡΟΣ

655 ἓν ἔτι ζητῶ· πῶς ἤν τις ὄφλῃ παρὰ τοῖς ἄρχουσι
δίκην τῳ;
πόθεν ἐκτείσει ταύτην; οὐ γὰρ τῶν κοινῶν γ᾽ ἐστὶ
δίκαιον.

ΠΡΑΞΑΓΟΡΑ

ἀλλ᾽ οὐδὲ δίκαι πρῶτον ἔσονται.

ΒΛΕΠΤΡΟΣ

τουτὶ τοὔπος σ᾽ ἐπιτρίψει.

ΓΕΙΤΩΝ

κἀγὼ ταύτην γνώμην ἐθέμην.

ΠΡΑΞΑΓΟΡΑ

τοῦ γὰρ τάλαν οὕνεκ᾽ ἔσονται;

ΒΛΕΠΤΡΟΣ

πολλῶν οὕνεκα, νὴ τὸν Ἀπόλλω· πρῶτον δ᾽ ἑνὸς
οὕνεκα δήπου,

PRAXAGORA

The slaves. Your only concern will be to get slicked up and
head for dinner when the shadow stick's at ten feet.

BLEPYRUS

Then about overcoats, who will supply them? It's a reason-
able question.

PRAXAGORA

Your current supply will do for now; later we'll weave you
new ones.

BLEPYRUS

One more question: what happens if someone loses a law-
suit to somebody before the archons? How will he pay the
judgment? It wouldn't be fair to take that from the com-
mon pool.

PRAXAGORA

But there won't be any lawsuits in the first place.

BLEPYRUS

That statement will be your undoing.

NEIGHBOR

That's my verdict too.

PRAXAGORA

But what, poor dear, will they sue over?

BLEPYRUS

My god, lots of things. Foremost, of course, is when a

ARISTOPHANES

ἤν τις ὀφείλων ἐξαρνῆται.

ΠΡΑΞΑΓΟΡΑ

660   πόθεν οὖν ἐδάνεισ᾽ ὁ δανείσας,
ἐν τῷ κοινῷ πάντων ὄντων; κλέπτων δήπου ᾽στ᾽
   ἐπίδηλος.

ΓΕΙΤΩΝ

νὴ τὴν Δήμητρ᾽, εὖ γε διδάσκεις.

ΒΛΕΠΤΡΟΣ

           τουτὶ τοίνυν φρασάτω μοι,
τῆς αἰκείας οἱ τύπτοντες πόθεν ἐκτείσουσιν, ἐπειδὰν
εὐωχηθέντες ὑβρίζωσιν; τοῦτο γὰρ οἶμαί σ᾽
   ἀπορήσειν.

ΠΡΑΞΑΓΟΡΑ

665 ἀπὸ τῆς μάζης ἧς σιτεῖται· ταύτης γὰρ ὅταν τις
   ἀφαιρῇ,
οὐχ ὑβριεῖται φαύλως οὕτως αὖθις τῇ γαστρὶ
   κολασθείς.

ΒΛΕΠΤΡΟΣ

οὐδ᾽ αὖ κλέπτης οὐδεὶς ἔσται;

ΠΡΑΞΑΓΟΡΑ

           πῶς γὰρ κλέψει μετὸν αὐτῷ;

ΒΛΕΠΤΡΟΣ

οὐδ᾽ ἀποδύσουσ᾽ ἄρα τῶν νυκτῶν;

ΓΕΙΤΩΝ

           οὐκ ἢν οἴκοι γε καθεύδῃς.

debtor refuses to pay.

PRAXAGORA

But where did the creditor get the money to lend, all funds being in common? He's obviously a thief—of course!

NEIGHBOR

By golly, that's right.

BLEPYRUS

But let her answer me this: when people act rowdy after a dinner party and get into fights, how will they pay their fines for assault? That one, I think, will stump you.

PRAXAGORA

He'll pay out of his own bread ration. A decrease there will hit him right in the belly, so he'll think twice before he gets rowdy again.

BLEPYRUS

And will no one be a thief?

PRAXAGORA

Of course not: how can anyone steal what he's got a share in?

BLEPYRUS

So no more muggers at night?

NEIGHBOR

Not if you sleep at home!

ΠΡΑΞΑΓΟΡΑ

οὐδ᾽ ἤν γε θύραζ᾽ ὥσπερ πρότερον· βίοτος γὰρ
πᾶσιν ὑπάρξει.

670 ἤν δ᾽ ἀποδύῃ γ᾽, αὐτὸς δώσει· τί γὰρ αὐτῷ πρᾶγμα
μάχεσθαι;
ἔτερον γὰρ ἰὼν ἐκ τοῦ κοινοῦ κρεῖττον ἐκείνου
κομιεῖται.

ΒΛΕΠΤΡΟΣ

οὐδὲ κυβεύσουσ᾽ ἄρ᾽ ἄνθρωποι;

ΠΡΑΞΑΓΟΡΑ

περὶ τοῦ γὰρ τοῦτο ποιήσει;

ΒΛΕΠΤΡΟΣ

τὴν δὲ δίαιταν τίνα ποιήσεις;

ΠΡΑΞΑΓΟΡΑ

κοινὴν πᾶσιν. τὸ γὰρ ἄστυ
μίαν οἴκησίν φημι ποιήσειν συρρήξασ᾽ εἰς ἒν
ἅπαντα,
ὥστε βαδίζειν εἰς ἀλλήλων.

ΒΛΕΠΤΡΟΣ

675 τὸ δὲ δεῖπνον ποῦ παραθήσεις;

ΠΡΑΞΑΓΟΡΑ

τὰ δικαστήρια καὶ τὰς στοιὰς ἀνδρῶνας πάντα
ποιήσω.

ΒΛΕΠΤΡΟΣ

τὸ δὲ βῆμα τί σοι χρήσιμον ἔσται;

PRAXAGORA

Not even when you go out as you used to, for all will be content with their condition. If someone tries to steal a cloak, the victim will let him have it. Why should he put up a fight? He can go to the common store and get a better one.

BLEPYRUS

And people won't gamble at dice?

PRAXAGORA

What would they use for stakes?

BLEPYRUS

And what standard of living will you establish?

PRAXAGORA

The same for all. I mean to convert the city into one household by breaking down all partitions to make one dwelling, so that everyone can walk into everyone else's space.

BLEPYRUS

And where will you serve dinner?

PRAXAGORA

I'll turn all the courthouses and porticoes into dining rooms.

BLEPYRUS

What will you do with the speakers' platform?

ARISTOPHANES

ΠΡΑΞΑΓΟΡΑ

τοὺς κρατῆρας καταθήσω
καὶ τὰς ὑδρίας, καὶ ῥαψῳδεῖν ἔσται τοῖς
παιδαρίοισιν
τοὺς ἀνδρείους ἐν τῷ πολέμῳ, κεί τις δειλὸς
γεγένηται,
ἵνα μὴ δειπνῶσ᾽ αἰσχυνόμενοι.

ΒΛΕΠΤΡΟΣ

680   νὴ τὸν Ἀπόλλω χάριέν γε.
τὰ δὲ κληρωτήρια ποῖ τρέψεις;

ΠΡΑΞΑΓΟΡΑ

          εἰς τὴν ἀγορὰν καταθήσω,
κᾆτα στήσασα παρ᾽ Ἁρμοδίῳ κληρώσω πάντας,
ἕως ἂν
εἰδὼς ὁ λαχὼν ἀπίῃ χαίρων ἐν ὁποίῳ γράμματι
δειπνεῖ.
καὶ κηρύξει τοὺς ἐκ τοῦ βῆτ᾽ ἐπὶ τὴν στοιὰν
ἀκολουθεῖν
685   τὴν βασίλειον δειπνήσοντας, τὸ δὲ θῆτ᾽ εἰς τὴν
παρὰ ταύτην,
τοὺς δ᾽ ἐκ τοῦ κάππ᾽ ἐς τὴν στοιὰν χωρεῖν τὴν
ἀλφιτόπωλιν.

ΒΛΕΠΤΡΟΣ

ἵνα κάπτωσιν;

ΠΡΑΞΑΓΟΡΑ

μὰ Δί᾽, ἀλλ᾽ ἵν᾽ ἐκεῖ δειπνῶσιν.

PRAXAGORA

I'll use it to store mixing bowls and water jugs, and the children can use it to recite poetry about brave men in battle, or about anyone who was cowardly, so they'll be ashamed to share the meal.

BLEPYRUS

An absolutely charming idea! And what will you do with the ballot boxes?

PRAXAGORA

I'll have them set up in the marketplace by Harmodius' statue[54] and have everyone draw lots, till each one has got his letter and gone off happily to whatever dining hall it assigns. Thus the Herald will instruct everyone with the letter R to proceed to dinner at the Royal Stoa; the Thetas will go to the one next to it; and the G's to the Grain Market.

BLEPYRUS

G as in guzzle?

PRAXAGORA

No, as in gourmandise.

---

[54] Located near the center of the marketplace.

ΒΛΕΠΤΡΟΣ

ὅτῳ δὲ τὸ γράμμα
μὴ ’ξελκυσθῇ καθ’ ὃ δειπνήσει, τούτους ἀπελῶσιν
ἅπαντες;

ΠΡΑΞΑΓΟΡΑ

ἀλλ’ οὐκ ἔσται τοῦτο παρ’ ἡμῖν·
690   πᾶσι γὰρ ἄφθονα πάντα παρέξομεν,
ὥστε μεθυσθεὶς αὐτῷ στεφάνῳ
πᾶς τις ἄπεισιν τὴν δᾷδα λαβών.
αἱ δὲ γυναῖκες κατὰ τὰς διόδους
προσπίπτουσαι τοῖς ἀπὸ δείπνου
695   τάδε λέξουσιν· "δεῦρο παρ’ ἡμᾶς·
ἐνθάδε μεῖράξ ἐσθ’ ὡραία."
"παρ’ ἐμοὶ δ’ ἑτέρα,"
φήσει τις ἄνωθ’ ἐξ ὑπερῴου,
"καὶ καλλίστη καὶ λευκοτάτη·
700   πρότερον μέντοι δεῖ σε καθεύδειν
αὐτῆς παρ’ ἐμοί."
702a τοῖς εὐπρεπέσιν δ’ ἀκολουθοῦντες
702b καὶ μειρακίοις οἱ φαυλότεροι
τοιάδ’ ἐροῦσιν· "ποῖ θεῖς οὗτος;
πάντως οὐδὲν δράσεις ἐλθών.
705   τοῖς γὰρ σιμοῖς καὶ τοῖς αἰσχροῖς
ἐψήφισται προτέροις βινεῖν,
ὑμᾶς δὲ τέως θρῖα λαβόντας
διφόρου συκῆς
ἐν τοῖς προθύροισι δέφεσθαι."

BLEPYRUS

But people who draw no letter for dinner, will everyone push them away from the table?

PRAXAGORA

That won't happen with us; we'll provide everything for everyone unstintingly. Every single man will leave drunk, garland still on and torch in hand, and along the streets as they come from dinner the ladies will accost them like this: "Come here to our place; there's a lovely girl in here." "And over here," another one will cry from a second storey window, "is a very fine and exquisitely pale girl. Of course, you'll have to sleep with me before her." And the inferior men will chase after the handsome lads, saying "Hey you, where do you think you're off to? You're going to get nothing anyway: the law says that the the pug-nosed and the ugly get first fuck, while you grab the petals of your double-hung fig branch and jerk off in the doorway!" So

φέρε νυν φράσον μοι, ταῦτ' ἀρέσκει σφῷν;

BΛΕΠΤΡΟΣ καὶ ΓΕΙΤΩΝ

710   πάνυ.

ΠΡΑΞΑΓΟΡΑ

βαδιστέον τἄρ' ἐστὶν εἰς ἀγορὰν ἐμοί,
ἵν' ἀποδέχωμαι τὰ προσιόντα χρήματα,
λαβοῦσα κηρύκαιναν εὔφωνόν τινα.
ἐμὲ γὰρ ἀνάγκη ταῦτα δρᾶν ᾑρημένην
715 ἄρχειν, καταστῆσαί τε τὰ ξυσσίτια,
ὅπως ἂν εὐωχῆσθε πρῶτον τήμερον.

ΒΛΕΠΤΡΟΣ

ἤδη γὰρ εὐωχησόμεσθα;

ΠΡΑΞΑΓΟΡΑ
                      φήμ' ἐγώ.
ἔπειτα τὰς πόρνας καταπαῦσαι βούλομαι
ἁπαξαπάσας.

ΒΛΕΠΤΡΟΣ
       ἵνα τί;

ΓΕΙΤΩΝ
           δῆλον τουτογί·
720 ἵνα τῶν νέων ἔχωσιν αὗται τὰς ἀκμάς.

ΠΡΑΞΑΓΟΡΑ

καὶ τάς γε δούλας οὐχὶ δεῖ κοσμουμένας
τὴν τῶν ἐλευθέρων ὑφαρπάζειν Κύπριν,
ἀλλὰ παρὰ τοῖς δούλοισι κοιμᾶσθαι μόνον,
κατωνάκην τὸν χοῖρον ἀποτετιλμένας.

tell me, does my plan meet with your approval?

BLEPYRUS AND NEIGHBOR

Very much so!

PRAXAGORA

Then I'll be going off to the marketplace to receive the goods as they come in, after I pick up a girl with a strong voice to be my herald. These are my duties as the woman elected to office. I must also organize the communal dinners, so you can have your first banquet this very day.

BLEPYRUS

The banquets are to start right away?

PRAXAGORA

That's what I'm telling you. Then I want to put all the prostitutes out of business.

BLEPYRUS

Why?

NEIGHBOR

(*indicating Praxagora and the Chorus*) That's obvious: so that these women can have their prick of the young men!

PRAXAGORA

What's more, slave girls will no longer be allowed to wear makeup and steal away the fond hearts of the free boys. They'll be allowed to sleep only with slaves, with their pussies trimmed like a woollen barn jacket.

ΒΛΕΠΤΡΟΣ

725 φέρε νυν ἐγώ σοι παρακολουθῶ πλησίον,
ἵν᾽ ἀποβλέπωμαι καὶ λέγωσιν ἐμὲ ταδί,
"τὸν τῆς στρατηγοῦ τοῦτον οὐ θαυμάζετε;"

ΓΕΙΤΩΝ

ἐγὼ δ᾽, ἵν᾽ εἰς ἀγοράν γε τὰ σκεύη φέρω,
προχειριοῦμαι κἀξετάσω τὴν οὐσίαν.

ΧΟΡΟΥ

ΓΕΙΤΩΝ

730 χώρει σὺ δεῦρο, κιναχύρα, καλὴ καλῶς
τῶν χρημάτων θύραζε πρώτη τῶν ἐμῶν,
ὅπως ἂν ἐντετριμμένη κανηφορῇς,
πολλοὺς κάτω δὴ θυλάκους στρέψασ᾽ ἐμούς.
ποῦ 'σθ᾽ ἡ διφροφόρος; ἡ χύτρα, δεῦρ᾽ ἔξιθι·
735 νὴ Δία μέλαινά γ᾽, ὡς ἂν εἰ τὸ φάρμακον
ἕψουσ᾽ ἔτυχες ᾧ Λυσικράτης μελαίνεται.
ἴστω παρ᾽ αὐτήν· δεῦρ᾽ ἴθ᾽, ἡ κομμώτρια.
φέρε δεῦρο ταύτην τὴν ὑδρίαν, ὑδριαφόρε,
ἐνταῦθα. σὺ δὲ δεῦρ᾽ ἡ κιθαρῳδός, ἔξιθι,
740 πολλάκις ἀναστήσασά μ᾽ εἰς ἐκκλησίαν
ἀωρὶ νύκτωρ διὰ τὸν ὄρθριον νόμον.
ὁ τὴν σκάφην λαβὼν προΐτω· τὰ κηρία
κόμιζε, τοὺς θαλλοὺς καθίστη πλησίον,

---

55 The utensils are arrayed like participants in a major ritual procession such as the Panathenaea.
56 The scholia identify this utensil as a hand mill.

BLEPYRUS

Say, I'd like to tag along at your side, and share the spotlight, with people saying, "Look, that's none other than the Lady Commander's husband!"

Exit PRAXAGORA and BLEPYRUS.

NEIGHBOR

As for me, if I'm to be taking my possessions to the marketplace, I'd better collect them and take inventory of what I've got.

Exit NEIGHBOR into his house.

The Chorus sing a brief song, not preserved; then NEIGHBOR comes out of his house, followed by two slaves, Sicon and Parmenon, who bring out household utensils and line them up in the street.

NEIGHBOR

You there, my pretty bran sieve, first of my possessions, come prettily outside here, so you can be the Basket Bearer,[55] since you're so well powdered by all those bags of my flour that you've emptied. Where's the Chair Bearer? Cooking Pot, come outside here. My God, you're black, as if it was you that boiled the concoction Lysicrates uses to dye his hair! You stand next to her. Come here, my Maid in Waiting. Jug Bearer, bring that jug over here. And you come out here and be our Musician, since you've so often gotten me up for Assembly with your morning song at an ungodly hour of the night.[56] Whoever's got the Tray come forward; bring the honeycombs, and put the olive

καὶ τὼ τρίποδ᾽ ἐξένεγκε καὶ τὴν λήκυθον.
745 τὰ χυτρίδι᾽ ἤδη καὶ τὸν ὄχλον ἀφίετε.

ΑΝΗΡ
ἐγὼ καταθήσω τἀμά; κακοδαίμων ἄρα
ἀνὴρ ἔσομαι καὶ νοῦν ὀλίγον κεκτημένος.
μὰ τὸν Ποσειδῶ γ᾽ οὐδέποτ᾽, ἀλλὰ βασανιῶ
πρώτιστον αὐτὰ πολλάκις καὶ σκέψομαι.
750 οὐ γὰρ τὸν ἐμὸν ἱδρῶτα καὶ φειδωλίαν
οὐδὲν πρὸς ἔπος οὕτως ἀνοήτως ἐκβαλῶ,
πρὶν ἐκπύθωμαι πᾶν τὸ πρᾶγμ᾽ ὅπως ἔχει.
οὗτος, τί τὰ σκευάρια ταυτὶ βούλεται;
πότερον μετοικιζόμενος ἐξενήνοχας
αὔτ᾽ ἢ φέρεις ἐνέχυρα θήσων;

ΓΕΙΤΩΝ
755   οὐδαμῶς.

ΑΝΗΡ
τί δῆτ᾽ ἐπὶ στοίχου ᾽στὶν οὕτως; οὔ τι μὴν
Ἱέρωνι τῷ κήρυκι πομπὴν πέμπετε;

ΓΕΙΤΩΝ
μὰ Δί᾽, ἀλλ᾽ ἀποφέρειν αὐτὰ μέλλω τῇ πόλει
ἐς τὴν ἀγορὰν κατὰ τοὺς δεδογμένους νόμους.

ΑΝΗΡ
μέλλεις ἀποφέρειν;

ΓΕΙΤΩΝ
πάνυ γε.

branches down beside them; bring out the two Tripods and the Oil Flask. Now let the throng of little pots follow along.

Enter SELFISH MAN.

SELFISH MAN
Imagine me turning in my stuff! I'd be a sorry excuse for a man, and virtually brainless. Never, by god! No, first of all I'll have to test and study the situation very carefully. On the strength of mere words I'm hardly about to throw away the fruits of my sweat and thrift in this sort of mindless way, until I've made thorough inquiries about the whole situation. You there, what's the point of these utensils? Are you moving? Do you mean to pawn them?

NEIGHBOR
Certainly not.

SELFISH MAN
Then why are they lined up like this? You're not arranging a procession for Hieron[57] the auctioneer, are you?

NEIGHBOR
God no! We're getting them ready to go to the marketplace for surrender to the state: it's the law of the land.

SELFISH MAN
You mean to turn them in?

NEIGHBOR
Of course.

[57] Otherwise unknown.

ΑΝΗΡ

760   κακοδαίμων ἄρ᾽ εἶ,
νὴ τὸν Δία τὸν σωτῆρα.

ΓΕΙΤΩΝ
πῶς;

ΑΝΗΡ
      πῶς; ῥᾳδίως.

ΓΕΙΤΩΝ
τί δ᾽; οὐχὶ πειθαρχεῖν με τοῖς νόμοισι δεῖ;

ΑΝΗΡ
ποίοισιν, ὦ δύστηνε;

ΓΕΙΤΩΝ
      τοῖς δεδογμένοις.

ΑΝΗΡ
δεδογμένοισιν; ὡς ἀνόητος ἦσθ᾽ ἄρα.

ΓΕΙΤΩΝ
ἀνόητος;

ΑΝΗΡ
765   οὐ γάρ; ἠλιθιώτατος μὲν οὖν
ἁπαξαπάντων.

ΓΕΙΤΩΝ
     ὅτι τὸ ταττόμενον ποιῶ;

ΑΝΗΡ
τὸ ταττόμενον γὰρ δεῖ ποιεῖν τὸν σώφρονα;

350

SELFISH MAN

Then, Zeus save us, you're a loser!

NEIGHBOR

How so?

SELFISH MAN

It's easy to see.

NEIGHBOR

Really? I'm not supposed to obey the laws?

SELFISH MAN

What laws, you sadsack?

NEIGHBOR

The laws that have been duly enacted.

SELFISH MAN

Duly enacted! How stupid can you get?

NEIGHBOR

Stupid?

SELFISH MAN

Well, aren't you? And not just stupid, but the biggest simpleton in the world?

NEIGHBOR

Because I do what I'm told?

SELFISH MAN

So you think the man of sense ought to do what he's told?

ΓΕΙΤΩΝ

μάλιστα πάντων.

ΑΝΗΡ

τὸν μὲν οὖν ἀβέλτερον.

ΓΕΙΤΩΝ

σὺ δ᾽ οὐ καταθεῖναι διανοεῖ;

ΑΝΗΡ

φυλάξομαι,

770 πρὶν ἄν γ᾽ ἴδω τὸ πλῆθος ὅ τι βουλεύεται.

ΓΕΙΤΩΝ

τί γὰρ ἄλλο γ᾽ ἢ φέρειν παρεσκευασμένοι
τὰ χρήματ᾽ εἰσίν;

ΑΝΗΡ

ἀλλ᾽ ἰδὼν ἐπειθόμην.

ΓΕΙΤΩΝ

λέγουσι γοῦν ἐν ταῖς ὁδοῖς.

ΑΝΗΡ

λέξουσι γάρ.

ΓΕΙΤΩΝ

καί φασιν οἴσειν ἀράμενοι.

ΑΝΗΡ

φήσουσι γάρ.

ΓΕΙΤΩΝ

ἀπολεῖς ἀπιστῶν πάντ᾽.

NEIGHBOR
Above everything else.

SELFISH MAN
No, that's what the imbecile does.

NEIGHBOR
So you don't intend to turn in your goods?

SELFISH MAN
I intend to be cautious, until I see what most people do.

NEIGHBOR
Why, they're getting ready to turn in their goods, of course.

SELFISH MAN
Well, I'll believe that when I see it.

NEIGHBOR
That's what they're saying around town, anyway.

SELFISH MAN
Say it? Sure they will.

NEIGHBOR
They're promising to bring their stuff in personally.

SELFISH MAN
Promise? Sure they will.

NEIGHBOR
You'll be the death of me with your total skepticism!

ΑΝΗΡ

775   ἀπιστήσουσι γάρ.

ΓΕΙΤΩΝ

ὁ Ζεύς σέ γ᾽ ἐπιτρίψειεν.

ΑΝΗΡ

     ἐπιτρίψουσι γάρ.
οἴσειν δοκεῖς τιν᾽ ὅστις αὐτῶν νοῦν ἔχει;
οὐ γὰρ πάτριον τοῦτ᾽ ἐστίν.

ΓΕΙΤΩΝ

       ἀλλὰ λαμβάνειν
ἡμᾶς μόνον δεῖ;

ΑΝΗΡ

     νὴ Δία· καὶ γὰρ οἱ θεοί.
780 γνώσει δ᾽ ἀπὸ τῶν χειρῶν γε τῶν ἀγαλμάτων·
ὅταν γὰρ εὐχώμεσθα διδόναι τἀγαθά,
ἕστηκεν ἐκτείνοντα τὴν χεῖρ᾽ ὑπτίαν,
οὐχ ὥς τι δώσοντ᾽ ἀλλ᾽ ὅπως τι λήψεται.

ΓΕΙΤΩΝ

ὦ δαιμόνι᾽ ἀνδρῶν, ἔα με τῶν προὔργου τι δρᾶν.
785 ταυτὶ γάρ ἐστι συνδετέα. ποῦ μοῦσθ᾽ ἱμάς;

ΑΝΗΡ

ὄντως γὰρ οἴσεις;

ΓΕΙΤΩΝ

     ναὶ μὰ Δία, καὶ δὴ μὲν οὖν
τωδὶ ξυνάπτω τὼ τρίποδε.

SELFISH MAN

Be skeptical? Sure they will.

NEIGHBOR

God damn you!

SELFISH MAN

Damn? Sure they will. Do you really think that anyone with a brain is going to turn it in? That's not in our national character.

NEIGHBOR

You mean we should only take?

SELFISH MAN

Absolutely. That's what the gods do too. You can tell by the hands on their statues: whenever we pray for blessings, they stand there with their hands out, palm up, plainly not to give something, but to get something.

NEIGHBOR

Listen, wacko, let me get on with my business here. These things need to be packed. Where's my strap?

SELFISH MAN

So you're really going to surrender them?

NEIGHBOR

Yes indeed. In fact, I'm tying up these two tripods now.

ΑΝΗΡ

τῆς μωρίας,
τὸ μηδὲ περιμείναντα τοὺς ἄλλους ὅ τι
δράσουσιν εἶτα τηνικαῦτ᾽ ἤδη—

ΓΕΙΤΩΝ

τί δρᾶν;

ΑΝΗΡ

790 ἐπαναμένειν, ἔπειτα διατρίβειν ἔτι.

ΓΕΙΤΩΝ

ἵνα δὴ τί;

ΑΝΗΡ

σεισμὸς εἰ γένοιτο πολλάκις,
ἢ πῦρ ἀπότροπον, ἢ διάξειεν γαλῆ,
παύσαιντ᾽ ἂν ἐσφέροντες, ὠμβρόντητε σύ.

ΓΕΙΤΩΝ

χαρίεντα γοῦν πάθοιμ᾽ ἄν, εἰ μὴ 'χοιμ᾽ ὅποι
ταῦτα καταθείην.

ΑΝΗΡ

795 μὴ γὰρ οὐ λάβοις ὅποι;
θάρρει, καταθήσεις, κἂν ἕνης ἔλθῃς.

ΓΕΙΤΩΝ

τιή;

ΑΝΗΡ

ἐγᾦδα τούτους χειροτονοῦντας μὲν ταχύ,
ἅττ᾽ ἂν δὲ δόξῃ, ταῦτα πάλιν ἀρνουμένους.

SELFISH MAN

What foolishness, not to wait and see what others are going to do, and then and only then—

NEIGHBOR

Do what?

SELFISH MAN

Wait a little longer, then put it off.

NEIGHBOR

The object being what?

SELFISH MAN

There might be an earthquake, or some ill-omened lightning, or a black cat darting across the street. That would put a stop to their depositions, you mental case!

NEIGHBOR

I'd be in a fine mess if I found no room left to deposit this stuff.

SELFISH MAN

Ah, no more room. Don't worry, they'll take your deposit even if you wait a couple of days.

NEIGHBOR

What do you mean?

SELFISH MAN

I know these people: they're quick to vote on something, then they turn around and refuse to abide by whatever it was.

ΓΕΙΤΩΝ

οἴσουσιν, ὦ τᾶν.

ΑΝΗΡ

ἢν δὲ μὴ κομίσωσι, τί;

ΓΕΙΤΩΝ

ἀμέλει, κομιοῦσιν.

ΑΝΗΡ

800   ἢν δὲ μὴ κομίσωσι, τί;

ΓΕΙΤΩΝ

μαχούμεθ᾽ αὐτοῖς.

ΑΝΗΡ

ἢν δὲ κρείττους ὦσι, τί;

ΓΕΙΤΩΝ

ἄπειμ᾽ ἐάσας.

ΑΝΗΡ

ἢν δὲ πωλῶσ᾽ αὐτά, τί;

ΓΕΙΤΩΝ

διαρραγείης.

ΑΝΗΡ

ἢν διαρραγῶ δέ, τί;

ΓΕΙΤΩΝ

καλῶς ποιήσεις.

ΑΝΗΡ

σὺ δ᾽ ἐπιθυμεῖς εἰσφέρειν;

NEIGHBOR

They'll bring in their stuff, pal.

SELFISH MAN

And what if they don't?

NEIGHBOR

Don't worry, they will.

SELFISH MAN

And what if they don't?

NEIGHBOR

We'll fight them.

SELFISH MAN

And what if they outnumber you?

NEIGHBOR

I'll walk away and leave them to it.

SELFISH MAN

And if they sell your stuff?

NEIGHBOR

Blast you to bits!

SELFISH MAN

And if I do blast to bits?

NEIGHBOR

You'll be doing a great service.

SELFISH MAN

Do you really want to surrender your stuff?

ΓΕΙΤΩΝ

805 ἔγωγε· καὶ γὰρ τοὺς ἐμαυτοῦ γείτονας
ὁρῶ φέροντας.

ΑΝΗΡ

πάνυ γ' ἂν οὖν Ἀντισθένης
αὔτ' εἰσενέγκοι· πολὺ γὰρ ἐμμελέστερον
πρότερον χέσαι πλεῖν ἢ τριάκονθ' ἡμέρας.

ΓΕΙΤΩΝ

οἴμωζε.

ΑΝΗΡ

Καλλίμαχος δ' ὁ χοροδιδάσκαλος
αὐτοῖσιν εἰσοίσει τι;

ΓΕΙΤΩΝ

810   πλείω Καλλίου.

ΑΝΗΡ

ἄνθρωπος οὗτος ἀποβαλεῖ τὴν οὐσίαν.

ΓΕΙΤΩΝ

δεινόν γε λέγεις.

ΑΝΗΡ

τί δεινόν; ὥσπερ οὐχ ὁρῶν
ἀεὶ τοιαῦτα γιγνόμενα ψηφίσματα.
οὐκ οἶσθ' ἐκεῖν' οὕδοξε τὸ περὶ τῶν ἁλῶν;

ΓΕΙΤΩΝ

ἔγωγε.

NEIGHBOR

I do. And I see that my own neighbors are doing it too.

SELFISH MAN

Antisthenes would contribute his stuff—sure! It would suit him much better to take a month-long shit first!

NEIGHBOR

Go to hell!

SELFISH MAN

And Callimachus the chorus master,[58] would he contribute anything?

NEIGHBOR

More than Callias.[59]

SELFISH MAN

(*aside*) This guy's gonna lose everything he has!

NEIGHBOR

That's putting it pretty drastically.

SELFISH MAN

What's so drastic? As if I don't see decrees like this all the time! Don't you remember the one about salt?

NEIGHBOR

Sure.

---

[58] Otherwise unknown.
[59] See *Frogs* 429 n.

ARISTOPHANES

ΑΝΗΡ

815
τοὺς χαλκοῦς δ' ἐκείνους ἡνίκα
ἐψηφισάμεθ', οὐκ οἶσθα;

ΓΕΙΤΩΝ

καὶ κακόν γέ μοι
τὸ κόμμ' ἐγένετ' ἐκεῖνο. πωλῶν γὰρ βότρυς
μεστὴν ἀπῆρα τὴν γνάθον χαλκῶν ἔχων,
κἄπειτ' ἐχώρουν εἰς ἀγορὰν ἐπ' ἄλφιτα.
820
ἔπειθ', ὑπέχοντος ἄρτι μου τὸν θύλακον,
ἀνέκραγ' ὁ κῆρυξ· "μὴ δέχεσθαι μηδένα
χαλκὸν τὸ λοιπόν· ἀργύρῳ γὰρ χρώμεθα."

ΑΝΗΡ

τὸ δ' ἔναγχος οὐχ ἅπαντες ἡμεῖς ὤμνυμεν
τάλαντ' ἔσεσθαι πεντακόσια τῇ πόλει
825
τῆς τετταρακοστῆς, ἣν ἐπόρισ' Εὐριπίδης;
κεὐθὺς κατεχρύσου πᾶς ἀνὴρ Εὐριππίδην.
ὅτε δὴ δ' ἀνασκοπουμένοις ἐφαίνετο
ὁ Διὸς Κόρινθος καὶ τὸ πρᾶγμ' οὐκ ἤρκεσεν,
πάλιν κατεπίττου πᾶς ἀνὴρ Εὐριππίδην.

ΓΕΙΤΩΝ

830
οὐ ταὐτόν, ὦ τᾶν. τότε μὲν ἡμεῖς ἤρχομεν,
νῦν δ' αἱ γυναῖκες.

ΑΝΗΡ

ἅς γ' ἐγὼ φυλάξομαι,
νὴ τὸν Ποσειδῶ, μὴ κατουρήσωσί μου.

362

SELFISH MAN

And when we voted for those copper coins, remember that?[60]

NEIGHBOR

Yes, that coinage was certainly bad for me. After selling my grapes I shoved off with a mouthful of those coppers to the market for barley, and as soon as I held out my bag the herald shouted, "no one is to take any more copper; we're using silver now."

SELFISH MAN

And didn't we all recently swear that the city would raise five hundred talents from the two and a half percent tax levied by Heurippides?[61] And how Heurippides was everyone's golden boy? But finally we looked into the matter more carefully, and it turned out to be just "Corinthus son of Zeus,"[62] a quite inadequate measure; then Heurippides became everyone's tarbaby.

NEIGHBOR

That's different, pal: we were in power then; now the women are.

SELFISH MAN

And I mean to keep an eye on them, so help me Poseidon, so they don't piss all over me!

---

[60] See *Frogs* 718–37. [61] Son of Adeimantus of Myrrhinus and protege of Conon; after the failure of his tax plan, his name came to denote a score of forty in games of dice.

[62] See *Frogs* 439 n.

825–29 Εὐριππίδης Bergk: Εὐριπίδης a
946 δράσει Brunck: δράσοι Γ: δράσεις R Λ

ARISTOPHANES

ΓΕΙΤΩΝ

οὐκ οἶδ' ὅ τι ληρεῖς. φέρε σὺ τἀνάφορον, ὁ παῖς.

ΚΗΡΥΚΑΙΝΑ

ὦ πάντες ἀστοί, νῦν γὰρ οὕτω ταῦτ' ἔχει,
835 χωρεῖτ', ἐπείγεσθ' εὐθὺ τῆς στρατηγίδος,
ὅπως ἂν ὑμῖν ἡ τύχη κληρουμένοις
φράσῃ καθ' ἕκαστον ἄνδρ' ὅποι δειπνήσετε·
ὡς αἱ τράπεζαί γ' εἰσὶν ἐπινενημέναι
ἀγαθῶν ἁπάντων καὶ παρεσκευασμέναι,
840 κλῖναί τε σισυρῶν καὶ δαπίδων νενασμέναι.
κρατῆρας ἐγκιρνᾶσιν, αἱ μυροπώλιδες
ἑστᾶσ' ἐφεξῆς, τὰ τεμάχη ῥιπίζεται,
λαγῷ' ἀναπηγνύασι, πόπανα πέττεται,
στέφανοι πλέκονται, φρύγεται τραγήματα,
845 χύτρας ἔτνους ἕψουσιν αἱ νεώταται·
Σμοῖος δ' ἐν αὐταῖς ἱππικὴν στολὴν ἔχων
τὰ τῶν γυναικῶν διακαθαίρει τρύβλια·
Γέρων δὲ χωρεῖ χλανίδα καὶ κονίποδας
ἔχων, καχάζων μεθ' ἑτέρου νεανίου·
850 ἐμβὰς δὲ κεῖται καὶ τρίβων ἐρριμμένος.
πρὸς ταῦτα χωρεῖθ', ὡς ὁ τὴν μᾶζαν φέρων
ἕστηκεν· ἀλλὰ τὰς γνάθους διοίγετε.

ΑΝΗΡ

οὐκοῦν βαδιοῦμαι δῆτα. τί γὰρ ἕστηκ' ἔχων
ἐνταῦθ', ἐπειδὴ ταῦτα τῇ πόλει δοκεῖ;

364

NEIGHBOR

I don't know what you're going on about. Hoist that baggage, boy.

Enter HERALD.

HERALD

Now here this, all you citizens—yes, all are included now: get a move on and go straight to the Lady Commander's place, so that the luck of the draw can determine where each man among you will dine. The tables are set and heaped high with every kind of treat, and the couches are draped with cushions and coverlets. They're mixing the wine in bowls, and the scent girls are standing by. The fish fillets are on the grill; they're spitting hares; the rolls are abake, garlands plaited, munchies roasting; the littlest girls are boiling pots of pea soup, and Smoeus[63] is with them in his riding suit, licking the women's bowls clean. And Geron's[64] there wearing a new suit and fashionable pumps, joking with another young blade, his cheap boots and shabby cloak tossed aside. This is what you're invited to, so come along! The slaves are waiting with your daily bread; just open your mouths!

Exit HERALD.

SELFISH MAN

Well then, I'm ready to go! Why stand around here when the city has ratified all this?

[63] Noted for cunnilingus.
[64] Otherwise unknown; the name means "oldster."

ΓΕΙΤΩΝ

855 καὶ ποῖ βαδιεῖ σὺ μὴ καταθεὶς τὴν οὐσίαν;

ΑΝΗΡ

ἐπὶ δεῖπνον.

ΓΕΙΤΩΝ

οὐ δῆτ᾽, ἤν γ᾽ ἐκείναις νοῦς ἐνῇ,
πρίν ἄν γ᾽ ἀπενέγκῃς.

ΑΝΗΡ

ἀλλ᾽ ἀποίσω.

ΓΕΙΤΩΝ

πηνίκα;

ΑΝΗΡ

οὐ τοὐμόν, ὦ τᾶν, ἐμποδὼν ἔσται.

ΓΕΙΤΩΝ

τί δαί;

ΑΝΗΡ

ἑτέρους ἀποίσειν φήμ᾽ ἔθ᾽ ὑστέρους ἐμοῦ.

ΓΕΙΤΩΝ

βαδιεῖ δὲ δειπνήσων ὅμως;

ΑΝΗΡ

860   τί γὰρ πάθω;
τὰ δυνατὰ γὰρ δεῖ τῇ πόλει ξυλλαμβάνειν
τοὺς εὖ φρονοῦντας.

ΓΕΙΤΩΝ

ἢν δὲ κωλύσωσι, τί;

NEIGHBOR

Just where do you think you're going? You haven't turned in your goods.

SELFISH MAN

To dinner.

NEIGHBOR

Oh no you don't! If the women have any sense they won't feed you till you've brought in your property.

SELFISH MAN

Don't worry, I will.

NEIGHBOR

When?

SELFISH MAN

It won't be me that holds anyone up, my man.

NEIGHBOR

Meaning what?

SELFISH MAN

I mean others are bound to turn their stuff in even later than me.

NEIGHBOR

And you mean to go to dinner anyway?

SELFISH MAN

Sure, how can I help but go? All right-minded people should assist the state to the best of their ability.

NEIGHBOR

And what if they won't let you in?

ΑΝΗΡ

ὀμόσ᾽ εἶμι κύψας.

ΓΕΙΤΩΝ

ἢν δὲ μαστιγῶσι, τί;

ΑΝΗΡ

καλούμεθ᾽ αὐτάς.

ΓΕΙΤΩΝ

ἢν δὲ καταγελῶσι, τί;

ΑΝΗΡ

ἐπὶ ταῖς θύραις ἑστώς—

ΓΕΙΤΩΝ

τί δράσεις; εἰπέ μοι.

ΑΝΗΡ

τῶν ἐσφερόντων ἁρπάσομαι τὰ σιτία.

ΓΕΙΤΩΝ

βάδιζε τοίνυν ὕστερος· σὺ δ᾽, ὦ Σίκων
καὶ Παρμένων, αἴρεσθε τὴν παμπησίαν.

ΑΝΗΡ

φέρε νυν ἐγώ σοι ξυμφέρω.

ΓΕΙΤΩΝ

μή, μηδαμῶς.

δέδοικα γὰρ μὴ καὶ παρὰ τῇ στρατηγίδι,
ὅταν κατατιθῶ, προσποιῇ τῶν χρημάτων.

ΑΝΗΡ

νὴ τὸν Δία δεῖ γοῦν μηχανήματός τινος,
ὅπως τὰ μὲν ὄντα χρήμαθ᾽ ἕξω, τοῖσδέ τε

SELFISH MAN

I'll lower my head and charge them.

NEIGHBOR

And if they beat you like a slave?

SELFISH MAN

I'll sue them.

NEIGHBOR

And if they laugh at your threats?

SELFISH MAN

I'll stand in the doorway—

NEIGHBOR

And do what, I'd like to know.

SELFISH MAN

—and snatch the food that they bring in.

NEIGHBOR

In that case you'd better go in after me. You there, Sicon, and you too, Parmenon, hoist my estate.

SELFISH MAN

Let me help you carry that.

NEIGHBOR

No, no thanks! I don't want to bring my contribution to the Lady Commander and have you pretending it's yours.

Exit NEIGHBOR and Slaves.

SELFISH MAN

I definitely need some kind of scheme to save the property

τῶν ματτομένων κοινῇ μεθέξω πως ἐγώ.
875   ὀρθῶς, ἔμοιγε φαίνεται· βαδιστέον
ὁμόσ᾿ ἐστὶ δειπνήσοντα κοὐ μελλητέον.

ΧΟΡΟΥ

ΓΡΑΥΣ Α

τί ποθ᾿ ἄνδρες οὐχ ἥκουσιν; ὥρα δ᾿ ἦν πάλαι.
ἐγὼ δὲ καταπεπλασμένη ψιμυθίῳ
ἕστηκα καὶ κροκωτὸν ἠμφιεσμένη
880   ἀργός, μινυρομένη τι πρὸς ἐμαυτὴν μέλος,
παίζουσ᾿ ὅπως ἂν περιλάβοιμ᾿ αὐτῶν τινα
παριόντα. Μοῦσαι, δεῦρ᾿ ἴτ᾿ ἐπὶ τοὐμὸν στόμα
μελύδριον εὑροῦσαί τι τῶν Ἰωνικῶν.

ΝΕΑΝΙΣ

νῦν μέν με παρακύψασα προὔφθης, ὦ σαπρά.
885   ᾤου δ᾿ ἐρήμας οὐ παρούσης ἐνθάδε
ἐμοῦ τρυγήσειν καὶ προσάξεσθαί τινα
ᾄδουσ᾿· ἐγὼ δ᾿, ἢν τοῦτο δρᾷς, ἀντᾴσομαι.
κεἰ γὰρ δι᾿ ὄχλου τοῦτ᾿ ἐστὶ τοῖς θεωμένοις,
ὅμως ἔχει τερπνόν τι καὶ κωμῳδικόν.

ΓΡΑΥΣ Α

890   τούτῳ διαλέγου κἀποχώρησον· σὺ δέ,
φιλοττάριον αὐλητά, τοὺς αὐλοὺς λαβὼν
ἄξιον ἐμοῦ καὶ σοῦ προσαύλησον μέλος.

εἴ τις ἀγαθὸν βούλεται πα-
        θεῖν τι, παρ᾿ ἐμοὶ χρὴ καθεύδειν·
οὐ γὰρ ἐν νέαις τὸ σοφὸν ἔν-

I've got and also share in the treats being whipped up for these people. I think I've got it; I must commence Operation Dinner, and on the double!

Exit SELFISH MAN.

The Chorus sing a brief song, not preserved.

FIRST OLD WOMAN appears in the central doorway of the stage house, while a GIRL appears at the window of the house next door; both look up and down the street.

FIRST OLD WOMAN

What can be keeping the men? They're long overdue. Here I am, all plastered with makeup and wearing a party dress, just standing around, whistling myself a song, and my trap all set to snag one of them as he passes. Ye Muses, come sit on my lips, and find me some spicy Ionian tune.

GIRL

This time you're on lookout ahead of me, old moldy. You thought you'd strip an unwatched vineyard when I wasn't around, and entice some guy with your singing. If you try it, I'll sing a song of my own. And even if the audience finds this boring, there's still something pleasantly comic about it.

FIRST OLD WOMAN

(*presenting her rump*) Put your complaints in here, and get lost! (*to the piper*) You, my dear little piper, pick up your pipes and blow a tune that'll do us both proud.

> Whoever wants to have a good time
> should sleep with me.
> For finesse dwells not in girls

371

895 ἐστιν, ἀλλ' ἐν ταῖς πεπείροις.
 οὐδέ τοι στέργειν ἂν ἐθέλοι μᾶλλον ἢ 'γὼ
τὸν φίλον ᾧπερ ξυνείην,
ἀλλ' ἐφ' ἕτερον ἂν πέτοιτο.

NEANIΣ

900 μὴ φθόνει ταῖσιν νέαισι·
τὸ τρυφερὸν γὰρ ἐμπέφυκε
τοῖς ἁπαλοῖσι μηροῖς,
κἀπὶ τοῖς μήλοις ἐπαν-
θεῖ· σὺ δ', ὦ γραῦ, παραλέλεξαι κἀντέτριψαι
905 τῷ Θανάτῳ μέλημα.

ΓΡΑΤΣ Α

ἐκπέσοι σου τὸ τρῆμα
τό τ' ἐπίκλιντρον ἀποβάλοις
βουλομένη σποδεῖσθαι.
κἀπὶ τῆς κλίνης ὄφιν προσελκύσαιο
910 βουλομένη φιλῆσαι.

NEANIΣ

αἰαῖ, τί ποτε πείσομαι;
οὐχ ἥκει μοὐταῖρος·
μόνη δ' αὐτοῦ λείπομ'· ἡ
γάρ μοι μήτηρ ἄλλη βέβηκεν.
καὶ τἆλλα μ' οὐδὲν τὰ μετὰ ταῦτα δεῖ λέγειν.
915 ἀλλ', ὦ μαῖ, ἱκετεύομαι,
κάλει τὸν Ὀρθαγόραν,
917a ὅπως σαυτῆς ἂν κατόναι',
917b ἀντιβολῶ σε.

but in ripe women.
You can bet she's no readier than I
to cherish the boyfriend I'm with,
but more likely to flit to another.

GIRL

Don't despise the girls,
for softness resides
in their tender thighs
and blossoms on their boobs.
But you, old bag, are tweezed and plastered,
the Grim Reaper's heartthrob.

FIRST OLD WOMAN

I hope your twat falls off,
and when you hanker for humping
you can't find your back seat.
And in bed when you hanker for smooching
I hope you take a snake in your arms.

GIRL

Ah, what will become of me?
My boyfriend hasn't come,
and I'm left here alone,
for my mother's out somewhere,
and I needn't say what comes next.
Well, nanny, I beg you,
call Doctor Dildo
so you can enjoy yourself.
Pretty please!

ΓΡΑΤΣ Α

ἤδη τὸν ἀπ᾽ Ἰωνίας
τρόπον, τάλαινα, κνησιᾷς.
920 δοκεῖς δέ μοι καὶ λάβδα κατὰ τοὺς Λεσβίους.

ΝΕΑΝΙΣ

ἀλλ᾽ οὐκ ἄν ποθ᾽ ὑφαρπάσαι-
ο τἀμὰ παίγνια· τὴν δ᾽
923a   ἐμὴν ὥραν οὐκ ἀπολεῖς
923b   οὐδ᾽ ἀπολήψει.

ΓΡΑΤΣ Α

ᾆδ᾽ ὁπόσα βούλει καὶ παράκυφθ᾽ ὥσπερ γαλῆ·
925 οὐδεὶς γὰρ ὡς σὲ πρότερον εἴσεισ᾽ ἀντ᾽ ἐμοῦ.

ΝΕΑΝΙΣ

οὔκουν ἐπ᾽ ἐκφοράν γε· καινόν γ᾽, ὦ σαπρά.

ΓΡΑΤΣ Α

οὐ δῆτα.

ΝΕΑΝΙΣ

τί γὰρ ἂν γραῒ καινά τις λέγοι;

ΓΡΑΤΣ Α

οὐ τοὐμὸν ὀδυνήσει σε γῆρας.

ΝΕΑΝΙΣ

ἀλλὰ τί;
ἔγχουσα μᾶλλον καὶ τὸ σὸν ψιμύθιον;

ΓΡΑΤΣ Α

τί μοι διαλέγει;

FIRST OLD WOMAN

Poor thing, you're already
itching for the Ionian toy,[65]
and I think you also want to do the L, like the
    Lesbians.[66]

GIRL

But you'll never snatch
my boytoys away,
never spoil my youth
or poach a share.

FIRST OLD WOMAN

Well, sing any tune you like, and peer out like a cat, because no man's going to visit you before me.

GIRL

Not for my funeral, anyway. Hey, that's a new one, old moldy!

FIRST OLD WOMAN

No it isn't.

GIRL

No, who could tell an old lady anything new?

FIRST OLD WOMAN

It's not my age that'll hurt you.

GIRL

What then? Your makeup and rouge?

FIRST OLD WOMAN

Why do you keep talking to me?

---

[65] I.e., a dildo.
[66] With whom classical Greeks associated fellatio.

ΝΕΑΝΙΣ
σὺ δὲ τί διακύπτεις;

ΓΡΑΥΣ Α

930   ἐγώ;
ᾄδω πρὸς ἐμαυτὴν Ἐπιγένει τὠμῷ φίλῳ.

ΝΕΑΝΙΣ
σοὶ γὰρ φίλος τίς ἐστιν ἄλλος ἢ Γέρης;

ΓΡΑΥΣ Α
δείξει γε καὶ σοί. τάχα γὰρ εἴσιν ὡς ἐμέ.
ὁδὶ γὰρ αὐτός ἐστιν.

ΝΕΑΝΙΣ
               οὐ σοῦ γ᾽, ὦλεθρε,
δεόμενος οὐδέν.

ΓΡΑΥΣ Α

935   νὴ Δί᾽, ὦ φθίνυλλα σύ.

ΝΕΑΝΙΣ
δείξει τάχ᾽ αὐτός, ὡς ἔγωγ᾽ ἀπέρχομαι.

ΓΡΑΥΣ Α
κἄγωγ᾽, ἵνα γνῷς ὡς πολύ σου μεῖζον φρονῶ.

ΕΠΙΓΕΝΗΣ
εἴθ᾽ ἐξῆν παρὰ τῇ νέᾳ καθεύδειν
καὶ μὴ ᾽δει πρότερον διασποδῆσαι

---

67 Identified by ancient commentators as the Geres of *Acharnians* 605, who would now be at least seventy; alternatively, the name may merely suggest *geron* ("old man").

GIRL

And why are you still peering around?

FIRST OLD WOMAN

Me? I'm humming a tune for my sweetheart Epigenes.

GIRL

You've got a sweetheart? You must mean Geres.[67]

FIRST OLD WOMAN

You'll see for yourself, since he'll soon be coming to visit me. In fact, here he comes now!

Enter EPIGENES, *wearing a garland and holding a torch.*

GIRL

Not for any business with you, old pest!

FIRST OLD WOMAN

Au contraire, miss twiggy!

GIRL

He'll soon settle this himself; I'll be off now.

GIRL *goes inside.*

FIRST OLD WOMAN

Me too, just so you'll see how much surer I am than you.

FIRST OLD WOMAN *goes inside.*

EPIGENES

How I wish I could sleep with the girl
and didn't first have to bang

940 ἀνάσιμον ἢ πρεσβυτέραν·
οὐ γὰρ ἀνασχετὸν τοῦτό γ᾽ ἐλευθέρῳ.

ΓΡΑΥΣ Α

οἰμώζων ἄρα νὴ Δία σποδήσεις·
οὐ γὰρ τἀπὶ Χαριξένης τάδ᾽ ἐστίν.
κατὰ τὸν νόμον ταῦτα ποιεῖν
945 ἔστι δίκαιον, εἰ δημοκρατούμεθα.

ἀλλ᾽ εἶμι τηρήσουσ᾽ ὅ τι καὶ δράσει ποτέ.

ΕΠΙΓΕΝΗΣ

εἴθ᾽, ὦ θεοί, λάβοιμι τὴν καλὴν μόνην,
ἐφ᾽ ἣν πεπωκὼς ἔρχομαι πάλαι ποθῶν.

ΝΕΑΝΙΣ

ἐξηπάτησα τὸ κατάρατον γρᾴδιον·
950 φρούδη γάρ ἐστιν οἰομένη μ᾽ ἔνδον μένειν.
ἀλλ᾽ οὑτοσὶ γὰρ αὐτὸς οὗ 'μεμνήμεθα.

(στρ.)   δεῦρο δή, δεῦρο δή,
952b   φίλον ἐμόν, δεῦρό μοι
               πρόσελθε καὶ ξύνευνος
954a   τὴν εὐφρόνην ὅπως ἔσει.
954b   πάνυ γάρ τις ἔρως με δονεῖ
955   τῶνδε τῶν σῶν βοστρύχων.

952–68 horum carminum etsi textus (praecipue in antistropha)
per periphrasin depravatus est, sensus tamen satis perspicuus
961a suppl. Wilamowitz, cf. ad 963

a pug-nose or a crone!
This doesn't sit well with a free man.

FIRST OLD WOMAN reappears.

FIRST OLD WOMAN

Then by heaven you'll bang to your sorrow;
this isn't Charixene's heyday.[68]
If we still live under democracy,
we've got to do this legal and proper!

But I'll go inside to see what he ends up doing.

FIRST OLD WOMAN goes back inside.

EPIGENES

Ye gods, let me catch this pretty girl alone! It's her I've
come for in my cups, her I've long desired.

GIRL reappears in her window.

GIRL

I've completely foxed the little old lady, damn her; she's
gone, thinking that I was going to stay inside. But here's the
very boy we were talking about.

Hither now, hither now,
my dear one, hither
come to me and promise to be
my bedmate through the night.
A powerful passion sets me awhirl
for those curly locks of yours.

[68] Evidently a courtesan of the pre-democratic era, cf.
Cratinus fr. 153, Theopompus com. fr. 51.

ἄτοπος δ' ἔγκειταί μοί τις πόθος,
ὅς με διακναίσας ἔχει.
μέθες, ἱκνοῦμαί σ', Ἔρως,
959a   καὶ ποίησον τόνδ' ἐς εὐνὴν
959b   τὴν ἐμὴν ἱκέσθαι.

ΕΠΙΓΕΝΗΣ

(ἀντ.)   δεῦρο δή, δεῦρο δή,
961a   ⟨φίλον ἐμόν,⟩ καὶ σύ μοι
961b   καταδραμοῦσα τὴν θύραν
961c   τήνδ' ἄνοιξον· εἰ δὲ μή,
       καταπεσὼν κείσομαι.
       ἀλλ' ἐν σῷ βούλομ' ἐγὼ κόλπῳ
       πληκτίζεσθαι μετὰ τῆς πυγῆς.
965   Κύπρι, τί μ' ἐκμαίνεις ἐπὶ ταύτῃ;
       μέθες, ἱκνοῦμαί σ', Ἔρως,
968a   καὶ ποίησον τήνδ' ἐς εὐνὴν
968b   τὴν ἐμὴν ἱκέσθαι.

(στρ.)   καὶ ταῦτα μέντοι μετρίως
       πρὸς τὴν ἐμὴν ἀνάγκην
       εἰρημέν' ἐστίν. σὺ δέ μοι,
970   φίλτατον, ὦ ἱκετεύω,
       ἄνοιξον, ἀσπάζου με·
       διά τοι σὲ πόνους ἔχω.

(ἀντ.)   ὦ χρυσοδαίδαλτον ἐμὸν
       μέλημα, Κύπριδος ἔρνος,

A strange longing besets me
and grinds me in its grip.
Release me, Eros, I beg you!
Please make this boy
come to my very own bed.

EPIGENES

Hither now, hither now,
you too, my dear one,
run down to this door for me
and open it wide; if you don't,
I'll fall flat on the doorstep!
But I'd rather lie in your lap
and swap strokes with your butt.
Aphrodite, why drive me mad for this girl?
Release me, Eros, I beg you!
Please make this girl
come to my very own bed.

Yet these words of mine
can but blandly express
my actual compulsion. But now,
my darling, oh, I beg you,
open up and welcome me.
It's you I'm hurting for!

Ah my fine-wrought golden
prize, bud of Aphrodite,

---

963 ἀλλ' Wilamowitz: φίλον, ἀλλ' a
963 σῷ βούλομ' ἐγὼ Wilamowitz: τῷ σῷ βούλομαι a
987 πεττοῖς (πετοῖς Γ) Γ A: Παιτοῖς R Λ Schol.

μέλιττα Μούσης, Χαρίτων
 θρέμμα, Τρυφῆς πρόσωπον,
975a ἄνοιξον, ἀσπάζου με.
975b διά τοι σὲ πόνους ἔχω.

ΓΡΑΤΣ Α

οὗτος, τί κόπτεις; μῶν ἐμὲ ζητεῖς;

ΕΠΙΓΕΝΗΣ

πόθεν;

ΓΡΑΤΣ Α

καὶ τὴν θύραν γ᾽ ἤραττες.

ΕΠΙΓΕΝΗΣ

ἀποθάνοιμ᾽ ἄρα.

ΓΡΑΤΣ Α

τοῦ δαὶ δεόμενος δᾷδ᾽ ἔχων ἐλήλυθας;

ΕΠΙΓΕΝΗΣ

Ἀναφλύστιον ζητῶν τιν᾽ ἄνθρωπον.

ΓΡΑΤΣ Α

τίνα;

ΕΠΙΓΕΝΗΣ

980 οὐ τὸν Σεβῖνον, ὃν σὺ προσδοκᾷς ἴσως.

ΓΡΑΤΣ Α

νὴ τὴν Ἀφροδίτην, ἤν τε βούλῃ γ᾽ ἤν τε μή.

honeybee of the Muses, nurseling
of the Graces, personification of Pleasure,
open up and welcome me.
Its you I'm hurting for!

Enter FIRST OLD WOMAN *from her door.*

FIRST OLD WOMAN

Hey you, what's this knocking? Not looking for me, are
you?

EPIGENES

Surely you jest!

FIRST OLD WOMAN

Well, you certainly battered on my door.

EPIGENES

I'll be damned if I did!

FIRST OLD WOMAN

Then what are you after, with the torch and all?

EPIGENES

I'm looking for a fellow from Wankton.[69]

FIRST OLD WOMAN

Which one?

EPIGENES

Not Mr. Humpus, whom you're probably expecting.

FIRST OLD WOMAN

(*seizing him*) Yes, by Aphrodite, whether you like it or not.

[69] See *Frogs* 427 n.

ARISTOPHANES

ΕΠΙΓΕΝΗΣ

ἀλλ᾽ οὐχὶ νυνὶ τὰς ὑπερεξηκοντέτεις
εἰσάγομεν, ἀλλ᾽ εἰσαῦθις ἀναβεβλήμεθα·
τὰς ἐντὸς εἴκοσιν γὰρ ἐκδικάζομεν.

ΓΡΑΤΣ Α

985 ἐπὶ τῆς προτέρας ἀρχῆς γε ταῦτ᾽ ἦν, ὦ γλύκων·
νυνὶ δὲ πρῶτον εἰσάγειν ἡμᾶς δοκεῖ.

ΕΠΙΓΕΝΗΣ

τῷ βουλομένῳ γε κατὰ τὸν ἐν πεττοῖς νόμον.

ΓΡΑΤΣ Α

ἀλλ᾽ οὐδ᾽ ἐδείπνεις κατὰ τὸν ἐν πεττοῖς νόμον.

ΕΠΙΓΕΝΗΣ

οὐκ οἶδ᾽ ὅ τι λέγεις· τηνδεδί μοι κρουστέον.

ΓΡΑΤΣ Α

990 ὅταν γε κρούσῃς τὴν ἐμὴν πρῶτον θύραν.

ΕΠΙΓΕΝΗΣ

ἀλλ᾽ οὐχὶ νυνὶ κρησέραν αἰτούμεθα.

ΓΡΑΤΣ Α

οἶδ᾽ ὅτι φιλοῦμαι· νῦν δὲ θαυμάζεις ὅτι
θύρασί μ᾽ ηὗρες. ἀλλὰ πρόσαγε τὸ στόμα.

ΕΠΙΓΕΝΗΣ

ἀλλ᾽ ὦ μέλ᾽ ὀρρωδῶ τὸν ἐραστήν σου.

ΓΡΑΤΣ Α

τίνα;

384

ASSEMBLYWOMEN

EPIGENES

(*shaking her off*) Wait: we're entering no hearings for cases
over sixty just now; we've tabled them for future consider-
ation, while we clear our docket of cases under twenty.

FIRST OLD WOMAN

That was true under the old system, my sweet; but under
current law you've got to enter us first.

EPIGENES

It's dealer's choice, by the rules of play.

FIRST OLD WOMAN

But you didn't eat dinner by those rules of play.

EPIGENES

I don't know what you're talking about. I've got to beat on
this door.

FIRST OLD WOMAN

Not until you first beat on mine!

EPIGENES

No thanks, we're not after a beater just now.

FIRST OLD WOMAN

I know I'm loved; you were just surprised to find me out-
side. Come on, give us a kiss.

EPIGENES

No ma'am; I'm terrified of your lover.

FIRST OLD WOMAN

Who's that?

1043 λόγον Le Febvre: νόμον a

ΕΠΙΓΕΝΗΣ

τὸν τῶν γραφέων ἄριστον.

ΓΡΑΤΣ Α

995   οὗτος δ᾽ ἐστὶ τίς;

ΕΠΙΓΕΝΗΣ

ὃς τοῖς νεκροῖσι ζωγραφεῖ τὰς ληκύθους.
ἀλλ᾽ ἄπιθ᾽, ὅπως μή σ᾽ ἐπὶ θύραισιν ὄψεται.

ΓΡΑΤΣ Α

οἶδ᾽, οἶδ᾽ ὅ τι βούλει.

ΕΠΙΓΕΝΗΣ

           καὶ γὰρ ἐγὼ σέ, νὴ Δία.

ΓΡΑΤΣ Α

μὰ τὴν Ἀφροδίτην, ἥ μ᾽ ἔλαχε κληρουμένη,
μὴ ᾽γώ σ᾽ ἀφήσω.

ΕΠΙΓΕΝΗΣ

1000   παραφρονεῖς, ὦ γρᾴδιον.

ΓΡΑΤΣ Α

ληρεῖς· ἐγὼ δ᾽ ἄξω σ᾽ ἐπὶ τἀμὰ στρώματα.

ΕΠΙΓΕΝΗΣ

τί δῆτα κρεάγρας τοῖς κάδοις ὠνοίμεθ᾽ ἄν,
ἐξὸν καθέντα γρᾴδιον τοιουτονὶ
ἐκ τῶν φρεάτων τοὺς κάδους ξυλλαμβάνειν;

ΓΡΑΤΣ Α

1005 μὴ σκῶπτέ μ᾽, ὦ τάλαν, ἀλλ᾽ ἕπου δεῦρ᾽ ὡς ἐμέ.

EPIGENES

The best-selling painter.

FIRST OLD WOMAN

And who's that?

EPIGENES

The one who decorates funeral urns.[70] Better scram before he spots you in the doorway.

FIRST OLD WOMAN

I know what you're after, I know.

EPIGENES

And I certainly know what *you're* after!

FIRST OLD WOMAN

By Aphrodite, who gave me the luck of the draw, I'm not giving you up!

EPIGENES

You're crazy, old lady.

FIRST OLD WOMAN

Nonsense! I'm going to escort you to my bed.

EPIGENES

Why should we buy tongs for our buckets, when we could run a crone like this down the well and use her to haul up those buckets?

FIRST OLD WOMAN

No more teasing, my boy; just come this way to my place.

---

[70] I.e., Death.

ΕΠΙΓΕΝΗΣ

ἀλλ' οὐκ ἀνάγκη μοὐστίν, εἰ μὴ τῶν ἐμῶν
τὴν πεντακοσιοστὴν κατέθηκας τῇ πόλει.

ΓΡΑΤΣ Α

νὴ τὴν Ἀφροδίτην, δεῖ γε μέντοι σ'· ὡς ἐγὼ
τοῖς τηλικούτοις ξυγκαθεύδουσ' ἥδομαι.

ΕΠΙΓΕΝΗΣ

1010   ἐγὼ δὲ ταῖς γε τηλικαύταις ἄχθομαι,
κοὐκ ἂν πιθοίμην οὐδέποτ'.

ΓΡΑΤΣ Α

                          ἀλλὰ νὴ Δία
ἀναγκάσει τουτί σε.

ΕΠΙΓΕΝΗΣ

                    τοῦτο δ' ἐστὶ τί;

ΓΡΑΤΣ Α

ψήφισμα, καθ' ὅ σε δεῖ βαδίζειν ὡς ἐμέ.

ΕΠΙΓΕΝΗΣ

λέγ' αὐτὸ τί ποτε κᾆστι.

ΓΡΑΤΣ Α

                    καὶ δή σοι λέγω.

1015   "ἔδοξε ταῖς γυναιξίν, ἢν ἀνὴρ νέος
νέας ἐπιθυμῇ, μὴ σποδεῖν αὐτὴν πρὶν ἂν
τὴν γραῦν προκρούσῃ πρῶτον. ἢν δὲ μὴ 'θέλῃ
πρότερον προκρούειν, ἀλλ' ἐπιθυμῇ τῆς νέας,
ταῖς πρεσβυτέραις γυναιξὶν ἔστω τὸν νέον
1020   ἕλκειν ἀνατεὶ λαβομένας τοῦ παττάλου."

EPIGENES

No! I don't have to, unless you've paid the city the .2% tax on me.

FIRST OLD WOMAN

By Aphrodite, you do have to. I just love sleeping with boys your age.

EPIGENES

And I just hate sleeping with women your age! I'll never consent.

FIRST OLD WOMAN

(*producing a scroll*) But this will make you.

EPIGENES

What's that?

FIRST OLD WOMAN

A decree that says you've got to come to my house.

EPIGENES

Read out what it actually says.

FIRST OLD WOMAN

All right, I shall. (*reading*) "The women have decreed: if a young man desires a young woman he may not hump her until he bangs an old woman first. Should he in his desire for the young woman refuse to do this preliminary banging, the older women shall be entitled with impunity to drag the young man off by his pecker."

ΕΠΙΓΕΝΗΣ
οἴμοι, Προκρούστης τήμερον γενήσομαι.

ΓΡΑΥΣ Α
τοῖς γὰρ νόμοις τοῖς ἡμετέροισι πειστέον.

ΕΠΙΓΕΝΗΣ
τί δ’ ἢν ἀφαιρῆταί μ’ ἀνὴρ τῶν δημοτῶν
ἢ τῶν φίλων ἐλθών τις;

ΓΡΑΥΣ Α
        ἀλλ’ οὐ κύριος
1025 ὑπὲρ μέδιμνόν ἐστ’ ἀνὴρ οὐδεὶς ἔτι.

ΕΠΙΓΕΝΗΣ
ἐξωμοσία δ’ οὐκ ἔστιν;

ΓΡΑΥΣ Α
        οὐ γὰρ δεῖ στροφῆς.

ΕΠΙΓΕΝΗΣ
ἀλλ’ ἔμπορος εἶναι σκήψομαι.

ΓΡΑΥΣ Α
        κλάων γε σύ.

ΕΠΙΓΕΝΗΣ
τί δῆτα χρὴ δρᾶν;

ΕΠΙΓΕΝΗΣ
        δεῦρ’ ἀκολουθεῖν ὡς ἐμέ.

ΕΠΙΓΕΝΗΣ
καὶ ταῦτ’ ἀνάγκη μούστί;

EPIGENES

Dear me, this very day I'm to play Procrustes![71]

FIRST OLD WOMAN

Our laws must be obeyed.

EPIGENES

What if one of my demesmen or friends comes and offers bail for me?

FIRST OLD WOMAN

No man is any longer permitted to transact business over the one-bushel limit.[72]

EPIGENES

Can't I swear off my duty?

FIRST OLD WOMAN

You can't squirm out of this duty!

EPIGENES

I'll get myself exempted as a merchant.

FIRST OLD WOMAN

You'll be sorry if you do!

EPIGENES

So what am I to do?

FIRST OLD WOMAN

Come along this way to my place.

EPIGENES

Is it an absolute necessity?

[71] A legendary robber who fitted his victims to a bed by stretching those who were too short and trimming those who were too long; there is a pun on the verb *prokrouein* "to bang first."

[72] Citing a law that in actuality applied to women.

ΓΡΑΥΣ Α

Διομήδειά γε.

ΕΠΙΓΕΝΗΣ

1030 ὑποστόρεσαί νυν πρῶτα τῆς ὀριγάνου
καὶ κλήμαθ᾽ ὑπόθου συγκλάσασα τέτταρα
καὶ ταινίωσαι καὶ παράθου τὰς ληκύθους
ὕδατός τε κατάθου τοὔστρακον πρὸ τῆς θύρας.

ΓΡΑΥΣ Α

ἦ μὴν ἔτ᾽ ὠνήσει σὺ καὶ στεφάνην ἐμοί.

ΕΠΙΓΕΝΗΣ

1035 νὴ τὸν Δί᾽, ἤνπερ ᾖ γέ που τῶν κηρίνων·
οἶμαι γὰρ ἔνδον διαπεσεῖσθαί σ᾽ αὐτίκα.

ΝΕΑΝΙΣ

ποῖ τοῦτον ἕλκεις;

ΓΡΑΥΣ Α

τόνδ᾽ ἐμαυτῆς εἰσάγω.

ΝΕΑΝΙΣ

οὐ σωφρονοῦσά γ᾽· οὐ γὰρ ἡλικίαν ἔχει
παρὰ σοὶ καθεύδειν τηλικοῦτος ὤν, ἐπεὶ
1040 μήτηρ ἂν αὐτῷ μᾶλλον εἴης ἢ γυνή.
ὥστ᾽ εἰ καταστήσεσθε τοῦτον τὸν νόμον,
τὴν γῆν ἅπασαν Οἰδιπόδων ἐμπλήσετε.

ΓΡΑΥΣ Α

ὦ παμβδελυρά, φθονοῦσα τόνδε τὸν λόγον

1112 δὲ γῆ Dobree: δ᾽ ἐγώ a

392

FIRST OLD WOMAN

Diomedes' necessity![73]

EPIGENES

Then strew the bier with marjoram, break four vine branches to lay underneath, deck it with ribbons, put the urns alongside, and set the water jug before your doorway.

FIRST OLD WOMAN

I bet you'll end up buying me a wedding garland too!

EPIGENES

I sure will, if I can find a waxen one somewhere,[74] because I think you're going to disintegrate pretty quickly in there!

Enter GIRL.

GIRL

Where are you dragging him off to?

FIRST OLD WOMAN

This is my own man I'm bringing home.

GIRL

That's not very prudent. He's the wrong age to be sleeping with you—you're more his mother than his wife. If you people start enforcing a law like this, you'll fill the whole country with Oedipuses.

FIRST OLD WOMAN

You dirty slut, you've thought up this objection out of pure

---

[73] The origin of this proverb, indicating ultimate compulsion, is variously explained by ancient scholars.

[74] Waxen garlands were used in funerals.

ἐξηῦρες· ἀλλ᾽ ἐγώ σε τιμωρήσομαι.

ΕΠΙΓΕΝΗΣ

1045 νὴ τὸν Δία τὸν σωτῆρα, κεχάρισαί γέ μοι,
ὦ γλυκύτατον, τὴν γραῦν ἀπαλλάξασά μου.
ὥστ᾽ ἀντὶ τούτων τῶν ἀγαθῶν εἰς ἑσπέραν
μεγάλην ἀποδώσω καὶ παχεῖάν σοι χάριν.

ΓΡΑΤΣ Β

αὕτη σύ, ποῖ τονδὶ παραβᾶσα τὸν νόμον
1050 ἕλκεις, παρ᾽ ἐμοὶ τῶν γραμμάτων εἰρηκότων
πρότερον καθεύδειν αὐτόν;

ΕΠΙΓΕΝΗΣ

οἴμοι δείλαιος.
πόθεν ἐξέκυψας, ὦ κάκιστ᾽ ἀπολουμένη;
τοῦτο γὰρ ἐκείνου τὸ κακὸν ἐξωλέστερον.

ΓΡΑΤΣ Β

βάδιζε δεῦρο.

ΕΠΙΓΕΝΗΣ

μηδαμῶς με περιίδης
ἑλκόμενον ὑπὸ τῆσδ᾽, ἀντιβολῶ σ᾽.

ΓΡΑΤΣ Β

1055   ἀλλ᾽ οὐκ ἐγώ,
ἀλλ᾽ ὁ νόμος ἕλκει σ᾽.

ΕΠΙΓΕΝΗΣ

οὐκ ἐμέ γ᾽, ἀλλ᾽ Ἔμπουσά τις,
ἐξ αἵματος φλύκταιναν ἠμφιεσμένη.

envy. But I'll make you pay for it!

FIRST OLD WOMAN goes inside.

EPIGENES
By Zeus the Savior, sweetest, you've done me a favor by getting that crone off my back. For that, come evening, I'll slip you a big, juicy token of my gratitude!

Enter SECOND OLD WOMAN.

SECOND OLD WOMAN
Hey you! Where are you taking this man, in violation of the law? It's plainly stated that he's got to sleep with me first.

EPIGENES
Good grief, where did you pop out of, you apparition of damnation? This horror is more revolting than the last one!

SECOND OLD WOMAN
Get over here!

EPIGENES
Don't let her drag me away, I beg you!

GIRL runs away.

SECOND OLD WOMAN
It's not me but the law that drags you away.

EPIGENES
No, it's some kind of Empusa[75] covered with one big blood blister.

---

[75] A horrible bogey-woman; for a description cf. *Frogs* 288–96.

ΓΡΑΥΣ Β

ἕπου, μαλακίων, δεῦρ᾽ ἀνύσας καὶ μὴ λάλει.

ΕΠΙΓΕΝΗΣ

ἴθι νυν ἔασον εἰς ἄφοδον πρώτιστά με
1060 ἐλθόντα θαρρῆσαι πρὸς ἐμαυτόν· εἰ δὲ μή,
αὐτοῦ τι δρῶντα πυρρὸν ὄψει μ᾽ αὐτίκα
ὑπὸ τοῦ δέους.

ΓΡΑΥΣ Β

θάρρει, βάδιζ᾽· ἔνδον χεσεῖ.

ΕΠΙΓΕΝΗΣ

δέδοικα κἀγὼ μὴ πλέον γ᾽ ἢ βούλομαι.
ἀλλ᾽ ἐγγυητάς σοι καταστήσω δύο
ἀξιόχρεως.

ΓΡΑΥΣ Β

μή μοι καθίστη.

ΓΡΑΥΣ Γ

1065 ποῖ σύ, ποῖ
χωρεῖς μετὰ ταύτης;

ΕΠΙΓΕΝΗΣ

οὐκ ἔγωγ᾽, ἀλλ᾽ ἕλκομαι.
ἀτὰρ ἥτις εἶ γε, πόλλ᾽ ἀγαθὰ γένοιτό σοι,
ὅτι μ᾽ οὐ περιεῖδες ἐπιτριβέντ᾽. ὦ Ἡράκλεις,
ὦ Πᾶνες, ὦ Κορύβαντες, ὦ Διοσκόρω,
1070 τοῦτ᾽ αὖ πολὺ τούτου τὸ κακὸν ἐξωλέστερον.
ἀτὰρ τί τὸ πρᾶγμ᾽ ἔστ᾽, ἀντιβολῶ, τουτί ποτε;
πότερον πίθηκος ἀνάπλεως ψιμυθίου
ἢ γραῦς ἀνεστηκυῖα παρὰ τῶν πλειόνων;

SECOND OLD WOMAN

Come along, you sissy. This way. Make it snappy, and no
back talk.

EPIGENES

Wait! May I go to the bathroom first? It would help me get
hold of myself. If you don't let me, I'll do something right
here and you'll soon see me go brown with fear.

SECOND OLD WOMAN

Buck up and get moving; you can shit when we get in the
house.

EPIGENES

I'm afraid I'll do more than I want! (*indicating his testicles*)
But I'll be glad to deposit two valuable sureties with you!

SECOND OLD WOMAN

Don't bother.

Enter THIRD OLD WOMAN.

THIRD OLD WOMAN

Hey you! Where are you going with her?

EPIGENES

I'm not going anywhere; I'm being kidnapped! But who-
ever you are, bless you if you don't just stand by and watch
me be tormented. (*turning to see Third Old Woman*)
Heracles! Pan! Corybantes! Dioscuri! Here's another hor-
ror, and much more revolting than the last! Please, some-
one tell me what in the world it is! A monkey plastered with
makeup? A hag arisen from the underworld?

ΓΡΑΥΣ Γ

μὴ σκῶπτέ μ᾽, ἀλλὰ δεῦρ᾽ ἕπου.

ΓΡΑΥΣ Β

δευρὶ μὲν οὖν.

ΓΡΑΥΣ Γ

ὡς οὐκ ἀφήσω σ᾽ οὐδέποτ᾽.

ΓΡΑΥΣ Β

1075   οὐδὲ μὴν ἐγώ.

ΕΠΙΓΕΝΗΣ

διασπάσεσθέ μ᾽, ὦ κακῶς ἀπολούμεναι.

ΓΡΑΥΣ Β

ἐμοὶ γὰρ ἀκολουθεῖν σε δεῖ κατὰ τὸν νόμον.

ΓΡΑΥΣ Γ

οὔκ, ἢν ἑτέρα γε γραῦς ἔτ᾽ αἰσχίων φανῇ.

ΕΠΙΓΕΝΗΣ

ἢν οὖν ὑφ᾽ ὑμῶν πρῶτον ἀπόλωμαι κακῶς,
1080   φέρε πῶς ἐπ᾽ ἐκείνην τὴν καλὴν ἀφίξομαι;

ΓΡΑΥΣ Γ

αὐτὸς σκόπει σύ· τάδε δέ σοι ποιητέον.

ΕΠΙΓΕΝΗΣ

ποτέρας προτέρας οὖν κατελάσας ἀπαλλαγῶ;

ΓΡΑΥΣ Γ

οὐκ οἶσθα; βαδιεῖ δεῦρ᾽.

ΕΠΙΓΕΝΗΣ

ἀφέτω νύν μ᾽ αὑτηί.

THIRD OLD WOMAN
Cut the jokes and follow me.

SECOND OLD WOMAN
Oh no you don't; come along this way.

THIRD OLD WOMAN
I'll never let you go.

SECOND OLD WOMAN
Me neither!

EPIGENES
You're going to rip me in half, you hellbound creatures!

SECOND OLD WOMAN
The law says you've got to follow me.

THIRD OLD WOMAN
No it doesn't, not if an old woman appears who's even uglier.

EPIGENES
So tell me, if I'm miserably done in by you two, how will I get to that pretty girl?

THIRD OLD WOMAN
That's your problem. (*lewdly gesturing*) Just now you've got to do this.

EPIGENES
So which one do I have to poke first in order to get away?

THIRD OLD WOMAN
Isn't it obvious? Come this way!

EPIGENES
Then make this one let go of me.

ΓΡΑΤΣ Β

δευρὶ μὲν οὖν ἴθ᾽ ὡς ἔμ᾽.

ΕΠΙΓΕΝΗΣ

ἢν ἡδί μ᾽ ἀφῇ.

ΓΡΑΤΣ Γ

ἀλλ᾽ οὐκ ἀφήσω μὰ Δία σ᾽.

ΓΡΑΤΣ Β

1085   οὐδὲ μὴν ἐγώ.

ΕΠΙΓΕΝΗΣ

χαλεπαί γ᾽ ἂν ἦστε γενόμεναι πορθμῆς.

ΓΡΑΤΣ Β

τιή;

ΕΠΙΓΕΝΗΣ

ἕλκοντε τοὺς πλωτῆρας ἂν ἀπεκναίετε.

ΓΡΑΤΣ Γ

σιγῇ βάδιζε δεῦρο.

ΓΡΑΤΣ Β

μὰ Δί᾽, ἀλλ᾽ ὡς ἐμέ.

ΕΠΙΓΕΝΗΣ

τουτὶ τὸ πρᾶγμα κατὰ τὸ Καννωνοῦ σαφῶς
1090 ψήφισμα· βινεῖν δεῖ με διαλελημμένον.
πῶς οὖν δικωπεῖν ἀμφοτέρας δυνήσομαι;

ΓΡΑΤΣ Β

καλῶς, ἐπειδὰν καταφάγῃς βολβῶν χύτραν.

SECOND OLD WOMAN

No! Come this way with me!

EPIGENES

If she'll let go.

THIRD OLD WOMAN

I certainly will not!

SECOND OLD WOMAN

Nor will I!

EPIGENES

You two would make rough ferryboat captains.

SECOND OLD WOMAN

How's that?

EPIGENES

You'd tug your passengers hard enough to wear them out.

THIRD OLD WOMAN

Shut up and get moving. This way!

SECOND OLD WOMAN

No, this way!

EPIGENES

This is obviously Cannonus' Law put into practice: I've got to appear in irons and fuck my accusers![76] But how can I manage to man two boats with a single oar?

SECOND OLD WOMAN

Just fine—after you've wolfed down a potful of love bulbs.

[76] Cannonus' Law, datable to the era of the Persian Wars, ordered that those accused of injuring the Athenian people be bound and face (not fuck!) the charge before the people.

ΕΠΙΓΕΝΗΣ

οἴμοι κακοδαίμων· ἐγγὺς ἤδη τῆς θύρας
ἑλκόμενός εἰμ'—

ΓΡΑΥΣ Γ

ἀλλ' οὐδὲν ἔσται σοι πλέον·
ξυνεσπεσοῦμαι γὰρ μετὰ σοῦ.

ΕΠΙΓΕΝΗΣ

1095   μὴ πρὸς θεῶν·
ἑνὶ γὰρ ξυνέχεσθαι κρεῖττον ἢ δυοῖν κακοῖν.

ΓΡΑΥΣ Γ

νὴ τὴν Ἑκάτην, ἐάν τε βούλῃ γ' ἤν τε μή.

ΕΠΙΓΕΝΗΣ

ὦ τρισκακοδαίμων, εἰ γυναῖκα δεῖ σαπρὰν
βινεῖν ὅλην τὴν νύκτα καὶ τὴν ἡμέραν,
1100 κἄπειτ', ἐπειδὰν τῆσδ' ἀπαλλαγῶ, πάλιν
φρύνην ἔχουσαν λήκυθον πρὸς ταῖς γνάθοις.
ἆρ' οὐ κακοδαίμων εἰμί; βαρυδαίμων μὲν οὖν,
νὴ τὸν Δία τὸν σωτῆρ', ἀνὴρ καὶ δυστυχής,
ὅστις τοιούτοις θηρίοις συνείρξομαι.
1105 ὅμως δ', ἐάν τι πολλὰ πολλάκις πάθω
ὑπὸ τοῖνδε τοῖν κασαλβάδοιν δεῦρ' ἐσπλέων,
θάψαι μ' ἐπ' αὐτῷ τῷ στόματι τῆς ἐσβολῆς,
καὶ τήνδ' ἄνωθεν ἐπιπολῆς τοῦ σήματος
ζῶσαν καταπιττώσαντες, εἶτα τὼ πόδε
1110 μολυβδοχοήσαντες κύκλῳ περὶ τὰ σφυρὰ
ἄνω 'πιθεῖναι πρόφασιν ἀντὶ ληκύθου.

EPIGENES

Oh, what a sorry end! I'm dragged to the very threshold!

THIRD OLD WOMAN

That's not going to help you: I'm going to fall in right be-
hind you.

EPIGENES

God no: better to grapple with one evil than two!

THIRD OLD WOMAN

By Hecate, you've got no choice in the matter.

EPIGENES

(*to the spectators*) I'm damned three ways from Sunday if I
have to fuck an old bag all night and all day, and after I get
free of her, start in again on an old toad with a funeral urn
already standing by her chops! So aren't I damned? Nay, a
man heavily doomed, by Zeus the Savior, and unlucky, to
be closeted with such creatures as these! But if the very
worst really does befall me as I put into port atop these two
floozies, bury me right where I penetrated the channel.
(*indicating Third Old Woman*) As for her, while she's still
alive, cover her with pitch all over and put her feet in
molten lead up to her ankles, then stick her over my grave
instead of an urn!

SECOND and THIRD OLD WOMEN *drag Epigenes into the
house and slam the door behind them.*

Enter a tipsy MAID.

ΘΕΡΑΠΑΙΝΑ

ὦ μακάριος μὲν δῆμος, εὐδαίμων δὲ γῆ,
αὐτή τέ μοι δέσποινα μακαριωτάτη,
ὑμεῖς θ' ὅσαι παρέστατ' ἐπὶ ταῖσιν θύραις,
1115 οἱ γείτονές τε πάντες οἵ τε δημόται,
ἐγώ τε πρὸς τούτοισιν ἡ διάκονος,
ἥτις μεμύρισμαι τὴν κεφαλὴν μυρώμασιν
ἀγαθοῖσιν, ὦ Ζεῦ. πολὺ δ' ὑπερπέπαικεν αὖ
τούτων ἁπάντων τὰ Θάσι' ἀμφορείδια·
1120 ἐν τῇ κεφαλῇ γὰρ ἐμμένει πολὺν χρόνον,
τὰ δ' ἄλλ' ἀπανθήσαντα πάντ' ἀπέπτατο,
ὥστ' ἐστὶ πολὺ βέλτιστα, πολὺ δῆτ', ὦ θεοί.
κέρασον ἄκρατον· εὐφρανεῖ τὴν νύχθ' ὅλην
ἐκλεγομένας ὅ τι ἂν μάλιστ' ὀσμὴν ἔχῃ.
1125 ἀλλ', ὦ γυναῖκες, φράσατέ μοι τὸν δεσπότην,
τὸν ἄνδρ', ὅπου 'στί, τῆς ἐμῆς κεκτημένης.

ΚΟΡΥΦΑΙΑ

αὐτοῦ μένουσ' ἡμῖν γ' ἂν ἐξευρεῖν δοκεῖς.
μάλισθ' ὁδὶ γὰρ ἐπὶ τὸ δεῖπνον ἔρχεται.

ΘΕΡΑΠΑΙΝΑ

ὦ δέσποτ', ὦ μακάριε καὶ τρισόλβιε.

ΒΛΕΠΥΡΟΣ

ἐγώ;

ΘΕΡΑΠΑΙΝΑ

1130   σὺ μέντοι, νὴ Δί', ὥς γ' οὐδεὶς ἀνήρ.
τίς γὰρ γένοιτ' ἂν μᾶλλον ὀλβιώτερος,
ὅστις πολιτῶν πλεῖον ἢ τρισμυρίων

MAID

Blessed citizenry! Favored land! And most blessed of all,
our mistress herself, and all you women who stand at our
door, and all our neighbors and fellow demesmen, and me
too, the maid, with my head perfumed with fine perfumes,
Zeus be praised! But far surpassing all these fragrances
are those nice little bottles of Thasian wine: they stay in
your head a long time, when those others have lost their
bouquet and completely evaporated. So they're far the
best, yes by far, the gods be praised! Pour it neat and it'll
make you merry all night long, if you pick the one with the
best bouquet! Women, tell me where master is, I mean my
mistress' husband.

CHORUS LEADER

If you wait right here you're bound to run into him. Yes
indeed, here he is on his way to dinner now.

Enter BLEPYRUS, *garlanded and embracing two Girls.*

MAID

Oh master! You happy, you triple-lucky man!

BLEPYRUS

Who, me?

MAID

Sure you, by Zeus, beyond anyone else in the world. Who
could be luckier? Out of more than thirty thousand citi-

1166–67 lacunam posuit Meineke, suppl. e.g. Sommerstein

ὄντων τὸ πλῆθος οὐ δεδείπνηκας μόνος;

ΚΟΡΥΦΑΙΑ

εὐδαιμονικόν γ᾽ ἄνθρωπον εἴρηκας σαφῶς.

ΘΕΡΑΠΑΙΝΑ

ποῖ ποῖ βαδίζεις;

ΒΛΕΠΤΡΟΣ

1135   ἐπὶ τὸ δεῖπνον ἔρχομαι.

ΘΕΡΑΠΑΙΝΑ

νὴ τὴν Ἀφροδίτην, πολύ γ᾽ ἁπάντων ὕστατος.
ὅμως δ᾽ ἐκέλευε συλλαβοῦσάν μ᾽ ἡ γυνὴ
ἄγειν σε καὶ τασδὶ μετὰ σοῦ τὰς μείρακας.
οἶνος δὲ Χῖός ἐστι περιλελειμμένος
1140 καὶ τἄλλ᾽ ἀγαθά. πρὸς ταῦτα μὴ βραδύνετε,
καὶ τῶν θεατῶν εἴ τις εὔνους τυγχάνει
καὶ τῶν κριτῶν εἰ μή τις ἑτέρωσε βλέπει,
ἴτω μεθ᾽ ἡμῶν· πάντα γὰρ παρέξομεν.

ΒΛΕΠΤΡΟΣ

οὔκουν ἅπασι δῆτα γενναίως ἐρεῖς
1145 καὶ μὴ παραλείψεις μηδέν᾽, ἀλλ᾽ ἐλευθέρως
καλεῖς γέροντα, μειράκιον, παιδίσκον; ὡς
τὸ δεῖπνον αὐτοῖς ἔστ᾽ ἐπεσκευασμένον
ἁπαξάπασιν—ἢν ἀπίωσιν οἴκαδε.
ἐγὼ δὲ πρὸς τὸ δεῖπνον ἤδη ᾽πείξομαι·
1150 ἔχω δέ τοι καὶ δᾷδα ταυτηνὶ καλῶς.

ΚΟΡΥΦΑΙΑ

τί δῆτα διατρίβεις ἔχων, ἀλλ᾽ οὐκ ἄγεις

zens you're the only one who hasn't had dinner.

CHORUS LEADER

Yes, you make him sound quite a happy fellow.

MAID

Hey, where can you be off to now?

BLEPYRUS

Why, I'm off to dinner.

MAID

By Aphrodite, you're the last one by a mile. Still, your wife told me to gather you up and escort you there, and these girls with you. There's some Chian wine left over, and some other good stuff. So don't be late. And any of you spectators who favor us, and any of you judges who's not looking elsewhere, come along with us: we'll supply everything.

BLEPYRUS

Why don't you be a lady and address all of them, leaving no one out? Be liberal, invite the old man, the boy, the little child: there's dinner specially made for all of them—if they hurry home! Me, I'm shoving off to my own dinner now; (*indicating one of the Girls*) and fortunately I've got this little torch here to light my way!

CHORUS LEADER

Then why waste time here? Come on, take these girls and

τασδὶ λαβών; ἐν ὅσῳ δὲ καταβαίνεις, ἐγὼ
ἐπᾴσομαι μέλος τι μελλοδειπνικόν.
σμικρὸν δ᾽ ὑποθέσθαι τοῖς κριταῖσι βούλομαι·

1155 τοῖς σοφοῖς μὲν τῶν σοφῶν μεμνημένοις κρίνειν
         ἐμέ,
         τοῖς γελῶσι δ᾽ ἡδέως διὰ τὸν γέλων κρίνειν ἐμέ—
         σχεδὸν ἅπαντας οὖν κελεύω δηλαδὴ κρίνειν ἐμέ—
         μηδὲ τὸν κλῆρον γενέσθαι μηδὲν ἡμῖν αἴτιον,
         ὅτι προείληχ᾽· ἀλλὰ πάντα ταῦτα χρὴ μεμνημένους
1160 μὴ ᾽πιορκεῖν, ἀλλὰ κρίνειν τοὺς χοροὺς ὀρθῶς ἀεί,
         μηδὲ ταῖς κακαῖς ἑταίραις τὸν τρόπον προσεικέναι,
         αἳ μόνον μνήμην ἔχουσι τῶν τελευταίων ἀεί.

ΧΟΡΟΣ

ὢ ὤ, ὥρα δή,
ὦ φίλαι γυναῖκες, εἴπερ μέλλομεν τὸ χρῆμα δρᾶν,
1165 ἐπὶ τὸ δεῖπνον ὑπανακινεῖν. Κρητικῶς οὖν τὼ πόδε
καὶ σὺ κίνει.

ΒΛΕΠΤΡΟΣ

τοῦτο δρῶ.

ΧΟΡΟΣ

καὶ τάσδε νῦν ‹τὰς μείρακας
χρὴ συνυπάγειν κοῦφα› λαγαρὰς τοῖν σκελίσκοιν
         τὸν ῥυθμόν.
τάχα γὰρ ἔπεισι

1176 τρέχε Blaydes: ταχὺ a

get going! And while you're on your way down there, I'll sing a little pre-dinner tune.

BLEPYRUS, MAID, and Girls descend into the orchestra.

But first I have a small suggestion for the judges: if you're intelligent, remember the intelligent parts and vote for me; if you've got a sense of humor, remember the jokes and vote for me. Yes, it's virtually all of you that I'm asking to vote for me. And don't hold it against me that the luck of the draw has put me onstage first. So, bearing all this in mind, don't break your oath, but always judge the choruses fairly. Don't act like dishonest courtesans, who only remember their latest companions.

CHORUS

Hey, hey, it's time,
dear ladies, to shake a leg and hop off to dinner,
if we mean to do it at all. So you start moving your
    feet too,
to a Cretan tune.[77]

BLEPYRUS

That's what I'm doing!

CHORUS

                                And these girls too,
so lithe, should join us in lightly moving their gams to
    the rhythm.
For soon there'll be served

[77] Cretans were renowned dancers.

λοπαδοτεμαχοσελαχογαλεο-
1170 κρανιολειψανοδριμυποτριμματο-
σιλφιολιπαρομελιτοκατακεχυμενο-
κιχλεπικοσσυφοφαττοπεριστερα-
λεκτρυονοπτοπιφαλλιδοκιγκλοπε-
λειολαγωοσιραιοβαφητραγα-
1175 λοπτερυγών. σὺ δὲ ταῦτ' ἀκροασάμε-
νος τρέχε καὶ ταχέως λαβὲ τρύβλιον.
εἶτα κόνισαι λαβὼν
λέκιθον, ἵν' ἐπιδειπνῇς.

BΛΕΠΤΡΟΣ

ἀλλὰ λαιμάττουσί που.

ΧΟΡΟΣ
1180 αἴρεσθ' ἄνω, ἰαί, εὐαί·
δειπνήσομεν, εὐοῖ, εὐαί,
εὐαί, ὡς ἐπὶ νίκῃ.
εὐαί, εὐαί, εὐαί, εὐαί.

limpets and saltfish and sharksteak and dogfish
and mullets and oddfish with savory pickle sauce
and thrushes with blackbirds and various pigeons
and roosters and pan-roasted wagtails and larks
and nice chunks of hare marinated in mulled wine
and all of it drizzled with honey and silphium
and vinegar, oil, and spices galore![78] Now that you've
    heard
what awaits you, run grab your plate quickly,
then raise the dust, but take
some porridge for dinner!

BLEPYRUS

I'm sure that they're stuffing it in.

CHORUS

Lift your legs aloft, hey hey,
We're off to dinner, hoy hoy,
and victory, hurray!
Hurray hurrah!

---

[78] In the Greek this list of foods is combined into one huge word.

WEALTH

INTRODUCTORY NOTE

Wealth was produced in 388 by Aristophanes in competition with Nicochares' *Spartans*, Aristomenes' *Admetus*, Nicophon's *Adonis*, and Alcaeus' *Pasiphae*, but the festival and prize are unreported. It was his last production in his own name; his final plays, *Cocalus* and *Aeolosicon*, were subsequently produced by his son, Araros.

Hellenistic scholars possessed a homonymous play by Aristophanes whose production they dated to 408. The fragments do not help us decide whether our play is a revision (like the extant *Clouds*) or a new play.[1] Its theme of wealth and justice would have been topical at either date, since the poverty of ordinary people is often mentioned in earlier plays and, for all we know, was an even more pressing issue in 408 than it was twenty years later. Comparative comments preserved in the scholia (at 115, 119, 173, 972, 1146) suggest that the two plays were similar enough (at least in part) to be confused, and while our play does contain passages datable after 408 (several topical allusions and the play's single choral song, 290–321), they are not integral to the plot and so could have been added in a revision. On the other hand, the structure and complexion of

---

[1] Fr. 458 may indicate the motif of blindness healed (as in our play), fr. 465 an Ionian or Doric speaker (not in our play).

our play are more typical of comedy in the fourth than in the fifth century. Its parodos and agon are truncated and unbalanced; there is no parabasis; and though the chorus is present throughout, it has only occasional lines of dialogue and only one song. As in later comedy, places where a choral song divided episodes are indicated by the note *chorou* ("place for a chorus"); presumably these *entr'actes* were not composed by Aristophanes. That ancient commentators mention this change particularly in regard to *Wealth* (cf. *Life*, T 1.51–54) may indicate that it was the first play to dispense with integrated choral songs. Also pointing to later comedy are the play's bland humor, linguistic simplicity, straightforward morality, relative lack of topicality and satirical animus, and the characters' commonplace names and personalities. Indeed these were the features that made *Wealth* the most popular of Aristophanes' works in later eras.

A noteworthy departure from Aristophanes' fifth-century practice is his changed moral stance toward economic inequality: whereas in earlier plays the poor as a class are often presumed to be wicked and the wealthy virtuous, in *Wealth* we find just the opposite; and when their economic situations are miraculously reversed, both poverty and injustice disappear. Noteworthy too is the prominence of Cario, the slave of the protagonist Chremylus, who is present throughout and plays an integral role in the plot. As in later comedy, master and resourceful slave share the main initiatives. Cario's cheeky vivacity counterpoints Chremylus' gloomy sobriety, and the scurrility that in earlier plays was an element of the protagonist's character is here concentrated largely in Cario, leaving Chremylus more dignified. Finally, the action of the play is unusually

concentrated: everything takes place before Chremylus'
house, and three actors can play all the roles.

Chremylus, a farmer on the poor end of the landed
class, has become so cynical as to doubt the value of hon-
esty, and to wonder whether it would not be best to raise
his beloved only son to be a criminal. He has travelled with
Cario to Delphi to put this question to Apollo, who advised
him to take home the first man he met on leaving the sanc-
tuary. This turns out to be the god Wealth, an old and de-
crepit figure who reveals that Zeus had long ago blinded
him so that he could not distinguish good men from bad.
Chremylus decides to remedy this situation by restoring
Wealth's sight. The Greeks typically imagined Wealth as
being a young child of Demeter,[2] but here his decrepitude
suits the allegory: it emphasizes that the unjust distribu-
tion of wealth has been going on a long time, and prepares
for the god's rejuvenation.

Cario summons Chremylus' friends, a Chorus of im-
poverished farmers, while Chremylus fetches his friend
Blepsidemus. After reassuring them at some length that
his motives are altruistic and that he has not enriched him-
self dishonestly, Chremylus prepares to take Wealth to
Asclepius' temple for the cure. But he is interrupted by the
appearance of the horrible hag Poverty, who condemns his
plan by pointing to her beneficial role in human society:
without the fear of poverty as a motivation, humanity
would produce and create nothing, so that there would be
nothing for money to buy. Chremylus replies by vividly de-
scribing the hard life of the poor. Poverty counters by

[2] Cf. Hesiod, *Theogony* 969–74, Homeric *Hymn to Demeter*
488–89.

drawing a distinction between poverty and beggary, and predicting that after a redistribution of wealth his life would be even harder than it already is. Chremylus mockingly replies that for poor people life simply cannot get any harder and that all mankind prefers wealth to poverty. To Poverty's complaint that "you're using ridicule and caricature and not taking this seriously," Chremylus replies, "you won't persuade me even if you convince me," and brusquely dismisses her.

Though Chremylus does not cogently refute Poverty at the theoretical level, his rebuttal is effective nonetheless: her arguments, which probably reflect contemporary economic theories, are palpably sophistic, and her physical ugliness and callous attitude are designed to be unsympathetic. As in earlier literature, she is portrayed as an unmitigated evil and a motivator of shameful acts,[3] and can have won no sympathy from the majority of spectators. As she exits she predicts that "you'll summon me back here one day, both of you," but the subsequent success of Chremylus' plan proves her wrong.

Chremylus and Cario now take Wealth to the sanctuary of Asclepius for his cure, described by Cario in an exceptionally long and vivid narrative (653–747), and upon their return we meet a series of visitors who exemplify the consequences. The first two visitors illustrate the play's initial premise that the restoration of Wealth's eyesight will enrich the good and impoverish the bad (cf. 95–7): a good man comes to thank Wealth, and an Informer comes to complain. The Informer claims (rather like Poverty) that

[3] Cf. Alcaeus 364 (sister of Helplessness), Theognis 351–54, 384–85, 649–52, Herodotus 8.111.3.

his activities benefit Athens, but his final vow to prosecute Wealth will not have helped his case in the eyes of the spectators. The Informer is the play's only representative of the political world; otherwise the issue of wealth and justice is viewed from the perspective of private lives, not as a political but a social problem, whose remedy is framed in intellectual and moral rather than political terms.

The next pair of visitors, a wealthy Old Woman and her former gigolo, illustrate a different outcome of Wealth's cure, that everyone is now wealthy: the Old Woman has not been impoverished (she can still offer gifts: 995–97), and the Young Man, newly enriched, no longer needs her. But the justice of this outcome is less clear: although Chremylus had expressed the hope (reminiscent of Praxagora's in *Assemblywomen*) that everyone will now become good once wickedness is no longer profitable (496–7), it is never implied that the Old Woman had been wicked or the Young Man good; indeed the Young Man comes off as a boorish ingrate, while Chremylus expresses sympathy for the Old Woman (1071–75) and obliges the Young Man to keep his promise to visit her that night (1200–01).

It remains to settle the old problem of Zeus' hostility to mankind. Hermes arrives to threaten divine vengeance, since people no longer sacrifice to the gods (recall the situation in *Birds*), but in his hungry condition is easily recruited to Chremylus' kitchen staff. A hungry Priest follows and offers to abandon Zeus for Wealth. But Chremylus proclaims that Zeus and Wealth are after all identical, and proposes to install Wealth "where he used to be," on the Acropolis as guardian of Athena's treasury (a reference to the bygone days of Athens' imperial prosperity), making it clear that all Athenians will benefit and portraying Chremylus as a civic benefactor not unlike Trygaeus in *Peace*.

Text

Seven papyri preserve fragments of *Wealth*; five of them are not cited in the notes: *POxy.* 4519 (III), partially preserving lines 1–16; *PBerol.* 13231 + 21202 (V/VI), partially preserving lines 134–38, 140–44, 171–73, 289–93, 311–19, 327–31, 347–55; *PAnt.* 180 (V/VI), partially preserving lines 466–67, 476–77, 499–501, 510–11, 806–8, 842–45; *POxy.* 4520 (V), partially preserving lines 635–679, 698–738; and *PLaur.* III.319 (V/VI), partially preserving lines 1135–39.

The transmission of *Wealth* has yet to be systematically investigated. There are over 150 medieval MSS, most of them late and only a few yet collated. Some 30 MSS (represented in this edition by A M U) are pre-Triclinian in their readings but are affected by horizontal contamination to such an extent that none show usefully consistent affinities; R and V separately and together are the most consistent source of good readings.

Sigla

Π1	*POxy.* 1617 (V), parts of lines 1–19, 22–25, 32–56
Π2	*POxy.* 4521 (II), parts of lines 687–705, 726–31, 957–70
R	Ravennas 429 (*c.* 950)
V	Venetus Marcianus 474 (XI/XII)
S	readings found in the Suda
A	Parisinus gr. 2712 (XIV[in])

M   Ambrosianus L 39 sup. (XIV[in])
U   Vaticanus Urbinas 141 (XIV)
a   the consensus of R V A M U
t   readings found only in Triclinian MSS

Annotated Editions

A. von Velsen (Leipzig 1881).
F. H. M. Blaydes (Halle 1886).
J. van Leeuwen (Leiden 1904).
B. B. Rogers (London 1907), with English translation.
K. Holzinger (Vienna/Leipzig 1940), commentary only.
A. H. Sommerstein (Warminster 2001), with English translation.

ΤΑ ΤΟΥ ΔΡΑΜΑΤΟΣ ΠΡΟΣΩΠΑ

ΚΑΡΙΩΝ οἰκέτης
  Χρεμύλου
ΧΡΕΜΥΛΟΣ
ΠΛΟΥΤΟΣ
ΒΛΕΨΙΔΗΜΟΣ φίλος
  Χρεμύλου
ΠΕΝΙΑ
ΓΥΝΗ Χρεμύλου
ΔΙΚΑΙΟΣ ΑΝΗΡ
ΣΥΚΟΦΑΝΤΗΣ
ΓΡΑΥΣ
ΝΕΑΝΙΑΣ
ΕΡΜΗΣ
ΙΕΡΕΥΣ Διὸς Σωτῆρος

ΧΟΡΟΣ ἀγροίκων

ΚΩΦΑ ΠΡΟΣΩΠΑ
ΠΑΙΔΑΡΙΟΝ τοῦ
  Δικαίου Ἀνδρός
ΜΑΡΤΥΣ
ΟΙΚΕΤΑΙ

DRAMATIS PERSONAE

CARIO, slave of
  Chremylus
CHREMYLUS
WEALTH
BLEPSIDEMUS, friend
  of Chremylus
POVERTY
WIFE of Chremylus
JUST MAN
INFORMER
OLD WOMAN
YOUNG MAN
HERMES
PRIEST of Zeus the
  Savior

CHORUS of farmers

SILENT CHARACTERS
CHILD of Just Man
WITNESS
SLAVES

ΠΛΟΥΤΟΣ

ΚΑΡΙΩΝ

ὡς ἀργαλέον πρᾶγμ᾽ ἐστίν, ὦ Ζεῦ καὶ θεοί,
δοῦλον γενέσθαι παραφρονοῦντος δεσπότου·
ἢν γὰρ τὰ βέλτισθ᾽ ὁ θεράπων λέξας τύχῃ,
δόξῃ δὲ μὴ δρᾶν ταῦτα τῷ κεκτημένῳ,
5 μετέχειν ἀνάγκη τὸν θεράποντα τῶν κακῶν·
τοῦ σώματος γὰρ οὐκ ἐᾷ τὸν κύριον
κρατεῖν ὁ δαίμων, ἀλλὰ τὸν ἐωνημένον.
καὶ ταῦτα μὲν δὴ ταῦτα· τῷ δὲ Λοξίᾳ,
ὃς θεσπιῳδεῖ τρίποδος ἐκ χρυσηλάτου,
10 μέμψιν δικαίαν μέμφομαι ταύτην, ὅτι
ἰατρὸς ὢν καὶ μάντις, ὥς φασιν, σοφὸς
μελαγχολῶντ᾽ ἀπέπεμψέ μου τὸν δεσπότην,
ὅστις ἀκολουθεῖ κατόπιν ἀνθρώπου τυφλοῦ,
τοὐναντίον δρῶν ἢ προσῆκ᾽ αὐτῷ ποιεῖν.
15 οἱ γὰρ βλέποντες τοῖς τυφλοῖς ἡγούμεθα,
οὗτος δ᾽ ἀκολουθεῖ, κἀμὲ προσβιάζεται,
καὶ ταῦτ᾽ ἀποκρινόμενος τὸ παράπαν οὐδὲ γρῦ.
ἐγὼ μὲν οὖν οὐκ ἔσθ᾽ ὅπως σιγήσομαι,
ἢν μὴ φράσῃς ὅ τι τῷδ᾽ ἀκολουθοῦμέν ποτε,

---

17 -μενος Bentley: -μένῳ R: -μένου cett. Π1 S

424

WEALTH

A street in Athens, outside Chremylus' house. A blind and ragged old man enters from a wing, followed by Chremylus and his slave, Cario; both wear laurel wreaths, and Cario carries some sacrificial meat.

CARIO

Gods in heaven, it's a tough job slaving for a master who's out of his mind! The servant might offer the best advice, but if his owner decides not to follow it, the servant will surely share the grief. It's his fate that mastery of his own body is denied him, but belongs to his purchaser. And that's how things stand. But against Apollo, "who from a tripod of beaten gold dispenses prophecies,"[1] I have a valid complaint, and here it is: people claim that he's a healer and sage prophet, yet he discharged my master in a deranged condition. There he goes, following a blind person, exactly the opposite of what he should be doing: we who can see should lead the blind, but he keeps following, and makes me follow too, all the while giving my questions nary a peep in reply. (*to Chremylus*) Well, I certainly don't intend to keep quiet, master, not unless you tell me why

---

[1] From an unknown tragedy.

20 ὦ δέσποτ', ἀλλά σοι παρέξω πράγματα.
οὐ γάρ με τυπτήσεις στέφανον ἔχοντά γε.

ΧΡΕΜΥΛΟΣ

μὰ Δί' ἀλλ' ἀφελὼν τὸν στέφανον, ἢν λυπῇς τί με,
ἵνα μᾶλλον ἀλγῇς.

ΚΑΡΙΩΝ

          λῆρος· οὐ γὰρ παύσομαι
πρὶν ἂν φράσῃς μοι τίς ποτ' ἐστὶν οὑτοσί·
25 εὔνους γὰρ ὢν σοι πυνθάνομαι πάνυ σφόδρα.

ΧΡΕΜΥΛΟΣ

ἀλλ' οὔ σε κρύψω· τῶν ἐμῶν γὰρ οἰκετῶν
πιστότατον ἡγοῦμαί σε καὶ κλεπτίστατον.
ἐγὼ θεοσεβὴς καὶ δίκαιος ὢν ἀνὴρ
κακῶς ἔπραττον καὶ πένης ἦν.

ΚΑΡΙΩΝ

          οἶδά τοι.

ΧΡΕΜΥΛΟΣ

30 ἕτεροι δ' ἐπλούτουν, ἱερόσυλοι, ῥήτορες
καὶ συκοφάνται καὶ πονηροί.

ΚΑΡΙΩΝ

          πείθομαι.

ΧΡΕΜΥΛΟΣ

ἐπερησόμενος οὖν ᾠχόμην ὡς τὸν θεόν,
τὸν ἐμὸν μὲν αὐτοῦ τοῦ ταλαιπώρου σχεδὸν
ἤδη νομίζων ἐκτετοξεῦσθαι βίον,
35 τὸν δ' υἱόν, ὅσπερ ὢν μόνος μοι τυγχάνει,

we're following this fellow; I'll just give you a hard time.
And you wouldn't dare beat me when I'm wearing a
wreath.[2]

CHREMYLUS

True enough, but if you pester me at all, I'll rip that wreath
off, and you'll get it even worse.

CARIO

Nonsense. I won't give up until you tell me who this fellow
is. I only ask with your welfare in mind, very much so.

CHREMYLUS

All right, I won't keep you in the dark; I consider you the
most trustworthy of my slaves, and the most larcenous. I'm
a just and godfearing man, and yet I've always been poor
and unsuccessful.

CARIO

As I well know.

CHREMYLUS

While others have prospered: temple robbers, politicians,
informers, rascals.

CARIO

I agree.

CHREMYLUS

And that's why I went to consult the god, not for my own
miserable sake—at this point in my life I've shot all my
arrows—but for my son, my only son. I wanted to find out if

_____

[2] As coming from an oracular consultation at Delphi.

ARISTOPHANES

πευσόμενος εἰ χρὴ μεταβαλόντα τοὺς τρόπους
εἶναι πανοῦργον, ἄδικον, ὑγιὲς μηδὲ ἕν,
ὡς τῷ βίῳ τοῦτ᾽ αὐτὸ νομίσας ξυμφέρειν.

ΚΑΡΙΩΝ
"τί δῆτα Φοῖβος ἔλακεν ἐκ τῶν στεμμάτων;"

ΧΡΕΜΥΛΟΣ
40 πεύσει. σαφῶς γὰρ ὁ θεὸς εἶπέ μοι ταδί·
ὅτῳ ξυναντήσαιμι πρῶτον ἐξιών,
ἐκέλευε τούτου μὴ μεθίεσθαί μ᾽ ἔτι,
πείθειν δ᾽ ἐμαυτῷ ξυνακολουθεῖν οἴκαδε.

ΚΑΡΙΩΝ
καὶ τῷ ξυναντᾷς δῆτα πρώτῳ;

ΧΡΕΜΥΛΟΣ
τουτῳί.

ΚΑΡΙΩΝ
45 εἶτ᾽ οὐ ξυνίης τὴν ἐπίνοιαν τοῦ θεοῦ
φράζουσαν, ὦ σκαιότατέ, σοι σαφέστατα
ἀσκεῖν τὸν υἱὸν τὸν ἐπιχώριον τρόπον;

ΧΡΕΜΥΛΟΣ
τῷ τοῦτο κρίνεις;

ΚΑΡΙΩΝ
δῆλον ὁτιὴ καὶ τυφλῷ
γνῶναι δοκεῖ τοῦθ᾽, ὡς σφόδρ᾽ ἐστὶ συμφέρον
50 τὸ μηδὲν ἀσκεῖν ὑγιὲς ἐν τῷ νῦν γένει.

50 γένει γρV: βίῳ R: ἔτει V: χρόνῳ Π1 γρV cett.

he should change his ways and become a criminal, unjust,
completely unwholesome, considering that that's the way
to get ahead in life.

CARIO

"What then did Phoebus pronounce from his holy
wreaths?"[3]

CHREMYLUS

You'll find out. Here's what the god told me in plain terms:
the first person I encountered on leaving the shrine I was
told to stick to, and persuade to come home with me.[4]

CARIO

And whom did you encounter first?

CHREMYLUS

Him!

CARIO

Well, don't you see the god's point, which tells you quite
plainly, you supreme dummy, to raise your son according
to the local norm?

CHREMYLUS

How do you figure that?

CARIO

It's so obvious, even a blind man could see it: in our age, the
key to real success is to avoid every wholesome practice.

---

[3] From an unknown tragedy.
[4] A motif from folklore, cf. Euripides, *Ion* 534–36.

ΧΡΕΜΤΛΟΣ

οὐκ ἔσθ᾽ ὅπως ὁ χρησμὸς εἰς τοῦτο ῥέπει,
ἀλλ᾽ εἰς ἕτερόν τι μεῖζον. ἢν δ᾽ ἡμῖν φράσῃ
ὅστις ποτ᾽ ἐστὶν οὑτοσὶ καὶ τοῦ χάριν
καὶ τοῦ δεόμενος ἦλθε μετὰ νῷν ἐνθαδί,
55   πυθοίμεθ᾽ ἂν τὸν χρησμὸν ἡμῶν ὅ τι νοεῖ.

ΚΑΡΙΩΝ

ἄγε δή, σὺ πότερον σαυτὸν ὅστις εἶ φράσεις,
ἢ τἀπὶ τούτοις δρῶ; λέγειν χρὴ ταχὺ πάνυ.

ΠΛΟΥΤΟΣ

ἐγὼ μὲν οἰμώζειν λέγω σοι.

ΚΑΡΙΩΝ
                    μανθάνεις

ὅς φησιν εἶναι;

ΧΡΕΜΤΛΟΣ
                    σοὶ λέγει τοῦτ᾽, οὐκ ἐμοί·
60   σκαιῶς γὰρ αὐτοῦ καὶ χαλεπῶς ἐκπυνθάνει.
ἀλλ᾽ εἴ τι χαίρεις ἀνδρὸς εὐόρκου τρόποις,
ἐμοὶ φράσον.

ΠΛΟΥΤΟΣ
            κλάειν ἔγωγέ σοι λέγω.

ΚΑΡΙΩΝ

δέχου τὸν ἄνδρα καὶ τὸν ὄρνιν τοῦ θεοῦ.

ΧΡΕΜΤΛΟΣ

οὔ τοι μὰ τὴν Δήμητρα χαιρήσεις ἔτι.

CHREMYLUS

That can't be the oracle's drift; no, it must be something loftier. Now if this fellow would just tell us who he is, and the why and wherefore of his coming here with us, we'd soon find out what our oracle means.

CARIO

All right you, are you going to identify yourself, or must I take additional steps? You'd better talk, and pretty fast.

WEALTH

My answer to you is, go to hell.

CARIO

Did you get who he said he is?

CHREMYLUS

He said it to you, not me. You did question him in a rude and clumsy way. (*to Wealth*) Now if you appreciate the manners of a man who keeps his word, please answer the question for me.

WEALTH

You can go to hell too.

CARIO

There you have the god's man and message.

CHREMYLUS

(*to Wealth*) By heaven, you won't get away with this!

ΚΑΡΙΩΝ

65 εἰ μὴ φράσεις γάρ, ἀπό σ' ὀλῶ κακὸν κακῶς.

ΠΛΟΥΤΟΣ

ὦ τᾶν, ἀπαλλάχθητον ἀπ' ἐμοῦ.

ΧΡΕΜΥΛΟΣ

πώμαλα.

ΚΑΡΙΩΝ

καὶ μὴν ὃ λέγω βέλτιστόν ἐστ', ὦ δέσποτα.
ἀπολῶ τὸν ἄνθρωπον κάκιστα τουτονί.
ἀναθεὶς γὰρ ἐπὶ κρημνόν τιν' αὐτὸν καταλιπὼν
70 ἄπειμ', ἵν' ἐκεῖθεν ἐκτραχηλισθῇ πεσών.

ΧΡΕΜΥΛΟΣ

ἀλλ' αἶρε ταχέως.

ΠΛΟΥΤΟΣ

μηδαμῶς.

ΧΡΕΜΥΛΟΣ

οὔκουν ἐρεῖς;

ΠΛΟΥΤΟΣ

ἀλλ' ἢν πύθησθέ μ' ὅστις εἴμ', εὖ οἶδ' ὅτι
κακόν τί μ' ἐργάσεσθε κοὐκ ἀφήσετον.

ΧΡΕΜΥΛΟΣ

νὴ τοὺς θεοὺς ἡμεῖς γ', ἐὰν βούλῃ γε σύ.

ΠΛΟΥΤΟΣ

μέθεσθέ νύν μου πρῶτον.

CARIO

If you don't start talking, I'm going to put a miserable end
to your miserable life.

WEALTH

Mister, leave me alone, the both of you.

CHREMYLUS

Fat chance.

CARIO

My suggestion is the best, master: let me put a miserable
end to this character. I'll plant him at the edge of some cliff
and leave him there, so he can fall off and break his neck.

CHREMYLUS

All right, haul him off right now.

WEALTH

No!

CHREMYLUS

You'll talk, then?

WEALTH

But if you discover my identity, I'm sure you'll do some-
thing bad to me, and never let me go.

CHREMYLUS

I swear we will, if that's what you want.

WEALTH

Then take your hands off me first.

ΧΡΕΜΥΛΟΣ

75   ἦν, μεθίεμεν.

ΠΛΟΥΤΟΣ

ἀκούετον δή· δεῖ γάρ, ὡς ἔοικέ, με
λέγειν ἃ κρύπτειν ἢ παρεσκευασμένος.
ἐγὼ γάρ εἰμι Πλοῦτος.

ΚΑΡΙΩΝ

                        ὦ μιαρώτατε
ἀνδρῶν ἀπάντων, εἶτ᾽ ἐσίγας Πλοῦτος ὤν;

ΧΡΕΜΥΛΟΣ

80 σὺ Πλοῦτος, οὕτως ἀθλίως διακείμενος;
ὦ Φοῖβ᾽ Ἄπολλον καὶ θεοὶ καὶ δαίμονες
καὶ Ζεῦ, τί φῄς; ἐκεῖνος ὄντως εἶ σύ;

ΠΛΟΥΤΟΣ

                                    ναί.

ΧΡΕΜΥΛΟΣ

ἐκεῖνος αὐτός;

ΠΛΟΥΤΟΣ

        αὐτότατος.

ΧΡΕΜΥΛΟΣ

                    πόθεν οὖν, φράσον,
αὐχμῶν βαδίζεις;

ΠΛΟΥΤΟΣ

                    ἐκ Πατροκλέους ἔρχομαι,
85 ὃς οὐκ ἐλούσατ᾽ ἐξ ὅτουπερ ἐγένετο.

CHREMYLUS

All right, they're off.

WEALTH

Now listen; it seems I must tell you what I was prepared to conceal. You see, I'm Wealth.

CARIO

You scum of the earth, you weren't going to tell us that you're Wealth?

CHREMYLUS

You're Wealth, in such a miserable state? By Phoebus Apollo, Zeus, and all the gods and spirits, what are you saying? Are you really who you say?

WEALTH

Yes.

CHREMYLUS

The very one himself?

WEALTH

None other.

CHREMYLUS

Then how come you look so grubby?

WEALTH

I've been visiting Patrocles, who hasn't taken a bath since he was born.[5]

---

[5] Identity uncertain; mentioned also in Aristophanes' *Storks* (fr. 455) as a wealthy miser.

ΧΡΕΜΥΛΟΣ

τουτὶ δὲ τὸ κακὸν πῶς ἔπαθες; κάτειπέ μοι.

ΠΛΟΥΤΟΣ

ὁ Ζεύς με ταῦτ᾽ ἔδρασεν ἀνθρώποις φθονῶν.
ἐγὼ γὰρ ὢν μειράκιον ἠπείλησ᾽ ὅτι
ὡς τοὺς δικαίους καὶ σοφοὺς καὶ κοσμίους
90   μόνους βαδιοίμην· ὁ δέ μ᾽ ἐποίησεν τυφλόν,
ἵνα μὴ διαγιγνώσκοιμι τούτων μηδένα.
οὕτως ἐκεῖνος τοῖσι χρηστοῖσι φθονεῖ.

ΧΡΕΜΥΛΟΣ

καὶ μὴν διὰ τοὺς χρηστούς γε τιμᾶται μόνους
καὶ τοὺς δικαίους.

ΠΛΟΥΤΟΣ

ὁμολογῶ σοι.

ΧΡΕΜΥΛΟΣ

φέρε, τί οὖν;
95   εἰ πάλιν ἀναβλέψειας, ὥσπερ καὶ πρὸ τοῦ,
φεύγοις ἂν ἤδη τοὺς πονηρούς;

ΠΛΟΥΤΟΣ

φήμ᾽ ἐγώ.

ΧΡΕΜΥΛΟΣ

ὡς τοὺς δικαίους δ᾽ ἂν βαδίζοις;

ΠΛΟΥΤΟΣ

πάνυ μὲν οὖν·
πολλοῦ γὰρ αὐτοὺς οὐχ ἑόρακά πω χρόνου.

WEALTH

CHREMYLUS

But how did you fall on such hard times, I'd like to know?

WEALTH

Zeus did this to me because he resents mankind. You see, when I was a boy I vowed that I'd only visit the houses of just, wise, and decent people, so Zeus made me blind, to keep me from recognizing any of them.[6] That's how much he resents good people.

CHREMYLUS

But it's only the good and the just that honor him!

WEALTH

I agree with you.

CHREMYLUS

All right now, suppose you regained your sight, just as it was before, would you start shunning the wicked?

WEALTH

Yes I would.

CHREMYLUS

And you'd visit the just?

WEALTH

Absolutely. It's been quite a while since I've laid eyes on them.

[6] The blindness of wealth was an old motif, cf. Hipponax 36.

ΚΑΡΙΩΝ
καὶ θαῦμά γ᾽ οὐδέν· οὐδ᾽ ἐγὼ γὰρ ὁ βλέπων.

ΠΛΟΥΤΟΣ
100 ἄφετόν με νῦν· ἴστον γὰρ ἤδη τἀπ᾽ ἐμοῦ.

ΧΡΕΜΥΛΟΣ
μὰ Δί᾽, ἀλλὰ πολλῷ μᾶλλον ἑξόμεσθά σου.

ΠΛΟΥΤΟΣ
οὐκ ἠγόρευον ὅτι παρέξειν πράγματα
ἐμέλλετόν μοι;

ΧΡΕΜΥΛΟΣ
    καὶ σύ γ᾽, ἀντιβολῶ, πιθοῦ
καὶ μή μ᾽ ἀπολίπῃς· οὐ γὰρ εὑρήσεις ἐμοῦ
105 ζητῶν ἔτ᾽ ἄνδρα τοὺς τρόπους βελτίονα.

ΚΑΡΙΩΝ
μὰ τὸν Δί᾽, οὐ γὰρ ἔστιν ἄλλος πλὴν ἐγώ.

ΠΛΟΥΤΟΣ
ταυτὶ λέγουσι πάντες· ἡνίκ᾽ ἂν δέ μου
τύχωσ᾽ ἀληθῶς καὶ γένωνται πλούσιοι,
ἀτεχνῶς ὑπερβάλλουσι τῇ μοχθηρίᾳ.

ΧΡΕΜΥΛΟΣ
110 ἔχει μὲν οὕτως, εἰσὶ δ᾽ οὐ πάντες κακοί.

ΠΛΟΥΤΟΣ
μὰ Δί᾽, ἀλλ᾽ ἀπαξάπαντες.

ΚΑΡΙΩΝ
    οἰμώξει μακρά.

CARIO

That's no surprise: neither have I, and I can see!

WEALTH

Now let me go; you've heard my story.

CHREMYLUS

Oh no, we want to hold on to you all the more!

WEALTH

Didn't I predict that you two would make trouble for me?

CHREMYLUS

No, please hear me out, and don't run off; you'll never find
a man with a better character than mine.

CARIO

No indeed, there's none better, except for me.

WEALTH

That's what they all say. But once they get their hands on
me for real and become rich, their wickedness knows abso-
lutely no bounds.

CHREMYLUS

True, that's how it is, but not everyone is bad.

WEALTH

Oh yes they are, all of them!

CARIO

You're really going to get it!

ΧΡΕΜΥΛΟΣ

σοὶ δ᾽ ὡς ἂν εἰδῇς ὅσα, παρ᾽ ἡμῖν ἢν μένῃς,
γενήσετ᾽ ἀγαθά, πρόσεχε τὸν νοῦν ἵνα πύθῃ.
οἶμαι γάρ, οἶμαι—ξὺν θεῷ δ᾽ εἰρήσεται—
115 ταύτης ἀπαλλάξειν σε τῆς ὀφθαλμίας
βλέψαι ποιήσας.

ΠΛΟΥΤΟΣ
            μηδαμῶς τοῦτ᾽ ἐργάσῃ·
οὐ βούλομαι γὰρ πάλιν ἀναβλέψαι.

ΧΡΕΜΥΛΟΣ
                        τί φῄς;

ΚΑΡΙΩΝ
ἄνθρωπος οὗτός ἐστιν ἄθλιος φύσει.

ΠΛΟΥΤΟΣ
ὁ Ζεὺς μὲν οὖν εἰδὼς τὰ τούτων μῶρ᾽, ἔμ᾽, εἰ
πύθοιτ᾽, ἂν ἐπιτρίψειε.

ΧΡΕΜΥΛΟΣ
120   νῦν δ᾽ οὐ τοῦτο δρᾷ,
ὅστις σε προσπταίοντα περινοστεῖν ἐᾷ;

ΠΛΟΥΤΟΣ
οὐκ οἶδ᾽· ἐγὼ δ᾽ ἐκεῖνον ὀρρωδῶ πάνυ.

ΧΡΕΜΥΛΟΣ
ἄληθες, ὦ δειλότατε πάντων δαιμόνων;
οἴει γὰρ εἶναι τὴν Διὸς τυραννίδα
125 καὶ τοὺς κεραυνοὺς ἀξίους τριωβόλου,
ἐὰν ἀναβλέψῃς σὺ κἂν σμικρὸν χρόνον;

WEALTH

CHREMYLUS

If you only knew what blessings you stand to gain if you stay with us! Just pay attention and you'll find out. Because I think, yes I think, and I hope to god it's true, that I can cure this sickness in your eyes and restore your sight.

WEALTH

Please don't do that! I don't want my sight back.

CHREMYLUS

You don't?

CARIO

This fellow's a congenital loser.

WEALTH

No, Zeus is well aware of the foolishness of these people, and it's me he would torment if he found out.

CHREMYLUS

But isn't he doing that already, leaving you to stumble about from place to place?

WEALTH

Maybe, but all I know is that he scares the pants off me.

CHREMYLUS

Really? Of all divinities you're the most faint-hearted! Do you think that Zeus' rule and all his thunderbolts would be worth a dime if you regained your sight even for a moment?

ΠΛΟΥΤΟΣ

ἆ, μὴ λέγ᾽, ὦ πόνηρε, ταῦτ᾽.

ΧΡΕΜΥΛΟΣ

ἔχ᾽ ἥσυχος·
ἐγὼ γὰρ ἀποδείξω σε τοῦ Διὸς πολὺ
μεῖζον δυνάμενον.

ΠΛΟΥΤΟΣ

ἐμὲ σύ;

ΧΡΕΜΥΛΟΣ

νὴ τὸν οὐρανόν.
130 αὐτίκα γὰρ ἄρχει διὰ τί ὁ Ζεὺς τῶν θεῶν;

ΚΑΡΙΩΝ

διὰ τἀργύριον· πλεῖστον γάρ ἐστ᾽ αὐτῷ.

ΧΡΕΜΥΛΟΣ

φέρε,
τίς οὖν ὁ παρέχων ἐστὶν αὐτῷ τοῦθ᾽;

ΚΑΡΙΩΝ

ὁδί.

ΧΡΕΜΥΛΟΣ

θύουσι δ᾽ αὐτῷ διὰ τίν᾽; οὐ διὰ τουτονί;

ΚΑΡΙΩΝ

καὶ νὴ Δί᾽ εὔχονταί γε πλουτεῖν ἄντικρυς.

ΧΡΕΜΥΛΟΣ

135 οὔκουν ὅδ᾽ ἐστὶν αἴτιος καὶ ῥᾳδίως
παύσειεν, εἰ βούλοιτο, ταῦτ᾽ ἄν;

WEALTH

Oh no, you rascal, don't say that!

CHREMYLUS

Calm down, because I'm going to show you that you're far more powerful than Zeus.

WEALTH

Me, you say?

CHREMYLUS

Heavens yes! (*to Cario*) Now then, how come Zeus rules over the gods?

CARIO

Because of his riches; he's got the most.

CHREMYLUS

Very good. Now who is it that supplies it to him?

CARIO

(*indicating Wealth*) Him.

CHREMYLUS

And for whose sake do people sacrifice to Zeus? Isn't it for his sake?

CARIO

Quite right, and their very first prayer is for wealth.

CHREMYLUS

So isn't he responsible for all this? And couldn't he put a stop to it if he wanted?

ΠΛΟΥΤΟΣ

ὅτι τί δή;

ΧΡΕΜΥΛΟΣ

ὅτι οὐδ' ἂν εἷς θύσειεν ἀνθρώπων ἔτι
οὐ βοῦν ἄν, οὐχὶ ψαιστόν, οὐκ ἀλλ' οὐδὲ ἕν,
μὴ βουλομένου σοῦ.

ΠΛΟΥΤΟΣ

πῶς;

ΧΡΕΜΥΛΟΣ

ὅπως; οὐκ ἔσθ' ὅπως
140   ὠνήσεται δήπουθεν, ἢν σὺ μὴ παρὼν
αὐτὸς διδῷς τἀργύριον, ὥστε τοῦ Διὸς
τὴν δύναμιν, ἢν λυπῇ τι, καταλύσεις μόνος.

ΠΛΟΥΤΟΣ

τί λέγεις; δι' ἐμὲ θύουσιν αὐτῷ;

ΧΡΕΜΥΛΟΣ

φήμ' ἐγώ.
καὶ νὴ Δί' εἴ τί γ' ἐστὶ λαμπρὸν καὶ καλὸν
145   ἢ χαρίεν ἀνθρώποισι, διὰ σὲ γίγνεται.
ἅπαντα τῷ πλουτεῖν γάρ ἐσθ' ὑπήκοα.

ΚΑΡΙΩΝ

ἔγωγέ τοι διὰ μικρὸν ἀργυρίδιον
δοῦλος γεγένημαι πρότερον ὢν ἐλεύθερος.

ΧΡΕΜΥΛΟΣ

καὶ τάς γ' ἑταίρας φασὶ τὰς Κορινθίας,
150   ὅταν μὲν αὐτάς τις πένης πειρῶν τύχῃ,

WEALTH

How do you mean?

CHREMYLUS

Well, no one would sacrifice another ox, or a barley cake, or anything else, if you weren't amenable.

WEALTH

How's that?

CHREMYLUS

Why, they could never buy it in the first place unless you were there to supply the money. So if Zeus gives you any trouble, you'll abolish his power all by yourself.

WEALTH

Are you telling me that I'm the reason they sacrifice to him?

CHREMYLUS

That's right. And what's more, it's through you that people have anything radiant, fine, or charming. Everything's in the service of wealth.

CARIO

In my case, it was for small change that I lost my freedom and became a slave.[7]

CHREMYLUS

And I've heard that Corinthian courtesans, when a poor

---

[7] Since in Aristophanes' time Athenian citizens were not enslaved for debt, we are probably to think of Cario as a metic unable to pay a debt or a captive unable to pay his ransom.

οὐδὲ προσέχειν τὸν νοῦν· ἐὰν δὲ πλούσιος,
τὸν πρωκτὸν αὐτὰς εὐθὺς ὡς τοῦτον τρέπειν.

ΚΑΡΙΩΝ
καὶ τούς γε παῖδάς φασι ταὐτὸ τοῦτο δρᾶν
οὐ τῶν ἐραστῶν ἀλλὰ τἀργυρίου χάριν.

ΧΡΕΜΤΛΟΣ
155 οὐ τούς γε χρηστούς, ἀλλὰ τοὺς πόρνους· ἐπεὶ
αἰτοῦσιν οὐκ ἀργύριον οἱ χρηστοί.

ΚΑΡΙΩΝ
τί δαί;

ΧΡΕΜΤΛΟΣ
ὁ μὲν ἵππον ἀγαθόν, ὁ δὲ κύνας θηρευτικάς.

ΚΑΡΙΩΝ
αἰσχυνόμενοι γὰρ ἀργύριον αἰτεῖν ἴσως
ὀνόματι περιπέττουσι τὴν μοχθηρίαν.

ΧΡΕΜΤΛΟΣ
160 τέχναι δὲ πᾶσαι διὰ σὲ καὶ σοφίσματα
ἐν τοῖσιν ἀνθρώποισίν ἐσθ᾽ ηὑρημένα.
ὁ μὲν γὰρ ἡμῶν σκυτοτομεῖ καθήμενος,
ἕτερος δὲ χαλκεύει τις, ὁ δὲ τεκταίνεται,
ὁ δὲ χρυσοχοεῖ γε χρυσίον παρὰ σοῦ λαβών—

ΚΑΡΙΟΝ
165 ὁ δὲ λωποδυτεῖ γε, νὴ Δί᾽, ὁ δὲ τοιχωρυχεῖ,—

ΧΡΕΜΤΛΟΣ
ὁ δὲ κναφεύει γ᾽,

man makes a pass at them, pay him no mind, but if he's
rich, they right away offer him their arse.

CARIO

And I've heard that boys do the same thing, not for their
lovers' sake but for the money.

CHREMYLUS

But not the decent ones, only the whores; the decent ones
don't ask for money.

CARIO

For what then?

CHREMYLUS

A good horse, or hunting dogs.

CARIO

No doubt they're ashamed to ask for money, and cover up
their sluttiness with fancy words.

CHREMYLUS

All crafts and skills known to mankind were invented for
your sake. For you, people sit and make shoes, or work
bronze, or do carpentry, or smelt gold that they obtain
from you—

CARIO

or mug people, by heaven, or break into houses—

CHREMYLUS

or make clothing—

ΚΑΡΙΩΝ
ὁ δέ γε πλύνει κῴδια,—

ΧΡΕΜΥΛΟΣ
ὁ δὲ βυρσοδεψεῖ γ᾽—

ΚΑΡΙΩΝ
ὁ δέ γε πωλεῖ κρόμμυα,—

ΧΡΕΜΥΛΟΣ
ὁ δ᾽ ἁλούς γε μοιχὸς διὰ σέ που παρατίλλεται.

ΠΛΟΥΤΟΣ
οἴμοι τάλας, ταυτί μ᾽ ἐλάνθανεν πάλαι.

ΚΑΡΙΩΝ
170 μέγας δὲ βασιλεὺς οὐχὶ διὰ τοῦτον κομᾷ;
ἐκκλησία δ᾽ οὐχὶ διὰ τοῦτον γίγνεται;

ΧΡΕΜΥΛΟΣ
τί δαὶ τριήρεις; οὐ σὺ πληροῖς; εἰπέ μοι.

ΚΑΡΙΩΝ
τὸ δ᾽ ἐν Κορίνθῳ ξενικὸν οὐχ οὗτος τρέφει;
ὁ Πάμφιλος δ᾽ οὐχὶ διὰ τοῦτον κλαύσεται;

ΧΡΕΜΥΛΟΣ
175 ὁ βελονοπώλης δ᾽ οὐχὶ μετὰ τοῦ Παμφίλου;

ΚΑΡΙΩΝ
Ἀγύρριος δ᾽ οὐχὶ διὰ τοῦτον πέρδεται;

---

8 Peltasts garrisoned there by the Athenian commander Iphicrates after a Spartan attack in 390 (Xenophon, *Hellenica* 4.5, 8).

CARIO

or launder woollens—

CHREMYLUS

or tan hides—

CARIO

or sell onions—

CHREMYLUS

or get caught in adultery and plucked, for your sake.

WEALTH

Dear me, I never realized all this!

CARIO

Doesn't the Great King preen on his account? And on his account doesn't the Assembly meet?

CHREMYLUS

And what about triremes? Tell me, isn't it you who fill them?

CARIO

And doesn't he provision the mercenary force in Corinth?[8] And won't Pamphilus[9] come to grief on his account?

CHREMYLUS

And the needle seller too, after Pamphilus?[10]

CARIO

And isn't he the source of Agyrrhius' happy farts?

[9] Mentioned by the comic poet Plato (fr. 14) in connection with the theft of public funds, a charge probably made after his expedition against Aegina in 389, cf. Xenophon, *Hellenica* 5.1, Demosthenes 40.22.   [10] Identified in a scholium as one Aristoxenus, otherwise unknown.

449

ΧΡΕΜΤΛΟΣ

Φιλέψιος δ' οὐχ ἕνεκα σοῦ μύθους λέγει;
ἡ ξυμμαχία δ' οὐ διὰ σὲ τοῖς Αἰγυπτίοις;
ἐρᾷ δὲ Λαῒς οὐ διὰ σὲ Φιλωνίδου;

ΚΑΡΙΩΝ

ὁ Τιμοθέου δὲ πύργος—

ΧΡΕΜΤΛΟΣ

180   ἐμπέσοι γέ σοι.
τὰ δὲ πράγματ' οὐχὶ διὰ σὲ πάντα πράττεται;
μονώτατος γὰρ εἶ σὺ πάντων αἴτιος
καὶ τῶν κακῶν καὶ τῶν ἀγαθῶν, εὖ ἴσθ' ὅτι.

ΚΑΡΙΩΝ

κρατοῦσι γοῦν κἂν τοῖς πολέμοις ἑκάστοτε
185 ἐφ' οἷς ἂν οὗτος ἐπικαθέζηται μόνον.

ΠΛΟΥΤΟΣ

ἐγὼ τοσαῦτα δυνατός εἰμ' εἷς ὢν ποιεῖν;

ΧΡΕΜΤΛΟΣ

καὶ ναὶ μὰ Δία τούτων γε πολλῷ πλείονα·
ὥστ' οὐδὲ μεστός σου γέγον' οὐδεὶς πώποτε.
τῶν μὲν γὰρ ἄλλων ἐστὶ πάντων πλησμονή·
ἔρωτος,—

---

11 Probably the Philepsius of Lamptrae cited by Demosthenes (24.134), along with Agyrrhius, as a prominent politician; cf. also Plato com. fr. 238.

CHREMYLUS

And doesn't Philepsius tell tall tales for your sake?[11] And isn't the alliance with Egypt for your sake?[12] And isn't it for your sake that Lais loves Philonides?[13]

CARIO

And Timotheus' tower—[14]

CHREMYLUS

May it fall on your head! (*to Wealth*) Aren't all activities undertaken for your sake? Yes, it's you and you alone who motivate everything, the good and the bad alike; you can be sure of that.

CARIO

In warfare it's certainly true that the side he sits on invariably wins.

WEALTH

Can I do all that, and single-handedly?

CHREMYLUS

Absolutely, and lots more besides. No one ever gets their fill of you. There can be too much of anything else: of love—

---

[12] Athens sided with Evagoras of Cyprus, who in 391 had revolted against the Persians and allied himself with a fellow rebel, the Egyptian Pharaoh Acoris (reigned 392–79).

[13] Lais was a celebrated courtesan born in 422/1 and now resident in Corinth; Philonides of Melite is ridiculed elsewhere as rich, corpulent, and foolish (Nicochares fr. 4, Philyllius fr. 22, Plato com. fr. 65.1.5–6, Theopompus fr. 5).

[14] Son of the great general Conon, recently deceased, who would later enjoy a great political and military career.

ΚΑΡΙΩΝ

ἄρτων,—

ΧΡΕΜΤΛΟΣ

μουσικῆς,—

ΚΑΡΙΩΝ

190   τραγημάτων,—

ΧΡΕΜΤΛΟΣ

τιμῆς,—

ΚΑΡΙΩΝ

πλακούντων,—

ΧΡΕΜΤΛΟΣ

ἀνδραγαθίας,—

ΚΑΡΙΩΝ

ἰσχάδων,—

ΧΡΕΜΤΛΟΣ

φιλοτιμίας,—

ΚΑΡΙΩΝ

μάζης,—

ΧΡΕΜΤΛΟΣ

στρατηγίας,—

ΚΑΡΙΩΝ

φακῆς.

ΧΡΕΜΤΛΟΣ

σοῦ δ᾽ ἐγένετ᾽ οὐδεὶς μεστὸς οὐδεπώποτε.
ἀλλ᾽ ἦν τάλαντά τις λάβῃ τριακαίδεκα,

CARIO

of loaves—

CHREMYLUS

of the arts—

CARIO

of munchies—

CHREMYLUS

of honor—

CARIO

of cakes—

CHREMYLUS

of manliness—

CARIO

of figs—

CHREMYLUS

of ambition—

CARIO

of barley bread—

CHREMYLUS

of generalship—

CARIO

of lentil soup.

CHREMYLUS

But no one ever gets his fill of you. If someone gets his

195 πολὺ μᾶλλον ἐπιθυμεῖ λαβεῖν ἑκκαίδεκα·
κἂν ταῦθ' ἀνύσηται, τετταράκοντα βούλεται,
ἢ φησὶν οὐ βιωτὸν αὐτῷ τὸν βίον.

ΠΛΟΥΤΟΣ

εὖ τοι λέγειν ἔμοιγε φαίνεσθον πάνυ·
πλὴν ἓν μόνον δέδοικα—

ΧΡΕΜΥΛΟΣ

φράζε, τοῦ πέρι;

ΠΛΟΥΤΟΣ

200 ὅπως ἐγὼ τὴν δύναμιν ἣν ὑμεῖς φατε
ἔχειν με, ταύτης δεσπότης γενήσομαι.

ΧΡΕΜΥΛΟΣ

νὴ τὸν Δί', ἀλλὰ καὶ λέγουσι πάντες ὡς
δειλότατόν ἐσθ' ὁ πλοῦτος.

ΠΛΟΥΤΟΣ

ἥκιστ', ἀλλά με
τοιχωρύχος τις διέβαλ'· εἰσδὺς γάρ ποτε
205 οὐκ εἶχεν εἰς τὴν οἰκίαν οὐδὲν λαβεῖν,
εὑρὼν ἁπαξάπαντα κατακεκλημένα·
εἶτ' ὠνόμασέ μου τὴν πρόνοιαν δειλίαν.

ΧΡΕΜΥΛΟΣ

μή νυν μελέτω σοι μηδέν· ὡς ἐὰν γένῃ
ἀνὴρ πρόθυμος αὐτὸς εἰς τὰ πράγματα,
210 βλέποντ' ἀποδείξω σ' ὀξύτερον τοῦ Λυγκέως.

ΠΛΟΥΤΟΣ

πῶς οὖν δυνήσει τοῦτο δρᾶσαι θνητὸς ὤν;

hands on thirteen talents, he hankers all the more to get sixteen; and if he achieves that, he wants forty, or else he says life isn't worth living.

WEALTH

You've both made a very convincing case, yet there's one thing that worries me.

CHREMYLUS

Please, what's that?

WEALTH

Just how I'm to become master of the power you say I have.

CHREMYLUS

Ah yes, everyone says that nothing's more cowardly than wealth.

WEALTH

Not true! That's a burglar's slander. You see, he broke into the house but had nothing to snatch, because he found everything under lock and key, so he called my precautions cowardice.

CHREMYLUS

Don't worry about a thing: if you'll just throw yourself wholeheartedly into this job, I'll give you better eyesight than Lynceus![15]

WEALTH

And how will you manage that? You're a mere mortal.

---

[15] A sharp-eyed Argonaut, cf. Apollonius of Rhodes 1.153–55.

ΧΡΕΜΥΛΟΣ

ἔχω τιν᾽ ἀγαθὴν ἐλπίδ᾽ ἐξ ὧν εἶπέ μοι
ὁ Φοῖβος αὐτὸς Πυθικὴν σείσας δάφνην.

ΠΛΟΥΤΟΣ

κἀκεῖνος οὖν ξύνοιδε ταῦτα;

ΧΡΕΜΥΛΟΣ

φήμ᾽ ἐγώ.

ΠΛΟΥΤΟΣ

ὁρᾶτε—

ΧΡΕΜΥΛΟΣ

215   μὴ φρόντιζε μηδέν, ὦγαθέ·
ἐγὼ γάρ, εὖ τοῦτ᾽ ἴσθι, κἂν δῇ μ᾽ ἀποθανεῖν,
αὐτὸς διαπράξω ταῦτα.

ΚΑΡΙΩΝ

κἂν βούλῃ γ᾽, ἐγώ.

ΧΡΕΜΥΛΟΣ

πολλοὶ δ᾽ ἔσονται χἄτεροι νῷν ξύμμαχοι,
ὅσοις δικαίοις οὖσιν οὐκ ἦν ἄλφιτα.

ΠΛΟΥΤΟΣ

220   παπαῖ· πονηρούς γ᾽ εἶπας ἡμῖν ξυμμάχους.

ΧΡΕΜΥΛΟΣ

οὔκ, ἤν γε πλουτήσωσιν ἐξ ἀρχῆς πάλιν.
ἀλλ᾽ ἴθι σὺ μὲν ταχέως δραμών—

ΚΑΡΙΩΝ

τί δρῶ; λέγε.

CHREMYLUS

I have high hopes, after what Phoebus told me, "when he personally shook the Pythian laurel bough."[16]

WEALTH

You mean he's in on this too?

CHREMYLUS

That's right.

WEALTH

Watch out now—

CHREMYLUS

Don't worry about a thing, my friend. Please rest assured that I'll pull this off, even if it means my death.

CARIO

I'll lend a hand, if you like.

CHREMYLUS

And we'll have many others for allies, righteous people who've gone without their daily bread.

WEALTH

Good grief, it's pretty poor allies you've assigned us.

CHREMYLUS

No, not once they've recovered their original wealth. (*to Cario*) Now you run off on the double—

CARIO

To do what, please?

---

16 From an unknown tragedy.

ΧΡΕΜΤΛΟΣ

τοὺς ξυγγεώργους κάλεσον,—εὑρήσεις δ᾽ ἴσως
ἐν τοῖς ἀγροῖς αὐτοὺς ταλαιπωρουμένους,—
225 ὅπως ἂν ἴσον ἕκαστος ἐνταυθοῖ παρὼν
ἡμῖν μετάσχῃ τοῦδε τοῦ Πλούτου μέρος.

ΚΑΡΙΩΝ

καὶ δὴ βαδίζω. τουτοδὶ τὸ κρεάδιον
τῶν ἔνδοθέν τις εἰσενεγκάτω λαβών.

ΧΡΕΜΤΛΟΣ

ἐμοὶ μελήσει τοῦτό γ᾽· ἀλλ᾽ ἀνύσας τρέχε.
230 σὺ δ᾽, ὦ κράτιστε Πλοῦτε πάντων δαιμόνων,
εἴσω μετ᾽ ἐμοῦ δεῦρ᾽ εἴσιθ᾽· ἡ γὰρ οἰκία
αὕτη ᾽στὶν ἣν δεῖ χρημάτων σε τήμερον
μεστὴν ποιῆσαι καὶ δικαίως κἀδίκως.

ΠΛΟΥΤΟΣ

ἀλλ᾽ ἄχθομαι μὲν εἰσιών, νὴ τοὺς θεούς,
235 εἰς οἰκίαν ἑκάστοτ᾽ ἀλλοτρίαν πάνυ·
ἀγαθὸν γὰρ ἀπέλαυσ᾽ οὐδὲν αὐτοῦ πώποτε.
ἢν μὲν γὰρ εἰς φειδωλὸν εἰσελθὼν τύχω,
εὐθὺς κατώρυξέν με κατὰ τῆς γῆς κάτω·
κἄν τις προσέλθῃ χρηστὸς ἄνθρωπος φίλος
240 αἰτῶν λαβεῖν τι σμικρὸν ἀργυρίδιον,
ἔξαρνός ἐστι μηδ᾽ ἰδεῖν με πώποτε.
ἢν δ᾽ ὡς παραπλῆγ᾽ ἄνθρωπον εἰσελθὼν τύχω,
πόρναισι καὶ κύβοισι παραβεβλημένος
γυμνὸς θύραζ᾽ ἐξέπεσον ἐν ἀκαρεῖ χρόνου.

WEALTH

CHREMYLUS

Summon my fellow farmers—you'll probably find them laboring away in their fields—so that each one of them may join us here for his share of what Wealth has for us.

CARIO

I'm on my way. Let one of the household slaves come and take this piece of meat inside.

CHREMYLUS

I'll take care of that; you get a move on.

Exit CARIO.

Now, Wealth, most puissant of all divinities, please come inside here with me, because this is the house you've got to fill up with riches this very day, by fair means or foul.

WEALTH

By heaven, I really hate going into a strange house; it's never yet brought me any benefit. If I find myself in a pauper's house, he immediately digs a hole and puts me underground, and if a good friend of his comes to call and asks for a little loan, he swears he's never even laid eyes on me. And if I find myself in a degenerate's house, I'm thrown away on whores and dice, and in no time I'm out on the street shirtless.

ΧΡΕΜΥΛΟΣ

245 μετρίου γὰρ ἀνδρὸς οὐκ ἐπέτυχες πώποτε.
ἐγὼ δὲ τούτου τοῦ τρόπου πῶς εἰμ᾽ ἀεί·
χαίρω τε γὰρ φειδόμενος ὡς οὐδεὶς ἀνὴρ
πάλιν τ᾽ ἀναλῶν, ἡνίκ᾽ ἂν τούτου δέῃ.
ἀλλ᾽ εἰσίωμεν, ὡς ἰδεῖν σε βούλομαι
250 καὶ τὴν γυναῖκα καὶ τὸν υἱὸν τὸν μόνον,
ὃν ἐγὼ φιλῶ μάλιστα μετὰ σέ.

ΠΛΟΥΤΟΣ

πείθομαι.

ΧΡΕΜΥΛΟΣ

τί γὰρ ἄν τις οὐχὶ πρὸς σὲ τἀληθῆ λέγοι;

ΚΑΡΙΩΝ

ὦ πολλὰ δὴ τῷ δεσπότῃ ταὐτὸν θύμον φαγόντες,
ἄνδρες φίλοι καὶ δημόται καὶ τοῦ πονεῖν ἐρασταί,
255 ἴτ᾽, ἐγκονεῖτε, σπεύδεθ᾽, ὡς ὁ καιρὸς οὐχὶ μέλλειν,
ἀλλ᾽ ἔστ᾽ ἐπ᾽ αὐτῆς τῆς ἀκμῆς, ᾗ δεῖ παρόντ᾽
ἀμύνειν.

ΚΟΡΥΦΑΙΟΣ

οὔκουν ὁρᾷς ὁρμωμένους ἡμᾶς πάλαι προθύμως,
ὡς εἰκός ἐστιν ἀσθενεῖς γέροντας ἄνδρας ἤδη;
σὺ δ᾽ ἀξιοῖς ἴσως με θεῖν, πρὶν ταῦτα καὶ φράσαι
μοι
260 ὅτου χάριν μ᾽ ὁ δεσπότης ὁ σὸς κέκληκε δεῦρο.

ΚΑΡΙΩΝ

οὔκουν πάλαι δήπου λέγω; σὺ δ᾽ αὐτὸς οὐκ ἀκούεις.

CHREMYLUS

That's because you've never met a moderate man, but that's the character I've pretty much always had. No one's fonder of frugality than me, or of spending money either, when that's called for. Come on, let's go inside; I want to introduce you to my wife and only son, whom I love more than anything, except you.

WEALTH

That I can believe.

CHREMYLUS

Well, why would anyone lie to you?

Exit CHREMYLUS and WEALTH into the house; then CARIO reappears, leading the CHORUS of farmers.

CARIO

Friends, fellow demesmen, and lovers of hard labor, who like my master have many a time made a meal of thyme leaves, come ahead, raise some dust, hurry along; there's no time for tarrying, for this is the hour of decision, and you must lend a ready hand.

CHORUS LEADER

Surely you can see that we've been hustling eagerly the whole time, as much as can be expected of feeble old men. Maybe you think I should be running, before I've even heard the reason why that master of yours has summoned us here.

CARIO

Surely I've been telling you the whole time; it's you who

ὁ δεσπότης γάρ φησιν ὑμᾶς ἡδέως ἅπαντας
ψυχροῦ βίου καὶ δυσκόλου ζήσειν ἀπαλλαγέντας.

ΚΟΡΥΦΑΙΟΣ

ἔστιν δὲ δὴ τί καὶ πόθεν τὸ πρᾶγμα τοῦθ᾽ ὅ φησιν;

ΚΑΡΙΩΝ

265 ἔχων ἀφῖκται δεῦρο πρεσβύτην τιν᾽, ὦ πόνηροι,
ῥυπῶντα, κυφόν, ἄθλιον, ῥυσόν, μαδῶντα, νωδόν·
οἶμαι δέ, νὴ τὸν οὐρανόν, καὶ ψωλὸν αὐτὸν εἶναι.

ΚΟΡΥΦΑΙΟΣ

ὦ χρυσὸν ἀγγείλας ἐπῶν, πῶς φῄς; πάλιν φράσον
μοι.
δηλοῖς γὰρ αὐτὸν σωρὸν ἥκειν χρημάτων ἔχοντα.

ΚΑΡΙΩΝ

270 πρεσβυτικῶν μὲν οὖν κακῶν ἔγωγ᾽ ἔχοντα σωρόν.

ΚΟΡΥΦΑΙΟΣ

μῶν ἀξιοῖς φενακίσας ἔπειτ᾽ ἀπαλλαγῆναι
ἀζήμιος, καὶ ταῦτ᾽ ἐμοῦ βακτηρίαν ἔχοντος;

ΚΑΡΙΩΝ

πάντως γὰρ ἄνθρωπον φύσει τοιοῦτον εἰς τὰ πάντα
ἡγεῖσθέ μ᾽ εἶναι, κοὐδὲν ἂν νομίζεθ᾽ ὑγιὲς εἰπεῖν;

ΚΟΡΥΦΑΙΟΣ

275 ὡς σεμνὸς οὑπίτριπτος. αἱ κνῆμαι δέ σου βοῶσιν
"ἰοὺ ἰού," τὰς χοίνικας καὶ τὰς πέδας ποθοῦσαι.

haven't listened. My master says you're all going to live nicely and be rid of your chill and disagreeable way of life.

CHORUS LEADER

But what's it all about? And where's the wherewithal for his claim?

CARIO

Very well, you rascals: he's brought an oldster home, grubby, stooped, pitiable, shrivelled, mangy, toothless, and by heaven, I think he's even circumcised.[17]

CHORUS LEADER

O harbinger of golden news, what's that you say? Tell me again! Obviously you're saying he's come with a mound of money.

CARIO

Not I; rather a mound of mature malaise.

CHORUS LEADER

So you think you'll hoodwink us and get away with it? And me with my walking stick in hand?

CARIO

Do you really think I'm invariably that sort of person? And do you think I'm incapable of talking sense?

CHORUS LEADER

The scamp's pretty smug! Your shins are just asking for the stocks and chains, and will soon be yelling "ouch"!

---

[17] As only barbarians were; here comically climaxing the list of physical debasements.

ARISTOPHANES

ΚΑΡΙΩΝ

ἐν τῇ σορῷ νυνὶ λαχὸν τὸ γράμμα σου δικάζειν,
σὺ δ' οὐ βαδίζεις; ὁ δὲ Χάρων τὸ ξύμβολον
   δίδωσιν.

ΚΟΡΥΦΑΙΟΣ

διαρραγείης. ὡς μόθων εἶ καὶ φύσει κόβαλος,
280 ὅστις φενακίζεις, φράσαι δ' οὔπω τέτληκας ἡμῖν,
οἳ πολλὰ μοχθήσαντες οὐκ οὔσης σχολῆς
   προθύμως
δεῦρ' ἤλθομεν, πολλῶν θύμων ῥίζας διεκπερῶντες.

ΚΑΡΙΩΝ

ἀλλ' οὐκέτ' ἂν κρύψαιμι. τὸν Πλοῦτον γάρ, ὦνδρες,
   ἥκει
285 ἄγων ὁ δεσπότης, ὃς ὑμᾶς πλουσίους ποιήσει.

ΚΟΡΥΦΑΙΟΣ

ὄντως γὰρ ἔστι πλουσίοις ἡμῖν ἄπασιν εἶναι;

ΚΑΡΙΩΝ

νὴ τοὺς θεούς, Μίδαις μὲν οὖν, ἢν ὦτ' ὄνου λάβητε.

ΚΟΡΥΦΑΙΟΣ

ὡς ἥδομαι καὶ τέρπομαι καὶ βούλομαι χορεῦσαι
ὑφ' ἡδονῆς, εἴπερ λέγεις ὄντως σὺ ταῦτ' ἀληθῆ.

281 = v. 260 repetunt A M U: del. Bergk
285 ὑμᾶς cett: ἡμᾶς R M
287 Μίδαις Kuster: Μίδας a

CARIO

And you've drawn the token marked Court of the Coffin.[18]
You better get going; Charon will give you your ticket.

CHORUS LEADER

Blow yourself to bits! You're an imp and a rascal to play us
for suckers, and you haven't yet bothered to explain any-
thing to us, when we've taken great pains to be here, and
time we can't afford to lose, passing right by innumerable
thyme plants.

CARIO

All right, I won't keep you in the dark any longer. Gentle-
men, my master's brought Wealth home with him, and he's
going to make you wealthy.

CHORUS LEADER

You mean it's really possible for us to be wealthy?

CARIO

So help me god, you'll be Midases if you can find a pair of
ass's ears![19]

CHORUS LEADER

I'm so happy and so glad, I want to dance for joy, if what
you're saying is really true.

---

[18] Jurors, who were often impecunious elders, were assigned
to courts by tokens drawn from an allotment machine.

[19] The legendary Phrygian king Midas got from Dionysus the
power to turn whatever he touched to gold, but ass's ears from
Apollo for voting against him in a musical contest.

ΚΑΡΙΩΝ

(στρ.)   καὶ μὴν ἐγὼ βουλήσομαι—θρεττανελο—τὸν
        Κύκλωπα

291   μιμούμενος καὶ τοῖν ποδοῖν ὡδὶ παρενσαλεύων
    ὑμᾶς ἄγειν. ἀλλ᾽ εἷα, τέκεα, θαμίν᾽ ἐπαναβοῶντες
    βληχώμενοί τε προβατίων
    αἰγῶν τε κιναβρώντων μέλη

295   ἔπεσθ᾽ ἀπεψωλημένοι·
    τράγοι δ᾽ ἀκρατιεῖσθε.

ΧΟΡΟΣ

(ἀντ)   ἡμεῖς δέ γ᾽ αὖ ζητήσομεν—θρεττανελο—τὸν
        Κύκλωπα

    βληχώμενοι σὲ τουτονὶ πεινῶντα καταλαβόντες,
    πήραν ἔχοντα λάχανά τ᾽ ἄγρια δροσερά,
    κραιπαλῶντα
    ἡγούμενον τοῖς προβατίοις,

300   εἰκῇ δὲ καταδαρθόντα που
    μέγαν λαβόντες ἠμμένον
    σφηκίσκον ἐκτυφλῶσαι.

ΚΑΡΙΩΝ

(στρ)   ἐγὼ δὲ τὴν Κίρκην γε, τὴν τὰ φάρμακ᾽
       ἀνακυκῶσαν,
    ἣ τοὺς ἑταίρους τοῦ Φιλωνίδου ποτ᾽ ἐν Κορίνθῳ

297 βληχώμενοι σὲ] βληχώμενόν τε V
300 -θόντα Porson: -θέντα a

CARIO[20]

As for me, I'm ready—ta dum da dum—to do a
    takeoff on the Cyclops
and lead you in dance, hopping with both feet like
    this!
Hey now, kids, sing out after me loud and clear:
bleating songs of little lambs
and stinky goats,
follow me with pricks unsheathed:
you goats will have your breakfast.

CHORUS

Now it's our turn—ta dum da dum—to pull
    something on the Cyclops
(that's you): bleating away, we'll find you feeling
    famished,
toting a pouch of fresh wild herbs, hung over
as you lead your little lambs;
then as you carelessly curl up somewhere,
we'll hoist a big burning
stake and put out your eye.

CARIO[21]

Then I'll do Circe, the mixer of potions,
who one day in Corinth convinced Philonides'
    companions

---

[20] A parody of a dithyramb by Philoxenus of Cythera, *Cyclops or Galateia* (frs. 815–24 Campbell), composed after he had fled the court of Dionysius of Syracuse, who came to power in 406. Cario sings the role of the Cyclops, the Chorus the role of Odysseus and his companions (cf. *Odyssey* 9.105–566). [21] Cario switches to the story of Odysseus and Circe (cf. *Odyssey* 10.210–574), for whom he substitutes Philonides and Lais (179 n.).

ἔπεισεν ὡς ὄντας κάπρους
305 μεμαγμένον σκῶρ ἐσθίειν,—αὐτὴ δ' ἔματτεν
αὐτοῖς,—
μιμήσομαι πάντας τρόπους·
ὑμεῖς δὲ γρυλλίζοντες ὑπὸ φιληδίας
ἔπεσθε μητρί, χοῖροι.

ΧΟΡΟΣ

(ἀντ) οὐκοῦν σέ, τὴν Κίρκην γε τὴν τὰ φάρμακ'
ἀνακυκῶσαν
310 καὶ μαγγανεύουσαν μολύνουσάν τε τοὺς ἑταίρους
λαβόντες ὑπὸ φιληδίας
τὸν Λαρτίου μιμούμενοι τῶν ὄρχεων κρεμῶμεν,
μινθώσομέν θ' ὥσπερ τράγου
τὴν ῥῖνα· σὺ δ' Ἀρίστυλλος ὑποχάσκων ἐρεῖς·
315 "ἔπεσθε μητρί, χοῖροι."

ΚΑΡΙΩΝ

ἀλλ' εἶά νυν τῶν σκωμμάτων ἀπαλλαγέντες ἤδη
ὑμεῖς ἐπ' ἄλλ' εἶδος τρέπεσθ'·
ἐγὼ δ' ἰὼν ἤδη λάθρα
βουλήσομαι τοῦ δεσπότου
320 λαβών τιν' ἄρτον καὶ κρέας
μασώμενος τὸ λοιπὸν οὕτω τῷ κόπῳ ξυνεῖναι.

ΧΟΡΟΥ

ΧΡΕΜΥΛΟΣ

"χαίρειν" μὲν ὑμᾶς ἐστιν, ὦνδρες δημόται,

---

318 ἤδη] εἴσω Bamberg

to behave like swine
and eat shit cakes—she kneaded them herself;
I'll act out the whole story,
while you grunt gaily
and follow your mother, piggies!

CHORUS

Now that you're Circe, the mixer of potions,
who's bewitching and befouling those companions,
we'll grab you gaily,
doing a takeoff on Laertes' son, and hang you by the
    balls,
and rub your nose in shit
like a goat; and you'll play Aristyllus, and say,
"follow your mother, piggies!"

CARIO

Whoa now, it's time to cut short your jibes
and form up a different dance.
Me, I'm set to sneak off,
filch from my master
some bread and meat,
and spend the day working at gobbling it up.

Exit CARIO.

The Chorus performs an entr'acte.

Enter CHREMYLUS *from the house.*

CHREMYLUS

To offer you "greetings," fellow demesmen, is now old-

ἀρχαῖον ἤδη προσαγορεύειν καὶ σαπρόν·
"ἀσπάζομαι" δ' ὁτιὴ προθύμως ἥκετε
325 καὶ συντεταμένως κοὐ κατεβλακευμένως.
ὅπως δέ μοι καὶ τἄλλα συμπαραστάται
ἔσεσθε καὶ σωτῆρες ὄντως τοῦ θεοῦ.

ΚΟΡΥΦΑΙΟΣ

θάρρει· βλέπειν γὰρ ἄντικρυς δόξεις μ' Ἄρη.
δεινὸν γὰρ εἰ τριωβόλου μὲν οὕνεκα
330 ὠστιζόμεσθ' ἑκάστοτ' ἐν τἠκκλησίᾳ,
αὐτὸν δὲ τὸν Πλοῦτον παρείην τῳ λαβεῖν.

ΧΡΕΜΥΛΟΣ

καὶ μὴν ὁρῶ καὶ Βλεψίδημον τουτονὶ
προσιόντα· δῆλος δ' ἐστὶν ὅτι τοῦ πράγματος
ἀκήκοέν τι τῇ βαδίσει καὶ τῷ τάχει.

ΒΛΕΨΙΔΗΜΟΣ

335 τί ἂν οὖν τὸ πρᾶγμ' εἴη; πόθεν καὶ τίνι τρόπῳ
Χρεμύλος πεπλούτηκ' ἐξαπίνης; οὐ πείθομαι.
καίτοι λόγος γ' ἦν, νὴ τὸν Ἡρακλέα, πολὺς
ἐπὶ τοῖσι κουρείοισι τῶν καθημένων,
ὡς ἐξαπίνης ἀνὴρ γεγένηται πλούσιος.
340 ἔστιν δέ μοι τοῦτ' αὐτὸ θαυμάσιον, ὅπως
χρηστόν τι πράττων τοὺς φίλους μεταπέμπεται.
οὔκουν ἐπιχώριόν γε πρᾶγμ' ἐργάζεται.

ΧΡΕΜΥΛΟΣ

ἀλλ' οὐδὲν ἀποκρύψας ἐρῶ. νὴ τοὺς θεούς,
ὦ Βλεψίδημ', ἄμεινον ἢ χθὲς πράττομεν,
345 ὥστε μετέχειν ἔξεστιν· εἶ γὰρ τῶν φίλων.

470

fashioned and worn out; but I do "salute" you for turning up here so eagerly, so painstakingly, and so energetically. Please be my supporters also in the work that lies ahead, and the true saviors of the god.

CHORUS LEADER

Never fear, you'll look at me and see Ares himself. It would be bizarre of us to push and shove at every Assembly to get our three obols, and then let somebody take Wealth himself away from us!

CHREMYLUS

And here comes Blepsidemus too; the way he's striding and hurrying along, he's obviously heard something about what's going on.

Enter BLEPSIDEMUS.

BLEPSIDEMUS

All right, what's going on? How has Chremylus managed to become wealthy all of a sudden? I can't believe it, and yet, by Heracles, the loungers in the barbershops are talking plenty about it, how the man's become wealthy all of a sudden. And I'm really surprised that, achieving some prosperity, he's calling for his friends; that's not normal practice in this country.

CHREMYLUS

Well, I won't hold anything back. By heaven, Blepsidemus, we're doing better than we were yesterday, which means that you'll get a share, as one of our friends.

ΒΛΕΨΙΔΗΜΟΣ

γέγονας δ' ἀληθῶς, ὡς λέγουσι, πλούσιος;

ΧΡΕΜΥΛΟΣ

ἔσομαι μὲν οὖν αὐτίκα μάλ', ἢν θεὸς θέλῃ·
ἔνι γάρ τις, ἔνι κίνδυνος ἐν τῷ πράγματι.

ΒΛΕΨΙΔΗΜΟΣ

ποῖός τις;

ΧΡΕΜΥΛΟΣ

οἷος—

ΒΛΕΨΙΔΗΜΟΣ

λέγ' ἀνύσας ὅ τι φῄς ποτε.

ΧΡΕΜΥΛΟΣ

350 ἢν μὲν κατορθώσωμεν, εὖ πράττειν ἀεί·
ἢν δὲ σφαλῶμεν, ἐπιτετρῖφθαι τὸ παράπαν.

ΒΛΕΨΙΔΗΜΟΣ

τουτὶ πονηρὸν φαίνεται τὸ φορτίον
καί μ' οὐκ ἀρέσκει. τό τε γὰρ ἐξαίφνης ἄγαν
οὕτως ὑπερπλουτεῖν τό τ' αὖ δεδοικέναι
355 πρὸς ἀνδρὸς οὐδὲν ὑγιές ἐστ' εἰργασμένου.

ΧΡΕΜΥΛΟΣ

πῶς οὐδὲν ὑγιές;

ΒΛΕΨΙΔΗΜΟΣ

εἴ τι κεκλοφὼς νὴ Δία
ἐκεῖθεν ἥκεις ἀργύριον ἢ χρυσίον
παρὰ τοῦ θεοῦ, κἄπειτ' ἴσως σοι μεταμέλει.

WEALTH

BLEPSIDEMUS
You've really become wealthy, just as they say?

CHREMYLUS
No, but I very soon will be, God willing. You see, there's a certain, well, risk in the plan.

BLEPSIDEMUS
What sort of risk?

CHREMYLUS
Well—

BLEPSIDEMUS
Come right out with what you mean to say.

CHREMYLUS
If we succeed, we'll be prosperous forever; if we fail, we'll be completely wiped out.

BLEPSIDEMUS
There's something shady about this merchandise, and I don't like it. Such very sudden wealth combined with trepidation suggests a man who's up to no good.

CHREMYLUS
What do you mean, no good?

BLEPSIDEMUS
Maybe you've come back from there with silver or gold you've stolen from the god, yes, and now you're worried.

ΧΡΕΜΥΛΟΣ

Ἄπολλον ἀποτρόπαιε, μὰ Δί' ἐγὼ μὲν οὔ.

ΒΛΕΨΙΔΗΜΟΣ

360 παῦσαι φλυαρῶν, ὦγάθ'· οἶδα γὰρ σαφῶς.

ΧΡΕΜΥΛΟΣ

σὺ μηδὲν εἰς ἔμ' ὑπονόει τοιουτονί.

ΒΛΕΨΙΔΗΜΟΣ

φεῦ,
ὡς οὐδὲν ἀτεχνῶς ὑγιές ἐστιν οὐδενός,
ἀλλ' εἰσὶ τοῦ κέρδους ἅπαντες ἥττονες.

ΧΡΕΜΥΛΟΣ

οὔ τοι, μὰ τὴν Δήμητρ', ὑγιαίνειν μοι δοκεῖς.

ΒΛΕΨΙΔΗΜΟΣ

365 ὡς πολὺ μεθέστηχ' ὧν πρότερον εἶχεν τρόπων.

ΧΡΕΜΥΛΟΣ

μελαγχολᾷς, ὦνθρωπε, νὴ τὸν οὐρανόν.

ΒΛΕΨΙΔΗΜΟΣ

ἀλλ' οὐδὲ τὸ βλέμμ' αὐτὸ κατὰ χώραν ἔχει,
ἀλλ' ἐστὶν ἐπίδηλόν τι πεπανουργηκότι.

ΧΡΕΜΥΛΟΣ

σὺ μὲν οἶδ' ὃ κρώζεις· ὡς ἐμοῦ τι κεκλοφότος
ζητεῖς μεταλαβεῖν.

ΒΛΕΨΙΔΗΜΟΣ

370   μεταλαβεῖν ζητῶ; τίνος;

CHREMYLUS

Apollo save us, I swear I haven't!

BLEPSIDEMUS

Stop blustering, my friend; I know what's up.

CHREMYLUS

How dare you suspect me of such a thing!

BLEPSIDEMUS

Dear me, there's no trace of goodness in anyone; the lust for profit rules the world.

CHREMYLUS

By Demeter, you sound deranged to me.

BLEPSIDEMUS

He's changed so much from the way he used to be!

CHREMYLUS

By heaven, you're crazy, mister.

BLEPSIDEMUS

Why, even the look in his eye is shifty; yes, he's obviously done something bad.

CHREMYLUS

I know what *you're* clucking about: you think I've stolen something and want a cut.

BLEPSIDEMUS

Me want a cut? Of what?

ΧΡΕΜΥΛΟΣ

τὸ δ᾽ ἐστὶν οὐ τοιοῦτον ἀλλ᾽ ἑτέρως ἔχον.

ΒΛΕΨΙΔΗΜΟΣ

μῶν οὐ κέκλοφας, ἀλλ᾽ ἥρπακας;

ΧΡΕΜΥΛΟΣ

κακοδαιμονᾷς.

ΒΛΕΨΙΔΗΜΟΣ

ἀλλ᾽ οὐδὲ μὴν ἀπεστέρηκάς γ᾽ οὐδένα;

ΧΡΕΜΥΛΟΣ

οὐ δῆτ᾽ ἔγωγ᾽.

ΒΛΕΨΙΔΗΜΟΣ

ὦ Ἡράκλεις, φέρε, ποῖ τις ἂν
375   τράποιτο; τἀληθὲς γὰρ οὐκ ἐθέλει φράσαι.

ΧΡΕΜΥΛΟΣ

κατηγορεῖς γὰρ πρὶν μαθεῖν τὸ πρᾶγμά μου.

ΒΛΕΨΙΔΗΜΟΣ

ὦ τᾶν, ἐγώ σοι τοῦτ᾽ ἀπὸ σμικροῦ πάνυ
ἐθέλω διαπρᾶξαι πρὶν πυθέσθαι τὴν πόλιν,
τὸ στόμ᾽ ἐπιβύσας κέρμασιν τῶν ῥητόρων.

ΧΡΕΜΥΛΟΣ

380   καὶ μὴν φίλος γ᾽ ἄν μοι δοκεῖς, νὴ τοὺς θεούς,
τρεῖς μνᾶς ἀναλώσας λογίσασθαι δώδεκα.

ΒΛΕΨΙΔΗΜΟΣ

ὁρῶ τιν᾽ ἐπὶ τοῦ βήματος καθεδούμενον
ἱκετηρίαν ἔχοντα μετὰ τῶν παιδίων

CHREMYLUS

It's not like that; it's something else entirely.

BLEPSIDEMUS

Maybe you aren't a thief, but a robber.

CHREMYLUS

You're possessed!

BLEPSIDEMUS

You haven't even defrauded anybody?

CHREMYLUS

I certainly haven't.

BLEPSIDEMUS

By Heracles, where do we go from here? He refuses to tell the truth!

CHREMYLUS

You're levelling charges before you've heard the facts from me.

BLEPSIDEMUS

Listen, friend, for a very small consideration I'm ready to pull this off before the whole town gets wind of it, by plugging the politicians' mouths with coins.

CHREMYLUS

Heavens yes, and I'm sure you'd be a real pal about it too, spending three minas and then charging me twelve.

BLEPSIDEMUS

I'm looking at a man who'll end up sitting in the dock, holding a suppliant's olive branch with his wife and children,

καὶ τῆς γυναικός, κοὐ διοίσοντ᾽ ἄντικρυς
385 τῶν Ἡρακλειδῶν οὐδ᾽ ὁτιοῦν τῶν Παμφίλου.

ΧΡΕΜΤΛΟΣ
οὔκ, ὦ κακόδαιμον, ἀλλὰ τοὺς χρηστοὺς ἐγὼ
καὶ τοὺς δικαίους τούς τε σώφρονας μόνους
ἀπαρτὶ πλουτῆσαι ποιήσω.

ΒΛΕΨΙΔΗΜΟΣ
τί σὺ λέγεις;
οὕτω πάνυ πολλὰ κέκλοφας;

ΧΡΕΜΤΛΟΣ
οἴμοι τῶν κακῶν,
ἀπολεῖς.

ΒΛΕΨΙΔΗΜΟΣ
390 σὺ μὲν οὖν σεαυτόν, ὥς γ᾽ ἐμοὶ δοκεῖς.

ΧΡΕΜΤΛΟΣ
οὐ δῆτ᾽, ἐπειδὴ Πλοῦτον, ὦ μόχθηρε σύ,
ἔχω.

ΒΛΕΨΙΔΗΜΟΣ
σὺ πλοῦτον; ποῖον;

ΧΡΕΜΤΛΟΣ
αὐτὸν τὸν θεόν.

ΒΛΕΨΙΔΗΜΟΣ
καὶ ποῦ 'στιν;

ΧΡΕΜΤΛΟΣ
ἔνδον.

absolute dead ringers for "The Children of Heracles" by
Pamphilus.[22]

CHREMYLUS
On the contrary, you jinx, I'm going to make good, just, and
well behaved people wealthy, and only them.

BLEPSIDEMUS
What's that you say? Have you stolen that much?

CHREMYLUS
Damn it all, you'll be the death of me!

BLEPSIDEMUS
You'll be your own, is my guess.

CHREMYLUS
Oh no I won't, you rascal, because I've got Wealth.

BLEPSIDEMUS
You've got wealth? What sort of wealth?

CHREMYLUS
The god himself.

BLEPSIDEMUS
Then where is he?

CHREMYLUS
Inside.

[22] After his death, Heracles' children, with their grandmother
Alcmene and family friend Iolaus, took refuge at Athens from
their persecutor, Eurystheus. The identity of this Pamphilus is un-
certain; the famous painter of that name from Amphipolis (cf.
Pliny, *Natural History* 35.36.7) is not known to have treated this
subject.

ΒΛΕΨΙΔΗΜΟΣ
ποῦ;

ΧΡΕΜΥΛΟΣ
παρ᾽ ἐμοί.

ΒΛΕΨΙΔΗΜΟΣ
παρὰ σοί;

ΧΡΕΜΥΛΟΣ
πάνυ.

ΒΛΕΨΙΔΗΜΟΣ
οὐκ ἐς κόρακας; Πλοῦτος παρὰ σοί;

ΧΡΕΜΥΛΟΣ
νὴ τοὺς θεούς.

ΒΛΕΨΙΔΗΜΟΣ
λέγεις ἀληθῆ;

ΧΡΕΜΥΛΟΣ
φημί.

ΒΛΕΨΙΔΗΜΟΣ
395   πρὸς τῆς Ἑστίας;

ΧΡΕΜΥΛΟΣ
νὴ τὸν Ποσειδῶ.

ΒΛΕΨΙΔΗΜΟΣ
τὸν θαλάττιον λέγεις;

ΧΡΕΜΥΛΟΣ
εἰ δ᾽ ἔστιν ἕτερός τις Ποσειδῶν, τὸν ἕτερον.

BLEPSIDEMUS

Inside where?

CHREMYLUS

In my house.

BLEPSIDEMUS

In your house?

CHREMYLUS

That's right.

BLEPSIDEMUS

Like hell he is! Wealth in your house?

CHREMYLUS

The gods be my witness.

BLEPSIDEMUS

You're telling the truth?

CHREMYLUS

I am.

BLEPSIDEMUS

You swear by Hestia?

CHREMYLUS

By Poseidon, yes.

BLEPSIDEMUS

The sea god, right?

CHREMYLUS

If there's another Poseidon, I swear by him too.

ΒΛΕΨΙΔΗΜΟΣ
εἶτ᾽ οὐ διαπέμπεις καὶ πρὸς ἡμᾶς, τοὺς φίλους;

ΧΡΕΜΤΛΟΣ
οὐκ ἔστι πω τὰ πράγματ᾽ ἐν τούτῳ.

ΒΛΕΨΙΔΗΜΟΣ
τί φῄς;
οὐ τῷ μεταδοῦναι;

ΧΡΕΜΤΛΟΣ
μὰ Δία· δεῖ γὰρ πρῶτα—

ΒΛΕΨΙΔΗΜΟΣ

400
τί;

ΧΡΕΜΤΛΟΣ
βλέψαι ποιῆσαι νῷν—

ΒΛΕΨΙΔΗΜΟΣ
τίνα βλέψαι; φράσον.

ΧΡΕΜΤΛΟΣ
τὸν Πλοῦτον, ὥσπερ πρότερον, ἑνί γέ τῳ τρόπῳ.

ΒΛΕΨΙΔΗΜΟΣ
τυφλὸς γὰρ ὄντως ἐστί;

ΧΡΕΜΤΛΟΣ
νὴ τὸν οὐρανόν.

ΒΛΕΨΙΔΗΜΟΣ
οὐκ ἐτὸς ἄρ᾽ ὡς ἔμ᾽ ἦλθεν οὐδεπώποτε.

ΧΡΕΜΤΛΟΣ
405 ἀλλ᾽ ἢν θεοὶ θέλωσι, νῦν ἀφίξεται.

BLEPSIDEMUS

And you're not sending him to visit us, your friends?

CHREMYLUS

Things haven't quite reached that stage.

BLEPSIDEMUS

What stage? The sharing stage?

CHREMYLUS

Exactly. You see, first—

BLEPSIDEMUS

What?

CHREMYLUS

we two must restore his sight—

BLEPSIDEMUS

Whose sight, please?

CHREMYLUS

Wealth's, as it was before, by whatever means.

BLEPSIDEMUS

You mean he's really blind?

CHREMYLUS

Heavens yes.

BLEPSIDEMUS

No wonder he's never visited my house!

CHREMYLUS

But, the gods willing, he'll come now.

ΒΛΕΨΙΔΗΜΟΣ
οὔκουν ἰατρὸν εἰσαγαγεῖν ἐχρῆν τινά;

ΧΡΕΜΥΛΟΣ
τίς δῆτ' ἰατρός ἐστι νῦν ἐν τῇ πόλει;
οὔτε γὰρ ὁ μισθὸς οὐδέν ἐστ' οὔθ' ἡ τέχνη.

ΒΛΕΨΙΔΗΜΟΣ
σκοπῶμεν.

ΧΡΕΜΥΛΟΣ
ἀλλ' οὐκ ἔστιν.

ΒΛΕΨΙΔΗΜΟΣ
οὐδ' ἐμοὶ δοκεῖ.

ΧΡΕΜΥΛΟΣ
410 μὰ Δί', ἀλλ' ὅπερ πάλαι παρεσκευαζόμην
ἐγώ, κατακλίνειν αὐτὸν εἰς Ἀσκληπιοῦ
κράτιστόν ἐστι.

ΒΛΕΨΙΔΗΜΟΣ
πολὺ μὲν οὖν, νὴ τοὺς θεούς.
μή νυν διάτριβ', ἀλλ' ἄννε πράττων ἕν γέ τι.

ΧΡΕΜΥΛΟΣ
καὶ δὴ βαδίζω.

ΒΛΕΨΙΔΗΜΟΣ
σπεῦδέ νυν.

ΧΡΕΜΥΛΟΣ
τοῦτ' αὐτὸ δρῶ.

---

23 Why this should be the case is unclear.

BLEPSIDEMUS
So shouldn't we call in a doctor?

CHREMYLUS
Is there any such thing as a doctor in this town? There's no money in it, and so no practice.[23]

BLEPSIDEMUS
(*scanning the audience*) Let's look for one.

CHREMYLUS
I don't see one.

BLEPSIDEMUS
I don't either.

CHREMYLUS
No, let's try something I'd already planned, to bed him down in Asclepius' temple.[24] That's best.

BLEPSIDEMUS
Yes, that's really a much better idea. Don't waste any time, now; hurry up and get something underway.

CHREMYLUS
I'm on my way.

BLEPSIDEMUS
Good, hurry up.

CHREMYLUS
That's what I'm doing.

Enter POVERTY, *a hideous hag.*

---

[24] Probably to be imagined as the one at Zea, near Athens and close to the sea (cf. 656); for the cult see S. B. Aleshire, *The Athenian Asclepieion* (Baltimore 1989).

ΠΕΝΙΑ

415 ὦ θερμὸν ἔργον κἀνόσιον καὶ παράνομον
τολμῶντε δρᾶν ἀνθρωπαρίω κακοδαίμονε,
ποῖ ποῖ τί φεύγετον; οὐ μενεῖτον;

ΒΛΕΨΙΔΗΜΟΣ

Ἡράκλεις.

ΠΕΝΙΑ

ἐγὼ γὰρ ὑμᾶς ἐξολῶ κακοὺς κακῶς·
τόλμημα γὰρ τολμᾶτον οὐκ ἀνασχετόν,
420 ἀλλ᾽ οἷον οὐδεὶς ἄλλος οὐδεπώποτε
οὔτε θεὸς οὔτ᾽ ἄνθρωπος. ὥστ᾽ ἀπολώλατον.

ΧΡΕΜΥΛΟΣ

σὺ δ᾽ εἶ τίς; ὠχρὰ μὲν γὰρ εἶναί μοι δοκεῖς.

ΒΛΕΨΙΔΗΜΟΣ

ἴσως Ἐρινύς ἐστιν ἐκ τραγῳδίας·
βλέπει γέ τοι μανικόν τι καὶ τραγῳδικόν.

ΧΡΕΜΥΛΟΣ

ἀλλ᾽ οὐκ ἔχει γὰρ δᾷδας.

ΒΛΕΨΙΔΗΜΟΣ

425 οὐκοῦν κλαύσεται.

ΠΕΝΙΑ

οἴεσθε δ᾽ εἶναι τίνα με;

ΧΡΕΜΥΛΟΣ

πανδοκεύτριαν
ἢ λεκιθόπωλιν· οὐ γὰρ ἂν τοσουτονὶ
ἀνέκραγες ἡμῖν οὐδὲν ἠδικημένη.

POVERTY

How dare you do such a brazen, unholy, and lawless deed,
you pair of lilliputian losers! Hey, just where do you mean
to run off to? Stay where you are!

BLEPSIDEMUS

Holy Heracles!

POVERTY

Yes, I'm going give you the miserable death you deserve,
for daring to commit an intolerable outrage, such as no
one, human or divine, has ever dared before. So prepare to
die!

CHREMYLUS

But who are you? You look pretty sickly to me.

BLEPSIDEMUS

Maybe she's a Fury from tragedy; she does have a rather
crazed and tragic look.

CHREMYLUS

But she's got no torches.

BLEPSIDEMUS

Then she'll be very sorry!

POVERTY

But who do you think I am?

CHREMYLUS

An innkeeper or a gruel monger; otherwise you wouldn't
have raised such a yelp when we'd done you no wrong.

ΠΕΝΙΑ

ἄληθες; οὐ γὰρ δεινότατα δεδράκατον
430 ζητοῦντες ἐκ πάσης με χώρας ἐκβαλεῖν;

ΧΡΕΜΥΛΟΣ

οὔκουν ὑπόλοιπον τὸ βάραθρόν σοι γίγνεται;
ἀλλ᾿ ἥτις εἶ λέγειν σ᾿ ἐχρῆν αὐτίκα μάλα.

ΠΕΝΙΑ

ἢ σφὼ ποιήσω τήμερον δοῦναι δίκην
ἀνθ᾿ ὧν ἐμὲ ζητεῖτον ἐνθένδ᾿ ἀφανίσαι.

ΒΛΕΨΙΔΗΜΟΣ

435 ἆρ᾿ ἐστὶν ἡ καπηλὶς ἡκ τῶν γειτόνων,
ἢ ταῖς κοτύλαις ἀεί με διαλυμαίνεται;

ΠΕΝΙΑ

Πενία μὲν οὖν, ἢ σφῶν ξυνοικῶ πόλλ᾿ ἔτη.

ΒΛΕΨΙΔΗΜΟΣ

ἄναξ Ἄπολλον καὶ θεοί, ποῖ τις φύγῃ;

ΧΡΕΜΥΛΟΣ

οὗτος, τί δρᾷς; ὦ δειλότατον σὺ θηρίον,
οὐ παραμενεῖς;

ΒΛΕΨΙΔΗΜΟΣ

ἥκιστα πάντων.

ΧΡΕΜΥΛΟΣ
440   οὐ μενεῖς;
ἀλλ᾿ ἄνδρε δύο γυναῖκα φεύγομεν μίαν;

POVERTY

No wrong? Aren't you two behaving terribly by seeking to kick me out of the country altogether?

CHREMYLUS

Well, don't you have the death pit as a last alternative? But you've got to tell us here and now just who you are.

POVERTY

The one who's going to punish you this very day for seeking my banishment.

BLEPSIDEMUS

Wait, is she the barmaid from the neighborhood who's always cheating me on the drinks?

POVERTY

No, I'm Poverty, a resident of your community for many years.

BLEPSIDEMUS

Lord Apollo and all the gods, how do we get out of here?

CHREMYLUS

Hey, what's the matter with you? You cowardly critter, you stay right here!

BLEPSIDEMUS

That's the last thing I'll do!

CHREMYLUS

Stay. Are two men going to run away from one woman?

ΒΛΕΨΙΔΗΜΟΣ

Πενία γάρ ἐστιν, ὦ πόνηρ', ἧς οὐδαμοῦ
οὐδὲν πέφυκε ζῷον ἐξωλέστερον.

ΧΡΕΜΥΛΟΣ

στῆθ', ἀντιβολῶ σε, στῆθι.

ΒΛΕΨΙΔΗΜΟΣ

μὰ Δί' ἐγὼ μὲν οὔ.

ΧΡΕΜΥΛΟΣ

445 καὶ μὴν λέγω, δεινότατον ἔργον παρὰ πολὺ
ἔργων ἁπάντων ἐργασόμεθ', εἰ τὸν θεὸν
ἔρημον ἀπολιπόντε ποι φευξούμεθα
τηνδὶ δεδιότε, μηδὲ διαμαχούμεθα.

ΒΛΕΨΙΔΗΜΟΣ

ποίοισιν ὅπλοις ἢ δυνάμει πεποιθότε;
450 ποῖον γὰρ οὐ θώρακα, ποίαν δ' ἀσπίδα
οὐκ ἐνέχυρον τίθησιν ἡ μιαρωτάτη;

ΧΡΕΜΥΛΟΣ

θάρρει· μόνος γὰρ ὁ θεὸς οὗτος οἶδ' ὅτι
τροπαῖον ἂν στήσαιτο τῶν ταύτης τρόπων.

ΠΕΝΙΑ

γρύζειν δὲ καὶ τολμᾶτον, ὦ καθάρματε,
455 ἐπ' αὐτοφώρῳ δεινὰ δρῶντ' εἰλημμένω;

ΧΡΕΜΥΛΟΣ

σὺ δ', ὦ κάκιστ' ἀπολουμένη, τί λοιδορεῖ
ἡμῖν προσελθοῦσ' οὐδ' ὁτιοῦν ἀδικουμένη;

BLEPSIDEMUS

But she's Poverty, you dog; there's no creature more destructive anywhere!

CHREMYLUS

Hold on, please hold on.

BLEPSIDEMUS

Not me, by god!

CHREMYLUS

I tell you, we'll be doing far the most dastardly deed ever done, if we run off and leave the god deserted here, just because we're afraid of her and won't put up a fight.

BLEPSIDEMUS

Relying on what weapons or power? Is there a breastplate, is there a shield that the miserable bitch hasn't put in pawn?

CHREMYLUS

Take heart, because I'm sure this god will single-handedly score a victory over her evil ways.

POVERTY

You trash, you've still got the nerve to grumble after being caught red-handed in a terrible deed?

CHREMYLUS

And why, damn and blast you, do you come yelling at us when we've done you absolutely no wrong?

ΠΕΝΙΑ

οὐδὲν γάρ, ὦ πρὸς τῶν θεῶν, νομίζετε
ἀδικεῖν με τὸν Πλοῦτον ποιεῖν πειρωμένῳ
βλέψαι πάλιν;

ΧΡΕΜΥΛΟΣ

460   τί οὖν ἀδικοῦμεν τοῦτό σε,
εἰ πᾶσιν ἀνθρώποισιν ἐκπορίζομεν
ἀγαθόν;

ΠΕΝΙΑ

τί δ᾽ ἂν ὑμεῖς ἀγαθὸν ἐξεύροιθ᾽;

ΧΡΕΜΥΛΟΣ

ὅ τι;
σὲ πρῶτον ἐκβαλόντες ἐκ τῆς Ἑλλάδος—

ΠΕΝΙΑ

ἔμ᾽ ἐκβαλόντες; καὶ τί ἂν νομίζετον
κακὸν ἐργάσασθαι μεῖζον ἀνθρώποις;

ΧΡΕΜΥΛΟΣ

465   ὅ τι;
εἰ τοῦτο δρᾶν μέλλοντες ἐπιλαθοίμεθα.

ΠΕΝΙΑ

καὶ μὴν περὶ τούτου σφῷν ἐθέλω δοῦναι λόγον
τὸ πρῶτον αὐτοῦ· κἂν μὲν ἀποφήνω μόνην
ἀγαθῶν ἁπάντων οὖσαν αἰτίαν ἐμὲ
470 ὑμῖν δι᾽ ἐμέ τε ζῶντας ὑμᾶς· εἰ δὲ μή,
ποιεῖτον ἤδη τοῦθ᾽ ὅ τι ἂν ὑμῖν δοκῇ.

POVERTY

Good gods, do you really think that by trying to restore
Wealth's eyesight you do me no wrong?

CHREMYLUS

How do we wrong you if we can bring good to the whole
human race?

POVERTY

What good could you two come up with?

CHREMYLUS

Want to know? When we've first kicked you out of
Greece—

POVERTY

Kicked me out? And what do you think would do the hu-
man race more harm than that?

CHREMYLUS

More harm? If we abandoned what we plan to do.

POVERTY

Well now, that's an issue I'm ready to debate with you right
on the spot. Either I'll demonstrate that I'm the sole
source of all your blessings, and it's I who give you a life, or
else go right ahead and do whatever you please.

ΧΡΕΜΥΛΟΣ

ταυτὶ σὺ τολμᾷς, ὦ μιαρωτάτη, λέγειν;

ΠΕΝΙΑ

καὶ σύ γε διδάσκου· πάνυ γὰρ οἶμαι ῥᾳδίως
ἅπανθ᾽ ἁμαρτάνοντά σ᾽ ἀποδείξειν ἐγώ,
475 εἰ τοὺς δικαίους φῇς ποιήσειν πλουσίους.

ΧΡΕΜΥΛΟΣ

ὦ τύμπανα καὶ κύφωνες, οὐκ ἀρήξετε;

ΠΕΝΙΑ

οὐ δεῖ σχετλιάζειν καὶ βοᾶν πρὶν ἂν μάθῃς.

ΧΡΕΜΥΛΟΣ

καὶ τίς δύναιτ᾽ ἂν μὴ βοᾶν "ἰοὺ ἰοὺ"
τοιαῦτ᾽ ἀκούων;

ΠΕΝΙΑ

ὅστις ἐστὶν εὖ φρονῶν.

ΧΡΕΜΥΛΟΣ

480 τί δῆτά σοι τίμημ᾽ ἐπιγράψω τῇ δίκῃ,
ἐὰν ἁλῶς;

ΠΕΝΙΑ

ὅ τι σοι δοκεῖ.

ΧΡΕΜΥΛΟΣ

καλῶς λέγεις.

ΠΕΝΙΑ

τὸ γὰρ αὖτ᾽, ἐὰν ἡττᾶσθε, καὶ σφὼ δεῖ παθεῖν.

CHREMYLUS
You vile witch, how dare you make such a case!

POVERTY
I do, and you pay attention to it, because I think I can easily show that you're completely wrong if you propose to make the just people rich.

CHREMYLUS
Oh cudgels and pillories, I need you here!

POVERTY
There's no need to curse and yell before you've heard me out.

CHREMYLUS
But who could help but yell "yuk yuk" at hearing such talk?

POVERTY
Someone with good sense.

CHREMYLUS
And what penalty shall I impose if you lose your case?

POVERTY
Whatever you like.

CHREMYLUS
Excellent.

POVERTY
But the same applies to you two if you lose.

ΧΡΕΜΥΛΟΣ

ἱκανοὺς νομίζεις δῆτα θανάτους εἴκοσιν;

ΒΛΕΨΙΔΗΜΟΣ

ταύτῃ γε· νῶν δὲ δύ᾽ ἀποχρήσουσιν μόνω.

ΠΕΝΙΑ

485 οὐκ ἂν φθάνοιτε τοῦτο πράττοντες· τί γὰρ
ἔχοι τις ἂν δίκαιον ἀντειπεῖν ἔτι;

ΚΟΡΥΦΑΙΟΣ

ἀλλ᾽ ἤδη χρῆν τι λέγειν ὑμᾶς σοφὸν ᾧ νικήσετε
τηνδὶ
ἐν τοῖσι λόγοις ἀντιλέγοντες, μαλακὸν δ᾽ ἐνδώσετε
μηδέν.

ΧΡΕΜΥΛΟΣ

φανερὸν μὲν ἔγωγ᾽ οἶμαι γνῶναι τοῦτ᾽ εἶναι πᾶσιν
ὁμοίως,
490 ὅτι τοὺς χρηστοὺς τῶν ἀνθρώπων εὖ πράττειν ἐστὶ
δίκαιον,
τοὺς δὲ πονηροὺς καὶ τοὺς ἀθέους τούτων τἀναντία
δήπου.
τοῦτ᾽ οὖν ἡμεῖς ἐπιθυμοῦντες μόλις ηὕρομεν ὥστε
γενέσθαι
βούλευμα καλὸν καὶ γενναῖον καὶ χρήσιμον εἰς
ἅπαν ἔργον.
ἢν γὰρ ὁ Πλοῦτος νυνὶ βλέψῃ καὶ μὴ τυφλὸς ὢν
περινοστῇ,
495 ὡς τοὺς ἀγαθοὺς τῶν ἀνθρώπων βαδιεῖται κοὐκ
ἀπολείψει,

CHREMYLUS

(*to Blepsidemus*) Do you think twenty death penalties will suffice?

BLEPSIDEMUS

For her, yes; for us, two will be more than enough.

POVERTY

You won't be long in getting them, for who could fairly rebut my case?

CHORUS LEADER

Now it's time for you to make a competent case and defeat her in the debate, leaving her no weak point to attack.

CHREMYLUS

I'll begin with what I think is obvious to everyone alike: that in all fairness the good people of the world should prosper, and the wicked and godless, the opposite, of course. Now that's what we want, and we finally found a way to make it happen, a fine, noble, and comprehensively workable plan. Because if Wealth should regain his eyesight and cease to wander around blind, he'll visit the good people and not desert them, and he'll shun the wicked and

τοὺς δὲ πονηροὺς καὶ τοὺς ἀθέους φευξεῖται· κᾆτα
    ποιήσει
πάντας χρηστοὺς καὶ πλουτοῦντας δήπου τά τε θεῖα
    σέβοντας.
καίτοι τούτου τοῖς ἀνθρώποις τίς ἂν ἐξεύροι ποτ᾽
    ἄμεινον;

ΒΛΕΨΙΔΗΜΟΣ

οὐδείς· τούτου σοὶ μάρτυς ἐγώ· μηδὲν ταύτην γ᾽
    ἀνερώτα.

ΧΡΕΜΥΛΟΣ

500 ὡς μὲν γὰρ νῦν ἡμῖν ὁ βίος τοῖς ἀνθρώποις
    διάκειται,
τίς ἂν οὐχ ἡγοῖτ᾽ εἶναι μανίαν κακοδαιμονίαν τ᾽ ἔτι
    μᾶλλον;
πολλοὶ μὲν γὰρ τῶν ἀνθρώπων ὄντες πλουτοῦσι
    πονηροί,
ἀδίκως αὐτὰ ξυλλεξάμενοι· πολλοὶ δ᾽ ὄντες πάνυ
    χρηστοὶ
πράττουσι κακῶς καὶ πεινῶσιν μετὰ σοῦ τε τὰ
    πλεῖστα σύνεισιν.
505 οὔκουν εἶναί φημ᾽, εἰ παύσει ταύτην βλέψας ποθ᾽ ὁ
    Πλοῦτος,
ὁδὸν ἥντιν᾽ ἰὼν τοῖς ἀνθρώποις ἀγάθ᾽ ἂν μείζω
    πορίσειεν.

ΠΕΝΙΑ

ἀλλ᾽, ὦ πάντων ῥᾷστ᾽ ἀνθρώπων ἀναπεισθέντ᾽ οὐχ
    ὑγιαίνειν

godless, and that will make everyone good, and rich of course, and god-fearing. Now who could come up with anything better for mankind than that?

BLEPSIDEMUS
Nobody, I'll guarantee you that, and you needn't bother to ask *her*.

CHREMYLUS
Just consider the current state of our human existence; who wouldn't think it's madness, or even divine malevolence? It's a fact that many people are wealthy despite being scoundrels who've amassed it unjustly, while a good many worthy people fare badly and go hungry, and spend most of their time in *your* company. That's why I declare that if ever Wealth recovered his eyesight and put a stop to *her*, there could be no better way to provide mankind with greater blessings.

POVERTY
How very easily the both of you have been suckered into

δύο πρεσβύτα, ξυνθιασῶτα τοῦ ληρεῖν καὶ
    παραπαίειν,
εἰ τοῦτο γένοιθ᾽ ὃ ποθεῖθ᾽ ὑμεῖς, οὔ φημ᾽ ἂν
    λυσιτελεῖν σφῷν.
510   εἰ γὰρ ὁ Πλοῦτος βλέψειε πάλιν διανείμειέν τ᾽ ἴσον
    αὑτόν,
οὔτε τέχνην ἂν τῶν ἀνθρώπων οὔτ᾽ ἂν σοφίαν
    μελετῴη
οὐδείς· ἀμφοῖν δ᾽ ὑμῖν τούτοιν ἀφανισθέντοιν
    ἐθελήσει
τίς χαλκεύειν ἢ ναυπηγεῖν ἢ ῥάπτειν ἢ τροχοποιεῖν
ἢ σκυτοτομεῖν ἢ πλινθουργεῖν ἢ πλύνειν ἢ
    σκυλοδεψεῖν
515   ἢ γῆς ἀρότροις ῥήξας δάπεδον καρπὸν Δηοῦς
    θερίσασθαι
ἢν ἐξῇ ζῆν ἀργοῖς ὑμῖν τούτων πάντων ἀμελοῦσιν;

ΧΡΕΜΥΛΟΣ

λῆρον ληρεῖς. ταῦτα γὰρ ἡμῖν πάνθ᾽ ὅσα νυνδὴ
    κατέλεξας
οἱ θεράποντες μοχθήσουσιν.

ΠΕΝΙΑ

πόθεν οὖν ἕξεις θεράποντας;

ΧΡΕΜΥΛΟΣ

ὠνησόμεθ᾽ ἀργυρίου δήπου.

ΠΕΝΙΑ

τίς δ᾽ ἔσται πρῶτον ὁ πωλῶν,
ὅταν ἀργύριον κἀκεῖνος ἔχῃ;

500

derangement, you codgers, you members of the Blather
and Babble Society! If you get your wish, you'll not be the
better for it, I assure you. Because if Wealth regains his
sight and shares himself out equally, absolutely no one will
practice the arts and crafts, and once these vanish from
your midst, who will want to do smithing or ship building
or tailoring or wheelwrighting or shoemaking or bricklay-
ing or laundering or tanning? Who will want to till the soil
with ploughshares and reap Deo's[25] bounty, once you can
live idly and ignore all this?

CHREMYLUS
That's nonsense, because everything you counted off just
now will be the slaves' jobs.

POVERTY
And where will you get slaves?

CHREMYLUS
We'll buy them with money, of course.

POVERTY
But who will be the seller? He'll already have money.

[25] A poetic name for Demeter.

ARISTOPHANES

520   κερδαίνειν βουλόμενός τις
ἔμπορος ἥκων ἐκ Θετταλίας παρὰ πλείστων
   ἀνδραποδιστῶν.

ΠΕΝΙΑ

ἀλλ᾽ οὐδ᾽ ἔσται πρῶτον ἁπάντων οὐδεὶς οὐδ᾽
   ἀνδραποδιστὴς
κατὰ τὸν λόγον ὃν σὺ λέγεις δήπου. τίς γὰρ
   πλουτῶν ἐθελήσει
κινδυνεύων περὶ τῆς ψυχῆς τῆς αὑτοῦ τοῦτο
   ποιῆσαι;
525 ὥστ᾽ αὐτὸς ἀροῦν ἐπαναγκασθεὶς καὶ σκάπτειν
   τἄλλα τε μοχθεῖν
ὀδυνηρότερον τρίψεις βίοτον πολὺ τοῦ νῦν.

ΧΡΕΜΥΛΟΣ

                               ἐς κεφαλὴν σοί.

ΠΕΝΙΑ

ἔτι δ᾽ οὐχ ἕξεις οὔτ᾽ ἐν κλίνῃ καταδαρθεῖν, οὐ γὰρ
   ἔσονται,
οὔτ᾽ ἐν δάπισιν· τίς γὰρ ὑφαίνειν ἐθελήσει χρυσίου
   ὄντος;
οὔτε μύροισιν μυρίσαι στακτοῖς ὁπόταν νύμφην
   ἀγάγησθον,
530 οὔθ᾽ ἱματίων βαπτῶν δαπάναις κοσμῆσαι
   ποικιλομόρφων.
καίτοι τί πλέον πλουτεῖν ἐστιν τούτων πάντων
   ἀπορῶντα;

CHREMYLUS

Some merchant from Thessaly, the capital of slave traffickers, who's looking to make a profit.

POVERTY

But first of all, there won't be a single slave trafficker anywhere—by the logic of your own argument, of course. When someone has wealth, why would he want to risk his very life in that kind of business? No, you'll be forced to do your ploughing and digging and other chores all by yourself, and so lead a much harder life than you do now.

CHREMYLUS

I hope it happens to you!

POVERTY

And you won't sleep in beds any more, or under quilts, because there won't be any, for who'll want to weave them once they've got money? And when you two bring home brides, you won't be scenting them with drops of perfume, or adorning them with expensive robes intricately dyed and decorated. Yet what good is wealth if you don't have all

παρ' ἐμοῦ δ' ἐστὶν ταῦτ' εὔπορα πάνθ' ὑμῖν ὧν
   δεῖσθον· ἐγὼ γὰρ
τὸν χειροτέχνην ὥσπερ δέσποιν' ἐπαναγκάζουσα
   κάθημαι
διὰ τὴν χρείαν καὶ τὴν πενίαν ζητεῖν ὁπόθεν βίον
   ἕξει.

ΧΡΕΜΥΛΟΣ

535 σὺ γὰρ ἂν πορίσαι τί δύναι' ἀγαθὸν πλὴν φῴδων
   ἐκ βαλανείου
καὶ παιδαρίων ὑποπεινώντων καὶ γραϊδίων
   κολοσυρτόν;
φθειρῶν τ' ἀριθμὸν καὶ κωνώπων καὶ ψυλλῶν οὐδὲ
   λέγω σοι
ὑπὸ τοῦ πλήθους, αἳ βομβοῦσαι περὶ τὴν κεφαλὴν
   ἀνιῶσιν,
ἐπεγείρουσαι καὶ φράζουσαι· "πεινήσεις· ἀλλ'
   ἐπανίστω."
540 πρὸς δέ γε τούτοις ἀνθ' ἱματίου μὲν ἔχειν ῥάκος·
   ἀντὶ δὲ κλίνης
στιβάδα σχοίνων κόρεων μεστήν, ἢ τοὺς εὕδοντας
   ἐγείρει·
καὶ φορμὸν ἔχειν ἀντὶ τάπητος σαπρόν· ἀντὶ δὲ
   προσκεφαλαίου
λίθον εὐμεγέθη πρὸς τῇ κεφαλῇ· σιτεῖσθαι δ' ἀντὶ
   μὲν ἄρτων
μαλάχης πτόρθους, ἀντὶ δὲ μάζης φυλλεῖ' ἰσχνῶν
   ῥαφανίδων,

that? It's from me that you get everything you need, because I'm the one who sits by the artisan like a taskmaster, compelling him by the pinch of poverty to seek his livelihood.

CHREMYLUS

What benefits can *you* provide, except blisters in the bathhouse and masses of hungry children and old ladies? Not to mention the lice, gnats, and fleas, too numerous to enumerate, that annoy us by buzzing around our heads and waking us up with the warning, "get up or you'll go hungry!" And on top of that, you have us wearing rags, not coats, and sleeping not on a bed but a bug-infested twine mat that doesn't let you get any sleep, under threadbare burlap instead of a blanket, with our heads not on a pillow but a hefty stone. And to eat, not bread but mallow shoots, not cake but withered radish leaves. We sit not on chairs

---

532 ἐμοῦ cett.: ἐμοὶ Vᵖᶜ Mᵃᶜ

545 ἀντὶ δὲ θράνου στάμνου κεφαλὴν κατεαγότος, ἀντὶ
δὲ μάκτρας
πιθάκνης πλευρὰν ἐρρωγυῖαν καὶ ταύτην· ἆρά γε
πολλῶν
ἀγαθῶν πᾶσιν τοῖς ἀνθρώποις ἀποφαίνω σ᾽ αἴτιον
οὖσαν;

ΠΕΝΙΑ

σὺ μὲν οὐ τὸν ἐμὸν βίον εἴρηκας, τὸν τῶν πτωχῶν
δ᾽ ἐπεκρούσω.

ΧΡΕΜΤΛΟΣ

οὔκουν δήπου τῆς Πτωχείας Πενίαν φαμὲν εἶναι
ἀδελφήν;

ΠΕΝΙΑ

550 ὑμεῖς γ᾽ οἵπερ καὶ Θρασυβούλῳ Διονύσιον εἶναι
ὅμοιον.
ἀλλ᾽ οὐχ οὑμὸς τοῦτο πέπονθεν βίος οὐ μὰ Δί᾽,
οὐδέ γε μέλλει.
πτωχοῦ μὲν γὰρ βίος, ὃν σὺ λέγεις, ζῆν ἐστιν
μηδὲν ἔχοντα·
τοῦ δὲ πένητος ζῆν φειδόμενον καὶ τοῖς ἔργοις
προσέχοντα,
περιγίγνεσθαι δ᾽ αὐτῷ μηδέν, μὴ μέντοι μηδ᾽
ἐπιλείπειν.

ΧΡΕΜΤΛΟΣ

555 ὡς μακαρίτην, ὦ Δάματερ, τὸν βίον αὐτοῦ
κατέλεξας,

but on broken crocks, and instead of a kneading trough we get one side of a barrel, and that's broken too. Now haven't I revealed the many blessings you bring to all humanity?

POVERTY

That's not my life you've described; you've sneaked in the life of beggars.

CHREMYLUS

Well, don't we say that Poverty is the sister of Beggary?

POVERTY

And you're the ones who also say that Thrasybulus is the same as Dionysius![26] No, the life I represent is certainly nothing like that and never will be. You see, you're describing the beggar's life, which means living without possessions; by contrast, the poor man's life means being thrifty and hard working, and though he has nothing to spare, he doesn't lack the necessities either.

CHREMYLUS

By Demeter, how blessed you make his life sound, scrimp-

[26] The point is that Thrasybulus, a hero of the democracy (cf. 1146 n.) recently killed on campaign, could not be more different from Dionysius I, the stern tyrant of Syracuse; but some popular politician had evidently made the comparison.

εἰ φεισάμενος καὶ μοχθήσας καταλείψει μηδὲ
    ταφῆναι.

σκώπτειν πειρᾷ καὶ κωμῳδεῖν τοῦ σπουδάζειν
    ἀμελήσας,
οὐ γιγνώσκων ὅτι τοῦ Πλούτου παρέχω βελτίονας
    ἄνδρας
καὶ τὴν γνώμην καὶ τὴν ἰδέαν. παρὰ τῷ μὲν γὰρ
    ποδαγρῶντες
560 καὶ γαστρώδεις καὶ παχύκνημοι καὶ πίονές εἰσιν
    ἀσελγῶς,
παρ' ἐμοὶ δ' ἰσχνοὶ καὶ σφηκώδεις καὶ τοῖς ἐχθροῖς
    ἀνιαροί.

ἀπὸ τοῦ λιμοῦ γὰρ ἴσως αὐτοῖς τὸ σφηκῶδες σὺ
    πορίζεις.

περὶ σωφροσύνης ἤδη τοίνυν περανῶ σφῷν
    κἀναδιδάξω
ὅτι κοσμιότης οἰκεῖ μετ' ἐμοῦ, τοῦ Πλούτου δ' ἐστ'
    ἐνυβρίζειν.

565 πάνυ γοῦν κλέπτειν κόσμιόν ἐστιν καὶ τοὺς τοίχους
    διορύττειν.

[νὴ τὸν Δί', εἰ δεῖ λαθεῖν αὐτόν, πῶς οὐχὶ κόσμιόν
    ἐστιν;]

ing and toiling and then having nothing left for his own funeral!

POVERTY

You're using ridicule and caricature and not taking this seriously, since you're unaware that I produce better men than Wealth does in both mind and body. With him you'll find men with gout, potbellies, bloated legs, and disgustingly fat, while with me they're lean, wasp-waisted, and hard on the enemy.

CHREMYLUS

Perhaps it's by starvation that you give them that wasp waist.

POVERTY

Turning now to the issue of morality, I'll proceed to demonstrate that good behavior dwells with me, and arrogance with Wealth.

CHREMYLUS

And I suppose good behavior means stealing and burglary!

---

566 del. Bentley

ΠΕΝΙΑ

σκέψαι τοίνυν ἐν ταῖς πόλεσιν τοὺς ῥήτορας, ὡς
  ὁπόταν μὲν
ὦσι πένητες, περὶ τὸν δῆμον καὶ τὴν πόλιν εἰσὶ
  δίκαιοι,
πλουτήσαντες δ᾽ ἀπὸ τῶν κοινῶν παραχρῆμ᾽ ἄδικοι
  γεγένηνται,
570   ἐπιβουλεύουσί τε τῷ πλήθει καὶ τῷ δήμῳ
  πολεμοῦσιν.

ΧΡΕΜΤΛΟΣ

ἀλλ᾽ οὐ ψεύδει τούτων γ᾽ οὐδέν, καίπερ σφόδρα
  βάσκανος οὖσα.
ἀτὰρ οὐχ ἧττόν γ᾽ οὐδὲν κλαύσει, μηδὲν ταύτῃ γε
  κομήσῃς,
ὁτιὴ ζητεῖς τοῦτ᾽ ἀναπείσειν ἡμᾶς, ὡς ἔστιν ἄμεινον
πενία πλούτου.

ΠΕΝΙΑ

  καὶ σύ γ᾽ ἐλέγξαι μ᾽ οὔπω δύνασαι περὶ τούτου,
ἀλλὰ φλυαρεῖς καὶ πτερυγίζεις.

ΧΡΕΜΤΛΟΣ

  καὶ πῶς φεύγουσί σ᾽ ἅπαντες;
575

ΠΕΝΙΑ

ὅτι βελτίους αὐτοὺς ποιῶ. σκέψασθαι δ᾽ ἔστι
  μάλιστα
ἀπὸ τῶν παίδων· τοὺς γὰρ πατέρας φεύγουσι
  φρονοῦντας ἄριστα

POVERTY

Just observe the politicians in every state: when they're poor, they do right by the people and the state; but when they get rich on public funds, they immediately become wrongdoers, plotting against the masses and warring against the people.

CHREMYLUS

Well, you don't misrepresent anything there, even though you're quite the witch. But don't imagine that this will get you any milder punishment for trying to persuade us that poverty is better than wealth.

POVERTY

But you haven't yet been able to refute me on this point; all you do is jabber and flail about.

CHREMYLUS

All right, why does everyone shun you?

POVERTY

Because I improve them. The case of children is the most instructive example: they shun the fathers who have their

αὐτοῖς. οὕτω διαγιγνώσκειν χαλεπὸν πρᾶγμ᾽ ἐστὶ
δίκαιον.

ΧΡΕΜΥΛΟΣ

τὸν Δία φήσεις ἆρ᾽ οὐκ ὀρθῶς διαγιγνώσκειν τὸ
κράτιστον·
κἀκεῖνος γὰρ τὸν πλοῦτον ἔχει.

ΒΛΕΨΙΔΗΜΟΣ

580   ταύτην δ᾽ ἡμῖν ἀποπέμπει.

ΠΕΝΙΑ

ἀλλ᾽, ὦ Κρονικαῖς λήμαις ὄντως λημῶντες τὰς
φρένας ἄμφω,
ὁ Ζεὺς δήπου πένεται, καὶ τοῦτ᾽ ἤδη φανερῶς σε
διδάξω.
εἰ γὰρ ἐπλούτει, πῶς ἂν ποιῶν τὸν Ὀλυμπικὸν
αὐτὸς ἀγῶνα
ἵνα τοὺς Ἕλληνας ἅπαντας ἀεὶ δι᾽ ἔτους πέμπτου
ξυναγείρει,
585 ἀνεκήρυττεν τῶν ἀσκητῶν τοὺς νικῶντας
στεφανώσας
κοτίνου στεφάνῳ; καίτοι χρυσῷ μᾶλλον χρῆν, εἴπερ
ἐπλούτει.

ΧΡΕΜΥΛΟΣ

οὔκουν τούτῳ δήπου δηλοῖ τιμῶν τὸν πλοῦτον
ἐκεῖνος;
φειδόμενος γὰρ καὶ βουλόμενος τούτου μηδὲν
δαπανᾶσθαι,

best interests at heart. That's how difficult it is to appreci-
ate what's right.

CHREMYLUS

Will you then claim that Zeus doesn't appreciate what's
best? Because he too has wealth.

BLEPSIDEMUS

And sends *her* to us!

POVERTY

Oh, your wits are blinded by truly primeval sties, the both
of you! Zeus of course is actually poor, as I now will clearly
demonstrate. If he's wealthy, then why is it that when he
holds the Olympic Games, where every fourth year he
gathers all the Greeks together, he heralds the victorious
athletes by crowning them with wild olive? If he's wealthy,
he should crown them with gold.

CHREMYLUS

Doesn't that simply show that he values his wealth? Being
thrifty, and unwilling to squander any of his wealth, he

λήροις ἀναδῶν τοὺς νικῶντας τὸν πλοῦτον ἐᾷ παρ'
ἑαυτῷ.

ΠΕΝΙΑ

590 πολὺ τῆς πενίας πρᾶγμ' αἴσχιον ζητεῖς αὑτῷ
περιάψαι,
εἰ πλούσιος ὢν ἀνελεύθερός ἐσθ' οὑτωσὶ καὶ
φιλοκερδής.

ΧΡΕΜΥΛΟΣ

ἀλλὰ σέ γ' ὁ Ζεὺς ἐξολέσειεν κοτίνου στεφάνῳ
στεφανώσας.

ΠΕΝΙΑ

τὸ γὰρ ἀντιλέγειν τολμᾶν ὑμᾶς ὡς οὐ πάντ' ἔστ'
ἀγάθ' ὑμῖν
διὰ τὴν Πενίαν.

ΧΡΕΜΥΛΟΣ

παρὰ τῆς Ἑκάτης ἔξεστιν τοῦτο πυθέσθαι,
595 εἴτε τὸ πλουτεῖν εἴτε τὸ πεινῆν βέλτιον. φησὶ γὰρ
αὑτῇ
τοὺς μὲν ἔχοντας καὶ πλουτοῦντας δεῖπνον
προσάγειν κατὰ μῆνα,
τοὺς δὲ πένητας τῶν ἀνθρώπων ἁρπάζειν πρὶν
καταθεῖναι.
ἀλλὰ φθείρου καὶ μὴ γρύζῃς
ἔτι μηδ' ὁτιοῦν.
600 οὐ γὰρ πείσεις, οὐδ' ἢν πείσῃς.

adorns the winners with baubles and keeps the wealth for himself.

POVERTY

You're trying to impute to him something more disgraceful than poverty: being rich yet behaving like a greedy lowlife.

CHREMYLUS

I hope Zeus crowns *you* with a wild olive wreath, after he exterminates you!

POVERTY

How dare you keep denying that Poverty is the source of all your blessings?

CHREMYLUS

This is a question that Hecate can answer, whether it's better to be rich than poor. She'll tell you that every month the wealthy set out a meal for her, and that poor people snatch it up before it's even put down.[27] Now get lost and stop your grumbling; not another word! You won't persuade me even if you convince me.

[27] Hecate's shrines stood in the street before houses (*Wasps* 804); her "meals" were mere refuse, cf. Demosthenes 54.39.

---

[596] προσάγειν κατὰ μῆνα (κ. μ. π. R M γρV) Holzinger: κατὰ μῆν' ἀποπέμπειν (προσπ. U) cett.

ΠΕΝΙΑ

ὦ πόλις Ἄργους, κλύεθ᾽ οἷα λέγει.

ΧΡΕΜΤΛΟΣ

Παύσωνα κάλει τὸν ξύσσιτον.

ΠΕΝΙΑ

τί πάθω τλήμων;

ΧΡΕΜΤΛΟΣ

ἔρρ᾽ ἐς κόρακας θᾶττον ἀφ᾽ ἡμῶν.

ΠΕΝΙΑ

605   εἶμι δὲ ποῖ γῆς;

ΧΡΕΜΤΛΟΣ

εἰς τὸν κύφων᾽· ἀλλ᾽ οὐ μέλλειν
χρή σ᾽, ἀλλ᾽ ἀνύειν.

ΠΕΝΙΑ

ἦ μὴν ὑμεῖς γ᾽ ἔτι μ᾽ ἐνταυθοῖ
μεταπέμψεσθον.

ΧΡΕΜΤΛΟΣ

610   τότε νοστήσεις· νῦν δὲ φθείρου·
κρεῖττον γάρ μοι πλουτεῖν ἐστιν,
σὲ δ᾽ ἐᾶν κλάειν μακρὰ τὴν κεφαλήν.

ΒΛΕΨΙΔΗΜΟΣ

νὴ Δί᾽, ἔγωγ᾽ οὖν ἐθέλω πλουτῶν
εὐωχεῖσθαι μετὰ τῶν παίδων
615   τῆς τε γυναικός, καὶ λουσάμενος
λιπαρὸς χωρῶν ἐκ βαλανείου
τῶν χειροτεχνῶν

POVERTY

City of Argos, hearken to his words![28]

CHREMYLUS

Summon Pauson, your tablemate.[29]

POVERTY

This is terrible; what am I to do?

CHREMYLUS

Get the hell out of here, and fast!

POVERTY

Where in the world shall I go?

CHREMYLUS

To the pillory. Come on, you mustn't tarry; get a move on!

POVERTY

Mark my words, you'll summon me back here one day, both of you.

Exit POVERTY.

CHREMYLUS

That's when you'll come back; meanwhile, get lost. I'm better off being rich, and letting you go to blazes.

BLEPSIDEMUS

Hear hear! As for me, I'm ready to revel in wealth with my wife and kids, to take a bath, walk gleaming from the bath-

---

[28] From Euripides' *Telephus*, fr. 713, a hyperbolic request for witnesses to an outrageous claim, cf. *Knights* 813.

[29] Teased for poverty in *Acharnians* 854 and *Women at the Thesmophoria* 949.

καὶ τῆς Πενίας καταπαρδεῖν.

ΧΡΕΜΥΛΟΣ

αὕτη μὲν ἡμῖν ἠπίτριπτος οἴχεται.
620 ἐγὼ δὲ καὶ σύ γ᾽ ὡς τάχιστα τὸν θεὸν
ἐγκατακλινοῦντ᾽ ἄγωμεν εἰς Ἀσκληπιοῦ.

ΒΛΕΨΙΔΗΜΟΣ

καὶ μὴ διατρίβωμέν γε, μὴ πάλιν τις αὖ
ἐλθὼν διακωλύσῃ τι τῶν προὔργου ποιεῖν.

ΧΡΕΜΥΛΟΣ

παῖ Καρίων, τὰ στρώματ᾽ ἐκφέρειν ἐχρῆν
625 αὐτόν τ᾽ ἄγειν τὸν Πλοῦτον, ὡς νομίζεται,
καὶ τἄλλ᾽ ὅσ᾽ ἐστὶν ἔνδον εὐτρεπισμένα.

ΧΟΡΟΥ

ΚΑΡΙΩΝ

ὦ πλεῖστα Θησείοις μεμυστιλημένοι
γέροντες ἄνδρες ἐπ᾽ ὀλιγίστοις ἀλφίτοις,
ὡς εὐτυχεῖθ᾽, ὡς μακαρίως πεπράγατε,
630 ἄλλοι θ᾽ ὅσοις μέτεστι τοῦ χρηστοῦ τρόπου.

ΚΟΡΥΦΑΙΟΣ

τί δ᾽ ἐστίν, ὦ βέλτιστε τῶν σαυτοῦ φίλων;
φαίνει γὰρ ἥκειν ἄγγελος χρηστοῦ τινος.

ΚΑΡΙΩΝ

ὁ δεσπότης πέπραγεν εὐτυχέστατα,

house, and blow a fart at Poverty and her artisans!

CHREMYLUS

Well, we're rid of that damned witch. Now as quick as we can, let's you and I take the god to Asclepius' temple and bed him down.

BLEPSIDEMUS

Yes, let's waste no time, in case somebody else comes along and thwarts our enterprise.

CHREMYLUS

(*calling into the house*) Cario my boy, it's time to fetch the bedding and bring out the god himself, with due cere- mony, as well as the other things we've got ready.

CARIO and other Slaves bring out WEALTH *and items of bedding and baggage, and all march off stage.*

The Chorus performs an entr'acte.

Enter CARIO, *returned from Asclepius' shrine; it is now the following morning.*

CARIO

You old men, who at many a festival for Theseus have sopped up soup with the tiniest of crumbs, you're in luck! You're on easy street! And so is everyone else who shares your good character!

CHORUS LEADER

What's up, best of all your fellow slaves? You look to be the harbinger of something good.

CARIO

My master's had the greatest stroke of luck, and Wealth

519

μᾶλλον δ᾽ ὁ Πλοῦτος αὐτός· ἀντὶ γὰρ τυφλοῦ
635 ἐξωμμάτωται καὶ λελάμπρυνται κόρας,
Ἀσκληπιοῦ παιῶνος εὐμενοῦς τυχών.

ΚΟΡΥΦΑΙΟΣ
λέγεις μοι χαράν, λέγεις μοι βοάν.

ΚΑΡΙΩΝ
πάρεστι χαίρειν, ἤν τε βούλησθ᾽ ἤν τε μή.

ΚΟΡΥΦΑΙΟΣ
ἀναβοάσομαι τὸν εὔπαιδα καὶ
640 μέγα βροτοῖσι φέγγος Ἀσκληπιόν.

ΓΥΝΗ
τίς ἡ βοή ποτ᾽ ἐστίν; ἆρ᾽ ἀγγέλλεται
χρηστόν τι; τοῦτο γὰρ ποθοῦσ᾽ ἐγὼ πάλαι
ἔνδον κάθημαι περιμένουσα τουτονί.

ΚΑΡΙΩΝ
ταχέως, ταχέως φέρ᾽ οἶνον, ὦ δέσποιν᾽, ἵνα
645 καὐτὴ πίῃς—φιλεῖς δὲ δρῶσ᾽ αὐτὸ σφόδρα—
ὡς ἀγαθὰ συλλήβδην ἅπαντά σοι φέρω.

ΓΥΝΗ
καὶ ποῦ ᾽στιν;

ΚΑΡΙΩΝ
ἐν τοῖς λεγομένοις· εἴσει τάχα.

ΓΥΝΗ
πέραινε τοίνυν ὅ τι λέγεις ἀνύσας ποτέ.

himself even more so: "yes, from being blind he's now well-sighted, and his pupils are made bright, since he's found a kindly healer in Asclepius."[30]

CHORUS LEADER

Your news calls for joy, calls for cheers!

CARIO

Joy's in order, like it or not!

CHORUS LEADER

I'll lift a cheer for Asclepius, blessed in his children and a bright beacon for humankind!

Enter Chremylus' WIFE *from the house.*

WIFE

What's all this shouting? Has someone brought good news? That's what I've long desired, sitting in the house and waiting for this very man.

CARIO

Quickly, mistress, quickly fetch some wine, and you can have some too (you dearly love doing that), because I'm bringing you the whole gamut of blessings all at once!

WIFE

So where are they?

CARIO

In my report; you'll soon find out.

WIFE

Well, give me your report, and make it snappy!

---

[30] According to the scholiast, a quotation (at least in part) from Sophocles' *Phineus* (fr. 710).

ΚΑΡΙΩΝ

ἄκουε τοίνυν, ὡς ἐγὼ τὰ πράγματα
650 ἐκ τῶν ποδῶν εἰς τὴν κεφαλήν σοι πάντ' ἐρῶ.

ΓΥΝΗ

μὴ δῆτ' ἔμοιγ' εἰς τὴν κεφαλήν.

ΚΑΡΙΩΝ

μὴ τἀγαθὰ

ἃ νῦν γεγένηται;

ΓΥΝΗ

μὴ μὲν οὖν τὰ πράγματα.

ΚΑΡΙΩΝ

ὡς γὰρ τάχιστ' ἀφικόμεθα πρὸς τὸν θεὸν
ἄγοντες ἄνδρα τότε μὲν ἀθλιώτατον,
655 νῦν δ' εἴ τιν' ἄλλον μακάριον κεὐδαίμονα,
πρῶτον μὲν αὐτὸν ἐπὶ θάλατταν ἤγομεν,
ἔπειτ' ἐλοῦμεν.

ΓΥΝΗ

νὴ Δί', εὐδαίμων ἄρ' ἦν
ἀνὴρ γέρων ψυχρᾷ θαλάττῃ λούμενος.

ΚΑΡΙΩΝ

ἔπειτα πρὸς τὸ τέμενος ᾖμεν τοῦ θεοῦ.
660 ἐπεὶ δὲ βωμῷ πόπανα καὶ προθύματα
καθωσιώθη, πελανὸς Ἡφαίστου φλογί,
κατεκλίναμεν τὸν Πλοῦτον, ὥσπερ εἰκὸς ἦν·
ἡμῶν δ' ἕκαστος στιβάδα παρεκαττύετο.

CARIO

Then listen; I'll break the whole business to you from head to foot.

WIFE

Don't break anything on *my* head!

CARIO

Not even the good news?

WIFE

No, just not that business.

CARIO

Then listen. As soon as we got to the shrine with that fellow—then very miserable, but now the happiest and luckiest in the world—we took him first to the sea and washed him.

WIFE

Oh yes, what good luck for an old man, to be washed in freezing water!

CARIO

Then we went to the god's precinct, and after the cakes and first offerings were burnt, "matter for Hephaestus' flame,"[31] we bedded Wealth down in the proper fashion, and rigged up bunks for ourselves.

---

[31] Recalling some tragic source.

ΓΥΝΗ

ἦσαν δέ τινες κἄλλοι δεόμενοι τοῦ θεοῦ;

ΚΑΡΙΩΝ

665 εἷς μέν γε Νεοκλείδης, ὅς ἐστι μὲν τυφλός,
κλέπτων δὲ τοὺς βλέποντας ὑπερηκόντικεν·
ἕτεροί τε πολλοὶ παντοδαπὰ νοσήματα
ἔχοντες. ὡς δὲ τοὺς λύχνους ἀποσβέσας
ἡμῖν παρήγγειλεν καθεύδειν τοῦ θεοῦ
670 ὁ πρόπολος, εἰπών, ἤν τις αἴσθηται ψόφου,
σιγᾶν, ἅπαντες κοσμίως κατεκείμεθα.
κἀγὼ καθεύδειν οὐκ ἐδυνάμην, ἀλλά με
ἀθάρης χύτρα τις ἐξέπληττε κειμένη
ὀλίγον ἄπωθεν τῆς κεφαλῆς του γρᾳδίου,
675 ἐφ᾽ ἣν ἐπεθύμουν δαιμονίως ἐφερπύσαι.
ἔπειτ᾽ ἀναβλέψας ὁρῶ τὸν ἱερέα
τοὺς φθοῖς ἀφαρπάζοντα καὶ τὰς ἰσχάδας
ἀπὸ τῆς τραπέζης τῆς ἱερᾶς. μετὰ τοῦτο δὲ
περιῆλθε τοὺς βωμοὺς ἅπαντας ἐν κύκλῳ,
680 εἴ που πόπανον εἴη τι καταλελειμμένον·
ἔπειτα ταῦθ᾽ ἥγιζεν εἰς σάκταν τινά.
κἀγὼ νομίσας πολλὴν ὁσίαν τοῦ πράγματος
ἐπὶ τὴν χύτραν τὴν τῆς ἀθάρης ἀνίσταμαι.

ΓΥΝΗ

ταλάντατ᾽ ἀνδρῶν, οὐκ ἐδεδοίκεις τὸν θεόν;

ΚΑΡΙΩΝ

685 νὴ τοὺς θεοὺς ἔγωγε, μὴ φθάσειέ με
ἐπὶ τὴν χύτραν ἐλθὼν ἔχων τὰ στέμματα.

WIFE

Were there any other patients at the shrine?

CARIO

One was Neocleides, who's blind but has a sharper eye than the sighted when it comes to stealing; and there were many others, with all kinds of illnesses. Then the temple servant put out the lamps and told us all to go to sleep, and to be quiet if we heard any noise, and we all lay there in good order. But I couldn't get to sleep. A pot of porridge sitting just beside some old lady's head was driving me nuts; I had a supernatural desire to slink over and get it. Then I looked up and saw the temple servant snatch the pastries and figs from the sacred table, and then make the rounds of all the altars in search of any leftover cakes, which he consecrated right into a sack. I appreciated the holiness of this procedure, so I left my bed for that pot of porridge.

WIFE

You utterly benighted man, weren't you afraid of the god?

CARIO

I certainly *was* afraid—that he'd come out wearing his gar-

---

681 ἥγιζεν cett. S: ἥιτιζεν R: ἥικιζεν (κ in ras.) V

ὁ γὰρ ἱερεὺς αὐτοῦ με προὐδιδάξατο.
τὸ γρᾴδιον δ᾽ ὡς ᾐσθ⟨άν⟩ετό μου τὸν ψόφον,
τὴν χεῖρ᾽ ἐνείρει· κᾆτα συρίξας ἐγὼ
690 ὀδὰξ ἐλαβόμην ὡς παρείας ὢν ὄφις.
ἡ δ᾽ εὐθέως τὴν χεῖρα πάλιν ἀνέσπασεν
κατέκειτό θ᾽ αὑτὴν ἐντυλίξασ᾽ ἡσυχῇ
ὑπὸ τοῦ δέους βδέουσα δριμύτερον γαλῆς.
κἀγὼ τότ᾽ ἤδη τῆς ἀθάρης πολλὴν ἔφλων·
695 ἔπειτ᾽ ἐπειδὴ μεστὸς ἦν, ἀνεπαυόμην.

ΓΡΑΥΣ

ὁ δὲ θεὸς ὑμῖν οὐ προσῄειν;

ΚΑΡΙΩΝ

οὐδέπω.
μετὰ τοῦτο δ᾽ ἤδη καὶ γέλοιον δῆτά τι
ἐποίησα. προσιόντος γὰρ αὐτοῦ μέγα πάνυ
ἀπέπαρδον· ἡ γαστὴρ γὰρ ἐπεφύσητό μου.

ΓΡΑΥΣ

700 ἦ πού σε διὰ τοῦτ᾽ εὐθὺς ἐβδελύττετο.

ΚΑΡΙΩΝ

οὔκ, ἀλλ᾽ Ἰασὼ μέν τις ἀκολουθοῦσ᾽ ἅμα
ὑπηρυθρίασε χἠ Πανάκει᾽ ἀπεστράφη
τὴν ῥῖν᾽ ἐπιλαβοῦσ᾽· οὐ λιβανωτὸν γὰρ βδέω.

ΓΡΑΥΣ

αὐτὸς δ᾽ ἐκεῖνος;

ΚΑΡΙΩΝ

οὐ μὰ Δί᾽ οὐδ᾽ ἐφρόντισεν.

526

lands and beat me to the pot! His own priest had taught me
that one. Now when the old lady heard the sound I was
making, she stuck her hand into the pot; then with a hiss I
grabbed it in my teeth like a garter snake. She pulled back
that hand right quickly, and lay there quietly, all wrapped
up in the blanket, farting in terror, stinkier than a weasel.
That's when I took a big gobble of that porridge, and I
didn't stop till I was full.

WIFE

But didn't the god approach you?

CARIO

Not yet; first I did one more amusing thing. As he was ap-
proaching, I let off a very big fart; my stomach had bloated
on me.

WIFE

I'll bet that put you right on his shit list.

CARIO

No, but Iaso, who followed him in, blushed, and Panacea
held her nose and turned away;[32] my farts aren't incense,
you know!

WIFE

And the god himself?

CARIO

He paid absolutely no attention at all.

[32] Two of Asclepius' daughters.

---

689 ἐνείρει Fraenkel: ὑφήρει vel ὑφήρει a

ARISTOPHANES

ΓΤΝΗ

705 λέγεις ἄγροικον ἄρα σύ γ᾽ εἶναι τὸν θεόν;

ΚΑΡΙΩΝ

μὰ Δί᾽ οὐκ ἔγωγ᾽, ἀλλὰ σκατοφάγον.

ΓΤΝΗ

αἲ τάλαν.

ΚΑΡΙΩΝ

μετὰ ταῦτ᾽ ἐγὼ μὲν εὐθὺς ἐνεκαλυψάμην
δείσας, ἐκεῖνος δ᾽ ἐν κύκλῳ τὰ νοσήματα
σκοπῶν περιῄει πάντα κοσμίως πάνυ.
710 ἔπειτα παῖς αὐτῷ λίθινον θυείδιον
παρέθηκε καὶ δοίδυκα καὶ κιβώτιον.

ΓΤΝΗ

λίθινον;

ΚΑΡΙΩΝ

μὰ Δί᾽ οὐ δῆτ᾽, οὐχὶ τό γε κιβώτιον.

ΓΤΝΗ

σὺ δὲ πῶς ἑώρας, ὦ κάκιστ᾽ ἀπολούμενε,
ὃς ἐγκεκαλύφθαι φής;

ΚΑΡΙΩΝ

διὰ τοῦ τριβωνίου·
715 ὀπὰς γὰρ εἶχεν οὐκ ὀλίγας, μὰ τὸν Δία.
πρῶτον δὲ πάντων τῷ Νεοκλείδῃ φάρμακον
κατάπλαστον ἐνεχείρησε τρίβειν, ἐμβαλὼν
σκορόδων κεφαλὰς τρεῖς Τηνίων. ἔπειτ᾽ ἔφλα
ἐν τῇ θυείᾳ συμπαραμειγνύων ὀπὸν

528

WIFE

You're telling me the god's a bumpkin?

CARIO

Certainly not; he's just a shit eater.

WIFE

Ugh, you're awful!

CARIO

Well, after that I got scared and covered right up, while in very orderly fashion the god made his rounds, examining everyone's malady. Then his assistant brought him a mortar made of stone, a pestle, and a box.

WIFE

Made of stone?

CARIO

No, not the box, only the mortar.

WIFE

But you were covered up, you say, so how did you manage to see, damn and blast you?

CARIO

Through my cloak of course, since it's got quite a few peep holes. Now his very first job was grinding a poultice for Neocleides. He put in three heads of Tenian garlic, then added fig juice and squill, and pounded it in the mortar;

720 καὶ σχῖνον· εἶτ᾽ ὄξει διέμενος Σφηττίῳ
κατέπλασεν αὐτοῦ τὰ βλέφαρ᾽ ἐκτρέψας, ἵνα
ὀδυνῷτο μᾶλλον. ὁ δὲ κεκραγὼς καὶ βοῶν
ἔφευγ᾽ ἀνάξας· ὁ δὲ θεὸς γελάσας ἔφη·
"ἐνταῦθά νυν κάθησο καταπεπλασμένος,
725 ἵν᾽ ἐπομνύμενον παύσω σε τὰς ἐκκλησίας."

ΓΥΝΗ
ὡς φιλόπολίς τίς ἐσθ᾽ ὁ δαίμων καὶ σοφός.

ΚΑΡΙΩΝ
μετὰ τοῦτο τῷ Πλούτωνι παρεκαθέζετο,
καὶ πρῶτα μὲν δὴ τῆς κεφαλῆς ἐφήψατο,
ἔπειτα καθαρὸν ἡμιτύβιον λαβὼν
730 τὰ βλέφαρα περιέψησεν. ἡ Πανάκεια δὲ
κατεπέτασ᾽ αὐτοῦ τὴν κεφαλὴν φοινικίδι
καὶ πᾶν τὸ πρόσωπον· εἶθ᾽ ὁ θεὸς ἐπόππυσεν.
ἐξῃξάτην οὖν δύο δράκοντ᾽ ἐκ τοῦ νεὼ
ὑπερφυεῖ τὸ μέγεθος.

ΓΥΝΗ
ὦ φίλοι θεοί.

ΚΑΡΙΩΝ
735 τούτω δ᾽ ὑπὸ τὴν φοινικίδ᾽ ὑποδύνθ᾽ ἡσυχῇ
τὰ βλέφαρα περιέλειχον, ὥς γ᾽ ἐμοὶ δοκεῖ·
καὶ πρίν σε κοτύλας ἐκπιεῖν οἴνου δέκα,
ὁ Πλοῦτος, ὦ δέσποιν᾽, ἀνειστήκει βλέπων·
ἐγὼ δὲ τὼ χεῖρ᾽ ἀνεκρότησ᾽ ὑφ᾽ ἡδονῆς
740 τὸν δεσπότην τ᾽ ἤγειρον. ὁ θεὸς δ᾽ εὐθέως
ἠφάνισεν αὐτὸν οἵ τ᾽ ὄφεις εἰς τὸν νεών.

then he drenched it all with Sphettian vinegar, turned out his eyelids, and smeared it in, to make the sting more painful. Neocleides jumped up screaming and yelling and tried to run, but the god laughed and said, "You sit right here, all poulticed up; it'll stop you from obstructing assemblies with your affidavits."

WIFE

That god's a true patriot, and smart too!

CARIO

Next, he took a seat beside our dear Wealth, and felt his head, then took clean gauze and daubed around his eyelids; Panacea wrapped his head and whole face in crimson cloth. Then the god whistled, and two serpents darted from the temple, extraordinarily large ones.

WIFE

Good heavens!

CARIO

They slipped quietly beneath the crimson cloth and started licking around his eyelids, I suppose. And sooner than you could drink five pints of wine, mistress, our Wealth stood up and could see. I clapped my hands for sheer joy and woke my master, and the god immediately disappeared into the temple, the serpents too.[33] You can

---

[33] This line shows that the incubation was outside the temple.

721 ἐκτρέψας R V: ἐκστρέψας cett.
727 Πλούτῳ τι Meineke: γέροντι Kappeyne

οἱ δ' ἐγκατακείμενοι παρ' αὐτῷ πῶς δοκεῖς
τὸν Πλοῦτον ἠσπάζοντο καὶ τὴν νύχθ' ὅλην
ἐγρηγόρεσαν, ἕως διέλαμψεν ἡμέρα.
745 ἐγὼ δ' ἐπῄνουν τὸν θεὸν πάνυ σφόδρα,
ὅτι βλέπειν ἐποίησε τὸν Πλοῦτον ταχύ,
τὸν δὲ Νεοκλείδην μᾶλλον ἐποίησεν τυφλόν.

ΓΥΝΗ

ὅσην ἔχεις τὴν δύναμιν, ὦναξ δέσποτα.
ἀτὰρ φράσον μοι, ποῦ 'σθ' ὁ Πλοῦτος;

ΚΑΡΙΩΝ

ἔρχεται.

750 ἀλλ' ἦν περὶ αὐτὸν ὄχλος ὑπερφυὴς ὅσος.
οἱ γὰρ δίκαιοι πρότερον ὄντες καὶ βίον
ἔχοντες ὀλίγον αὐτὸν ἠσπάζοντο καὶ
ἐδεξιοῦνθ' ἅπαντες ὑπὸ τῆς ἡδονῆς·
ὅσοι δ' ἐπλούτουν οὐσίαν τ' εἶχον συχνὴν
755 οὐκ ἐκ δικαίου τὸν βίον κεκτημένοι,
ὀφρῦς ξυνῆγον ἐσκυθρώπαζόν θ' ἅμα.
οἱ δ' ἠκολούθουν κατόπιν ἐστεφανωμένοι
γελῶντες, εὐφημοῦντες· ἐκτυπεῖτο δὲ
ἐμβὰς γερόντων εὐρύθμοις προβήμασιν.
760 ἀλλ' εἶ', ἁπαξάπαντες ἐξ ἑνὸς λόγου
ὀρχεῖσθε καὶ σκιρτᾶτε καὶ χορεύετε·
οὐδεὶς γὰρ ὑμῖν εἰσιοῦσιν ἀγγελεῖ,
ὡς ἄλφιτ' οὐκ ἔνεστιν ἐν τῷ θυλάκῳ.

ΓΥΝΗ

νὴ τὴν Ἑκάτην, κἀγὼ δ' ἀναδῆσαι βούλομαι

imagine how everyone stayed up the whole night long,
hugging him till the new day lit up. I was especially loud in
my praises of the god, for giving Wealth his sight so
quickly, and for making that Neocleides even blinder!

WIFE

How great your power, my sovereign lord! But tell me,
where's Wealth now?

CARIO

He's on his way, but quite an immense crowd has collected
around him. All the people who formerly led upright but
meager lives wanted to greet him and shake his hand for
sheer joy, while the wealthy, who had heaps of possessions,
a living not acquired by upright means, were knitting their
brows and wearing frowns. The others followed behind
wearing garlands and laughing and voicing their blessings,
and the old men's shoes beat out a nice rhythm for the pa-
rade. *(to the Chorus)* Come on now, everyone all together
start dancing, skipping, and promenading, because you'll
never again come home to hear the news that there's no
more grain in your sack.

WIFE

By Hecate, I'd also like to drape a string of loaves around

765 εὐαγγέλιά σε κριβανιτῶν ὁρμαθῷ
τοιαῦτ᾿ ἀπαγγείλαντα.

ΚΑΡΙΩΝ

μή νυν μέλλ᾿ ἔτι,
ὡς ἄνδρες ἐγγύς εἰσιν ἤδη τῶν θυρῶν.

ΓΥΝΗ

φέρε νυν, ἰοῦσ᾿ εἴσω κομίσω καταχύσματα
ὥσπερ νεωνήτοισιν ὀφθαλμοῖς ἐγώ.

ΚΑΡΙΩΝ

770 ἐγὼ δ᾿ ἀπαντῆσαί γ᾿ ἐκείνοις βούλομαι.

ΧΟΡΟΥ

ΠΛΟΥΤΟΣ

καὶ προσκυνῶ γε πρῶτα μὲν τὸν ἥλιον,
ἔπειτα σεμνῆς Παλλάδος κλεινὸν πέδον
χώραν τε πᾶσαν Κέκροπος ἥ μ᾿ ἐδέξατο.
αἰσχύνομαι δὲ τὰς ἐμαυτοῦ συμφοράς,
775 οἵοις ἄρ᾿ ἀνθρώποις ξυνὼν ἐλάνθανον,
τοὺς ἀξίους δὲ τῆς ἐμῆς ὁμιλίας
ἔφευγον, εἰδὼς οὐδέν. ὦ τλήμων ἐγώ,
ὡς οὔτ᾿ ἐκεῖν᾿ ἄρ᾿ οὔτε ταῦτ᾿ ὀρθῶς ἔδρων.
ἀλλ᾿ αὐτὰ πάντα πάλιν ἀναστρέψας ἐγὼ
780 δείξω τὸ λοιπὸν πᾶσιν ἀνθρώποις ὅτι
ἄκων ἐμαυτὸν τοῖς πονηροῖς ἐπεδίδουν.

---

34 Sweets were customarily tossed over slaves first entering a
new master's house.

your neck for delivering such good news.

CARIO

Then don't delay, because the men are almost at the door.

WIFE

All right, I'll go in and fetch sweets, as for new-bought eyes![34]

CARIO

And me, I'm ready to greet the arrivals.

Exit CARIO *to a wing, and* WIFE *into the house.*

The Chorus performs an entr'acte.

Enter WEALTH *from a wing.*

WEALTH

Yes, [35] and first I bow to the sun, then to the famous soil of august Pallas[36] and all the country of Cecrops,[37] which has received me. I feel shame at my own misadventures, realizing the kind of people I used to associate with unawares, while in complete ignorance I shunned those who deserved my company. How pitiful that in both respects I acted wrongly! But I intend to reverse that situation completely, and show the world that I didn't mean to put myself in the hands of the wicked.

Enter CHREMYLUS *and* CARIO *from a wing.*

---

[35] Wealth apparently replies to the Chorus' song, which is not extant.

[36] Athena.

[37] The legendary first king of Athens.

ΧΡΕΜΥΛΟΣ

βάλλ᾽ ἐς κόρακας. ὡς χαλεπόν εἰσιν οἱ φίλοι
οἱ φαινόμενοι παραχρῆμ᾽ ὅταν πράττῃ τις εὖ.
νύττουσι γὰρ καὶ φλῶσι τἀντικνήμια,
785 ἐνδεικνύμενος ἕκαστος εὔνοιάν τινα.
ἐμὲ γὰρ τίς οὐ προσεῖπε; ποῖος οὐκ ὄχλος
περιεστεφάνωσεν ἐν ἀγορᾷ πρεσβυτικός;

ΓΥΝΗ

ὦ φίλτατ᾽ ἀνδρῶν, καὶ σὺ καὶ σύ, χαίρετον.
φέρε νυν, νόμος γάρ ἐστι, τὰ καταχύσματα
ταυτὶ καταχέω σου λαβοῦσα.

ΠΛΟΥΤΟΣ

790   μηδαμῶς.
ἐμοῦ γὰρ εἰσιόντος εἰς τὴν οἰκίαν
πρώτιστ᾽ ἀναβλέψαντος οὐδὲν ἐκφέρειν
πρεπῶδές ἐστιν, ἀλλὰ μᾶλλον εἰσφέρειν.

ΓΥΝΗ

εἶτ᾽ οὐχὶ δέξει δῆτα τὰ καταχύσματα;

ΠΛΟΥΤΟΣ

795 ἔνδον γε παρὰ τὴν ἑστίαν, ὥσπερ νόμος.
ἔπειτα καὶ τὸν φόρτον ἐκφύγοιμεν ἄν·
οὐ γὰρ πρεπῶδές ἐστι τῷ διδασκάλῳ
ἰσχάδια καὶ τρωγάλια τοῖς θεωμένοις
προβαλόντ᾽, ἐπὶ τούτοις εἶτ᾽ ἀναγκάζειν γελᾶν.

ΓΥΝΗ

800 εὖ πάνυ λέγεις· ὡς Δεξίνικός γ᾽ οὑτοσὶ
ἀνίσταθ᾽ ὡς ἁρπασόμενος τὰς ἰσχάδας.

CHREMYLUS

(*shouting behind him*) Damn you all! (*aside*) Friends are trouble if they're the sort who suddenly materialize when you're successful. They jostle you and bang your shins, each one making a show of his affection. Who failed to greet me? What bunch of oldsters failed to crown me in the marketplace?

Enter WIFE *from the house, with sweets.*

WIFE

Hello, dearest, and you also; hello to you both. (*to Wealth*) Now then, let's honor tradition: I'll take hold of you and pour on these sweets.

WEALTH

Please don't! The first time I enter your house with my sight restored, you shouldn't be bringing anything out, but rather taking something in.

WIFE

But don't you want the sweets?

WEALTH

Yes, but inside, at your hearth; that's traditional. (*indicating the spectators*) Plus, we'll avoid the lowbrow humor: our producer shouldn't be tossing figs and munchies to the spectators in hopes of forcing their laughter.

WIFE

That's good advice, because look, there's Dexinicus[38] standing up, ready to catch the figs.

[38] Unknown; the name is unattested elsewhere.

ΧΟΡΟΥ

ΚΑΡΙΩΝ

ὡς ἡδὺ πράττειν, ὦνδρές, ἐστ᾽ εὐδαιμόνως,
καὶ ταῦτα μηδὲν ἐξενεγκόντ᾽ οἴκοθεν.
ἡμῖν γὰρ ἀγαθῶν σωρὸς εἰς τὴν οἰκίαν
805   ἐπεισπέπαικεν οὐδὲν ἠδικηκόσιν.
805a οὕτω τὸ πλουτεῖν ἐστιν ἡδὺ πρᾶγμα δή.
ἡ μὲν σιπύη μεστή ᾽στι λευκῶν ἀλφίτων,
οἱ δ᾽ ἀμφορῆς οἴνου μέλανος ἀνθοσμίου.
ἅπαντα δ᾽ ἡμῖν ἀργυρίου καὶ χρυσίου
τὰ σκευάρια πλήρη ᾽στίν, ὥστε θαυμάσαι.
810   τὸ φρέαρ δ᾽ ἐλαίου μεστόν· αἱ δὲ λήκυθοι
μύρου γέμουσι, τὸ δ᾽ ὑπερῷον ἰσχάδων.
ὀξὶς δὲ πᾶσα καὶ λοπάδιον καὶ χύτρα
χαλκῆ γέγονε· τοὺς δὲ πινακίσκους τοὺς σαπροὺς
τοὺς ἰχθυηροὺς ἀργυροῦς πάρεσθ᾽ ὁρᾶν.
815   ὁ δ᾽ ἰπνὸς γέγον᾽ ἡμῖν ἐξαπίνης ἐλεφάντινος.
στατῆρσι δ᾽ οἱ θεράποντες ἀρτιάζομεν
χρυσοῖς· ἀποψώμεσθα δ᾽ οὐ λίθοις ἔτι,
ἀλλὰ σκοροδίοις ὑπὸ τρυφῆς ἑκάστοτε.
καὶ νῦν ὁ δεσπότης μὲν ἔνδον βουθυτεῖ
820   ὗν καὶ τράγον καὶ κριὸν ἐστεφανωμένος,
ἐμὲ δ᾽ ἐξέπεμψεν ὁ καπνός· οὐχ οἷός τε γὰρ
ἔνδον μένειν ἦν· ἔδακνε γὰρ τὰ βλέφαρά μου.

ΔΙΚΑΙΟΣ

ἕπου μετ᾽ ἐμοῦ, παιδάριον, ἵνα πρὸς τὸν θεὸν
ἴωμεν.

538

WEALTH

Exit WEALTH, CHREMYLUS, WIFE, *and* CARIO *into the house.*

The Chorus performs an entr'acte.

Enter CARIO *from the house.*

CARIO

Gentlemen, how nice it is to live happily, especially when there are no household expenses. A heap of goods has befallen our house, though we've done nothing bad! Yes, getting wealthy this way is mighty nice. Our grain tub's filled with white barley, our casks with dark fragrant wine, and all our purses are full of gold and silver like you wouldn't believe. Our well's full of olive oil, our jars are brimming with perfume, and the attic with figs. Our saucers, dishes, and pots have turned to bronze, and those worn-out fish platters are silvery to behold. Our kitchen's suddenly turned to ivory. We slaves pitch pennies with gold staters, and in our luxury we no longer use stones to wipe our bottoms, but cloves of garlic every time. Right now our master's in there all garlanded and offering up pig, goat, and ram, but the smoke's driven me outside here; I couldn't stand it in there, with the smoke stinging my eyes.

Enter JUST MAN, *accompanied by a Child carrying a tattered cloak and old shoes.*

JUST MAN

Come along, my child, so we can visit the god.

539

ARISTOPHANES

ΚΑΡΙΩΝ

ἔα, τίς ἐσθ' ὁ προσιὼν οὑτοσί;

ΔΙΚΑΙΟΣ

825 ἀνὴρ πρότερον μὲν ἄθλιος, νῦν δ' εὐτυχής.

ΚΑΡΙΩΝ

δῆλον ὅτι τῶν χρηστῶν τις, ὡς ἔοικας, εἶ.

ΔΙΚΑΙΟΣ

μάλιστ'.

ΚΑΡΙΩΝ

ἔπειτα τοῦ δέει;

ΔΙΚΑΙΟΣ

πρὸς τὸν θεὸν
ἥκω. μεγάλων γάρ μοὐστὶν ἀγαθῶν αἴτιος.
ἐγὼ γὰρ ἱκανὴν οὐσίαν παρὰ τοῦ πατρὸς
830 λαβὼν ἐπήρκουν τοῖς δεομένοις τῶν φίλων,
εἶναι νομίζων χρήσιμον πρὸς τὸν βίον.

ΚΑΡΙΩΝ

ἦ πού σε ταχέως ἐπέλιπεν τὰ χρήματα.

ΔΙΚΑΙΟΣ

κομιδῇ μὲν οὖν.

ΚΑΡΙΩΝ

οὐκοῦν μετὰ ταῦτ' ἦσθ' ἄθλιος.

ΔΙΚΑΙΟΣ

κομιδῇ μὲν οὖν. κἀγὼ μὲν ᾤμην οὓς τέως
835 εὐεργέτησα δεομένους ἕξειν φίλους

CARIO

Hey, who's this visitor?

JUST MAN

A man once ruined, but now fortunate.

CARIO

It's obvious at a glance that you're an honest man.

JUST MAN

That's right.

CARIO

So what are you after?

JUST MAN

I'm here to see the god; it's him I thank for my great blessings. You see, I had a sufficient inheritance from my father and used it to help my needy friends, considering this a responsible way to behave.

CARIO

Let me guess: your money quickly ran out.

JUST MAN

Exactly right.

CARIO

And then you were ruined.

JUST MAN

Exactly right. I used to think that the needy people I helped would be true friends if I ever needed their help,

ὄντως βεβαίους, εἰ δεηθείην ποτέ·
οἱ δ' ἐξετρέποντο κοὐκ ἐδόκουν ὁρᾶν μ' ἔτι.

ΚΑΡΙΩΝ

καὶ κατεγέλων γ', εὖ οἶδ' ὅτι.

ΔΙΚΑΙΟΣ

κομιδῇ μὲν οὖν·
αὐχμὸς γὰρ ὢν τῶν σκευαρίων μ' ἀπώλεσεν.
840   ἀλλ' οὐχὶ νῦν. ἀνθ' ὧν ἐγὼ πρὸς τὸν θεὸν
προσευξόμενος ἥκω δικαίως ἐνθάδε.

ΚΑΡΙΩΝ

τὸ τριβώνιον δὲ τί δύναται, πρὸς τῶν θεῶν,
ὃ φέρει μετὰ σοῦ τὸ παιδάριον τουτί; φράσον.

ΔΙΚΑΙΟΣ

καὶ τοῦτ' ἀναθήσων ἔρχομαι πρὸς τὸν θεόν.

ΚΑΡΙΩΝ

845   μῶν ἐνεμυήθης δῆτ' ἐν αὐτῷ τὰ μεγάλα;

ΔΙΚΑΙΟΣ

οὔκ, ἀλλ' ἐνερρίγωσ' ἔτη τριακαίδεκα.

ΚΑΡΙΩΝ

τὰ δ' ἐμβάδια;

ΔΙΚΑΙΟΣ

καὶ ταῦτα συνεχειμάζετο.

ΚΑΡΙΩΝ

καὶ ταῦτ' ἀναθήσων ἔφερες οὖν;

but they turned their backs on me and pretended they
didn't even know me any more.

CARIO

I'll bet they sneered at you, too.

JUST MAN

Exactly right. A drought that befell my coffers ruined me.
But not now. That's why I'm here to pay the god my due
respects.

CARIO

But what in heaven's name is that cloak doing here, the one
your child is carrying? Do explain it.

JUST MAN

I'm bringing this too, as a dedication to the god.

CARIO

That's not what you wore for your initiation at the Great
Mysteries, is it?[39]

JUST MAN

No, it's what I wore to freeze in for thirteen years!

CARIO

And those shoes?

JUST MAN

They too braved the winters with me.

CARIO

And you've brought them to dedicate as well?

39 At Eleusis, when it was customary to wear and then dedi-
cate ragged clothing, cf. *Frogs* 404–7.

ARISTOPHANES

ΔΙΚΑΙΟΣ

νὴ τὸν Δία.

ΚΑΡΙΩΝ

χαρίεντά γ᾽ ἥκεις δῶρα τῷ θεῷ φέρων.

ΣΥΚΟΦΑΝΤΗΣ

850 οἴμοι κακοδαίμων, ὡς ἀπόλωλα δείλαιος,
καὶ τρισκακοδαίμων καὶ τετράκις καὶ πεντάκις
καὶ δωδεκάκις καὶ μυριάκις· ἰοὺ ἰού.
οὕτω πολυφόρῳ συγκέκραμαι δαίμονι.

ΚΑΡΙΩΝ

Ἄπολλον ἀποτρόπαιε καὶ θεοὶ φίλοι,
855 τί ποτ᾽ ἐστὶν ὅ τι πέπονθεν ἄνθρωπος κακόν;

ΣΥΚΟΦΑΝΤΗΣ

οὐ γὰρ σχέτλια πέπονθα νυνὶ πράγματα,
ἀπολωλεκὼς ἅπαντα τἀκ τῆς οἰκίας
διὰ τὸν θεὸν τοῦτον, τὸν ἐσόμενον τυφλὸν
πάλιν αὖθις, ἤνπερ μὴ ᾽πιλίπωσιν αἱ δίκαι;

ΔΙΚΑΙΟΣ

860 ἐγὼ σχεδὸν τὸ πρᾶγμα γιγνώσκειν δοκῶ.
προσέρχεται γάρ τις κακῶς πράττων ἀνήρ,
ἔοικε δ᾽ εἶναι τοῦ πονηροῦ κόμματος.

ΚΑΡΙΩΝ

νὴ Δία, καλῶς τοίνυν ποιῶν ἀπόλλυται.

ΣΥΚΟΦΑΝΤΗΣ

ποῦ, ποῦ ᾽σθ᾽ ὁ μόνος ἅπαντας ἡμᾶς πλουσίους
865 ὑποσχόμενος οὗτος ποιήσειν εὐθέως,

JUST MAN

I certainly have.

CARIO

Charming gifts you've brought for the god!

Enter INFORMER with Witness.

INFORMER

Good heavens me, I'm cursed, I'm ruined and wretched, cursed thrice over, four times over, five times over, twelve times, infinite times! Boo hoo hoo! I've gotten mixed up with hundred-proof spirits!

CARIO

Healer Apollo and you kindly gods, I wonder what calamity this fellow's suffered?

INFORMER

Just tell me if my present sufferings aren't dire. I've lost everything I had in my house, and it's that god's fault, the one who's going to be blind again, if our courts don't fail us!

JUST MAN

I'm pretty sure I see what's going on here: our visitor's a man fallen on hard times, but he seems to be a bad penny.

CARIO

Yes indeed, and he does well to be ruined.

INFORMER

Where, oh where's the one who promised he'd single-handedly make us all wealthy on the spot, if ever he re-

εἰ πάλιν ἀναβλέψειεν ἐξ ἀρχῆς; ὁ δὲ
πολὺ μᾶλλον ἐνίους ἐστὶν ἐξολωλεκώς.

ΚΑΡΙΩΝ

καὶ τίνα δέδρακε δῆτα τοῦτ';

ΣΥΚΟΦΑΝΤΗΣ

ἐμὲ τουτονί.

ΚΑΡΙΩΝ

ἦ τῶν πονηρῶν ἦσθα καὶ τοιχωρύχων;

ΣΥΚΟΦΑΝΤΗΣ

870 μὰ Δί', οὐ μὲν οὖν ἐσθ' ὑγιὲς ὑμῶν οὐδενός,
κοὐκ ἔσθ' ὅπως οὐκ ἔχετέ μου τὰ χρήματα.

ΚΑΡΙΩΝ

ὡς σοβαρός, ὦ Δάματερ, εἰσελήλυθεν
ὁ συκοφάντης. δῆλον ὅτι βουλιμιᾷ.

ΣΥΚΟΦΑΝΤΗΣ

σὺ μὲν εἰς ἀγορὰν ἰὼν ταχέως οὐκ ἂν φθάνοις·
875 ἐπὶ τοῦ τροχοῦ γὰρ δεῖ σ' ἐκεῖ στρεβλούμενον
εἰπεῖν ἃ πεπανούργηκας.

ΚΑΡΙΩΝ

οἰμώξἄρα σύ.

ΔΙΚΑΙΟΣ

νὴ τὸν Δία τὸν σωτῆρα, πολλοῦ γ' ἄξιος
ἅπασι τοῖς Ἕλλησιν ὁ θεὸς οὗτος, εἰ
τοὺς συκοφάντας ἐξολεῖ κακοὺς κακῶς.

gained his original ability to see? But the fact is, there are some people he's totally ruined instead.

CARIO

Just whom has he treated that way?

INFORMER

Me, that's who.

CARIO

So you were one of the troublemakers and housebreakers?

INFORMER

Not at all; it's you people who are up to no good, and it must be you who've taken my goods.

CARIO

Ah Demeter, this informer makes quite a blustery entrance. It's a clear case of gluttonitis.

INFORMER

You, sir, had better report to the marketplace at once; that's where you'll be broken on the wheel and made to confess your crimes.

CARIO

You'll regret that!

JUST MAN

By Zeus the Savior, all Greece will be much obliged to our god if he puts these miserable informers to a miserable death!

ARISTOPHANES

ΣΥΚΟΦΑΝΤΗΣ

880 οἴμοι τάλας· μῶν καὶ σὺ μετέχων καταγελᾷς;
ἐπεὶ πόθεν θοἰμάτιον εἴληφας τοδί;
ἐχθὲς δ᾽ ἔχοντ᾽ εἶδόν σ᾽ ἐγὼ τριβώνιον.

ΔΙΚΑΙΟΣ

οὐδὲν προτιμῶ σου· φορῶ γὰρ πριάμενος
τὸν δακτύλιον τονδὶ παρ᾽ Εὐδάμου δραχμῆς.

ΚΑΡΙΩΝ

885 ἀλλ᾽ οὐδέν᾽ ἔστι συκοφάντου δήγματος.

ΣΥΚΟΦΑΝΤΗΣ

ἆρ᾽ οὐχ ὕβρις ταῦτ᾽ ἐστὶ πολλή; σκώπτετον,
ὅ τι δὲ ποιεῖτον ἐνθάδ᾽ οὐκ εἰρήκατον.
οὐκ ἐπ᾽ ἀγαθῷ γὰρ ἐνθάδ᾽ ἐστὸν οὐδενί.

ΚΑΡΙΩΝ

μὰ τὸν Δί᾽, οὔκουν τῷ γε σῷ, σάφ᾽ ἴσθ᾽ ὅτι.

ΣΥΚΟΦΑΝΤΗΣ

890 ἀπὸ τῶν ἐμῶν γὰρ ναὶ μὰ Δία δειπνήσετον.

ΔΙΚΑΙΟΣ

ὡς δὴ ᾽π᾽ ἀληθείᾳ σὺ μετὰ τοῦ μάρτυρος
διαρραγείης.

ΚΑΡΙΩΝ

μηδενός γ᾽ ἐμπλήμενος.

ΣΥΚΟΦΑΝΤΗΣ

ἀρνεῖσθον; ἔνδον ἐστίν, ὦ μιαρωτάτω,

⁸⁸⁴ -δήμου ΣV

548

INFORMER

Damn it, are you on their side too, and deriding me? Just
where did you get this cloak? Yesterday I saw you wearing a
jacket.

JUST MAN

I'm paying no attention to you; I'm wearing this amulet I
bought from Eudamus for a drachma.[40]

CARIO

But there's no antidote for an informer's bite!

INFORMER

Well, isn't this absolutely outrageous? You're both laugh-
ing at me, but you haven't said what you're up to here; I
think you're here for no good purpose.

CARIO

Not in your case we aren't, you can be sure of that.

INFORMER

In fact, it's my money that's going to pay for your dinner.

JUST MAN

I hope you literally bust a gut, and your witness too.

CARIO

An empty gut!

INFORMER

You won't own up? You scum of the earth, there's a whole

---

[40] Not inexpensive. The scholia say that this man was men-
tioned by Eupolis (fr. 96) and Ameipsias (fr. 26); perhaps also
(with the Attic form, Eudemus, a common name) by Cratinus (fr.
302) and Plato Com. (fr. 214).

πολὺ χρῆμα τεμαχῶν καὶ κρεῶν ὠπτημένων.
895 υυ υυ υυ υυ υυ υυ.

ΚΑΡΙΩΝ
κακόδαιμον, ὀσφραίνει τι;

ΔΙΚΑΙΟΣ
        τοῦ ψύχους γ᾽ ἴσως·
ἐπεὶ τοιοῦτόν γ᾽ ἀμπέχεται τριβώνιον.

ΣΥΚΟΦΑΝΤΗΣ
ταῦτ᾽ οὖν ἀνασχέτ᾽ ἐστίν, ὦ Ζεῦ καὶ θεοί,
τούτους ὑβρίζειν εἰς ἔμ᾽; οἴμ᾽ ὡς ἄχθομαι
900 ὅτι χρηστὸς ὢν καὶ φιλόπολις πάσχω κακῶς.

ΔΙΚΑΙΟΣ
σὺ φιλόπολις καὶ χρηστός;

ΣΥΚΟΦΑΝΤΗΣ
        ὡς οὐδείς γ᾽ ἀνήρ.

ΔΙΚΑΙΟΣ
καὶ μὴν ἐπερωτηθεὶς ἀπόκριναί μοι.

ΣΥΚΟΦΑΝΤΗΣ
        τὸ τί;

ΔΙΚΑΙΟΣ
γεωργὸς εἶ;

ΣΥΚΟΦΑΝΤΗΣ
μελαγχολᾶν μ᾽ οὕτως οἴει;

ΔΙΚΑΙΟΣ
ἀλλ᾽ ἔμπορος;

bunch of fish and meat being cooked in there! (*sniffs loudly*)

CARIO

Smell anything, sadsack?

JUST MAN

Maybe he's caught a cold, considering that jacket he's got on!

INFORMER

Gods above, must I put up with this, with their outrageous conduct toward me? I'm terribly hurt that an upstanding patriot like me should be mistreated.

JUST MAN

You, an upstanding patriot?

INFORMER

Second to none!

JUST MAN

Very well then, I have a question for you.

INFORMER

Ask away.

JUST MAN

Are you a farmer?

INFORMER

Do you think I'm crazy?

JUST MAN

A businessman, then?

ARISTOPHANES

ΣΥΚΟΦΑΝΤΗΣ
ναί, σκήπτομαί γ᾽, ὅταν τύχω.

ΔΙΚΑΙΟΣ
τί δαί; τέχνην τιν᾽ ἔμαθες;

ΣΥΚΟΦΑΝΤΗΣ
905   οὐ μὰ τὸν Δία.

ΔΙΚΑΙΟΣ
πῶς οὖν διέζης ἢ πόθεν μηδὲν ποιῶν;

ΣΥΚΟΦΑΝΤΗΣ
τῶν τῆς πόλεώς εἰμ᾽ ἐπιμελητὴς πραγμάτων
καὶ τῶν ἰδίων πάντων.

ΔΙΚΑΙΟΣ
σύ; τί μαθών;

ΣΥΚΟΦΑΝΤΗΣ
βούλομαι.

ΔΙΚΑΙΟΣ
πῶς οὖν ἂν εἴης χρηστός, ὦ τοιχωρύχε,
910   εἴ σοι προσῆκον μηδὲν εἶτ᾽ ἀπεχθάνει;

ΣΥΚΟΦΑΝΤΗΣ
οὐ γὰρ προσήκει τὴν ἐμαυτοῦ μοι πόλιν
εὐεργετεῖν, ὦ κέπφε, καθ᾽ ὅσον ἂν σθένω;

ΔΙΚΑΙΟΣ
εὐεργετεῖν οὖν ἐστι τὸ πολυπραγμονεῖν;

INFORMER

Sure; at least I claim to be when the occasion arises.[41]

JUST MAN

Well, did you learn a craft?

INFORMER

Certainly not.

JUST MAN

Then what did you live on without a livelihood?

INFORMER

I'm a manager of all affairs public and private.

JUST MAN

You are? What qualifies you?

INFORMER

I volunteer.[42]

JUST MAN

How can you be upstanding, you criminal, if you're loathed for meddling in what's none of your business?

INFORMER

None of my business, you bird brain, to benefit my own city with all my might?

JUST MAN

So being a busybody is beneficence?

[41] Merchants could claim exemptions from military and other duties, cf. *Assemblywomen* 1027.

[42] Under Attic law, a wrongdoer could be taken to court not only by an injured party but by any citizen, a provision which men like the Informer were thought to abuse for their own gain.

553

ARISTOPHANES

ΣΥΚΟΦΑΝΤΗΣ

τὸ μὲν οὖν βοηθεῖν τοῖς νόμοις τοῖς κειμένοις
915 καὶ μὴ 'πιτρέπειν ἐάν τις ἐξαμαρτάνῃ.

ΔΙΚΑΙΟΣ

οὔκουν δικαστὰς ἐξεπίτηδες ἡ πόλις
ἄρχειν καθίστησιν;

ΣΥΚΟΦΑΝΤΗΣ
κατηγορεῖ δὲ τίς;

ΔΙΚΑΙΟΣ

ὁ βουλόμενος.

ΣΥΚΟΦΑΝΤΗΣ
οὔκουν ἐκεῖνός εἰμ' ἐγώ;
ὥστ' εἰς ἔμ' ἥκει τῆς πόλεως τὰ πράγματα.

ΔΙΚΑΙΟΣ

920 νὴ Δία, πονηρόν γ' ἄρα προστάτην ἔχει.
ἐκεῖνο δ' οὐ βούλοι' ἄν, ἡσυχίαν ἔχων
ζῆν ἀργός;

ΣΥΚΟΦΑΝΤΗΣ
ἀλλὰ προβατίου βίον λέγεις,
εἰ μὴ φανεῖται διατριβή τις τῷ βίῳ.

ΔΙΚΑΙΟΣ

οὐδ' ἂν μεταμάθοις;

ΣΥΚΟΦΑΝΤΗΣ
οὐδ' ἂν εἰ δοίης γέ μοι
925 τὸν Πλοῦτον αὐτὸν καὶ τὸ Βάττου σίλφιον.

INFORMER

No, but upholding the established laws is, and not letting a wrongdoer get away with it.

JUST MAN

Doesn't the city charge juries with just this function?

INFORMER

But who prosecutes?

JUST MAN

The volunteer.

INFORMER

Isn't that what I am? That's how the city's affairs become my business.

JUST MAN

And that's exactly why it has a rotten patron indeed. Look, wouldn't you rather mind your own business and have no work to do?

INFORMER

No, that's a sheep's life, having no apparent purpose in one's life.

JUST MAN

And you won't change your mind?

INFORMER

Not even if you gave me Wealth himself, and all of Battus'[43] fennel.

---

[43] The founder of the prosperous North African city of Cyrene.

ΚΑΡΙΩΝ

κατάθου ταχέως θοἰμάτιον.

ΔΙΚΑΙΟΣ

οὗτος, σοὶ λέγει.

ΚΑΡΙΩΝ

ἔπειθ᾽ ὑπόλυσαι.

ΔΙΚΑΙΟΣ

πάντα ταῦτα σοὶ λέγει.

ΣΥΚΟΦΑΝΤΗΣ

καὶ μὴν προσελθέτω πρὸς ἔμ᾽ ὑμῶν ἐνθαδὶ
ὁ βουλόμενος.

ΚΑΡΙΩΝ

οὔκουν ἐκεῖνός εἰμ᾽ ἐγώ;

ΣΥΚΟΦΑΝΤΗΣ

930   οἴμοι τάλας, ἀποδύομαι μεθ᾽ ἡμέραν.

ΚΑΡΙΩΝ

σὺ γὰρ ἀξιοῖς τἀλλότρια πράττων ἐσθίειν;

ΣΥΚΟΦΑΝΤΗΣ

ὁρᾷς ἃ ποιεῖ; ταῦτ᾽ ἐγὼ μαρτύρομαι.

ΚΑΡΙΩΝ

ἀλλ᾽ οἴχεται φεύγων ὃν ἦγες μάρτυρα.

ΣΥΚΟΦΑΝΤΗΣ

οἴμοι, περιείλημμαι μόνος.

ΚΑΡΙΩΝ

νυνὶ βοᾷς;

CARIO

Remove your cloak at once!

JUST MAN

Hey, he's speaking to you!

CARIO

Now your shoes!

JUST MAN

He's still speaking to you.

INFORMER

All right, I dare any of you to come over here and get me, any volunteer.

CARIO

Isn't that what I am?

INFORMER

(*attacked*) Good grief, I'm being stripped in broad daylight!

CARIO

I'll teach you to gobble other people's goods for a living!

INFORMER

(*to Witness*) See what he's doing? I call you to witness!

Witness runs off.

CARIO

Well, that witness you brought has run off on you.

INFORMER

Dear me, I'm left all alone.

CARIO

Screaming now, eh?

ΣΥΚΟΦΑΝΤΗΣ

οἴμοι μάλ᾽ αὖθις.

ΚΑΡΙΩΝ

935   δὸς σύ μοι τὸ τριβώνιον,
ἵν᾽ ἀμφιέσω τὸν συκοφάντην τουτονί.

ΔΙΚΑΙΟΣ

μὴ δῆθ᾽· ἱερὸν γάρ ἐστι τοῦ Πλούτου πάλαι.

ΚΑΡΙΩΝ

ἔπειτα ποῦ κάλλιον ἀνατεθήσεται
ἢ περὶ πονηρὸν ἄνδρα καὶ τοιχωρύχον;
940 Πλοῦτον δὲ κοσμεῖν ἱματίοις σεμνοῖς πρέπει.

ΔΙΚΑΙΟΣ

τοῖς δ᾽ ἐμβαδίοις τί χρήσεταί τις; εἰπέ μοι.

ΚΑΡΙΩΝ

καὶ ταῦτα πρὸς τὸ μέτωπον αὐτίκα δὴ μάλα
ὥσπερ κοτίνῳ προσπατταλεύσω τουτῳί.

ΣΥΚΟΦΑΝΤΗΣ

ἄπειμι· γιγνώσκω γὰρ ἥττων ὢν πολὺ
945 ὑμῶν· ἐὰν δὲ σύζυγον λάβω τινὰ
κἂν σύκινον, τοῦτον τὸν ἰσχυρὸν θεὸν
ἐγὼ ποιήσω τήμερον δοῦναι δίκην,
ὁτιὴ καταλύει περιφανῶς εἷς ὢν μόνος
τὴν δημοκρατίαν, οὔτε τὴν βουλὴν πιθὼν
950 τὴν τῶν πολιτῶν οὔτε τὴν ἐκκλησίαν.

ΔΙΚΑΙΟΣ

καὶ μὴν ἐπειδὴ τὴν πανοπλίαν τὴν ἐμὴν

INFORMER

Dear me, I say!

CARIO

(*to Just Man*) Here, hand me that jacket; I want to put it on this informer.

JUST MAN

Please don't; it's already vowed to Wealth.

CARIO

What better place to dedicate it than a rotten criminal like this? Wealth deserves to be adorned in dignified garb.

JUST MAN

And what's to be done with the shoes, I ask you?

CARIO

Give me them too; I'll nail them right here on his forehead, like an offering on a wild olive tree.

INFORMER

I'll be leaving; I realize that I can't stand up to the pair of you. But if I find a teammate, no matter how ratty, I'll bring that mighty god of yours to justice this very day, for blatantly taking it upon himself alone to overthrow the democracy, without persuading the people's Council or the Assembly.

Exit INFORMER

JUST MAN

(*calling after*) Hey, since you're marching off in my gear,

ἔχων βαδίζεις, εἰς τὸ βαλανεῖον τρέχε·
ἔπειτ᾽ ἐκεῖ κορυφαῖος ἑστηκὼς θέρου.
κἀγὼ γὰρ εἶχον τὴν στάσιν ταύτην ποτέ.

ΚΑΡΙΩΝ

955 ἀλλ᾽ ὁ βαλανεὺς ἕλξει θύραζ᾽ αὐτὸν λαβὼν
τῶν ὀρχιπέδων· ἰδὼν γὰρ αὐτὸν γνώσεται
ὅτι ἔστ᾽ ἐκείνου τοῦ πονηροῦ κόμματος.
νὼ δ᾽ εἰσίωμεν, ἵνα προσεύξῃ τὸν θεόν.

ΓΡΑΥΣ

ἆρ᾽, ὦ φίλοι γέροντες, ἐπὶ τὴν οἰκίαν
960 ἀφίγμεθ᾽ ὄντως τοῦ νέου τούτου θεοῦ,
ἢ τῆς ὁδοῦ τὸ παράπαν ἡμαρτήκαμεν;

ΚΟΡΥΦΑΙΟΣ

ἀλλ᾽ ἴσθ᾽ ἐπ᾽ αὐτὰς τὰς θύρας ἀφιγμένη,
ὦ μειρακίσκη· πυνθάνει γὰρ ὡρικῶς.

ΓΡΑΥΣ

φέρε νυν, ἐγὼ τῶν ἔνδοθεν καλέσω τινά.

ΧΡΕΜΥΛΟΣ

965 μὴ δῆτ᾽· ἐγὼ γὰρ αὐτὸς ἐξελήλυθα.
ἀλλ᾽ ὅ τι μάλιστ᾽ ἐλήλυθας λέγειν σ᾽ ἐχρῆν.

ΓΡΑΥΣ

πέπονθα δεινὰ καὶ παράνομ᾽, ὦ φίλτατε·
ἀφ᾽ οὗ γὰρ ὁ θεὸς οὗτος ἤρξατο βλέπειν,
ἀβίωτον εἶναί μοι πεποίηκε τὸν βίον.

958 post h.v. spatium habet Π2, quae solum fines linearum
exhibet: χοροῦ t, ut scholia metrica recentiora ad v. 850

double-time it over to the baths; set yourself up as the squad leader there and get warm. That's the position that I once held.

CARIO

But the bathman will grab him by the balls and drag him outside; he'll take one look at him and know him for that bad penny. Now let's go inside so you can make your devotions to the god.

CARIO and JUST MAN enter the house.

Enter from a wing OLD WOMAN, with a Slave who carries a tray of food.

OLD WOMAN

So, my dear old men, have I really come to the dwelling of this new god, or have I taken a completely wrong turn?

CHORUS LEADER

No, rest assured that you've come to his very door, my girl (since you ask so girlishly).

OLD WOMAN

Well then, I'll just call one of them out here.

CHREMYLOS comes out.

CHREMYLUS

No need; I'm coming out anyway. Now you must tell me exactly why you're here.

OLD WOMAN

My dear man, I've suffered terrible injustices! Ever since this god regained his sight, he's made my life unlivable.

ARISTOPHANES

970 τί δ' ἐστίν; ἦ που καὶ σὺ συκοφάντρια
ἐν ταῖς γυναιξὶν ἦσθα;

ΓΡΑΥΣ

μὰ Δί', ἐγὼ μὲν οὔ.

ΧΡΕΜΥΛΟΣ

ἀλλ' οὐ λαχοῦσ' ἔπινες ἐν τῷ γράμματι;

ΓΡΑΥΣ

σκώπτεις· ἐγὼ δὲ κατακέκνισμαι δειλάκρα.

ΧΡΕΜΥΛΟΣ

οὔκουν ἐρεῖς ἀνύσασα τὸν κνισμὸν τίνα;

ΓΡΑΥΣ

975 ἄκουέ νυν. ἦν μοί τι μειράκιον φίλον,
πενιχρὸν μέν, ἄλλως δ' εὐπρόσωπον καὶ καλὸν
καὶ χρηστόν· εἰ γάρ του δεηθείην ἐγώ,
ἅπαντ' ἐποίει κοσμίως μοι καὶ καλῶς·
ἐγὼ δ' ἐκείνῳ ταὐτὰ πάνθ' ὑπηρέτουν.

ΧΡΕΜΥΛΟΣ

980 τί δ' ἦν ὅ τι σου μάλιστ' ἐδεῖθ' ἑκάστοτε;

ΓΡΑΥΣ

οὐ πολλά· καὶ γὰρ ἐκνομίως μ' ᾐσχύνετο.
ἀλλ' ἀργυρίου δραχμὰς ἂν ᾔτησ' εἴκοσιν
εἰς ἱμάτιον, ὀκτὼ δ' ἂν εἰς ὑποδήματα·
καὶ ταῖς ἀδελφαῖς ἀγοράσαι χιτώνιον
985 ἐκέλευσεν ἂν τῇ μητρί θ' ἱματίδιον·
πυρῶν τ' ἂν ἐδεήθη μεδίμνων τεττάρων.

CHREMYLUS

What's the matter? You're not another informer, are you, some kind of female version among the women?

OLD WOMAN

Certainly not!

CHREMYLUS

Then maybe you showed up for drinking service without a valid token?[44]

OLD WOMAN

You're making fun of me, but I'm all banged up, poor woman!

CHREMYLUS

Just what sort of banging are you talking about?

OLD WOMAN

Listen to this. I had a boyfriend, penniless but very good looking, fine, and honest. Whenever I asked him a favor, he accommodated me in fine fashion, and I did him all the same services.

CHREMYLUS

What did he typically want from you?

OLD WOMAN

Not much; he was extraordinarily modest. He'd request twenty silver drachmas for a coat, and eight for a pair of shoes; and he'd want me to buy little dresses for his sisters, and a little wrap for his mother; and he'd need four bushels of grain.

---

[44] A surprise for "jury service," for which volunteers were allotted tokens assigning them to a specific court and entitling them to payment.

ΧΡΕΜΥΛΟΣ

οὐ πολλὰ τοίνυν, μὰ τὸν Ἀπόλλω, ταῦτά γε
εἴρηκας· ἀλλὰ δῆλον ὅτι σ' ᾐσχύνετο.

ΓΡΑΥΣ

καὶ ταῦτα τοίνυν οὐχ ἕνεκα μισητίας
990 αἰτεῖν μ' ἔφασκεν, ἀλλὰ φιλίας οὕνεκα,
ἵνα τοὐμὸν ἱμάτιον φορῶν μεμνῇτό μου.

ΧΡΕΜΥΛΟΣ

λέγεις ἐρῶντ' ἄνθρωπον ἐκνομιώτατα.

ΓΡΑΥΣ

ἀλλ' οὐχὶ νῦν ὁ βδελυρὸς ἔτι τὸν νοῦν ἔχει
τὸν αὐτόν, ἀλλὰ πολὺ μεθέστηκεν πάνυ.
995 ἐμοῦ γὰρ αὐτῷ τὸν πλακοῦντα τουτονὶ
καὶ τἆλλα τἀπὶ τοῦ πίνακος τραγήματα
ἐπόντα πεμψάσης ὑπειπούσης θ' ὅτι
εἰς ἑσπέραν ἥξοιμι—

ΧΡΕΜΥΛΟΣ

     τί ἔδρασ'; εἰπέ μοι.

ΓΡΑΥΣ

ἄμητα προσαπέπεμψεν ἡμῖν τουτονί,
1000 ἐφ' ᾧτ' ἐκεῖσε μηδέποτέ μ' ἐλθεῖν ἔτι,
καὶ πρὸς ἐπὶ τούτοις εἶπεν ἀποπέμπων ὅτι
"πάλαι ποτ' ἦσαν ἄλκιμοι Μιλήσιοι."

ΧΡΕΜΥΛΟΣ

δῆλον ὅτι τοὺς τρόπους τις οὐ μοχθηρὸς ἦν,
ἔπειτα πλουτῶν οὐκέθ' ἥδεται φακῇ·

CHREMYLUS

That's certainly not very much, I agree; he was clearly being modest.

OLD WOMAN

And he'd stress that his reason for asking was not greed but affection: when he was wearing that coat he would think of me.

CHREMYLUS

There was a fellow extraordinarily in love.

OLD WOMAN

But nowadays that skunk hasn't got the same attitude; he's completely changed his tune. You see, when I sent him this pie and the other munchies on the tray here, with a message that I'd visit him this evening—

CHREMYLUS

What did he do, I'd like to know?

OLD WOMAN

He sent it all back, along with this cheese cake, on condition that I never visit him again, and on top of that he added, "Once upon a time the Milesians were formidable."[45]

CHREMYLUS

He obviously wasn't a person of shiftless character. Now that he's rich, he's lost his taste for lentil soup; before that,

[45] Proverbial of has-beens.

1005 πρὸ τοῦ δ' ὑπὸ τῆς πενίας ἅπαντ' ἂν ἤσθιεν.

ΓΡΑΤΣ

καὶ μὴν πρὸ τοῦ γ' ὁσημέραι, νὴ τὼ θεώ,
ἐπὶ τὴν θύραν ἐβάδιζεν ἀεὶ τὴν ἐμήν.

ΧΡΕΜΤΛΟΣ

ἔπ' ἐκφοράν;

ΓΡΑΤΣ

μὰ Δί', ἀλλὰ τῆς φωνῆς μόνον
ἐρῶν ἀκοῦσαι.

ΧΡΕΜΤΛΟΣ

τοῦ λαβεῖν μὲν οὖν χάριν.

ΓΡΑΤΣ

1010 καί, νὴ Δί', εἰ λυπουμένην αἴσθοιτό με,
νηττάριον ὑπεκορίζετ' ἂν καὶ φάττιον.

ΧΡΕΜΤΛΟΣ

ἔπειτ' ἴσως ᾔτησ' ἂν εἰς ὑποδήματα.

ΓΡΑΤΣ

μυστηρίοις δὲ τοῖς μεγάλοις ὀχουμένην
ἐπὶ τῆς ἁμάξης ὅτι προσέβλεψέν μέ τις,
1015 ἐτυπτόμην διὰ τοῦθ' ὅλην τὴν ἡμέραν.
οὕτω σφόδρα ζηλότυπος ὁ νεανίσκος ἦν.

ΧΡΕΜΤΛΟΣ

μόνος γὰρ ᾔδεθ', ὡς ἔοικεν, ἐσθίων.

ΓΡΑΤΣ

καὶ τάς γε χεῖρας παγκάλας ἔχειν μ' ἔφη.

poverty made him eat anything.

OLD WOMAN
Oh yes, before that he used to come to my door every day without fail.

CHREMYLUS
Hoping there'd be a funeral?

OLD WOMAN
Not at all; only because he loved to hear my voice.

CHREMYLUS
He loved to get things, is more like it.

OLD WOMAN
And when he saw that I was feeling blue, ah yes, he'd call me his ducky and his dovey.

CHREMYLUS
Then he'd maybe ask for shoes.

OLD WOMAN
Once at the Great Mysteries somebody glanced at me as I rode on my wagon, and that got me a day-long beating. That's how very jealous the boy was!

CHREMYLUS
It seems he liked to have his food all to himself.

OLD WOMAN
And he said I had very beautiful hands.

1005 ἅπαντ᾽ ἂν ἦσθ- Dobree: ἅπαντα γ ἦσθ- V Sʳ: ἅπανθ᾽ ὑπήσθ- R: ἅπαντα κατήσθ᾽ A M U: ἅπαντ᾽ ἐπ- Athenaeus 170d: ἅπαντα Sᴬ

1011 ὑπ. ἂν καὶ φάττιον (Bentley: βάτιον a) Porson: ἂν καὶ β. ὑπ. a

ARISTOPHANES

ΧΡΕΜΤΛΟΣ

ὁπότε προτείνοιέν γε δραχμὰς εἴκοσιν.

ΓΡΑΤΣ

1020 ὄζειν τε τῆς χροιᾶς ἔφασκεν ἡδύ μου.

ΧΡΕΜΤΛΟΣ

εἰ Θάσιον ἐνέχεις, εἰκότως γε, νὴ Δία.

ΓΡΑΤΣ

τὸ βλέμμα θ᾽ ὡς ἔχοιμι μαλακὸν καὶ καλόν.

ΧΡΕΜΤΛΟΣ

οὐ σκαιὸς ἦν ἄνθρωπος, ἀλλ᾽ ἠπίστατο
γραὸς καπρώσης τἀφόδια κατεσθίειν.

ΓΡΑΤΣ

1025 ταῦτ᾽ οὖν ὁ θεός, ὦ φίλ᾽ ἄνερ, οὐκ ὀρθῶς ποιεῖ,
φάσκων βοηθεῖν τοῖς ἀδικουμένοις ἀεί.

ΧΡΕΜΤΛΟΣ

τί γὰρ ποιήσει; φράζε, καὶ πεπράξεται.

ΓΡΑΤΣ

ἀναγκάσαι δίκαιόν ἐστι, νὴ Δία,
τὸν εὖ παθόνθ᾽ ὑπ᾽ ἐμοῦ πάλιν ⟨μ᾽⟩ ἀντ᾽ εὖ ποιεῖν.
1030 ἢ μηδ᾽ ὁτιοῦν ⟨μ᾽⟩ ἀγαθὸν δίκαιόν ἐστ᾽ ἔχειν;

ΧΡΕΜΤΛΟΣ

οὔκουν καθ᾽ ἑκάστην ἀπεδίδου τὴν νύκτα σοι;

ΓΡΑΤΣ

ἀλλ᾽ οὐδέποτέ με ζῶσαν ἀπολείψειν ἔφη.

CHREMYLUS
When they held out twenty drachmas, that is.

OLD WOMAN
And he said that my skin smelled nice.

CHREMYLUS
When you were pouring Thasian wine,[46] I'll bet.

OLD WOMAN
And that I had tender beauty in my eyes.

CHREMYLUS
He was no dummy, that one; he knew how to gobble up a horny old lady's assets!

OLD WOMAN
In this, my dear man, the god behaves improperly, since he staunchly claims to come to the aid of injured parties.

CHREMYLUS
Then what shall he do? He'll act as you instruct.

OLD WOMAN
It's only right to force the man I treated well to treat me well in return. Or is it fair that I get no benefit at all?

CHREMYLUS
Well, didn't he pay you back every single night?

OLD WOMAN
But he promised he'd never leave me as long as I live.

---

[46] A fine red.

ΧΡΕΜΤΛΟΣ

ὀρθῶς γε· νῦν δέ γ᾽ οὐκέτι σε ζῆν οἴεται.

ΓΡΑΤΣ

ὑπὸ τοῦ γὰρ ἄλγους κατατέτηκ᾽, ὦ φίλτατε.

ΧΡΕΜΤΛΟΣ

1035 οὔκ, ἀλλὰ κατασέσηπας, ὥς γ᾽ ἐμοὶ δοκεῖς.

ΓΡΑΤΣ

διὰ δακτυλίου μὲν οὖν ἐμέ γ᾽ ἂν διελκύσαις.

ΧΡΕΜΤΛΟΣ

εἰ τυγχάνοι γ᾽ ὁ δακτύλιος ὢν τηλίας.

ΓΡΑΤΣ

καὶ μὴν τὸ μειράκιον τοδὶ προσέρχεται,
οὗπερ πάλαι κατηγοροῦσα τυγχάνω·
1040 ἔοικε δ᾽ ἐπὶ κῶμον βαδίζειν.

ΧΡΕΜΤΛΟΣ

φαίνεται·
στεφάνους γέ τοι καὶ δᾷδ᾽ ἔχων πορεύεται.

ΝΕΑΝΙΑΣ

ἀσπάζομαι.

ΓΡΑΤΣ

τί φησιν;

ΝΕΑΝΙΑΣ

ἀρχαία φίλη,
πολιὰ γεγένησαι ταχύ γε, νὴ τὸν οὐρανόν.

CHREMYLUS

Quite rightly; but now he considers you no longer alive.

OLD WOMAN

In fact I'm pining away with grief, my dear man.

CHREMYLUS

No, you're rotting away, if you ask me.

OLD WOMAN

Why, you could pull me right through a ring.

CHREMYLUS

Provided the ring were the size of a barrel hoop.

OLD WOMAN

But look, here comes the young man now, the very one I've been castigating; he's probably off to a revel.

CHREMYLUS

He looks it; he's got garlands and a torch at any rate.

Enter from a wing YOUNG MAN.

YOUNG MAN

Salutations!

OLD WOMAN

What's he say?

YOUNG MAN

My ancient ladyfriend, how quickly you've turned grey; good heavens!

ΓΡΑΤΣ

τάλαιν᾽ ἐγὼ τῆς ὕβρεος ἧς ὑβρίζομαι.

ΧΡΕΜΥΛΟΣ

1045 ἔοικε διὰ πολλοῦ χρόνου σ᾽ ἑορακέναι.

ΓΡΑΤΣ

ποίου χρόνου, ταλάνταθ᾽, ὃς παρ᾽ ἐμοὶ χθὲς ἦν;

ΧΡΕΜΥΛΟΣ

τοὐναντίον πέπονθε τοῖς πολλοῖς ἄρα·
μεθύων γάρ, ὡς ἔοικεν, ὀξύτερον βλέπει.

ΓΡΑΤΣ

οὔκ, ἀλλ᾽ ἀκόλαστός ἐστιν ἀεὶ τοῖς τρόποις.

ΝΕΑΝΙΑΣ

1050 ὦ Ποντοπόσειδον καὶ θεοὶ πρεσβυτικοί,
ἐν τῷ προσώπῳ τῶν ῥυτίδων ὅσας ἔχει.

ΓΡΑΤΣ

ἆ ἆ,
τὴν δᾷδα μή μοι πρόσφερ᾽.

ΧΡΕΜΥΛΟΣ

εὖ μέντοι λέγει.
ἐὰν γὰρ αὐτὴν εἷς μόνος σπινθὴρ βάλῃ,
ὥσπερ παλαιὰν εἰρεσιώνην καύσεται.

ΝΕΑΝΙΑΣ

1055 βούλει διὰ χρόνου πρός με παῖσαι;

ΓΡΑΤΣ

ποῦ, τάλαν;

OLD WOMAN

Mercy me, the insults I'm subjected to!

CHREMYLUS

It seems he hasn't seen you for a long time.

OLD WOMAN

What do you mean, a long time? He was with me just yesterday!

CHREMYLUS

Then he's reacting differently than most people: it seems that drunkenness has sharpened his eyesight.

OLD WOMAN

No, his behavior has always been impudent.

YOUNG MAN

Poseidon of the Deep and ye other gods of old, what countless wrinkles her face contains!

OLD WOMAN

Hey now, keep that torch away from me!

CHREMYLUS

She's right: if just one spark hits her, she'll go up like an old harvest wreath.

YOUNG MAN

Would you like to play with me a while?

OLD WOMAN

But where?

ΝΕΑΝΙΣ
αὐτοῦ, λαβοῦσα κάρυα.

ΓΡΑΤΣ
παιδιὰν τίνα;

ΝΕΑΝΙΑΣ
πόσους ἔχεις ὀδόντας.

ΧΡΕΜΥΛΟΣ
ἀλλὰ γνώσομαι
κἄγωγ᾽· ἔχει γὰρ τρεῖς ἴσως ἢ τέτταρας.

ΝΕΑΝΙΣ
ἀπότεισον· ἕνα γὰρ γομφίον μόνον φορεῖ.

ΓΡΑΤΣ
1060 ταλάντατ᾽ ἀνδρῶν, οὐχ ὑγιαίνειν μοι δοκεῖς,
πλυνόν με ποιῶν ἐν τοσούτοις ἀνδράσιν.

ΝΕΑΝΙΣ
ὄναιο μέν γ᾽ ἄν, εἴ τις ἐκπλύνειέ σε.

ΧΡΕΜΥΛΟΣ
οὐ δῆτ᾽, ἐπεὶ νῦν μὲν καπηλικῶς ἔχει·
εἰ δ᾽ ἐκπλυνεῖται τοῦτο τὸ ψιμύθιον,
1065 ὄψει κατάδηλα τοῦ προσώπου τὰ ῥάκη.

ΓΡΑΤΣ
γέρων ἀνὴρ ὢν οὐχ ὑγιαίνειν μοι δοκεῖς.

ΝΕΑΝΙΣ
πειρᾷ μὲν οὖν ἴσως σε καὶ τῶν τιτθίων
ἐφάπτεταί σου λανθάνειν δοκῶν ἐμέ.

YOUNG MAN

Right here; have these nuts.

OLD WOMAN

What kind of play do you mean?

YOUNG MAN

Guessing how many teeth you have.

CHREMYLUS

Here, let me guess: I say three or four.

YOUNG MAN

Pay up: she's only got a single molar.

OLD WOMAN

You bastard, you must be unhinged, to soak me with abuse in front of all these men.

YOUNG MAN

A good soaking would do you good.

CHREMYLUS

No it wouldn't; she's got herself ready for sale. If that rouge were washed off, you'd see the tattered remnants of her face.

OLD WOMAN

Old age must have unhinged you.

YOUNG MAN

Maybe he's making a play for you, and trying to grab your tits when he thinks I'm not looking.

ARISTOPHANES

ΓΡΑΥΣ

μὰ τὴν Ἀφροδίτην, οὐκ ἐμοῦ γ', ὦ βδελυρὲ σύ.

ΧΡΕΜΥΛΟΣ

1070 μὰ τὴν Ἑκάτην, οὐ δῆτα· μαινοίμην γὰρ ἄν.
ἀλλ', ὦ νεανίσκ', οὐκ ἐῶ τὴν μείρακα
μισεῖν σε ταύτην.

ΝΕΑΝΙΑΣ

ἀλλ' ἔγωγ' ὑπερφιλῶ.

ΧΡΕΜΥΛΟΣ

καὶ μὴν κατηγορεῖ γέ σου.

ΝΕΑΝΙΑΣ

τί κατηγορεῖ;

ΧΡΕΜΥΛΟΣ

εἶναί σ' ὑβριστήν φησι καὶ λέγειν ὅτι
1075 "πάλαι ποτ' ἦσαν ἄλκιμοι Μιλήσιοι."

ΝΕΑΝΙΑΣ

ἐγὼ περὶ ταύτης οὐ μαχοῦμαί σοι.

ΧΡΕΜΥΛΟΣ

τὸ τί;

ΝΕΑΝΙΑΣ

αἰσχυνόμενος τὴν ἡλικίαν τὴν σήν· ἐπεὶ
οὐκ ἄν ποτ' ἄλλῳ τοῦτ' ἐπέτρεπον ἄν ποιεῖν.
νῦν δ' ἄπιθι χαίρων συλλαβὼν τὴν μείρακα.

ΧΡΕΜΥΛΟΣ

1080 οἶδ', οἶδα τὸν νοῦν· οὐκέτ' ἀξιοῖς ἴσως
εἶναι μετ' αὐτῆς.

OLD WOMAN

By Aphrodite, not mine you won't, you pig!

CHREMYLUS

By Hecate, I'd be insane to do that. But look here, young man, I won't allow you to hate this girl.

YOUNG MAN

Who me? I adore her!

CHREMYLUS

And yet she makes complaints about you.

YOUNG MAN

What complaints?

CHREMYLUS

She says you're insulting, and that you say, "Once upon a time the Milesians were formidable."

YOUNG MAN

I'll let you have her without a fight.

CHREMYLUS

Meaning what?

YOUNG MAN

Out of respect for your age; I certainly wouldn't have extended this offer to anyone else. Now take the girl with my compliments, and run along.

CHREMYLUS

I know what's on your mind, I know: perhaps you don't think she's worth being with any more.

ARISTOPHANES

ΝΕΑΝΙΑΣ
ὁ δ᾽ ἐπιτρέψων ἐστὶ τίς;
οὐκ ἂν διαλεχθείην διεσπλεκωμένῃ
ὑπὸ μυρίων ἐτῶν γε καὶ τρισχιλίων.

ΧΡΕΜΥΛΟΣ
ὅμως δ᾽ ἐπειδὴ καὶ τὸν οἶνον ἠξίους
1085 πίνειν, συνεκποτέ᾽ ἐστί σοι καὶ τὴν τρύγα.

ΝΕΑΝΙΑΣ
ἀλλ᾽ ἔστι κομιδῇ τρὺξ παλαιὰ καὶ σαπρά.

ΧΡΕΜΥΛΟΣ
οὐκοῦν τρύγοιπος ταῦτα πάντ᾽ ἰάσεται.
ἀλλ᾽ εἴσιθ᾽ εἴσω.

ΝΕΑΝΙΑΣ
τῷ θεῷ γοῦν βούλομαι
ἐλθὼν ἀναθεῖναι τοὺς στεφάνους τούσδ᾽ ὡς ἔχω.

ΓΡΑΥΣ
1090 ἐγὼ δέ γ᾽ αὐτῷ καὶ φράσαι τι βούλομαι.

ΝΕΑΝΙΑΣ
ἐγὼ δέ γ᾽ οὐκ εἴσειμι.

ΧΡΕΜΥΛΟΣ
θάρρει, μὴ φοβοῦ·
οὐ γὰρ βιάσεται.

ΝΕΑΝΙΑΣ
πάνυ καλῶς τοίνυν λέγεις·
ἱκανὸν γὰρ αὐτὴν πρότερον ὑπεπίττουν χρόνον.

YOUNG MAN

And who's going to make me? I don't want relations with a woman who's been boinked by thirteen thousand—seasons.

CHREMYLUS

Be that as it may, you did see fit to drink the wine, so you've got to drink up the dregs too.

YOUNG MAN

But these dregs are utterly ancient and putrid.

CHREMYLUS

A wine strainer will cure all that. Now go along inside.

YOUNG MAN

I'd certainly like to go in and dedicate these garlands to the god right away.

OLD WOMAN

And I've got something to say to him myself.

YOUNG MAN

Then I'm not going inside.

CHREMYLUS

Take it easy, and never fear; she's not going to rape you.

YOUNG MAN

Well, that's very good to hear; I've spent quite enough time caulking her bottom.

ARISTOPHANES

ΓΡΑΥΣ

βάδιζ'· ἐγὼ δέ σου κατόπιν εἰσέρχομαι.

ΧΡΕΜΥΛΟΣ

1095 ὡς εὐτόνως, ὦ Ζεῦ βασιλεῦ, τὸ γράδιον
ὥσπερ λεπὰς τῷ μειρακίῳ προσείχετο.

ΧΟΡΟΥ

ΚΑΡΙΩΝ

τίς ἔσθ' ὁ κόπτων τὴν θύραν; τουτὶ τί ἦν;
οὐδείς, ἔοικεν· ἀλλὰ δῆτα τὸ θύριον
φθεγγόμενον ἄλλως κλαυσιᾷ.

ΕΡΜΗΣ

σέ τοι λέγω,

ὁ Καρίων, ἀνάμεινον.

ΚΑΡΙΩΝ

1100 οὗτος, εἰπέ μοι,
σὺ τὴν θύραν ἔκοπτες οὑτωσὶ σφόδρα;

ΕΡΜΗΣ

μὰ Δί', ἀλλ' ἔμελλον· εἶτ' ἀνέῳξάς με φθάσας.
ἀλλ' ἐκκάλει τὸν δεσπότην τρέχων ταχύ,
ἔπειτα τὴν γυναῖκα καὶ τὰ παιδία,
1105 ἔπειτα τοὺς θεράποντας, εἶτα τὴν κύνα,
ἔπειτα σαυτόν, εἶτα τὴν ὗν.

1096 -είχετο R V: -ίσχεται cett.   post h.v. Χοροῦ statu-
erunt scholia metrica recentiora ad v. 1042

580

OLD WOMAN

Get moving; I'll be right behind you.

YOUNG MAN and OLD WOMAN go into the house.

CHREMYLUS

Lord Zeus, that little old lady sticks to the boy as tight as a barnacle!

CHREMYLUS goes into the house.

The Chorus performs an entr'acte.

Enter from a wing HERMES, who knocks on the door.

CARIO

(*emerging from the house*) Who's that banging on the door? (*looking around*) What's going on? No one around, apparently. This door will have plenty to cry about if it's making noise for nothing. (*turns to go back inside*)

HERMES

You there, Cario, hold on!

CARIO

Hey, was that you banging on the door so loud?

HERMES

Not at all, though I was just about to when you opened it up. Now run quick and get your master out here, and his wife and kids, and his slaves, and his dog, then yourself, and the pig too.

ΚΑΡΙΩΝ

εἰπέ μοι,

τί δ᾽ ἐστίν;

ΕΡΜΗΣ

ὁ Ζεύς, ὦ πόνηρε, βούλεται
εἰς ταὐτὸν ὑμᾶς συγκυκήσας τρύβλιον
ἁπαξάπαντας εἰς τὸ βάραθρον ἐμβαλεῖν.

ΚΑΡΙΩΝ

1110 ἡ γλῶττα τῷ κήρυκι τούτων τέμνεται.
ἀτὰρ διὰ τί δὴ ταῦτ᾽ ἐπιβουλεύει ποιεῖν
ἡμᾶς;

ΕΡΜΗΣ

ὅτιὴ δεινότατα πάντων πραγμάτων
εἴργασθ᾽. ἀφ᾽ οὗ γὰρ ἤρξατ᾽ ἐξ ἀρχῆς βλέπειν
ὁ Πλοῦτος, οὐδεὶς οὐ λιβανωτόν, οὐ δάφνην,
1115 οὐ ψαιστόν, οὐχ ἱερεῖον, οὐκ ἄλλ᾽ οὐδὲ ἐν
ἡμῖν ἔτι θύει τοῖς θεοῖς.

ΚΑΡΙΩΝ

μὰ Δί᾽, οὐδέ γε
θύσει· κακῶς γὰρ ἐπεμελεῖσθ᾽ ἡμῶν τότε.

ΕΡΜΗΣ

καὶ τῶν μὲν ἄλλων μοι θεῶν ἧττον μέλει,
ἐγὼ δ᾽ ἀπόλωλα κἀπιτέτριμμαι.

ΚΑΡΙΩΝ

σωφρονεῖς.

CARIO

What's up, I'd like to know?

HERMES

It's Zeus, you rascal: he's ready to mash up every last one of you in the same bowl and toss you into the executioner's pit!

CARIO

For this news the tongue gets sliced for the Herald.[47] But what's his reason for wanting to do that to us?

HERMES

Because you've committed the most terrible deeds. Ever since Wealth recovered his original sight, no one has offered us gods any sort of sacrifice: no incense, no bay, no barley cake, no victim, not a single thing.

CARIO

That's right, and they're not going to either, because you took bad care of us in the past.

HERMES

I'm not so worried about the other gods, but I myself am a goner, ruined!

CARIO

Very shrewd of you.

[47] As at an animal sacrifice.

ARISTOPHANES

ΕΡΜΗΣ

1120 πρότερον γὰρ εἶχον ἂν παρὰ ταῖς καπηλίσιν
πάντ' ἀγάθ' ἕωθεν εὐθύς, οἰνοῦτταν, μέλι,
ἰσχάδας, ὅσ' εἰκός ἐστιν Ἑρμῆν ἐσθίειν·
νυνὶ δὲ πεινῶν ἀναβάδην ἀναπαύομαι.

ΚΑΡΙΩΝ

οὔκουν δικαίως, ὅστις ἐποίεις ζημίαν
1125 ἐνίοτε τοιαῦτ' ἀγάθ' ἔχων;

ΕΡΜΗΣ

οἴμοι τάλας,
οἴμοι πλακοῦντος τοῦ 'ν τετράδι πεπεμμένου.

ΚΑΡΙΩΝ

"ποθεῖς τὸν οὐ παρόντα καὶ μάτην καλεῖς."

ΕΡΜΗΣ

οἴμοι δὲ κωλῆς ἣν ἐγὼ κατήσθιον—

ΚΑΡΙΩΝ

ἀσκωλίαζ' ἐνταῦθα πρὸς τὴν αἰθρίαν.

ΕΡΜΗΣ

1130 σπλάγχνων τε θερμῶν ὧν ἐγὼ κατήσθιον.

ΚΑΡΙΩΝ

ὀδύνη σε περὶ τὰ σπλάγχν' ἔοικέ τις στρέφειν.

ΕΡΜΗΣ

οἴμοι δὲ κύλικος ἴσον ἴσῳ κεκραμένης.

ΚΑΡΙΩΝ

ταύτην ἐπιπιὼν ἀποτρέχων οὐκ ἂν φθάνοις;

584

HERMES

In the past I'd get all sorts of goodies from the barmaids, bright and early: wine cake, honey, figs, everything Hermes likes to eat; but now I'm cooling my heels up there and going hungry.

CARIO

And doesn't it serve you right, for occasionally punishing the people who gave you those goodies?

HERMES

What grief, grief for the cake that's baked on the fourth of the month![48]

CARIO

"You pine and vainly cry for one now gone."[49]

HERMES

Grief for the ham that I used to eat!

CARIO

Ham it up here, out of doors.

HERMES

And for the hot innards that I used to eat!

CARIO

You seem to have an ache in your own innards.

HERMES

What grief for the tankard mixed one to one!

CARIO

Have a sip from this one, and then get lost.

[48] Hermes' traditional birthday, when he would be given special offerings; cf. Theophrastus, *Characters* 16.10.

[49] Addressed to Heracles, bereft of his beloved Hylas, in a lost tragedy (*TrGF* adesp. 63).

585

ARISTOPHANES

ΕΡΜΗΣ
ἆρ᾽ ὠφελήσαις ἄν τι τὸν σαυτοῦ φίλον;

ΚΑΡΙΩΝ
1135 εἴ του δέει γ᾽ ὧν δυνατός εἰμί σ᾽ ὠφελεῖν.

ΕΡΜΗΣ
εἴ μοι πορίσας ἄρτον τιν᾽ εὖ πεπεμμένον
δοίης καταφαγεῖν καὶ κρέας νεανικὸν
ὧν θύεθ᾽ ὑμεῖς ἔνδον.

ΚΑΡΙΩΝ
ἀλλ᾽ οὐκ ἐκφορά.

ΕΡΜΗΣ
καὶ μὴν ὁπότε τι σκευάριον τοῦ δεσπότου
1140 ὑφέλοι᾽, ἐγώ σ᾽ ἂν λανθάνειν ἐποίουν ἀεί.

ΚΑΡΙΩΝ
ἐφ᾽ ᾧτε μετέχειν καὐτός, ὦ τοιχωρύχε·
ἧκεν γὰρ ἄν σοι ναστὸς εὖ πεπεμμένος.

ΕΡΜΗΣ
ἔπειτα τοῦτόν γ᾽ αὐτὸς ἂν κατήσθιες.

ΚΑΡΙΩΝ
οὐ γὰρ μετεῖχες τὰς ἴσας πληγὰς ἐμοί,
1145 ὁπότε τι ληφθείην πανουργήσας ἐγώ.

ΕΡΜΗΣ
μὴ μνησικακήσῃς, εἰ σὺ Φυλὴν κατέλαβες.
ἀλλὰ ξύνοικον, πρὸς θεῶν, δέξασθέ με.

WEALTH

HERMES

Surely you'll give your old friend a little help?

CARIO

Provided I'm able to give you the help you want.

HERMES

How about fetching me some nicely baked bread to eat, and a hefty steak from the sacrifice you're making in there.

CARIO

This isn't carry-out!

HERMES

Yet when you would pilfer a dish from your master, I always helped you get away with it.

CARIO

On condition you got a share, you robber! Some nicely baked pastry always came your way.

HERMES

Which then you'd eat up yourself!

CARIO

Well, you never shared the whippings I got when I was caught doing something bad.

HERMES

Don't bear grudges, if you captured Phyle,[50] but in heaven's name, invite me to join your household!

---

[50] The capture of Phyle by Thrasybulus and the democratic exiles in 404/3 was the initial step in the overthrow of the Thirty, the restoration of the democracy, and a decree of general amnesty (Xenophon, *Hellenica* 2.4).

ARISTOPHANES

ΚΑΡΙΩΝ

ἔπειτ᾽ ἀπολιπὼν τοὺς θεοὺς ἐνθάδε μενεῖς;

ΕΡΜΗΣ

τὰ γὰρ παρ᾽ ὑμῖν ἐστι βελτίω πολύ.

ΚΑΡΙΩΝ

1150 τί δέ; ταὐτομολεῖν ἀστεῖον εἶναί σοι δοκεῖ;

ΕΡΜΗΣ

πατρὶς γάρ ἐστι πᾶσ᾽ ἵν᾽ ἂν πράττῃ τις εὖ.

ΚΑΡΙΩΝ

τί δῆτ᾽ ἂν εἴης ὄφελος ἡμῖν ἐνθάδ᾽ ὤν;

ΕΡΜΗΣ

παρὰ τὴν θύραν Στροφαῖον ἱδρύσασθέ με.

ΚΑΡΙΩΝ

Στροφαῖον; ἀλλ᾽ οὐκ ἔργον ἔστ᾽ οὐδὲν στροφῶν.

ΕΡΜΗΣ

ἀλλ᾽ Ἐμπολαῖον.

ΚΑΡΙΩΝ

1155 ἀλλὰ πλουτοῦμεν. τί οὖν
Ἑρμῆν παλιγκάπηλον ἡμᾶς δεῖ τρέφειν;

ΕΡΜΗΣ

ἀλλὰ Δόλιον τοίνυν.

ΚΑΡΙΩΝ

Δόλιον; ἥκιστά γε·
οὐ γὰρ δόλου νῦν ἔργον, ἀλλ᾽ ἁπλῶν τρόπων.

WEALTH

CARIO
You mean you'll abandon the gods and live here?

HERMES
You people do have it a lot better.

CARIO
Oh? Do you consider desertion such a nice thing?

HERMES
One's country is wherever one does well.[51]

CARIO
And what's in it for us if you're down here?

HERMES
Enshrine me at your door as Bracket God.

CARIO
Bracket God? But we've no use for bracketeering!

HERMES
God of Commerce then.

CARIO
But we're wealthy, so why should we subsidize Hermes the Reseller?

HERMES
In that case, God of Deceit.

CARIO
God of Deceit? Absolutely not: we now use not deceit but honest ways.

[51] Probably a quotation from tragedy, as also line 1158.

ΕΡΜΗΣ

ἀλλ᾽ Ἡγεμόνιον.

ΚΑΡΙΩΝ

ἀλλ᾽ ὁ θεὸς ἤδη βλέπει,
1160 ὥσθ᾽ ἡγεμόνος οὐδὲν δεησόμεσθ᾽ ἔτι.

ΕΡΜΗΣ

Ἐναγώνιος τοίνυν ἔσομαι. καὶ τί ἔτ᾽ ἐρεῖς;
Πλούτῳ γάρ ἐστι τοῦτο συμφορώτατον,
ποιεῖν ἀγῶνας μουσικοὺς καὶ γυμνικούς.

ΚΑΡΙΩΝ

ὡς ἀγαθόν ἐστ᾽ ἐπωνυμίας πολλὰς ἔχειν·
1165 οὗτος γὰρ ἐξηύρηκεν αὑτῷ βιότιον.
οὐκ ἐτὸς ἅπαντες οἱ δικάζοντες θαμὰ
σπεύδουσιν ἐν πολλοῖς γεγράφθαι γράμμασιν.

ΕΡΜΗΣ

οὐκοῦν ἐπὶ τούτοις εἰσίω;

ΚΑΡΙΩΝ

καὶ πλῦνέ γε
αὐτὸς προσελθὼν πρὸς τὸ φρέαρ τὰς κοιλίας,
1170 ἵν᾽ εὐθέως Διακονικὸς εἶναι δοκῇς.

ΙΕΡΕΤΣ

τίς ἂν φράσειε ποῦ ᾽στι Χρεμύλος μοι σαφῶς;

HERMES

Then Guide God.

CARIO

But our god can see again, so we'll have no further need of a guide.

HERMES

Then I'll be God of Contests. How can you object to that? Holding artistic and athletic contests is perfectly congenial to Wealth.[52]

CARIO

It's certainly convenient to have so many titles; he's devised a nice little livelihood for himself. No wonder all who serve on juries often contrive to get enrolled on several lists.[53]

HERMES

Shall I go inside on these terms?

CARIO

Yes, and go personally to the well and wash some tripe, to make your immediate debut as Servant God.

CARIO and HERMES go inside.

Enter PRIEST from a wing.

PRIEST

Can anyone tell me exactly where Chremylus lives?

CHREMYLUS comes outside.

---

[52] These were civic expenses undertaken by the wealthiest citizens.

[53] See 972 n.

ARISTOPHANES

ΧΡΕΜΤΛΟΣ

τί δ' ἐστίν, ὦ βέλτιστε;

ΙΕΡΕΤΣ

τί γὰρ ἄλλ' ἢ κακῶς;
ἀφ' οὗ γὰρ ὁ Πλοῦτος οὗτος ἤρξατο βλέπειν,
ἀπόλωλ' ὑπὸ λιμοῦ· καταφαγεῖν γὰρ οὐκ ἔχω,
1175 καὶ ταῦτα τοῦ σωτῆρος ἱερεὺς ὢν Διός.

ΧΡΕΜΤΛΟΣ

ἡ δ' αἰτία τίς ἐστιν, ὦ πρὸς τῶν θεῶν;

ΙΕΡΕΤΣ

θύειν ἔτ' οὐδεὶς ἀξιοῖ.

ΧΡΕΜΤΛΟΣ

τίνος οὕνεκα;

ΙΕΡΕΤΣ

ὅτι πάντες εἰσὶ πλούσιοι. καίτοι τότε,
ὅτ' εἶχον οὐδέν, ὁ μὲν ἂν ἥκων ἔμπορος
1180 ἔθυσεν ἱερεῖόν τι σωθείς, ὁ δέ τις ἂν
δίκην ἀποφυγών, ὁ δ' ἂν ἐκαλλιερεῖτό τις
κἀμέ γ' ἐκάλει τὸν ἱερέα· νῦν δ' οὐδὲ εἷς
θύει τὸ παράπαν οὐδὲν οὐδ' εἰσέρχεται,
πλὴν ἀποπατησόμενοί γε πλεῖν ἢ μύριοι.

ΧΡΕΜΤΛΟΣ

1185 οὔκουν τὰ νομιζόμενα σὺ τούτων λαμβάνεις;

ΙΕΡΕΤΣ

τὸν οὖν Δία τὸν σωτῆρα καὐτός μοι δοκῶ
χαίρειν ἐάσας ἐνθάδ' αὐτοῦ καταμένειν.

592

CHREMYLUS

What's up, my good man?

PRIEST

What else but trouble! Ever since this Wealth regained his
sight, I've been perishing of hunger; I've nothing to eat,
and me the priest of Zeus the Savior!

CHREMYLUS

Good heavens! And why is that?

PRIEST

Nobody bothers with sacrifices anymore.

CHREMYLUS

Why not?

PRIEST

Because everyone's wealthy. When they had nothing, the
merchant back safely from a voyage would make a sacri-
fice, and the man acquitted in court, and the man whose
sacrifice was auspicious would invite me over as priest. But
now not a single one sacrifices anything at all, or even
comes to the temple, except for countless thousands look-
ing for a toilet.

CHREMYLUS

So you don't claim your orthodox share of that?

PRIEST

That's why I myself intend to bid Zeus the Savior goodbye,
and settle down right here.

ΧΡΕΜΥΛΟΣ

θάρρει· καλῶς ἔσται γάρ, ἢν θεὸς θέλῃ.
ὁ Ζεὺς ὁ σωτὴρ γὰρ πάρεστιν ἐνθάδε,
αὐτόματος ἥκων.

ΙΕΡΕΥΣ

1190   πάντ᾽ ἀγαθὰ τοίνυν λέγεις.

ΧΡΕΜΥΛΟΣ

ἱδρυσόμεθ᾽ οὖν αὐτίκα μάλ᾽—ἀλλὰ περίμενε—
τὸν Πλοῦτον, οὗπερ πρότερον ἦν ἱδρυμένος,
τὸν ὀπισθόδομον ἀεὶ φυλάττων τῆς θεοῦ.
ἀλλ᾽ ἐκδότω τις δεῦρο δᾷδας ἡμμένας,
ἵν᾽ ἔχων προηγῇ τῷ θεῷ σύ.

ΙΕΡΕΥΣ

1195   πάνυ μὲν οὖν
δρᾶν ταῦτα χρή.

ΧΡΕΜΥΛΟΣ

τὸν Πλοῦτον ἔξω τις κάλει.

ΓΡΑΥΣ

ἐγὼ δὲ τί ποιῶ;

ΧΡΕΜΥΛΟΣ

τὰς χύτρας, αἷς τὸν θεὸν
ἱδρυσόμεσθα, λαβοῦσ᾽ ἐπὶ τῆς κεφαλῆς φέρε
σεμνῶς· ἔχουσα δ᾽ ἦλθες αὐτὴ ποικίλα.

ΓΡΑΥΣ

ὧν δ᾽ οὕνεκ᾽ ἦλθον;

CHREMYLUS

Cheer up! It's going to be all right, god willing, for Zeus the Savior is here with us; he's come of his own accord.

PRIEST

Well, you have nothing but good news!

CHREMYLUS

We're on our way right now to install Wealth—no, please stay—right where he was installed before, as permanent guardian of Athena's treasure chamber.[54] Now someone bring us lighted torches; you can lead the god's procession!

PRIEST

I'm very much obliged.

CHREMYLUS

Someone ask Wealth to come outside.

OLD WOMAN comes outside.

OLD WOMAN

And what may I do?

CHREMYLUS

Take the pots that we're going to use in the god's installation and carry them solemnly on your head. You've come wearing your own finery!

OLD WOMAN

But what about my problem?

[54] On the Acropolis.

ΧΡΕΜΥΛΟΣ

1200   πάντα σοι πεπράξεται.
ἥξει γὰρ ὁ νεανίσκος ὥς σ᾽ εἰς ἑσπέραν.

ΓΡΑΥΣ

ἀλλ᾽ εἴ γε μέντοι, νὴ Δί᾽, ἐγγυᾷ σύ μοι
ἥξειν ἐκεῖνον ὡς ἔμ᾽, οἴσω τὰς χύτρας.

ΧΡΕΜΥΛΟΣ

καὶ μὴν πολὺ τῶν ἄλλων χυτρῶν τἀναντία
1205 αὗται ποιοῦσιν· ταῖς μὲν ἄλλαις γὰρ χύτραις
ἡ γραῦς ἔπεστ᾽ ἀνωτάτω, ταύτης δὲ νῦν
τῆς γραὸς ἐπιπολῆς ἔπεισιν αἱ χύτραι.

ΧΟΡΟΣ

οὐκέτι τοίνυν εἰκὸς μέλλειν οὐδ᾽ ἡμᾶς, ἀλλ᾽
    ἀναχωρεῖν
εἰς τοὔπισθεν· δεῖ γὰρ κατόπιν τούτων ᾄδοντας
    ἕπεσθαι.

CHREMYLUS

It's all taken care of: your young man will visit you tonight.

OLD WOMAN

Well, if you really guarantee that he'll visit me, I'll carry the pots.

CHREMYLUS

Look, these pots are doing the opposite of other pots: in other pots the slag's on top, but in this case the pots are atop this slag!

Enter WEALTH, *followed by the rest of the household;* PRIEST *leads everyone off in procession.*

CHORUS

Well, we shouldn't be tarrying; let's take up the rear! We should follow along behind them in song.

INDEX OF PERSONAL NAMES

Reference is to play and line number. Italicized references are footnoted in the text.

INDEX

*Composed in ZephGreek and ZephText by
Technologies 'N Typography, Merrimac, Massachusetts.
Printed in Great Britain by St Edmundsbury Press Ltd,
Bury St Edmunds, Suffolk, on acid-free paper.
Bound by Hunter & Foulis Ltd, Edinburgh, Scotland.*